MAGDALENA'S SHADOW

E. E. ORME

MAGDALENA'S SHADOW

E. E. ORME

THE
WOW
HOUSE LLC

First Edition

Magdalena's Shadow
ISBN Print Edition: 978-0-9985953-1-3
ISBN eBook Edition: 978-0-9985953-0-6
IBSN Audiobook Edition: 978-0-9985953-2-0

THE WOW HOUSE LLC

Copyright © 2011 #TXu001787617
Publication Date: February 2017

Author Photo by Erin Ivankovich
Editing by Grammar Chick, www.grammarchick.com

Cover & Interior Design: Heather McIntyre, Cover&Layout
www.coverandlayout.com
Rose Artwork: Urban Soule, www.urbansoule.com

FOR SIERRA

MAGDALENA'S SHADOW

E. E. ORME

CHAPTER ONE

Morning crept unnoticed into the modern, minimalist expanse of Penthouse #2 where no clocks chimed or gonged to mark the hour. What threatened to be an ordinary morning of quiet routine was interrupted by the harsh sound of the usually silent buzzer. The noise erupted through the apartment like an attack. Coco stood frozen in the center of her bedroom still holding her mother's yellow chiffon dress like a favorite stuffed toy. Her first thought was to hide, but hiding wouldn't block out the noise; hiding wouldn't stop the intrusion. Warily, she laid the dress across her bed and moved toward the intercom, the lit button on the side indicating that the call came from the ground floor lobby.

Pressing the button, Coco heard the doorman's familiar voice ring in the gloom of Penthouse #2.

"Miss Rodriguez, there's a woman here who says she has a delivery for Eva Clark? I told her Eva doesn't work here anymore, but she says she spoke to her yesterday."

"She's not here, Benny. You know she quit years ago," Coco replied. Hearing Eva's name brought back memories. Eva had been the good nanny, the last nanny, the one paid employee who had effectively stood in place of Coco's absent mother, Magdalena.

E. E. ORME

"She says this is the address Eva gave her."

"Well, Eva isn't here. I don't know where she is." Coco felt the lingering uneasiness begin to take hold of her. The Keeper could arrive at the apartment any minute now, and she didn't allow Coco to touch the intercom.

"She says Eva needs to sign for it," Benny said. "She has to witness the signature. She says she talked to her yesterday? She's adamant."

Coco bit her lip. "Eva's gone. Just make her leave, okay, Benny?"

"Who are you talking to, Coco?" the Keeper asked, standing behind Coco. Coco hadn't heard her come in. Biting her lip even harder, Coco turned to look at her housekeeper. "Coco, go to your room and rest." Coco left the living room. From behind her bedroom door, Coco heard the Keeper dismiss Benny and then apologize to the woman for Coco's behavior, calling her a difficult and deeply troubled girl. "God alone knows how hard it is to care for a mentally challenged child," the Keeper added before buzzing the woman up to their floor. Angry, Coco slipped silently out of her bedroom and into the large sitting room that had been her mother's. Over the years when things had been broken, they were thrown away and replaced, but lately it seemed that items just went missing for no reason at all. Whole walls were empty of their photographs: unpublished proofs from one of Magdalena's Prada shoots had gone last week leaving only the signed Lichtenstein print Gianni Versace had given her mother simply because she had admired it. What would Magdalena say if she knew her things were disappearing?

Coco looked around the room. *Would Magdalena even notice the empty places and blank walls if she did come home?* The apartment was a mess, stacks of fashion magazines lined the walls and boxes of new clothes lay open and spilling over in nearly every room. Silk sundresses, linen jackets, and cotton designer tees lay tossed over the sofas, flung haphazardly across the matching chairs, left to spill in varying colors from the boxes of clothes sent to Magdalena – clothes that only her daughter would wear. Coco walked to the empty south wall where only her fashion collages now hung, letting her fingers trace silk swatches and couture evening gowns cut from Vogue and Elle. They lay one across the other, creating the framework of the life Coco hoped to someday inhabit. Through fashion she would find her freedom, her mother, and herself. She felt hope bloom in her chest, the bitter tears of loneliness stinging her eyes. Prada, Chanel, Valentino, Balenciaga: they were her haven, her home, and her hope. Coco walked toward her mother's portrait, a black and white photo taken on a beach when she first had signed with Prada. Coco looked just like her, just as tall, as thin, and as beautiful. Magdalena was a fashion icon, and Coco desperately wanted to follow in her footsteps. Kissing the tips of her fingers, Coco raised her hand to her mother's cheek.

"I have to get out of here," she said, her eyes fixed on her mother. "Please, Mama, I have to get out." Hearing the Keeper leave the apartment, Coco slipped out of the room and headed to the front door.

Standing just outside the light, Coco listened in shadow while the floor numbers above the elevator doors glowed one after the other, indicating the woman's steady upward approach. Coco raised her hood to hide her features, hiding her tall slender form in the shadows of the dark apartment. She was almost a woman, yet life with the Keeper had kept her small and powerless, denying her the maturity she had hoped to feel at sixteen. That was why she stayed quiet and hidden.

With a ding and a mechanized rumble the woman stepped out of the elevator. In one arm, she held a bundle of cloth with a document, in the other a paisley print cotton bag. Her eyes didn't smile when she spotted the Keeper waiting by the entryway table.

"Please sign here, Miss Clark." The woman's clipped syllables did not welcome argument. Coco watched the stranger place the bundle carefully on the sofa. On the table, she placed the document along with a pen, a pen the Keeper did not hesitate to pick up.

Coco wanted to explain how Eva Clark had quit three years ago, and that Magdalena, her super-model mother, was too busy jet-setting around the world to hire a new nanny or a proper housekeeper. But the Keeper didn't deal in truth like Coco did. She dealt in bruises, hard slaps, and gutting ridicule. Without hesitation, the Keeper signed the nanny's name to the paper.

"No." Coco felt a spark of courage, her voice coming of its own accord. She pushed open the door, taking a step into the hall, "Eva…Eva…."

"Yes," the Keeper said. "Yes, Coco, I'm right here." Both women watched Coco, the Keeper's eyes narrowing to a look of warning. "It's okay, Coco. I'll be with you in a moment. Please go back to your bedroom like I asked."

"Did you I.D. her?" Coco asked the woman. "How do you know she is who she says she is? She's not Eva Clark. Eva is gone."

"Coco, you are having an episode. Please go in and rest. I'll be with you shortly." The two women stared at Coco. "Again, I'm so sorry. She's bipolar and the drugs are having no effect," the Keeper added when Coco turned back toward the apartment.

"I'm not bipolar," Coco yelled over her shoulder. "And I'm not having an episode."

Retreating again behind the crack in the door, Coco watched the Keeper return the document without reading it. The woman didn't check her I.D. Instead she folded the document into her purse and dropped a copy next to the bundle on the sofa. Then she was gone.

"Coco," the Keeper said, "I know you're still there. Get over here now."

Biting her lip, Coco walked into the hallway. "I said, get your ass here NOW," the Keeper said, her voice rising. She ignored the bundle and bag on the couch, turning her full focus on Coco. "Don't you ever question me when I'm doing business! If I say I'm Eva Clark, then I am FUCKING Eva Clark. If I say I'm your mama, then I am your FUCKING mama. If I say I'm God, then I am MOTHER FUCKING GOD! Are we clear?"

"You don't have the right to pretend to be my mother or her absent employee. You don't have the right to forge other people's names. Eva quit. Benny knows Eva quit. If I tell him you signed her name and pretended to be her I could get you...." The Keeper's fist knocked Coco's head into the wall behind her.

"Don't you threaten me! What I do and don't do is between me and God and any little bitch who tries to interfere is gonna get her ass handed to her. You want your ass handed to you?" Coco didn't answer. The Keeper stared at her for a while. When Coco still didn't answer, she hit her a second time. "I asked you a question, Coco. You better answer me this time. I asked you if you want your fucking ass handed to you?"

E. E. ORME   5

"No," Coco whispered, holding her face where the Keeper had hit her.

"Well, then you take what that bitch brought and don't you let me see you or it again, not till tomorrow. And remember, that thing she brought is your problem, not mine." Coco looked at the package and then back up at the Keeper. "Go on and get it," the Keeper said, "and you better keep it quiet." She left Coco bruised and alone in the hallway. Angry and hurt, Coco walked to the couch and grabbed hold of the multicolored bundle.

Something heavy rolled out of the middle of the cloth, turning over once, twice, before landing with a soft thud on the fabric of the sofa. Black hair curled out from under pink fabric as the bundle became animated.

The cloth-covered lump moved and then whimpered. Coco stepped back in surprise. Two huge black eyes stared up at her while a large red mouth opened to stretch like an O. The ensuing scream bounced across ornate mirrors to reverberate off the marble walls of the entryway.

"You better shut that thing up," the Keeper said, returning with her coat and purse. "She's the only reason I came in today. You keep her quiet or you'll get worse than you just got." Coco stared at the baby, her head still ringing with the last punch, while behind her the Keeper stepped into the elevator and was gone.

Babies weren't wholly unknown to Coco. She had seen them on TV, smiling and looking sweet, but she had never been left alone with one.

After Coco's initial panic passed, she leaned over the couch. The baby looked up at her, its cry turning from a scream to a low whimper, accompanied by the rustling of fabric. Coco fixed her eyes on the baby, who stared up at her with a questioning expression.

"Hello." Coco reached out a tentative hand to stroke the child's cheek. Its slight size, delicate features, and luminous brown eyes created a person too tiny and beautiful to be real. The baby stared at her, flailing its hands wildly and kicking its feet, its little body wiggling against the red patterned fabric where it had been dumped.

"Hi, baby." Coco's words were a whisper in the spacious entryway. The baby sucked its fist and then flailed its arms again. Coco looked down on it in wonder, fresh tears stinging her eyes. "We need help." Her mind turned again to her mother. *I can't call her.* Coco had done everything she could to reach her mother, but her calls and letters, emails and IMs went unanswered. *There has to be someone I can call.* When Coco moved to find her unreliable cellphone, she heard an intake of breath followed by a tremendous shriek.

"No, no!" Coco soothed, hurrying back. "Don't do that, I'm not going away." The baby stopped screaming and stared up at her expectantly. "We need help." Coco moved back toward the door, grief filling her chest, restricting her breathing. She gulped back a sob. "I'm going to get my phone; just wait here." When she moved from sight the baby screamed again.

"Okay. Okay. You can come too. Just don't wiggle."

Coco slipped the baby carefully off the sofa into her arms. It weighed almost nothing. Coco felt the baby's tiny hand grasp onto her thumb, its dark eyes still peering into her face.

"Hi." Coco smiled, her tears running freely down her face. She felt lost in the dark depths of this tiny child's eyes, lost in the tender way the little stranger saw her and held her hand.

Coco's loneliness rose in her stomach, twisting her insides into knots while the baby kept staring, taking in every feature of her face until she felt that she was being memorized in the same way she had once memorized her own mother, Magdalena. Coco blinked away the thought, breaking the connection. *How is it possible that I'm standing here holding a baby?* With the break in eye contact, the baby began to cry again – not the harsh, high-pitched cries of abandonment but the soft whimpers of a person who is in some way disappointed.

Coco looked down again. Again, she felt the instant connection when her eyes met and were held by the liquid brown eyes of the child. In that second, she kissed the baby's head, breaking their gaze, her nose nuzzling the baby's cheek while she walked into the penthouse.

The Keeper came and went when she liked, doing as little as she chose to keep the penthouse in order. That day was no exception. Once, Coco remembered with bitterness, there had been cooks and maids, a nanny she loved, and friends to play with. Now there was just Rosa, the housekeeper, whom Coco called "the Keeper" because she was more jailer than maid. The Keeper never treated her like anything other than an inconvenient mental case that needed to be managed. She read Coco's emails, deleted numbers from her phone, and ran surveillance using parent protection apps on every call and text she made. Even little conversations with old friends had become impossible. Coco didn't know why the Keeper hated her or where so many of her mother's things had gone and she didn't dare ask. The Keeper was the only person who came to the apartment now. She was the only one who brought food, who kept the lights on and the apartment warm. Each time Coco had tried to tell anyone how the Keeper treated her, she was beaten and lied to until she actually believed she was as crazy and difficult as the Keeper told her she was.

After hours of Googling *how to care for babies,* Coco's resentment grew. How could she leave now with a baby to care for? She felt more trapped than ever. Worst still, the baby was crying and sucking its fingers. It looked tired and hungry and Coco didn't know how to help it. Around dinnertime, Coco remembered the paisley cotton bag the woman had left on the couch in the hallway. Retrieving it, Coco found it contained a large tin of dry formula, a bottle, a pacifier, diapers, and wipes.

Coco laid the baby on the sofa so it could watch her at the wet bar, a small kitchen with granite countertops where Coco made most of her food. She rarely entered the main kitchen where the Keeper spent her working hours eating and watching TV. The wet bar had a tiny fridge under the counter and a microwave, as well as dozens and dozens of bottles of alcohol with foreign labels, left over from the days when Magdalena still had lived there.

Coco put three scoops of formula into the bottle (as directed by the neatly printed instructions on the label) before adding water. She shook the contents and microwaved the bottle for a few seconds to warm it. While she worked, she could see the baby staring at her from the sofa, watching everything she did.

When the microwave beeped, the baby kicked its feet happily. Coco twisted the nipple onto the bottle as hard as she could before lifting the baby into her arms. It cooed and shook its fists, its pink mouth puckered in anticipation. At first the baby felt awkward in her lap, but with some small adjustments Coco brought its head to rest in the crook of her arm and raised the bottle to its expectant lips.

The baby latched on instantly, sending bubbles shooting up the center of the bottle as it fiercely sucked out the formula. Coco stared at the feeding infant and smiled. She was holding a baby, and she had actually managed to feed it. The baby drank and drank. Little bits of formula slid down its cheeks onto the red cotton of Coco's hoodie, leaving a wet mark that would dry to a hard chalk if it weren't washed out.

Coco didn't consider the shirt, nor the near silence that filled the room as Mozart played low in the background of a televised fashion show. For the first time in memory she was not troubled by the howl of the Chicago wind, a tortured sound that had frightened her since she had been a child. Instead, she considered the little person who ate with such hunger and looked with such contentment on her and the world she occupied.

When the bottle emptied, the baby's intense eyes slid closed. The milk that remained in its mouth ran down its cheek as the baby fell asleep. Coco stared silently, hardly breathing, hardly thinking, entirely enthralled by the person who had moved so inexplicably into her life.

The door slammed at noon the next day, signaling the Keeper's return to #2. Coco jumped at the sound, as did the baby who fell into hysterical screams.

"What the hell? I told you to keep that brat quiet," the Keeper barked, two bags of groceries hanging from her sausage-like fingers.

Coco kissed the baby's head, rocking the infant until it was silent.

"You startled her."

The Keeper glared, daring Coco to talk back again; her double chins wobbled while spit flecked her fat lips. Forcing her eyes from the repulsive woman, Coco reached inside the paisley diaper bag for the folded document, which she offered to the Keeper.

"Will you translate this for me? I want to know more about her, but the words are written in Spanish."

"No. I won't translate it. I'll just tell you what her nanny told me. That kid is just like you; she's another little nobody no one wants to deal with. And since Eva isn't here you will raise it. End of fucking story." The Keeper tossed the document back at Coco, who watched it flutter to the floor.

Just like me? Coco took a deep breath and tried to steady herself, her eyes fixed on the baby; from the corner of her eye she saw the document come to rest on the floor near her foot. The baby girl's hands wriggled out of her blanket and shook in the air as if she clutched an invisible rattle, while her face took on an intensely thoughtful expression. Coco adjusted the child onto her hip and leaned over to retrieve the piece of paper, her long dark hair slipping over her shoulder to the floor. Coco hadn't thought to translate the document herself; she didn't usually read anything that didn't pertain to fashion, and it had been years since she had read anything in Spanish. Now as she looked at the crinkled piece of paper she realized that it couldn't satisfy her curiosity. It was illegible, not because it was poorly printed, but because the words had long ago lost their meaning. Coco could make out the word *Argentina* and a date some seven months before, but the rest was in a language she no longer understood. Folding the document in half, she carefully returned it to the diaper bag's inside pocket.

The baby was a good baby. She seemed to prefer to watch the world than to scream at it. She rarely cried and slept most of the time. Inside the bag, Coco found a bottle with an eyedropper top. As long as Coco added the drops to the baby's bottle she was quiet, easy to manage, and instantly sleepy.

The worst part of parenting, Coco decided, was diapering. Unfortunately, by the end of the third day the diapers ran out and the Keeper refused to buy more.

"You think you're rich?" the Keeper yelled. "You're not; your mother hardly gives me enough money to feed you on. Get some dishtowels and make up some diapers on your own. You'll do it the way I had to in Mexico. You'll see what it's like to work, lazy *vaca*."

Coco didn't argue; she didn't dare. Instead she learned to diaper the hard way.

As the baby formula began to run low Coco became frightened that the Keeper wouldn't replace it either. How would she feed the child?

"Rosa?" The Keeper turned on Coco in surprise, her chins swaying with the motion. "Please buy more formula tomorrow morning."

There was no kindness in the fat lips that twisted slowly into a grin. "In Mexico, we breastfeed our kids. I suggest you try it."

"What?" Coco responded in confusion.

The Keeper laughed, shouldered her bags, and left for the night. The baby was Coco's new soft spot, a weakness that the Keeper wouldn't hesitate to exploit.

For some unknown reason the Keeper delighted in making Coco suffer. In the past, it was not unusual for Coco to come out of her bedroom and find every blind in the apartment raised and the TV and radio switched off. Coco would crawl on hands and knees to retrieve the remotes that drew the blinds, shielding her from the thousand-foot drop outside.

Vertigo crippled her. It made the floor ripple and the walls sway, causing a panic that took her hours to recover from. The terror intensified when coupled with the constantly roaring wind that tore around the Chicago high-rise. The wind had upset her for as long as she could remember.

The last time Coco had upset the Keeper, the fat cow had raised the blinds, turned off the TV, and hidden the remotes; Coco couldn't draw the blinds again or switch on the TV without them.

Surrounded by naked glass and a howling wind, Coco had faced the terror that surrounded her without success. She had felt the floor sway beneath her, seen the glass tremble, and heard the wind roar in shrill gusts around the thirty-story tower. It had proven too much. After several attempts to find the remotes Coco had fainted. No, it was no good upsetting the Keeper, so Coco kept quiet and dreamed of the day when the Keeper would be gone and the apartment only a distant memory.

Coco named the baby girl Bebe after the one word she recognized from the document. She pronounced it Bee-Bee, after the American fashion house. Bebe spent her time sleeping, eating, smiling, wriggling, and pooping; Coco had never been so busy in her life. Magazines were left unread, boxes of clothes arrived but were not opened, and she rarely changed out of her sweats as fashion was pushed from her mind. The best part of Bebe's arrival was that for the first time in years, Coco had someone she could talk to and care for.

Bebe slept in her arms during the day and in the crook of her arm at night. Coco loved watching the child sleep, her tiny hands clenched into fists close to her face, her eyes closed to lash-framed slits as she breathed little breaths and dreamed little baby dreams. Coco fell asleep to the sight of Bebe's chest as it rose and fell, memorizing each twitch of her fists, the kick of her foot, and the occasional smile.

The daydreams that once had lulled Coco to sleep no longer took her to exotic fashion shoots or the beaches of Argentina where Magdalena's beach house lay nestled on a bluff overlooking the Atlantic. Her mind no longer turned to the remembered scent of her mother's perfume or the gleaming sunshine of their life in South America. Instead her dreams were filled with Bebe, a curious kind of warm love and a sense of serenity she had long lived without.

The Keeper brought formula but not the kind that Bebe was used to. It was thin and watery. It tasted like sugar mixed with powdered milk. One week passed on the new formula and Bebe grew sickly.

"You're making this yourself, aren't you, Rosa?" Coco raised her eyes to the Keeper's face, but the woman looked away.

"I'm not buying that expensive stuff."

"But Bebe needs good formula, not this watered down stuff."

"She'll get what she gets. Now get out of my kitchen."

After another week Bebe could no longer sit up without help. She grew weaker by the day.

"Please, Rosa, I need you to buy the good formula. If you'll give me some money, I'll ask Benny to buy it."

The Keeper froze where she sat, her eyes fixed warily on Coco. Her expression changed as a new thought seemed to present itself. "You better give me something to sell, girl. If you do, I'll get you the expensive stuff. But you need to remember you are poor. You're also stupid and useless, and the doorman doesn't need to be bothered by you any more than I do. I work here and keep this place running on nothing. Be grateful."

Coco looked around the apartment; she had no idea what anything was worth. "What do you think you could sell?" Her voice rose with hope.

"Well, that painting for starters." The Keeper pointed to a large Campbell's Soup can painted in vivid reds and yellows. The painting had hung in Coco's life for as long as she could remember. Her heart sank at the thought of losing it. How many hours had she spent tracing its lines with her eyes? The sight of it was as comforting to her as a photo of Magdalena; yet when Coco looked at Bebe she knew she would part with it.

"Okay. Just make sure you get the good formula."

The Keeper smiled and nodded. From that moment on the Keeper became almost nice. She called Coco "Miss" and changed the sheets on her bed. But Coco didn't care what the Keeper did as long as the good formula was back and Bebe was well.

It took over a week for the color to come back to Bebe's cheeks. Another week passed and the baby was able to sit up again. Before Coco knew it, she was crawling.

On a Monday exactly three weeks after the painting had gone, the Keeper disappeared, too. Each call to her cellphone went straight to voicemail. Around five in the evening, Coco received a call from the agency the Keeper worked for. The administrator said that arrangements had been made and that a new housekeeper would arrive shortly. It was around that time that two men came to the apartment in security uniforms accompanied by Benny, the doorman. Coco retreated quietly to her room. She listened as the men returned her mother's painting to its place on the wall.

E. E. ORME   15

Benny knocked on Coco's bedroom door, opening it carefully when she didn't answer. He looked uncomfortable when he saw her staring fixedly from the bed, her eyes peering at him from the unlit room.

"Miss Rodriguez, do you have a moment?" He spoke gently, careful to look away from where Coco sat. Bebe lay unseen and asleep in a laundry basket next to the bed. "Mrs. Gonzalez tried to sell your mother's painting at a gallery." Coco remained silent. The doorman went on politely. "Were you aware that it was missing?" Coco remained still. "Mrs. Gonzalez also told the police that you gave her the painting. Is it true? Did you give it to her?"

Tears filled Coco's eyes. She needed to find her voice. She needed to answer. With one word, she could corroborate the Keeper's story and set her free. With another word, she could lock her away. "Miss Rodriguez," Benny pleaded, "these men represent the company who insures the painting. When the gallery ran the painting's history they learned that the piece belonged to your mother. Mrs. Gonzalez is in custody and your mother has been notified." Coco took a deep breath. She knew Benny. Benny was safe, but it had been years since she had visited the lobby. He looked older now but still, Benny was safe. "Your mother has been notified, Coco," Benny repeated, hoping to elicit some spark of understanding. "Coco, please...these men need to know what happened." When she didn't respond, he started to close the door.

"Benny," Coco whispered. "Tell them she took my mother's things, and she beat me when I tried to stop her. Every time I tried to tell someone she would threaten me. Tell them that, okay, Benny?"

"I'll tell them, Coco, and I'll see if management can get a hold of your mother. She should know. I wish I had known. I'm so sorry."

"It's okay… Mama's busy and I didn't know how to tell you. Besides, the agency is sending a new keeper so hopefully things will be better." Coco pulled her hood up over her head and faded back into the darkness, too worried and worn out to say more.

With the click of the front door she was alone. She had hated the Keeper. The Keeper had been a thief who had starved Bebe. She hurt children and Coco was glad she was in jail; she was glad she was gone and that Bebe was safe, but the glad stuck in Coco's throat and ran in bitter rivers down her cheeks. But what if the new keeper was even worse than the last? Tears stung Coco's eyes until she was nearly blinded. Closing them tightly, she let her fingers brush gently through Bebe's hair where she slept in the laundry basket. The wind tore around the tower, answering her fears with roaring howls.

18   MAGDALENA'S SHADOW

CHAPTER TWO

"Breakfast," a small voice called at eight o'clock the next morning. Coco blinked in the darkness of her bedroom, half awake and half asleep. Who was calling? Bebe didn't stir when Coco slipped out of bed to creep quietly down the hallway toward the kitchen. Concealed in the shadows of the hall, she could view the new keeper without being seen.

What Coco saw was a tiny brown skinned woman with snow-white hair standing near the range. Eggs, bacon, and toast sat on a white plate on the table. The scent of the fresh food rose in enchanting waves to where Coco stood watching. She tried not to enjoy it. Food was a battle she had waged with all the help.

"They told me you were a picky eater," the woman said, not looking at where Coco stood. Coco knew that "anorexic" was the word they had used. "So, I made you some good solid food. I would be happy if you would sit down and eat it."

Coco walked from the shadow and slid into her place at the table, careful not to make eye contact.

The woman sat down across from her with an equally filled plate and a cup of coffee. "Now I imagine you're shocked to see a new face in your house, but I'm with the agency. They said that you lost your last housekeeper so they sent me."

Coco nodded silently, sipping her juice and eyeing the slice of bacon next to the yellow scrambled eggs. The toast was thankfully plain, but when she lifted it to her lips she noticed the little woman staring at her. Coco quickly set the toast down again and looked away. "Thank you." The words felt strange when she said them. Coco looked at the side of her plate for a linen napkin before realizing she had wrapped the last one around Bebe's bottom the night before.

"You're welcome." The woman smiled and watched Coco nervously nibble the toast. Once she finished the toast, Coco rose to leave. "You know that's low-fat turkey bacon." The tiny woman's voice froze Coco mid-movement. "And I only put in half an egg yolk for color; nothing there will make you fat!"

Coco stared at her, realizing that this woman maneuvered in a way that none of the others had. The mothers from sitcoms like *Leave it to Beaver* and *The Brady Bunch* came to mind as Coco realized that this woman would try to make her eat what was put in front of her. She thought about going to her room and locking the door but didn't. Eva, the nice nanny, had begged and pleaded, offering up hugs and promises in an attempt to make Coco eat. The Keeper, in her malevolence, had added globs of oil and butter to Coco's food, because she knew grease repulsed her. The other maids and housekeepers hadn't cared if she ever ate again. This woman was different. What she cooked, she expected it to be eaten. Coco watched the woman open a newspaper, rustling it noisily in the large kitchen.

Everything about this new keeper seemed grounded and purposeful, like a mountain that time couldn't move. She had an antiquated quality, reflected in the blue checkered dress she wore complete with an apron. The look was very out of place in the modern steel and granite kitchen; she would have looked more at home near chrome and Formica.

A soft sigh escaped Coco's lips. She reclaimed her seat and drove a fork into the yellow egg. It was delicious, and when coupled with the slice of turkey bacon the taste was decadent. When she had finished half the food on her plate, the newspaper rustled again bringing two eyes to smile quietly over the top.

"Good?"

"Yes." Coco stood, ready to slip away again; the overwhelming guilt of having eaten felt terrible.

"My name is Lucia Brown." The woman's voice stopped Coco a second time. "But everyone – and I mean everyone – calls me Tia."

Coco stared at her. Now she wanted to have a conversation? Coco nodded, her eyes large with the realization that this new keeper wouldn't allow her to remain passively invisible. The long silence was broken by the noise of a commercial coming from the TV, which blared continually in the darkened living room. Coco nodded again and turned to go. She had almost succeeded in leaving the room when the woman's voice froze her a third time.

"Coco Rodriguez, you and I are going to be friends."

With that Coco knew that her days of quiet anonymity were over.

As if on cue Bebe awoke and wailed. At any moment when she didn't see Coco, she wailed. Tia stood quickly, her chair skidding out behind her on the granite floor. Coco remained frozen. The Keeper may have been evil, but she hadn't intruded into Coco's relationship with Bebe; this keeper would ask where Bebe had come from. She would be nosy and want to help.

Coco could feel Tia's eyes boring into the back of her head.

"Are you going to get the baby, or am I?" Tia's asked, her voice commanding.

Coco moved quickly to her room where Bebe screamed from her basket, angry and frightened at being left alone. Coco swept the sobbing baby into her arms; tears cascaded down both their cheeks. Bebe's shrieks lessened when she felt Coco around her, enfolding her in her warmth. Bebe's dark eyes searched Coco's face, taking in the tears and the anguished expression until Bebe began to cry again, not out of anger but confusion: Coco wasn't supposed to cry.

A long time passed before Coco felt Tia's presence. To her surprise, Tia tried to take Bebe from her, something the Keeper had never done. Coco resisted only slightly when the old woman lifted Bebe away, inspecting the child before walking to the bed. Bebe's struggling breath filled the silence. She fought Tia when the housekeeper tried to lay her on a blanket. Tia removed Bebe's clothes, her eyes scanning the baby's lean body before turning on Coco with a thin-lipped look of concern.

"Your baby looks underfed."

"I had trouble getting good formula."

"She should be eating solid food by now. She looks to be around nine months old."

"She'll be eleven months old next Thursday."

"Do you have a fresh diaper handy?"

"No." Numb with the fear that she could lose Bebe, Coco went into her bathroom where she had hung a clean cloth under the heat lamp to dry. Tia accepted the designer napkin with its embroidered fleur-de-lis pattern without saying a word. Coco watched her wrap the napkin around the struggling baby.

"This baby will need a bath after she eats." Tia lifted the infant up into Coco's arms before leaving the room with the soiled napkin.

Coco didn't hide from Tia that day. Instead she watched Tia call in a case of formula, a swing, a crib, a stroller, and five boxes of diapers all to be delivered to the apartment that day. Tia taught Coco how to properly wash Bebe in the sink instead of washing her in the shower the way she usually did. Then she taught Coco a better way of holding her when she fed.

In truth, Tia never stopped talking. Every word she said was directed at either Coco or Bebe. Nothing about either of them was ignored. Tia's words flowed like water from a spring, pure and constant. Whereas the Keeper had said things like, "You stupid little hussy, what did you do that for?" Tia said, "Coco, I want you to hold her head like this, elevated above her chest so that she can feed without getting as many bubbles in her tummy. When she's done with the bottle let's see if she'll eat a graham cracker."

Coco drank in the words, each one an education in child care, respect, and kindness. In the past, her teachers had spoken to her in a similar way, but they had never come home with her, never lived with her.

At the end of the day Tia and Coco set up the baby swing and unloaded the formula into the kitchen cupboards. At that point Coco began to cry.

"Tell me what's wrong," Tia said with real concern when she noticed Coco's tears. Coco shook her head and smiled, but Tia didn't look away. Her eyes shone with that same steadfast look of caring determination that made Coco eat; now that look made her talk.

"Don't leave...." Coco's hands began to shake. She wanted to lift the last tin of formula into the cupboard but found she couldn't. The room was silent except for the click of the swing and the rattle of Bebe's new toy as she swung it happily over her head.

Coco felt Tia's touch on her arm; she felt herself being turned to face the little woman, her thin shaking fingers held tightly in Tia's warm grasp.

"I have to go home. I have people who need me, but I'll be back tomorrow morning. I promise." Coco nodded, unable to look Tia in the eye. She was shocked that she had asked a keeper for something on the very first day.

Tia took Coco gently by the chin, lowering Coco's gaze to her own, trying for eye contact. "Everything's okay now," Tia assured her quietly.

"No, it's not, Tia. Sooner or later everyone leaves."

"Not me." Tia's voice was steady with certainty. "I don't leave, not unless I'm told to." After a long moment, Coco began to relax. Her breathing became less strained as the grief passed.

"Tomorrow morning?" Coco nodded her head. "You'll come back tomorrow morning?"

"That's right. I'll come in the morning. We'll have breakfast together."

"Okay." Coco looked away momentarily, her shoulders sagging.

The old woman held her hands until the shaking lessened and Coco was able again to make eye contact.

"Now," Tia buttoned her coat and shouldered her purse, "I'm going to go home to my people, and I'm going to tell them that I met a good person today, and at dinner we'll thank God for the introduction and ask him to bless you and...." Her voice trailed off as she turned her eyes to Bebe, "and your baby."

"Thank you." Coco's voice was no louder than a whisper. She followed Tia to the door beyond Bebe's line of vision; immediately they heard the baby sniffle and then cry. Coco turned back but Tia caught her arm.

"Let her cry, that baby has got you spinning in circles. You'll spoil her if you run every time she calls."

Coco nodded and saw Tia out. Once the door closed she hurried to Bebe and scooped her into her arms.

Tia came back as she had promised. On the following morning, she arrived with a chrome basket on wheels filled with fresh produce and lean meats. When Coco walked out of her bedroom the kitchen simmered with the scent of good things cooking. The table lay set with new linen napkins, cups, saucers, and silverware all perfectly placed. There was even a pot of tea. Coco ate whole grain toast, fried zucchini, and fried tomatoes with smoked salmon. It was the best breakfast she could ever remember eating even though the guilt of eating tore at her unmercifully.

"Thank you for breakfast, Tia." Coco looked to where Tia sat reading her paper. They had eaten together again that morning, an experience Coco enjoyed. She liked it when Tia read out interesting articles. She enjoyed the rustle of the newspaper when Tia turned the pages.

"I'm glad you liked it." Tia set down the paper and smiled at Coco.

"Can I ask you a question?" Coco asked.

"Yes."

"How did you pay for the formula and the crib and diapers for Bebe?"

Tia frowned, her eyes suddenly sad, her lips pursed as she regarded Coco. "Your mother gives you four thousand dollars a month for household expenses and four thousand dollars a month for personal use."

Coco stared at Tia for a long time, unable to comprehend what she had said. "But...." Her voice trailed off. "I thought... I was told...."

Tia nodded her head, encouraging Coco to keep talking. "What were you told, Coco?"

"I was told I was a poor girl, that there was hardly enough money to feed me let alone keep Bebe. The Keeper, I mean...the last housekeeper who worked here...she told me that Mama had mostly forgotten about me...and that I was poor. Where was all this money before? I've been living on nothing for years."

"It was always there; it's just been going to other people and not to you. If your last housekeeper hadn't been caught selling your painting no one would have known she was taking thousands of dollars a month from your household account. Only you can draw from your personal account though I'm sure she tried accessing that, too."

"She said I was poor. She made bad formula for Bebe; it made her thin and sick. It was only when I told her she could sell the painting that she started buying the good formula." Coco went quiet with rage. "I've been washing diapers," she added breaking the heavy silence.

"You have been washing diapers." Tia nodded her understanding. "It's built character I'm sure, but it's not a pleasant thing to have to do. There was no reason for you to ever have to go without, Coco. You were being robbed."

Coco nodded, her heart filled with anger as she realized that she had never dared to complain, and that Bebe had suffered needlessly. "I hate the Keeper." Coco glared at the table. "I hate her."

 26   MAGDALENA'S SHADOW

Tia watched quietly. "Yes," she nodded. "But I'm afraid hate is something other people do. It's something that 'the Keeper' does. Leave it to her and people like her to hate. You should pray that someday she feels remorse for what she's done to innocent children. You should pray that she can find forgiveness for her cruelty."

Coco looked angrily up at Tia, but when met by the older woman's soft sad eyes, all her rage melted and she was left with the simple wound of injustice, an ache she had known her entire life. Her eyes filled with tears and she cried noisily the way Bebe often did.

Bebe awoke in her nice new crib. The sound of the baby's babbling voice took Tia from the kitchen, leaving Coco alone to grieve. Raising her head, Coco listened for Bebe's voice, watching the elderly woman walk quietly to the room where Bebe fussed.

Coco's rage-filled crying stopped long before Tia returned to the kitchen. Though her eyes were red, Coco was up making Bebe's bottle. Instead of tears she sniffed the sniff of an injured woman who has decided on action instead of self-pity.

Tia saw the dishes sitting pre-washed in the sink along with a total lack of any of the kitchen items that had been used with breakfast. "Good," Tia said, placing Bebe in the new swing. "Always turn your rage into good works. Rage turned inward becomes sickness. You'll feel better soon."

Too angry to reply Coco walked to Bebe, reclined the seat, and gave her the bottle. The baby held it tightly between her hands and began to drink deeply. There was something relaxing in the sound of Bebe feeding. The noise settled over the room like a warm blanket, taking with it the last shreds of Coco's indignation. Leaning back, she sagged against the counter, the heels of her small hands resting on the granite behind her, her eyes fixed on the floor. Tia was right, she felt drained and tired but better than she had felt in years.

Already the world seemed less closed to her. She had money, a friend, a child she loved, and the hope that life could be more than the small existence she had been confined to. Anger replaced the fear instilled in her by the Keeper – the woman who had told her she was too stupid to leave the apartment, too poor to go shopping, and too naïve and skinny to defend herself in the world outside. Coco remembered now that there had been a bagel shop around the corner that she had loved to visit, and a hair salon, and a lot of fun shops she had enjoyed with her nanny. Three years had passed since Eva Clark had gone. What would the world look like now?

"Coco, Bebe needs new clothes." Tia spoke without looking up. "Someone cut the feet off her sleeper."

"That's the sleeper she came in," Coco answered, looking at where Tia folded the baby's ragged pant legs into cuffs. "I had to cut the feet off to make room for her long legs."

"Came in?" Tia asked. "What do you mean, came in?"

Coco didn't answer. In a panic, she stared down at her pink slippers trying to think quickly.

"Coco?" Tia asked with an authority that sent shivers down Coco's spine. "Where did Bebe come from?"

"I meant came *home* in… from the hospital…."

Tia only stared at her. "Coco, you didn't have Bebe yourself, did you?"

"No." Coco shook her head, her eyes leveled at the floor. After a moment, she left the kitchen to get the bag that held the document.

When she returned, Tia held Bebe over her shoulder, patting her back. Bebe burped loudly and happily before being returned to her swing with a graham cracker.

"This came with the woman who brought Bebe to me." Coco handed Tia the document. "She was still learning to sit up when she came; if the date on this document is her birthdate then she was only seven months old when she came." Coco ran her finger down the page, stopping on the date she believed was Bebe's birthday. "If this is right she'll turn one next month."

Tia studied the paper carefully before turning her eyes on Coco. "Why do you call her Bebe?"

"It says Bebe right here." Coco leaned over the document a second time, her honey brown eyes searching the page for the name she had recognized from her fashion magazines. "See." She pointed to the four small letters.

Tia smiled. "That's the Spanish word for baby. You have been calling her baby all this time. It's pronounced bay-bay."

Coco frowned. "Then what's her name?" She looked over the paper with worry.

"They didn't give her one. It just says 'Baby Rodriguez' – or to you, *Bebe* Rodriguez – 'born the seventh of March to M. Rodriguez of Miramar, Argentina.' Do you know an M. Rodriguez?"

Coco nodded slowly. "My mother is Magdalena Rodriguez, the fashion model. She has a beach house in Argentina, in Miramar. I used to visit there when I was little."

Tia nodded, looking at the baby who swung on happily. "So," she said with deliberate slowness, "Bebe is most likely your baby sister, Coco. You have given her such good care even though you didn't know she was related to you. Few people would have been as selfless."

Coco's eyes misted over with fresh tears. "That explains why the Keeper didn't give her to some orphanage. She knew Bebe was Magdalena's." Coco watched her tiny sister without words. Never had she dreamed that Bebe could be her sister; she had always seen her as the baby God had sent to help her in her loneliness.

CHAPTER THREE

"We don't have to leave the lobby today if it feels too soon," Tia said. "This could just be a practice run. We can shop for Bebe's clothes another day."

"I'm okay," Coco answered, her eyes fixed anxiously on her image starkly reflected in the elevator's mirrored walls. Her hands shook while she listened to the sound of the floors rushing by. She had spent two hours dressing for her first day out yet she still felt unprepared. Looking down she noticed her oversized feet, one of her two embarrassing features. Today they looked almost pretty in nude-colored sandals. Glancing up again she surveyed the scarf she wore over her ugly ears, her second embarrassing feature because of her attached earlobes.

"I'm okay," Coco murmured a second time, her eyes still trained on her reflection. With her two ugly features dealt with she almost felt okay.

Bebe sat in the stroller wearing Coco's wool barrette pulled jauntily down over her forehead. The barrette fit Bebe well, though it was meant for an older child. A silk and cashmere wrap concealed the outgrown baby clothes she wore.

The color of the wrap matched Coco's silk scarf and Stella McCartney dress. The dress was new. Like all the clothing that came to #2, it was tailored for Magdalena but fit Coco just as well.

Boxes arrived at the apartment each week. They came in every style, in every color, and from every corner of the earth – some from major fashion houses, others from labels just getting their start – small boutiques and designers who worked out of their basements. The boxes were gifts to Magdalena filled with hope that maybe Magdalena would wear their garments and put their designer on the map.

The downstairs lobby stood empty when they reached it. Outside, Coco discovered that the bagel shop was gone, replaced by a busy Starbucks that teemed with well-dressed Chicago natives looking for a caffeine fix. Coco was transfixed by the busy atmosphere of the new café, her eyes scanning the Starbucks' mermaid, the lights, and the people coming and going in a constant flow of movement.

While Coco took in the world, the world took in Coco with its usual hunger. Her natural beauty shone like a beacon in a sea of mediocrity. When still a child she had confused admiration with ridicule. Now, as a man twice her age looked on her with fixed admiration, she wished she had worn her red hoodie and jeans instead of the delicately beautiful Stella dress. Walking past the café, they turned down a side street toward the high-end boutique that sold baby clothes. Coco stuck close to Tia, never moving more than a few steps away from the baby stroller.

Halfway to the boutique, Coco stopped suddenly before a window to stare at the manikin behind the glass. It wore Dolce & Gabbana slacks, similar to a pair she owned. Coco admired the sight, her fingers grazing the surface of the glass. Posters of supermodels wavered in an artificial breeze, set in motion by the air conditioning inside the store. Coco passed manikin after manikin looking lovingly at the clothes until she stopped, turning a bright smile on Tia and Bebe.

Tia looked up at the window where Coco stood. A manikin dressed in Prada posed gracefully above them, back-dropped by a poster of a glossy-eyed sex-kitten of a model wearing the same outfit. She lounged lazily on a blisteringly bright rock, an expanse of endless desert sweeping out behind her. Tia noticed her cocoa-colored skin and thick, wavy dark hair, all too familiar to be mistaken. From the full lips to the heart-shaped face...this was Coco's mother, no doubt; this was Magdalena.

"Mama." Coco spoke the word with a touch of the Latin accent she had heard her mother speak with. "Look, Bebe, that's our mother." The baby rattled her toy and stared at the flow of cars reflected back to her in the glass. What did she know of scrawny supermodels and store front windows? Tia smiled at Bebe's innocence, while the look of unsurpassed admiration on Coco's young face drew her pity.

"Bebe will be tired soon," Tia said, hoping to refocus Coco's attention. "We need to get to the baby store."

Coco nodded, pulling her eyes from her mother before they walked down the avenue toward Bebe's new wardrobe.

Once inside the store Coco was immediately approached by a friendly salesgirl. One look at Coco and the girl's face lit with an expression which screamed, "Money, money, money!" To someone who worked on commission, Coco was a walking miracle. She bought sleepers and jumpers, dresses with matching hats and booties, as well as silk sweaters with matching silk lined pants all embroidered with silk and cashmere flowers. With a point of her finger or a quietly whispered request every dress was matched with tights, shoes, hats, and a stuffed toy in a matching outfit.

To Coco, fine clothes were a necessity; to Tia it was a shocking waste of money as Bebe would outgrow everything in no time.

Coco was in heaven. She sat on the living room floor and untied all the ribbons on the boxes of baby clothing that had been delivered to #2. In her newfound confidence, she had even allowed the delivery boy to bring the boxes through the door instead of leaving them with the doorman. Bebe slept soundly in her swing while Coco unwrapped each piece of clothing from its tissue paper. When she had finished, she surveyed Bebe's new things with a growing sense of pride.

The moment felt like Christmas as tissue paper and ribbon lay in piles on the floor around her. Coco glowed with confidence; she had gone shopping, braved the outside world, and returned home with her treasures. As she flung another empty box on the pile of tissue paper, she slowly became aware of the faraway look in Tia's eyes.

"This is my favorite." Coco raised the little pink dress up before her. Yet even this statement didn't draw Tia into the moment. "Tia, are you okay?"

The old lady laughed in a sudden startling way. "I was thinking… it's odd how being around you brings back old memories. The way you're sitting there now, surrounded with pink tissue paper and boxes – it reminds me of a time when I was little…." She shook her head, her thoughts fading off into the distance.

"Tell me. I don't know anything about your childhood."

"It was Christmas, and I had hidden to watch my mother's employers open their Christmas gifts. I could hear my mother calling me from the back garden but I ignored her. I wanted to see what rich people bought each other."

 34   MAGDALENA'S SHADOW

"Were you very poor?"

"Yes. I had one skirt, one shirt, and one pair of panties and that was all. My mother was a maid in this huge stone house in Nicaragua and I was not supposed to go near it. Unfortunately, I was headstrong and disobedient; I was always in trouble." Tia laughed again, the same quick, slightly uncomfortable laugh.

She leaned over and started collecting the tissue paper, folding it into fours, laying one piece on top of the other. Coco would have tossed it all, but Tia was going to keep it. In that moment, Coco glimpsed poverty for the first time. Even though she had been abandoned and neglected she knew she had never been the "poor girl" the Keeper had told her she was.

CHAPTER FOUR

All through the next day, Coco and Tia made a room for Bebe out of one of the guest bedrooms. A bed was dismantled and moved into storage along with several other pieces of furniture. After spending the entire day dusting and organizing, Bebe's new garments hung on pink silk-wrapped hangers, while her tiny shoes sat sweetly in the oversized cherry wood shoe rack next to hats, scarves, and a dozen other precious little items. Later that evening Coco laid Bebe in the new crib in her own room, a multicolored mobile spinning and singing *Imagine* above her.

The room was bright with toys, blankets, and the soft wall decals that Coco had purchased during their earlier excursion; animals and stars twinkled and grinned from the walls and ceiling. Tia switched off the light, causing hundreds of stars to shine through the room. Bebe instantly stopped rattling her toy and stared at the store-bought cosmos above her.

Thirty minutes later Coco stood in the kitchen putting up baby bottles next to the few remaining tins of formula. With Tia's help Bebe had begun eating solid foods. Soon the days of bottles and formula would be over.

"What will we put Bebe's vitamins in when she's off bottles?" Coco turned to Tia who was busy gathering her things to go. Coco glanced up at the bottle with the eyedropper top that sat next to the formula.

"I didn't know you were giving her vitamins." Tia glanced up at the bottle with its old label handwritten in Spanish. There was nothing interesting about the bottle, nothing out of the ordinary about it except for the fact that Coco alone knew it existed. "Is this what you have been giving her?" Tia took the bottle off the shelf.

"Yes, the bottle came with her. Rosa read me the directions; I'm to give her four drops three times a day."

Tia stared at the handwritten label and then examined the contents, holding the liquid up to the light. The bottle was only a quarter full. Tia translated the label aloud. "Reduce each feeding by one drop every seven days or use as necessary under a doctor's guidance. I don't suppose she read you that part."

Coco's face fell. She took the bottle from Tia's hand and stared at the Spanish words. "It was in her baby bag when she came." Coco handed it back to Tia.

"I understand." Tia unscrewed the top of the bottle and chemical fumes filled the air between them. Worse than the scent was the look of dismay on Tia's face.

"What's the matter, Tia?"

"This is a drug called laudanum, Coco. It's an opiate given to babies who were born addicted to heroin. Like heroin, it's also very addictive." There was a pause while both Coco and Tia contemplated the bottle. "Do you know if your mother was using during her pregnancy?"

"No, no, no.... Mama wouldn't do drugs when she was pregnant." Coco shook her head, dismissing the thought completely. "She wouldn't do that. No, Tia, there has to be another reason. She loves us. She...."

"Without medical records," Tia interrupted, "we can't know why Bebe was given laudanum. They could've started her on it for the trip to the U.S. It might have been prescribed to keep her calm on the plane. When I was a child in Nicaragua it was used to quiet sick people and children. Maybe it's still used in Argentina. I honestly don't know why they gave it to her."

A lingering silence settled over the room. When Coco raised her eyes to Tia, the old woman was still staring at the bottle. "Tia, I haven't been giving it to her regularly... sometimes I miss a dose... maybe I haven't been giving her enough to hurt her." Coco stared at Tia, her heart racing.

"Oh, God, Tia, why would anyone give Bebe laudanum?"

Tia pulled her eyes from the bottle. "Everything will be fine. Bebe will be fine." She handed the bottle to Coco and walked to the darkened living room, the glare from the wall mounted TV casting the furniture in long blinking shadows.

Coco lingered in the kitchen, turning the bottle over and over in her hands. On Bebe's arrival it had been full; now six months later, it was nearly empty. Bebe had to be addicted.

"Tia?" Coco's voice broke with emotion. She followed the old woman into the living room. "What do we do?" Coco stopped when she saw Tia standing before an un-blinded wall of windows. Chicago stretched out behind them, mile upon mile of city glaring a pinkish gray in the evening sun. Coco's vertigo froze her where she stood.

Tia looked out beyond the city, past the skyscrapers and the busy streets.

When she finally spoke, her voice came in hushed tones. "Bebe will cry, she'll be sick, she'll be angry, but she will recover. Tomorrow we will give her only three drops three times a day, and we will give her even less the week after. It must be a very slow withdrawal."

"Okay."

"When Bebe came did she arch her back and go stiff when you held her? Did she look in your eyes or did she avoid your face?"

"She looked in my eyes and she never arched away from me. She liked to be held. She liked to have me close."

"Did her hands shake? Did she cry a lot or have trouble catching her breath?

"No."

"Good."

"Why?"

"Babies born addicted to heroin don't make eye contact. They don't want to be touched. They can have tremors and irregular heartbeats. Some of them have trouble learning to roll over. Some have breathing problems. Of course, she was not a newborn when she came here. Her treatment may have been good in Argentina. Even still she should have been off the laudanum before she arrived. They must have prescribed it to keep her calm on the plane."

"That has to be it." Coco turned toward the kitchen, unable to face the possibility that Magdalena was a drug addict who would use during a pregnancy. Rumors of drug use cycled through the tabloids and magazines Coco read, but the TV had offered no solid evidence to support the rumors. Magdalena looked flawless in her ads and spoke perfectly in her interviews, and she had never once been listed among the celebrities in drug treatment programs. Coco shook the thought from her head.

It had been stupid to trust what the Keeper had read off the bottle. No wonder Bebe was such a good baby: she had been slightly stoned for the last six months. She rarely cried and demanded, and never for more than a moment. Bebe slept much of the time, and that made her very easy to care for.

Coco heard a click as the door opened and then closed. When she walked back to the living room she found Tia's old coat gone along with her chrome handcart. Tia had left for the night and Coco felt abandoned, frightened, and angry.

"It's not my fault!" Coco said the moment Tia walked into the kitchen the following morning.

"You're up early." Tia skipped the polite "good morning" they usually exchanged. Coco looked exhausted but more importantly, she looked afraid. "I know it's not your fault," Tia soothed. "I'm sorry if I seemed angry yesterday. I was shocked and upset; I needed fresh air to clear my mind."

Coco deflated slightly, her red eyes following Tia through the kitchen. Tia warmed the frying pan and got out eggs, bread, and fruit from the refrigerator. She was ignoring Coco, not on purpose but out of preoccupation.

"How did you know that smell?" Coco demanded.

"What smell?"

"The drops. The moment you smelled them you looked so shocked, like someone had hit you. How did you know that smell?"

Tia shook her head and began to slice a tomato. Coco watched her for a few minutes before repeating the question.

"Not today, I'm not in the mood. Maybe I'll tell you sometime but not today." Tia kept her back to Coco while she kept her fingers busy.

Coco went to get Bebe, who was sitting up and looking around her room.

"Good morning." Coco lifted her up into her arms and kissed her. Bebe smiled pleasantly, her soft brown eyes blinking in the morning sun. In the kitchen, Coco sat her in her swing before giving her the drops. *One, two, three,* she counted silently as the drops fell into the baby formula. Bebe sucked up her breakfast with happy relish.

Bebe seemed fine for the first part of the day, but by evening, even with the three dinnertime drops, she was restless and angry. Coco played with her, sang to her, and rocked her, but nothing she did could soothe away the signs of withdrawal.

"It'll be like this for a while." Tia moved through the house cleaning, tidying, and organizing.

By nine that evening Tia was gone and Bebe began to cry from withdrawal. Coco hadn't slept the night before, and she didn't sleep that night, either. Instead she watched Bebe go between exhausted crying to exhausted sleep and then back again.

When Tia walked in the next morning she found Bebe in her swing, staring at the TV while Coco lay passed out on the living room couch.

The days crept by in a cycle of sleepless hysteria until Coco began to cry as well from exhaustion.

"She doesn't sleep for more than an hour or two before she's back up screaming. I can't do this much longer, Tia. I can't."

"You can do this, Coco," Tia answered, gathering Bebe up into her arms.

"No, I can't."

"What other choice do you have? This is motherhood, Coco, it's not just diapers and playtime. Sometimes it's worry, exhaustion, and endurance. Most mothers have got past the

 42   MAGDALENA'S SHADOW

screaming all night stage by the third month. You're getting to experience it now, and this *is* the way things are, and there is nothing you can do but get through it. In life, you have no choice but to be strong."

Coco stared at Tia. She had expected sympathy not a lecture on the hardships of existence. "You are being cruel. I tell you I need help and you talk to me like I'm spoiled and whiny. I'm not whining, I'm tired. What's the matter with you?"

Tia stopped where she stood, turning with Bebe on her hip to face Coco. "You're right. I'm being cruel. But I'm not the only one. Your mother was cruel when she sent a drug addicted baby to another country to be raised by the sixteen-year-old she abandoned years before. That was cruel. It's also cruel that right now there are girls in the streets raising drug addicted babies without the luxury of a penthouse apartment or a four thousand dollar a month allowance."

"I'm doing the best job I can! I need to sleep and I need you to be nice. I thought you were my friend, Tia." Coco watched Tia deflate, and in that instant, she realized that nothing Tia had said since she had walked in the door had been directed at her. "What's going on with you?" Coco looked at her with concern.

"I'm sorry. I'm tired too. It's been rough… at home. It's hard to remember that tough love isn't always the answer. I'll watch Bebe while you get some sleep. Okay?"

"I don't know what kinds of problems you deal with outside of this apartment, Tia. All I do know is that I've always been nice to you. Remember that the next time you decide to pull this *tough love* act." Coco burst into tears and walked from the room.

When Bebe began to sleep through the night, they dropped her dose to two drops two times a day. Bebe became sick again and the screaming resumed. Coco learned to live without sleep and Tia did her best to counter her complaints and bolster her courage. The laudanum bottle was nearly empty three weeks later when they dropped the dose again. This time, the effects were not as severe and with time Bebe was off the drug completely.

CHAPTER FIVE

To Coco's shock and sadness, the Bebe she had loved and nurtured all those months was completely different from the Bebe she now had to raise. Where once Bebe was a happy contented baby, now she was demanding and dissatisfied. She dragged herself around the apartment with absolute determination, grabbing onto tabletops and sofa cushions to pull herself to standing. Everything within arm's reach went straight into her mouth and then onto the floor. Coco frantically baby-proofed the apartment, but no matter how hard she tried, things were still broken and the mess was constant. Bebe took off her clothes and she took off her diapers. She peed on the carpet and dug in the plants, and Coco found herself wishing she could escape the apartment and the life Magdalena had thrust upon her. Every day she thought up a reason to leave the apartment, sometimes for coffee at Starbucks, other times to buy a new piece of clothing at the store where she had seen her mother's picture in the window. Yet even these short escapes didn't revitalize her.

Worse still was how tired Tia seemed each day. There were days when leaving Bebe with her was not an option. Tia wouldn't discuss her seemingly disastrous home life, and without the bond of trust they had earlier shared, Coco felt unsupported and alone.

Coco's daydreams shifted from moments with Magdalena and the memory of her once sweet baby, to rich fantasies involving beautiful boys who kissed her in romantic, baby-free destinations. As the months dragged by and Bebe's newfound attitude developed, Coco's mind shifted further from reality, focusing less and less on the life she lived, a life that seemed harder to endure with each passing day.

One evening, while Tia and Coco sat on the living room couch, they heard the elevator ding and the doors slide open. It was a sound they would not have heard if Bebe hadn't been passed out in her crib. Coco rushed to the front door peephole in time to see the black-clad shoulders of a man vanish into #1, the apartment that had been empty ever since she was very little. When the door to #1 closed, Coco moved to the adjoining wall, listening for the sound of movement.

Tia laughed loudly when she saw Coco press her ear to the wall. Coco shushed her with a look and then pressed her ear back against the wall. She heard the TV switch on followed by the sound of running water. Cupboard doors opened and closed followed by silence.

Tia laughed again. "Girl, you need a vacation," she teased, watching Coco press her ear to a different part of the wall.

"Tia, you don't understand. No one has lived there in years. A family lived there when I was little. But I can hardly remember what they looked like. I wonder who this guy is?" Coco frowned and walked back to the sofa, her curiosity conjuring up a thousand stories. "I wonder when we'll get to meet him. I wonder what he looks like. Maybe he has a family?"

Tia shrugged. "If he's anything like my neighbors you'll never see him unless the power goes out."

CHAPTER SIX

"She's a monster," Coco told Tia the moment she walked in the door. It was still early morning but havoc had broken loose in #2. Coco was in the middle of washing baby poop off the walls. Bebe had taken her diaper off and played in the contents. When Coco grabbed her up and washed her she had screamed the whole time. The moment Bebe was clean she had run back to her art project and dived back in. Coco had washed her again before putting her into her crib with the safety tent fastened. Bebe's fingers scrambled over the tent while she tore at the fabric and screamed. Tia arrived as Coco, sponge in hand, began to cry.

"She's not a monster, she's asserting herself. Think of it as the terrible twos at a year and a half. It'll pass, I promise."

In the other room, there was a thud as Bebe hit the floor and began to cry. The safety tent was totally useless when faced with a toddler like Bebe.

"I'll get her." Tia turned toward Bebe's room leaving Coco alone. The scent of baby poop and disinfectant made Coco sick.

"No biting, Bebe." Tia's voice carried to where Coco cleaned. Coco could see Tia lift a struggling Bebe up into her arms. The baby grabbed the skin under Tia's chin and twisted, starting yellow and blue bruises on the old woman's neck. Tia grabbed her little fists. "No, Bebe." They stood staring at each other until Bebe's fists relaxed and she let go. "Now it's time to get dressed." Coco watched Tia set the child on her hip where she stood before the closet. Bebe reached her hand out and began tearing clothes off the hangers. "No, Bebe."

Turning away, Coco blinked back fresh tears. Bebe made everything hard. Even getting her dressed was difficult.

"I'm taking her to the park." Tia entered the living room with Bebe. "You take some time for yourself. You'll have to make your own breakfast, but you'll be alone."

"Thank you." Coco finished cleaning before heading for the shower.

While she stripped off her clothes she heard Bebe shriek as she was forced into her stroller. The screaming didn't stop until the elevator took them out of hearing range. Bebe hated her stroller; she wanted to run and she knew how to unbuckle the stroller harness in seconds. Tia must have restrained her with a climbing hook snapped across her chest straps. No matter how Bebe struggled she couldn't figure out how to unhook the climbing hook and set herself free.

Tears ran down Coco's cheeks. She stepped into the shower remembering the sweet baby she had loved. Where had her Bebe gone and how could that sweet child have become the terror of #2? Coco felt the hot water run down her back and closed her eyes as a new wave of grief overtook her.

In the past, dressing had been something Coco had enjoyed, something she had done with care, picking through her wardrobe for just the right look. Today she was not in the mood for a Prada suit or any of her other dressier clothes. She settled instead for comfort while she tried to remember what she used to do for fun. There were her unread magazines. The Fashion Channel and the storage room stuffed to capacity with all the gift boxes she hadn't made time to go through.

On entering the living room Coco tripped over a stuffed bear and then had to slide still more toys off the couch to make room to sit. The TV blinked on, pouring light and noise into the gloomy living room. Coco switched the channel from cartoons to the catwalks. Slowly she realized that New York's February Fashion Week had come and gone along with the last several months of her life. Model after model traipsed across the screen bringing her the latest fashions from a world she had completely lost touch with.

Feeling restless and irritable Coco switched off the TV. She felt like she was missing out on life, missing out on what was important, missing all the things she loved by staying in the apartment with Bebe day after day. Worse still was the idea that she should go out and get a life. *If only Magdalena hadn't dumped Bebe on me,* Coco thought. *But where would Bebe be if Magdalena hadn't dumped her here?*

Getting up angrily, Coco went to retrieve the storage room key only to be startled by her reflection in the entryway mirror. She wore an old Gucci T-shirt which reflected back the large GUCCI logo stretched across her breasts. It was stained pink on the shoulder where Bebe had burped up cough medicine. In the darkness, Coco could make out the lines of her beloved old Calvin Klein jeans looking as ragged and worn as the T-shirt. Ragged and worn: that was how she looked and felt. Biting her lip, she passed through the door toward the only fun she could think of.

The 30th floor entryway felt cold and empty when Coco stepped into it, her bare feet sank into the chill of the plush carpeting. The room felt far darker and colder than #2, existing as it did like a silent void: transitory and lifeless. Goosebumps rose on Coco's arms when she slid her key into the storage room lock. She heard the satisfying click of the bolt as the door handle moved in her hand.

Boxes lined the walls like works of art: colorful, glossy, smooth to the touch, all filled with beautifully designed garments and accessories. It was not uncommon for each carefully shipped item to be individually wrapped in silk tissue to preserve the piece. Valentino, Prada, Dior, Jacobs, Cole, Chanel, Dolce & Gabbana, any one of them could be there. The possibility of new furs, evening gowns, sundresses, cocktail dresses, shoes, purses, and lingerie thrilled her. Coco loved the storage room; it was a continual cornucopia of gifts and material pleasure, all addressed to a woman who would never see a single box let alone wear its contents.

Magdalena's assistant was supposed to collect the gift boxes but he never did. He was supposed to do a lot of things, like hire nannies to raise Coco and make her go to school, but he didn't do that, either. Coco and the penthouse she occupied where no longer on his schedule.

The first box Coco inspected was blue with orange stripes. The designer was unfamiliar, probably a young label with little clout. Coco set the box down but didn't discount it. Many of her favorite pieces came from small boutiques and independent tailors.

When she reached for a second box her long hair swung forward and caught on the shelf beside her. Coco carefully pulled the tress back, working it gently free from the bracket before winding it up high on her head. She shoved two pencils that lay forgotten on a shelf through the dark mass.

The next box was from Tommy Hilfiger; she set it aside and moved onto a blue box that she recognized as being from Prada. Everything that came from Prada was worth her time. Coco lifted the box into her arms and turned back out into the lobby, only to bump straight into a man who must have just exited the elevator.

Coco froze in shock. Her eyes met his and held them. How had she not heard him? How had he moved up so silently beside her? The man was beautiful – not like the male models from her magazines but like an action star or a soldier. He had an amazingly tall and powerful body. She felt herself being assessed in the quick glance of his sharp brown eyes. He was Latin like her, dark like her, but his brown eyes were not flecked with gold but with silver.

"Hello." He continued looking at Coco while she openly stared at him. The look in his eyes moved from curiosity to admiration, then to quiet restraint as he took her in. His black hair and bronzed skin paired beautifully with his perfectly tailored suit and black Burberry wool topcoat. Everything about him added up to perfection.

A sensuous shiver raised goosebumps along Coco's arms as something other than the cold passed over her. "Hi." Her voice was quick and nervous, embarrassingly high.

The attraction was instant. Coco felt a wave of dizziness hit her.

"I'm staying in #1 for a while." His words exuded confidence. His smile shrank to a slight one-sided grin.

Coco remained still, her heart making the only noise she was capable of. This was the man who had fired up her imagination, the mysterious neighbor who had arrived without warning. Trapped by his gaze, Coco felt more the deer-in-headlights than ever, but the idea of running him off with her shyness terrified her. "I live here," Coco blurted out. She stood half in, half out of the storage room with the box clutched protectively to her chest, her dark hair spilling wildly from the pencils that held the pile on top of her head.

"Bit cramped, isn't it?" The man's teasing smile twisted up both corners of his mouth while his eyes surveyed the storage room.

"Not really," Coco answered in confusion, her breath catching in her chest, making it ache.

Coco's new neighbor smelled like a mixture of expensive cologne and fine fabric, yet there was more to the fragrance. There was the scent of the man himself. A slow heat crept up from under Coco's T-shirt, spreading to her cheeks. She found herself wondering if he tasted as good as he smelled. The look he gave her said he knew exactly what she was thinking.

Coco's eyes dropped in embarrassment only to refocus on her bare feet. Never in her life had a man seen her huge ugly feet. She slid one foot over the other in an attempt to hide them before looking up nervously at her new neighbor. Lifting a finger, she brushed one stray strand of hair out of her eyes, tucking it behind her ear. In that moment, she realized that her ears were also exposed. This man had seen her two greatest defects and yet he was still looking, smiling and drinking her in.

"Hi," Coco said again, her voice now much lower. The man's smile only grew as a low chuckle rumbled in his chest. "Coco," she said, by way of introduction.

"Sure." The man nodded still looking amused. "Sounds good."

Coco laughed a high laugh that vibrated strangely in the small room, her lack of confidence becoming more evident. "No. I'm Coco," she corrected with more control.

"I would still like some." And with that she knew she was in trouble. He reached out, taking the box she held. "I'll follow you," he added, his voice thick with confidence. He stepped aside to let her out of the storage room.

Coco felt drunk and unsteady when she walked ahead of him toward #2. She felt his eyes on the swing of her hips and the curve of her back as she opened the door and let him into her flat.

Some small part of her rebelled in a voice that said, *don't let a strange and obviously interested man into your flat.* She felt the madness of her actions like a distant scream, but the warning was drowned out by years of quiet obedience and a need for attention.

The beautiful man's eyes flashed over the interior of #2, taking it all in with one glance. The penthouse was modern yet feminine; baby things lay everywhere. What stopped him where he stood was the enormous Salvador Dali that hung on the wall to his right.

"Dali's *Elephants.*" His voice was hushed and low.

"That one's my favorite." Coco drifted over to stand beside him, breathing in his scent with slow satisfaction. A spotlight hung above the painting, illuminating it with soft light as long-legged elephants danced before them. Coco felt the man's admiration, the bright colors glowing vividly before them.

"I'll make the chocolate," Coco offered shyly. She walked toward the kitchen wondering how this situation had come about and why on earth she was making hot chocolate.

Coco watched the man follow after her, his reflection multiplied in the black glass-fronted kitchen cabinets. He stopped again, this time admiring the Diego Rivera and the Warhol.

"You have expensive taste."

E. E. ORME   55

"Yes," Coco answered distractedly. She set a saucepan on the stovetop, hearing the woof of blue flame as the fire sparked on the gas range. He laughed at her response but didn't seem surprised.

His eyes regained their earlier look of casual appraisal. He watched Coco unwrap two squares of dark Belgian chocolate, his eyes never leaving her.

The two cubes of unsweetened chocolate melted quickly in the pan and were followed in slow succession by raw brown sugar crystals, a dash of cinnamon, and a pinch of red chili powder. Coco's fingers fumbled only when she glanced at her guest, finding the intensity in his gaze.

"You make hot chocolate like my mother used to."

"I learned this recipe from my housekeeper, Tia. It's Central American."

"You have lived here a long time," he stated more than questioned.

Coco's brow lifted. *How did he know?* She nodded, trying to stay focused as she answered,

"All my life."

The mixture began to simmer. Before it boiled, Coco whisked it to a froth, adding milk when all the chocolate and sugar crystals dissolved. Cooking Tia's recipes relaxed her. For a moment, she felt totally herself, forgetting the fact that soon she would have to make conversation. After dividing the hot chocolate into two cups the work was done. With nothing left to focus on, conversation became inevitable. Coco felt fidgety, but she moved with a slow, deliberate calm that belied her feelings. The new neighbor followed her to the couch.

"Strange having cocoa in the summer." She tucked her knees under her chin when she sat down across from him, feeling how pitiful her opening attempt at conversation was.

He seemed not to notice. "It's never summer in this place," he responded, indicating the skyscraper they lived in with a casual gesture. "They keep the air conditioning on so high I need a coat just to get to the apartment."

"Yes, all year round. Have you lived here before?" Her eyes rose to his, blinking nervously as her curiosity grew.

"Not for a long time. I just inherited the place from my father. He died last week."

"I'm so sorry." Coco had no way of knowing how to empathize with death. There was a pause as nether of them spoke. "Are you going to live here again? #1 has been empty for a long time. It would be nice to have a neighbor."

"I don't know. I haven't had time to think that far ahead."

"Of course not. I'm sorry you just lost your dad."

"Yes, well...." He shrugged before settling back into the couch, his eyes focused on his cup. "I'm Rob Banks." He smiled, looking up. Coco felt trapped by his gaze, unable to look away. "I sort of forgot the introduction part." Coco laughed. "Oh, the name," he grinned, his eyes dropping in embarrassment. "I don't usually shorten it the first time. It's why I'm a lawyer and not a banker. I don't think any bank would take me."

"No, probably not," Coco giggled. "I don't think your parents thought that one through." She traced her index finger over the rim of her mug, trying to stay calm.

"Oh, they did, Dad thought it was a riot. He always called me Rob."

"Well, if we're being formal," Coco said slowly, "I'm Coco Rodriguez."

Rob extended his hand to take hers. "Pleased to formally meet you," he grinned. His fingers felt warm. He kept her hand for a lingering moment before releasing her. The action was sweetly intimate and intensely stirring, especially for a young girl as isolated and sheltered as Coco.

Their conversation drifted from Chicago to the age and dignity of their building. Rob loved the location and Coco couldn't disagree. It was central to everything she loved, everything she knew. As they talked, Coco's hand still tingled from the earlier contact, short lived as the moment had been. When her heartbeat returned to near normal, she ventured to look up again. His eyes were as ever, glued to her with the same appraising look.

"How old are you?" Rob asked suddenly, his expression moving from interest to regret when he saw Coco's startled expression. "Sorry, that came out far differently than I had planned."

Coco shrugged, uncomfortable but determined to look nonchalant before looking away. If he knew her age, that she was legally a child, then none of this would be okay. Coco would be demoted from woman to girl and the relationship would become strained to nonexistent.

"It's just that I seem to remember you, but... I can't place it. The memory is so foggy and the timeline doesn't work. You are so totally familiar to me." He sighed as he watched her, lost for words. "I'm sorry," he repeated, "I didn't mean to be rude."

"You're not rude, you're fine. Don't worry about it. So, where's home?" She changed the subject sounding surprisingly confident, even relaxed. Coco shifted on the sofa to sit cross-legged, determined to look more at ease. The movement was purposefully executed with a languid grace. When she looked up again Rob was watching her, his eyes drifting over her with open admiration. "Where did you live before?" Coco restated the question, drawing his eyes back to hers.

"New York City."

Coco's smile shone like an instant beam of light, her shyness dissolving into excitement. "I've always wanted to go to New York. I want to go for Fashion Week. I would love to see the designers and all the models–" Rob nodded but looked lost. Then Coco remembered that she was supposed to be a wealthy woman who could travel freely if she wanted to.

"So, what's that?" Rob asked.

The shocked expression that transformed Coco's face made Rob laugh. In her world, it was impossible that anyone could live in New York and not know about Fashion Week.

She waved her hand at his mocking grin, shaking her head in annoyance. "A true New Yorker would know about Fashion Week."

"Maybe and maybe not. Where's your child?" He changed the subject, his eyes focusing on the toys strewn across the room.

"She's out with the housekeeper. She was more than I could handle today."

"How old is she?"

"Sixteen months."

"My daughter will be a year next week. She's a handful, too."

"What's her name?" Coco brightened at the idea of playdates and more time with Rob.

"Mila. Her mother named her after the actress."

Rob sighed, looking repulsed but Coco laughed. "I named Bebe after a fashion house, so I guess I'm no better. What's your wife's name?"

"Her name was Chloe."

"Oh, I'm sorry."

"Oh, don't be, we're divorced, nothing worse."

"Oh."

"What about Bebe's father? Does he live here?"

The question startled Coco; she hadn't thought about Bebe's father. She shifted uncomfortably in her seat, casting her eyes toward Dali's dancing elephants. "No, he's off... somewhere... in the world." Her words were slow but truthful. Who knew where Bebe's father was? Or *who* he was.

"He sounds like Chloe. Off somewhere doing God knows what." He shrugged before smiling his crooked smile, sending another sensuous shiver running through Coco's body.

A pause followed, which turned mildly uncomfortable. The initial attraction coupled with their missing spouses, both real and pretend, made further conversation difficult. Rob sipped his drink and Coco watched his hands as he held his mug. They were strong like the rest of him, and tan, darker even than her own. Their silence was interrupted by the sound of Tia's key in the latch. Rob and Coco watched the door slide open. Moments later Tia pushed a sleeping Bebe into the room.

"I wore her out," Tia proclaimed, smiling as she set her bag down and rolled the stroller into the living room. She scanned the sofa for Coco but found Rob instead.

"Hi," he smiled politely.

Tia stared at him, her smile fading. With pursed lips, she surveyed the pair before turning a suspicious eye on Coco. Leaving Bebe asleep in her stroller Tia walked quickly to the kitchen.

"She's not the friendly type, I take it?"

"Oh she is. She's just very protective of me. It's been hard living here alone with a small child."

"Well, I won't stay. Mila's flying in with her nanny tomorrow so I have a lot to do to get my place ready."

From the kitchen came the sound of dishes and saucepans being moved without care. Rob rose slowly to his feet, his expression preoccupied. He glanced toward the kitchen and then back at Coco as if trying to make sense of the situation. "I'm glad we met." Rob offered Coco his hand a second time.

"Me too." Another soft blush colored Coco's cheeks. She felt his fingers a second time before they slipped from her grasp. No part of her wanted him to leave, yet in a moment he was gone.

"That's our new neighbor."

Tia looked up from her work, catching sight of Coco's glowing complexion.

"Hmm..." Tia murmured.

"He's nice!"

"Did you happen to mention you're not yet seventeen?" Tia scowled with disapproval. Coco blushed but said nothing. "No, I didn't think so." Tia shook her head with dismay. "You need to be careful, not just for your sake but for his as well. You look so mature that you could easily confuse him and that would be wrong – totally and completely wrong."

Coco's heart sank in her chest. She liked Rob, but he was basically the first man she had talked to in years. "He's just a neighbor," she murmured as she left the room, the empty place in her heart expanding painfully as the momentary joy fled.

62   MAGDALENA'S SHADOW

CHAPTER SEVEN

August brought dry heat and that special kind of baked-city smell: a mixture of hot concrete and exhaust with the occasional addition of fried food, garbage, and industrial smoke. The mixed scents spun between pleasant and suffocating on the back of the constant breeze. The city looked dirty in the midsummer warmth, the smells mingling as they drifted over deep-fried donuts and a burning cigarette that sat on the curb, its smoke and ash blown lazily up into the breeze.

Coco felt the life around her – the roar of traffic and the jostle of moving bodies, everyone bent on their own plans and destinations. Bebe babbled in her stroller looking up at the tall buildings cast in hues of blue, grey, and purple by their far flung shadows. Coco breathed in the scent of the street and became part of the city, melding into the chaos and rumble of living. Like all the other ants with plans, she moved through the sea of humanity with a purpose that said *I belong here as much as you do*.

The park was her daily destination. If Bebe toddled around the slides and chased after the ducks all morning, she was far less aggressive and overactive in the afternoon. Coco walked the last two blocks to Lincoln Park feeling the sharp Chicago breeze lift her long dark hair and play in the folds of her skirt.

The stroller handles felt warm and comforting in her hands. She pushed Bebe the last hundred yards to the park, counting each of the white stripes of the crosswalk as she left the last urban shadow to emerge into gloriously blinding sunshine. Coco made the trip five times with Tia before coming to the point where she could make the journey alone. With each venture out into the world she moved with more confidence and less fear.

Lincoln Park buzzed with children, parents, and nannies. Coco compared the happy noise to the remembered chatter of the housemaids who once worked at #2 so many years ago. Like the maids, the park people chattered and gossiped, laughed and argued, filling the world with life while Coco listened, quietly enjoying the friendly flow of conversation.

Most of the other women were older than her. Some were nannies who raised other people's kids while others were mothers, aunties, and grandmothers. Many of these women had been lawyers, bankers, and journalists before they had refocused their lives around their families. They talked about everything from world events to local news and potty-training. Coco loved to listen to them talk; she listened to their conversations with rapt interest while she watched Bebe play in the sand and totter after the other kids.

Bebe walked well but she ran better. It sometimes seemed as if her large baby body gained coordination when she added speed. Coco never wore heels when she went out with Bebe; she had to be fast on her feet. When Bebe chased ducks, she did it with such gusto that falling into one of the Lincoln Park ponds was always a possibility.

The sun warmed them through the chilly breeze that blew off Lake Michigan. Coco unfastened the buckles on

Bebe's stroller and removed the climbing hook. In seconds Bebe rolled to her side, swung her legs over the stroller and landed on her feet running.

"Bebe," Coco called, holding the child's sunhat in her hand. But the girl was off, trotting at full speed around the play area looking for a child to chase.

"You have got to be fast to catch that one," Deborah, one of the park moms, teased.

Coco pushed the sunhat back into a stroller compartment where it would probably stay. They stood chatting – or rather Deborah chatted and Coco listened, saying "really" and "you're kidding" when conversation ebbed enough to allow her to speak. They were soon joined by Rachel and her daughter, Torrin.

Torrin, a quiet blonde haired girl with luminous blue eyes, wore glasses and talked about cats incessantly. She spent her days acting like a cat, her own stuffed kitty toy tucked lovingly under one arm. She was a gentle child who never screamed, hit, or bit.

Bebe spotted her in seconds, making a dash straight for her. "Play!" Bebe yelled as she sprang, knocking the quiet Torrin to the ground.

"No, Bebe." Coco picked her sister off the frightened child who lay flat on her back.

Rachel lifted Torrin off the ground and hugged her.

"No pushing, Bebe," Coco scolded, holding her sister's hands in her own while she tried to get Bebe to make eye contact.

"Play!" Bebe spluttered.

"Say sorry." Coco steered Bebe to stand before Torrin, whose crying intensified. Torrin shrank back as Bebe moved closer.

"Soss!" Bebe shouted before turning to run after

something that had caught her eye.

Rachel's face was red with irritation. Every day Bebe knocked someone down and it was usually Torrin.

"I'm so sorry," Coco apologized. "I don't know how to make her stop doing that."

"Maybe you should lock her in her stroller the next time she tackles someone?" Deborah suggested not five minutes later when she lifted her own son, Carson, off the ground. Bebe's second tackle of the day had taken place in the sandbox, effectively destroying the castle Carson had built. The boy spat sand from his mouth, his eyes leveled on Bebe with loathing.

Coco looked at Deborah with pleading eyes. "She'll hate me."

"That's motherhood," Deborah laughed, watching Carson run away from her, a glare of anger still marring his features.

Coco did her best to explain to Bebe that the next time she knocked someone down she was headed for the stroller. It took exactly six minutes for Bebe to spot an unfamiliar little black haired girl and flatten her like a pancake.

Sand clung to the girl's face and chest. Huge tears ran down her cheeks. Coco grabbed Bebe up off the little girl's back and carried her straight to the stroller. Bebe screamed like murder when she was buckled in, the climbing hook snapped over the otherwise useless shoulder straps. The little black haired girl lifted her arms into the air when her father came and picked her up; he dusted the sand from her face and clothes.

"Can I have a baby wipe?" The man carried his daughter toward Coco who glanced over her shoulder at the sobbing child, an apology already forming on her lips. A box of wipes sat open beside her, and as she passed him one she caught a glimpse of his face. Rob was every bit as gorgeous as Coco remembered. The moment she saw him she felt weak all over.

"Is this Mila?" Coco asked, her voice rising over Bebe's irate screams.

Rob looked up quickly, his brow creased before he realized who she was. "Hi, Coco." He looked suddenly surprised. "Yes, this is Mila." Rob brushed sand from the corners of Mila's eyes with the edge of the wipe.

Mila's cries ebbed. Once the sand was out of her eyes she tottered back to the sandbox to play.

"I'm so sorry Mila was knocked down." Coco glanced apologetically at Rob before refocusing on Bebe who was thrashing in her stroller screaming.

"Is that good for her?" Rob asked, looking at the struggling child with concern.

"I don't know. Mila is the third child she knocked down today. I'll let her go when she's calm."

Coco stroked Bebe's hair. The child turned fierce dark eyes on Coco but stopped screaming. Soon she stopped struggling. "Good girl," Coco whispered when Bebe quieted. The second Bebe became totally calm, Coco unsnapped the climbing hook. "No pushing, Bebe, or you go back in the stroller."

A second later Bebe was off and running. Mila saw her coming but instead of running to hide behind her father as Torrin would have, Mila rounded on Bebe knocking her flat. Bebe hit the ground with a thud. The one-year-old regained her place in the sandbox, leaving Bebe on her back staring in shock at the cloudless blue sky.

"That's a first," Deborah laughed. Coco fought the urge to help her sister up. Rob started to move to correct Mila but stopped when Coco touched his arm.

"Do you mind if we let them work it out? Bebe needed that." Together they watched Bebe roll onto her tummy and push herself to her feet. Rob shrugged before settling down on the bench next to Coco.

Standing in the middle of the playground, Bebe looked for Mila; when she found her she ran at her, stopping inches from where the girl sat. Bebe watched the baby as she dug with her hands, piling the sand onto her knees and feet. After a moment, Bebe sat down next to her and began digging.

Rob laughed, turning one of his brilliant smiles on Coco.

"They seem to have worked things out."

Coco liked the way his black hair shone in the sunlight. He looked incredible in a tight, faded green T-shirt and shorts. He was every bit the Hollywood action hero she had first imagined.

"How long is Mila staying with you?" Coco lowered her Chanel sunglasses from the top of her head to hide the hunger in her eyes.

"Forever as far as I know; Chloe's never tried to get custody."

Why's it so easy for some women to abandon their children? Coco wondered but said nothing.

She turned her attention back to where Mila and Bebe played. Bebe copied Mila action for action without noise, aggression, or any of her usual displays of erratic behavior. This moment marked the first time Bebe had ever played quietly with another child.

"They like each other." Coco glanced at Rob who smiled his half smile. He leaned forward to watch his daughter giving Coco an opportunity to examine him without notice. She studied the line of his cheekbone, memorized the shape of his nose, and the hard, inflexible set of his mouth and jaw. He was probably a force in a courtroom, she thought, remembering that he had said he was a lawyer.

"Are you hanging around this summer?" Rob turned suddenly toward Coco, catching her eyes on him.

"What?"

"Do you leave Chicago in the summer?"

"No...." Confusion filled her. The idea had never occurred to her. Simply getting to the park each day was a miracle.

"I'm asking because I've taken some time off to be with Mila. I would like to take you out."

The statement was so direct that Coco didn't have a second to be surprised, pleased, or even shy. Instead she heard herself agree to see him. She turned her eyes away, afraid that he would see the worry behind the sunglasses.

The instant Coco looked away, she caught their images reflected in the glass wall of a nearby boutique. In the reflected vision, she looked like a twenty-three-year-old mother enjoying a day at the park with her husband.

The thought thrilled her, but the thrill was short-lived. Tia was right: she was a walking illusion, a lie of maturity that would hurt more than her. If Rob knew her age, if he knew *her,* he would be shocked and angry. Then that hard, implacable jaw and those steely dark eyes would turn against her, and she already suspected there was a side to his character that didn't give second chances.

CHAPTER EIGHT

That day in the park changed Coco's life. She felt herself altered by the moment, feeling the girl she had been disappear in the wake of the vision she had seen so clearly in the window of the boutique. More than anything in the world she wanted to be the woman on Robert Banks' arm. She had attracted him as easily as a flower attracts a bee, yet when she pushed the stroller home that afternoon she felt afraid that he might see her for what she was the next time they met. No part of her wanted to lie to him – but if he wanted to take her out, then she would give him the woman he saw, not the girl she was.

Coco's attempt at perfected maturity began at seven o'clock the following morning and increased in strength as the week progressed. Coco rose early each morning to bathe in scented oils, apply her makeup, and straighten her hair. She chose her clothing with care, preparing for chance encounters, unexpected conversation, and a time when the nagging ache that lived inside her chest would be replaced by the adoration of a man she already felt she loved. Bebe and parenthood were pushed to the side while Coco became obsessed with beauty, clothing, and the crush that consumed her.

"Good morning, Coco."

Coco glanced up to see Tia enter the penthouse some four days after meeting Rob in Lincoln Park.

"Good morning, Tia," she replied, annoyed.

"Do you need help?" Tia watched Coco tidy away baby things at a feverish pace.

"No, I'm just picking up. I thought I would ask our new neighbors over if they're free. Rob's daughter and Bebe are friends so I thought we could have a... you know... a playdate."

"A playdate?" Tia asked, with more sarcasm than she had intended.

"Yes." Coco turned on her housekeeper. "Yes, a playdate! Is there anything wrong with that?"

"No." Tia looked surprised by how quickly Coco's mood shifted. "I just think you should call a thing what it is." Tia walked toward the kitchen to start breakfast.

"And what's that?"

"A date. Whatever you're calling it, don't use Bebe as your excuse. I saw that look in your eye when you got home after seeing him. Your new neighbor has you all aglow. I've half a mind to walk over there and tell him your age myself."

"You can't do that. I told you we're just friends."

"I can do that and I will. You glow every time you see him. Look at you. You're all dressed up for a playdate? You don't wear a thousand dollars' worth of designer clothes to play with toddlers, Coco."

"Tia, I'm wearing what I have. I can't help it if the clothes that come to the house are expensive."

"Last week I couldn't get you out of your stained T-shirt and jeans. Now look at you. You're wearing heels at eight-thirty in the morning, and you have been restricting your food again."

"I have not been restricting. I'm just not very hungry. I have a lot on my mind."

"Oh for heaven's sake, Coco! How long has this relationship been going on? Have you been seeing him when I go home at night?"

"No, of course not. I've only seen him twice – four days ago in the park, and that first time when you found us here in the living room talking."

"He's too old for you and far too worldly. If you want a boyfriend you need to find a boy your own age, someone with your same level of experience. That man needs to know you're still a child. I'll tell him if you won't."

"Mrs. Brown, I'm warning you. Don't tell him or I'll replace you."

The words flew out of Coco's mouth like a hiss. Tia's eyes flashed murder while Coco stood shocked to stillness by what she had said. Tia stared at Coco for a long moment; neither of them moved or spoke.

"Do you know what possession is?" Tia asked in a cold flat voice, her eyes focused on Coco. She watched Coco's quick defiance turn to confused uncertainty.

"Is that a trick question?" Coco's voice sounded weak and unsteady.

"It's when an evil voice echoes from the mouth of innocence. It's when a person is taken over by a thing wholly unnatural to them. Call it a demon, call it a drug, or in your case call it lust. Either way it's *bad*. Never did I think I would hear those words from you, Coco Rodriguez. I told you once I never leave unless I'm told to go. Well, I'm going now. I've no patience for vicious, lust-sick glamour queens!" Tia picked up her coat and her chrome wheeled basket and walked out of #2.

Coco watched Tia leave in silence. Her pride fastened her feet to the floor while her voice caught in her throat. Images of life without Tia flashed through her mind. *I should stop her. I have to stop her. I have to apologize.* The elevator dinged, the doors slid open, and Tia disappeared.

"Oh, God!" Coco slid down the living room wall, feeling tears spill down her cheeks while the glamazon she had been died a quick death. The apartment began to sway and rock, taking all of Coco's short-lived confidence with it. Who would sit and eat with her? Who would teach her how to cook? Who would make sure she didn't skip meals? Who would teach her how to raise Bebe? Who would teach her how to live? The old panic found her, bringing with it the usual terrors: abandonment, loneliness, and need.

Coco sat crying against the wall when she heard Bebe's low murmurs. If Coco didn't move quickly Bebe would be over the top of her crib, risking a fall. Bebe had chewed a hole through the safety tent and there was no point in replacing the useless thing. On entering the room Coco found her sister crawling down the side of the crib with all the dexterity of a gibbon monkey scaling a tree. The girl was strong, quick, and nimble in a frightening way.

"Good morning, Bebe." Coco watched Bebe drop to the floor and run past her. Coco followed her to the kitchen where the toddler stood in confusion.

"Tia!" Bebe called.

"No Tia, not today." Coco opened the refrigerator to begin breakfast.

"Tia!" Bebe yelled again as if calling louder would make the old woman appear. A moment later she ran out of the room.

Coco started breakfast, but stopped suddenly when the front door opened and the sound of Bebe's footfalls receded into the entryway. Coco's heart caught in her throat. She ran through the living room, out the front door, and into the lobby only to see Bebe standing in the open elevator, her tiny hand smacking all the buttons at once.

"No, Bebe!" Coco ran forward to stop her, her elegant Chanel heels catching in the deep carpeting. Coco fell to the floor, the elevator dinged, the doors closed, and Bebe began her descent. Coco threw one heel at the elevator door while she kicked off the other and sprang to her feet.

The old-fashioned lights above the door lit up one by one marking Bebe's stop on every descending floor.

"No!" Coco screamed, hitting the elevator button hard with her palm before running back to the old building phone on the entryway table. With Tia's dramatic exit, she had forgotten to fasten the chain on the door, the one thing that kept Bebe in.

Benny the doorman answered, "Miss Rodriguez, how can I help you?"

"Bebe, my baby girl, just got in the elevator alone. Please catch her before she makes it out of the building! She pushed all the buttons."

"Yes, Miss Rodriguez, we'll recall the car and set security on the doors. There are cameras on all the floors but it'll take time to review the footage. Try not to panic."

Coco turned back toward the elevator. Number 26 glowed above the door, marking the floor where the elevator stopped next. Coco's heart dropped when she realized that if Bebe had left the elevator she could be lost and wandering in any of the dozens of floors in the building. Frightened, she turned to #1 and pounded frantically at the door. It was opened by a middle-aged woman who had to be Mila's nanny, Karen.

"Is Mr. Banks in? I need help. My toddler just went down the elevator alone. Can you wait here in case someone returns her? The elevator stopped on the twenty-six floor. I'm going to start looking there."

Coco heard Rob's voice echo from inside as she ran for the stairs. Hitching up her black pencil skirt, she ran barefoot, skipping several steps at a time.

One floor, then another and another passed until a large black **26** came into view. "Bebe!" Coco called when she pulled the door open and ran into an empty hall. "Bebe!" she hollered again before running down the hall to the end. The child was nowhere in sight. Coco turned to the phone by the elevator that would connect her with the lobby.

A voice answered but it was not Benny's.

"Did you catch her?"

"No, the elevator was empty when it reached us. She stopped on several floors. I'm guarding the main exit, and we have staff going to the floors she stopped on."

"Thank you." Coco hung up the phone feeling breathless with terror before turning back to the stairs, only to bump into Rob.

"I thought I would help."

"Thank you," Coco answered, tears filling her eyes.

They continued down the levels, calling into each hallway, one after the other. When Coco stopped on the twenty-second floor Rob didn't follow. "I'll hit twenty-one." He slid past her, moving down the stairs to the next floor.

Coco ran down the hall of floor 22 looking behind the furniture, before hitting the end and swinging back to the stairwell in the grip of terror. With a hand pressed to her aching ribs, she moved toward the twenty-first floor; the pain of running stairs coupled with the panic was terrible. She wrenched open the door just as Rob backed out of the hallway.

His strong body hardly shuddered as Coco's slight weight hit him. He turned to face her, holding a struggling, angry Bebe.

"She was hiding behind the curtains. If she hadn't giggled I never would have found her."

Coco swept Bebe into her arms and slid down the wall to sit on the last step, clutching Bebe firmly to her chest.

The toddler stopped kicking and stared in confusion at her sister's anguished face. Coco rocked back and forth, tears streaming down her cheeks. She hardly noticed when Rob sat down next to them to rest.

Coco couldn't speak; she could hardly breathe. Slowly the terror that had gripped her turned to soft sobs. She felt Rob's arm around her shoulder, holding her close.

"She's safe, Coco. Everything's okay now." Coco leaned into him, her head resting on his shoulder, her sobs gradually lessening in intensity. After a while Rob rose to his feet. Stepping past them, he placed his hand on Coco's shoulder offering more gentle reassurance.

She could hear his voice, low and calm through the stairwell door, telling the tower employees that Bebe had been found.

Bebe stared at Coco, her face squished in apparent thought, her lips pressed tightly together.

"Do not ever leave me, Bebe." Coco held Bebe's gaze. "Do you understand?"

Bebe continued to stare, never breaking eye contact. She grabbed a hunk of Coco's dark ponytail and shoved it in her mouth.

"Coco sad baby," Bebe said, still staring at Coco.

Coco nodded and hugged her sister. Bebe patted her shoulder before jumping off her lap to climb the stairs and find Rob.

Rob hung up the phone and turned to see Bebe's little fingers trying to push the heavy steel door open to the twenty-first floor. Coco stared after her looking worn and sad as the determined child struggled for a new escape. Rob opened the door and picked Bebe up before he walked to Coco.

"Give me your hand."

Coco reached up, her slender fingers disappearing into his large hand as he pulled her to her feet. She felt his arm sliding around her waist as he steadied her, helping her reach the elevator door. When the car arrived, Benny stood panting and red-faced inside.

"There you are, you little... miracle." A strained smile spread across his sweaty face. His smile faded when he saw Coco looking pale beside Rob.

Back in #2, Coco sank onto the sofa when Rob let go of his hold around her waist. He strapped Bebe into her swing before going to the kitchen for a glass of water.

Coco's breathing was normal now but she still looked pale. She felt far away, as if an integral part of her had snapped.

Rob watched her with concern before offering her the water.

"Look at Bebe." He settled down on the couch beside Coco. "She loves to swing as much as Mila does."

Coco raised her unfocused eyes to the toddler, who swung her legs back and forth with such exuberance that the swing moved beyond its normal motion, rocking wildly front to back.

"I could have lost her. I don't know what I would have done if you hadn't..." A sob broke her words as fresh tears filled her eyes.

"You would have found her." His voice was certain, firm. "You were flying down those steps faster than I could have. You would have found her." Coco didn't seem to hear him. Her eyes were locked on Bebe as if she were afraid that the child might vanish a second time. "Do you have someone you can call? Someone who can come over?"

Coco shifted her gaze slowly to his face. "There's no one to call."

"Where's Tia?"

"We argued. I don't think she'll be back."

Rob rose reluctantly to his feet. "Unfortunately, I have a meeting I can't miss." Looking back at Coco he added, "I don't think you should be alone. You're still really pale. Don't you have anyone you could call?"

Coco shook her head. "It's just us."

"If you like, you can drop Bebe off with Karen. She would be happy to have a play friend for Mila, and that way you could get some rest." Rob still looked concerned but Coco hardly noticed. She felt dizzy and far away as if she might pass out at any minute.

"I'll be okay," she whispered. "I'm just shook up. Thanks for your help. I...."

"No need for thanks, Coco, I know you'd have found her."

"I wish I could believe that."

CHAPTER NINE

Coco fed and changed Bebe before walking her to #1. Rob was gone, but Karen was happy to take Bebe for a few hours. Returning to the wind tortured emptiness of #2, Coco remembered how Tia had filled the apartment with the feeling that a family lived there. Now empty, dark, and silent, the place resembled a mausoleum more than a home. Tia was gone, gone like Magdalena, gone like the nannies and the housemaids, gone, gone, gone....

So Bebe ran away, Coco thought. *She's back now and safe, everything's fine. So, Tia's gone. She'll be replaced just like all the others were.* Still, Coco couldn't shift the heavy grief.

A commercial blared noise, displaying happy teenagers chewing bubble gum on a California beach. That commercial was followed by a woman joyfully cradling her perfectly behaved child in a blindingly bright white room. As the jingle for a third commercial began Coco felt an additional sense of discontent, one that bordered on loathing. She felt hatred for the picture-perfect people who smiled from the screen.

With growing despair, she spotted the lie.

Through thick and thin she had held to the notion that somewhere – out there – people were happy, and that if she could talk, walk, or dress the right way everything would be okay. What a lie! Those beautiful people didn't really exist. They were not real. They were actors, hiding their flawed existences behind sets, products, and concepts they wanted you to believe would fulfill you. They were selling the *idea* of happy, not the reality.

Coco clutched at her chest, feeling the ache of years of loveless living. Tia was gone, and Bebe had nearly gone too. During those twenty horrifying minutes of searching, Coco had lived as she had for so many years, running blindly in grief to look for someone precious who had left her.

In that moment, Magdalena's face shone across the screen, peddling moisturizer to the masses with her seductive smile. Coco felt her hand flex around the remote, felt her knuckles blanch, the blood running from the pressure of her grip as she raised her hand far over her head, hurling the remote at her mother's flawless face.

"Bitch!" she screamed, her voice reverberating off the walls, clattering over the surfaces of the Dali, the Warhol, and the Rivera. Coco slumped back against the couch, shocked by her own violence. The damaged screen blinked strange distorted images into the room while Magdalena's soft Latin voice spoke through the advertisement, her careful syllables soothing away the last of Coco's sudden rage.

Through the disfigured screen, Magdalena smiled on her daughter, her eyes sparkling with warmth, kindness, and love. Coco drew her knees to her chest and wept for the loss of that warmth, for all the years she had been forced to live without her mother's love. Never in her life had she understood her abandonment. In the quiet recesses of her mind she replayed the rumors she had overheard of drug use, abusive boyfriends, and an unrelenting paparazzi. How long had she clung to these rumors as the real reasons for her mother's neglect? How long had she forgiven Magdalena for every missed Christmas and forgotten birthday? Through rage and confusion, she had hidden her misery behind the belief that something terrible had come between them.

Staring up at the broken screen, Coco could no longer live with the lie that their separation was an unfathomable act of God. Slowly she allowed herself to recognize what had been so obvious for so long.

As the commercial died, Coco understood that Magdalena had simply left her.

Karen returned Bebe three hours later exhausted but peculiarly pleasant. She didn't run, scream, kick, or demand anything from Coco. Instead Bebe simply went to her room and began to make a pile of toys on the carpet next to her crib. Coco rested against the door frame and watched.

The things Bebe loved best sat piled on the floor, creating a pyramid of everything she considered precious.

"Coco play," Bebe yawned. She added a plastic bug she had found at the park.

Coco crossed her ankles, sinking down on the floor opposite Bebe and her pile. She didn't play. For Bebe it was enough that she was there, watching; after all, the child knew what needed to be done. *Maybe this is what everyone does,* Coco thought while she watched her baby sister add a pacifier next to the big green plastic grasshopper. *Maybe we all build pyramids out of the things we love – only we call them homes, hobbies, careers….* When examining her own life by these standards, Coco realized her pyramid would be very small.

Coco slid deeper into depression with each conclusion she reached. Before Tia, before Bebe, she had been empty, finding joy in small insignificant things such as the arrival of a new *Vogue* or *Bazaar*. She had never before hurt the way she did now. Shaking her head, she tried to focus on Bebe and the moment, but her mind immediately strayed to the memory of Magdalena's face staring down at her from the ravaged flat screen.

I loved my mother. I still love her and always will, but is the pain of being left and forgotten worth the few years I had with her? Perhaps if she had never known Magdalena, she never would have wept for her, never missed her, and her life could have been bearable. Now nothing in life seemed certain – everything was transitory and fading.

Coco wiped away her tears while she watched her sister play. She realized that someday even she would go; that Bebe, like Tia and Magdalena, was impermanent. Quietly, Bebe took Coco's hand placing it firmly at the top of the pile. Startled by the action, Coco couldn't fail to understand its significance. The baby had put her at the top of her pyramid. In that moment, Coco knew she would never do anything to jeopardize her place in Bebe's world again.

Without Tia's mothering hand to organize them, the two sisters fell back into their old sleeping habits. Every moment with Bebe felt suddenly fragile, bittersweet, and fleeting. Bebe fell peacefully asleep in the crook of her sister's arm while Coco slept without rest, wading alone through the darkness in her mind. Depression crushed in from all sides, gnawing at her in sleep as it took the form of a dream too troubling to be believed.

The nightmare began with feelings of despair, loss, and futility. Coco stood alone in a shadowy open air garage, thirty stories above the earth. Luxury cars painted in primary colors sat in silent rows around her, their beautiful curves blurred by the screaming wind that tore at her hair and clothes, deafening her while whipping tears from her eyes.

Over the din, Coco heard a high sweet little laugh. She recognized it only when a dash of pink moved in the peripheral of her wind-stung eyes. When she shifted her gaze, it was gone. Further in the distance Coco saw it again, black-brown hair and the color pink coupled with the laugh. Bebe was playing a game, hiding behind the cars just out of sight.

"Bebe!" Coco called but the wind stole the name from her lips the moment it was spoken.

Coco ran to the end of the garage, to the spot where Bebe had stood only moments before. She blinked back tears as she scanned the garage looking for the baby who appeared on her left, a grin of ecstatic delight spread across her little face. Coco knew that grin; it was the *come and get me* grin.

"No," Coco ordered, trying to make herself heard over the wind. Bebe's grin broadened. She spun around, running to the far end of the garage toward an elevator door that hadn't existed moments earlier. It stood at the far end of the building, its red paint grimy with exhaust and age. A large button glowed to its right, illuminating one arrow which pointed down.

Bebe ran blindly, too filled with the joy of her game to stop or think. In less than a second the toddler reached the door, her small palm hitting the glowing button while she turned to face Coco. The elevator chimed, the door slid open, and Bebe's joyful grin grew mischievous. Raising her left foot, she stepped back into the empty shaft.

Coco screamed as she ran forward into the blackness, her outstretched fingers grazing Bebe's hand as the child fell, disappearing end over end into the bottomless blackness.

"Breakfast," a voice called into the silence, jerking Coco awake. A shivering full-body ache, stiff joints, and sweat soaked bedding told her she was ill. Every part of her body hurt.

Coco shivered in the 72-degree room, the darkened windows restraining the sunlight, maintaining the constant gloom that characterized #2.

"Breakfast," the voice called again.

Bebe rolled onto her side, pressing her fists into the mattress to raise her head. She moved to a crawling position before slithering backward over the edge of the mattress. Coco watched her sister rappel down the side of the bed, using the sheets like a climber's rope, her eyes still half closed from sleep. As always, Bebe managed a perfect landing before setting off at a steady trot to the kitchen.

"Tia!" Bebe squealed with delight.

Coco rolled onto her side and pulled the blankets up over her head.

Ten minutes later Tia poked her head into her room. "I've made breakfast."

"So you said." Coco pulled a pillow over her head and ignored her housekeeper. She had missed the old woman so much the day before that now she was angry with her for leaving.

"You okay?" Tia watched Coco sink low under the covers and disappear.

There was no answer. Coco didn't feel she owed Tia a response, not when the woman could disappear as easily as a curling twist of smoke in a Chicago wind. Tia closed the door as Coco pressed her face into the pillow and tried not to cry.

Almost an hour later Coco got up to run shakily to the bathroom. She hadn't eaten in so long that there was nothing to throw up. She gagged on misery until she could only crawl, her body so choked with bile that every muscle ached and she passed out.

"She's in here." Tia's voice echoed through the fog in Coco's head. "I can't lift her. That's why I called you."

The man walked forward but stopped, his cheap black vinyl shoes only inches from Coco's face. She lay curled in a ball on the floor, half in, half out of her bathroom. The man hesitated before stepping over her. Moments later she felt her shoulders lifted as the man pushed his arms through hers, pulling her to a limp standing position.

"Wish my wife was this light," the man commented when he had settled Coco on the mattress. Coco recognized the voice; it was Benny.

"You shouldn't," Tia scolded. "I doubt this child's eaten a thing since the day before yesterday." Tia pulled the blankets up, tucking them gently around Coco's shivering body.

"Stomach flu's going around," Benny said, as he walked from the room.

"Stomach flu," Tia muttered, her voice edged with doubt.

The miserable illness that gripped Coco had a teasing essence that toyed with her memories, painting the lonely insignificance of her life on a mental canvas to be jeered at and ridiculed. Faces smiled through half-forgotten memories: Magdalena laughed while a dark eyed boy stood crying at the door. The boy looked familiar but Coco couldn't remember his name. He had dark brown eyes and curling black hair. Before she could comfort him, he was gone, leaving her alone to be eaten by the darkness which fed on her. The darkness caused the lonely ache in her chest to expand until the vomiting returned in the form of dry heaves.

Tia held Coco in a sitting position, forcing a blue bucket into her lap. Nothing came up as long as the grief remained lodged.

"Cry it out," Tia urged, patting Coco hard on the back. "Just cry it out."

"Go to hell," Coco growled, her voice sounding hard and cruel. With the back of her hand Coco hit the bucket, sending it flying across the room. She shrugged Tia off, giving in to the convulsive shivers which overtook her.

Thankfully Bebe was not there to witness Coco's illness. Mila and Karen had arrived that morning to take Bebe to #1 to play.

"Stomach flu," the doctor said. "Give her as much fluid as she can keep down. If she's not better in twenty-four hours take her to the ER."

Tia bit her lip but was silent.

"So I left," Tia said, staring down at Coco an hour later, "and you lost Bebe for a *little* while. You're okay, I'm back, and Bebe is safe. What's this all about?"

"Stomach flu," Coco replied obstinately, not looking at Tia.

"I know, I know, it just seems like something different. It seems like... grief."

"What do I have to grieve about?"

"A lot of things," Tia soothed, her worn, cold hand coming to rest on the girl's arm. Coco was running a fever and her face was flushed. Tia watched her for some time, concerned.

"People leave sometimes, Coco. But sometimes they come back. Would you like me to try to contact Magdalena? I might be able to get a message to her through the agency." Tia knew Coco still wrote to her mother. She had seen the girl glow with excitement at the sight of a letter, only to disappear into her room when it proved to be another autograph or generic fan letter.

"And what, Mrs. Brown, would be the point of that?" The silence that followed was broken by a sob. "If my mother gave a damn she wouldn't have left me here to be raised by strangers. If she cared she wouldn't have sent Bebe here to be raised by a kid."

Tears welled up in Coco's eyes but refused to spill. Tia rubbed her back before pulling her into a hug. Convulsive sobs rocked Coco's body as the grief began to flow along with the tears.

When the worst of it subsided, Tia laid her back against the pillow and looked into Coco's eyes. "When I was a little girl, I lost my mother. I know what it feels like to have no one to turn to in the world. I know what it feels like to be lost and alone, to feel abandoned by everyone, even God. I promise that I'll never leave here angry again, that we'll always talk things out, that you'll always know that I'm coming back – and that no matter what happens in your life, you're never alone."

Tia's dark eyes sparkled in the poorly lit room. She held Coco's hand while she made the promise. Coco didn't answer; she just looked into Tia's sincere gaze and nodded.

"Okay," Tia said, getting to her feet, "I'm going to make you some soup, so try to sleep and I'll bring it in when it's ready."

When Tia turned to leave, Coco stopped her. "I'm sorry for what I said. I would never replace you."

Tia's smile was sad. She leaned over to smooth Coco's hair away from her face. "I know, sweetie. Try to sleep."

CHAPTER TEN

After three days of illness, Coco felt well enough to leave her room. Morning light peeked through the blinds as she ventured on unsteady legs toward the kitchen. There she found Bebe singing from her outgrown swing, kicking her feet wildly back and forth while Tia set toast and fruit on the table. Coco's diet had consisted of homemade chicken soup for so long that the sight of fresh fruit made her smile, the one smile she had allowed herself in days.

"I would like to take you out for a tour of this place. I think you'll love it there." Tia pointed to a pamphlet from a place called Gilman's School of Fashion.

Coco silently flipped through the pamphlet. Each page contained glossy photos of gorgeous gowns and smiling students. In the final photo, Mr. Gilman, the head of the school, stood in a perfectly cut suit surrounded by clothing forms displaying his students' designs. Every piece looked completely original, fresh, and well-crafted.

"When did you pick this up?"

"The day of the 'playdate.'" Coco's face grew sad. "You need something to do, Coco. I think you need to study something you love. I've looked over two other fashion schools and this one seems to be the best. It's close, small, and intimate. I think you'll like it."

"I'll learn to sew?"

"Yes – sew, cut, draw, and design."

"I didn't finish school," Coco sighed. "I doubt they'll take me."

"I'll look into that. Try not to worry yet."

Coco set the pamphlet aside as Tia spooned strawberries onto her plate.

The paperwork was staggering. Coco needed letters of introduction, character references, and an essay explaining what she felt she could offer the world of fashion. The essay was a terrifying proposition. *What can I offer anything?* Feeling overwhelmed, she walked away from the admittance forms to find her bed.

Coco cried each morning. There was no reason for the crying; it became something she did, like brushing her teeth or showering, just another morning ritual. For some reason the tears came after breakfast, exhausting her to the point that she was forced to take a pre-lunch nap.

Bebe saw her as a point of interest. After breakfast she watched her sister, waiting for the waterworks to begin. When the tears came and Coco retreated to her room, Bebe would invariably nod her head and say, "Coco sad baby," her tiny voice echoing into her sister's room.

On the seventh day after the proposed "playdate," Coco woke from a nap feeling slightly better. She lay in bed for a long while, watching the light creep around the corners of her blinds. It shone golden like the sunlight of evening. Glancing at the clock beside the bed, she realized she had slept all day. She felt disheveled in her sweatpants and matching hoodie, both dyed a gorgeous plum color that usually offset her golden-brown eyes and bronzed Latin skin. But now her eyes were red and puffy from crying all morning, while her skin lacked its usual luminescence. Getting out of bed she walked down the long hall to the living room. Halfway down the hall her pants slipped off her hips, forcing her to retie the drawstring. She had been painfully thin before the illness, now she was a skeleton.

"You're up," called a voice the moment she turned the corner into the living room. Coco's fingers froze on the drawstring, the front of her hoodie pulled half way up, leaving her ribs and stomach completely exposed. Rob sat quietly on the couch, Bebe on one knee, Mila on the other. Coco stared, a look of horror flickering through her eyes. Tia sat opposite Rob, her coffee cup resting in her hands.

Before her illness, Coco had spent days dressing and caring for herself in the hope of impressing Rob with her taste, sophistication, and beauty, yet this was the image she presented him: a sick, disheveled girl with puffy bloodshot eyes and an unattractively exposed midriff. Coco's first thought was to apologize. Her second thought was to turn back toward her room. In the end, she dropped her shirt and walked quietly to join them.

Bebe slid off Rob's knee, hurling herself onto Coco before she even sat down.

"Hello, you." Coco lifted the toddler up into her lap and kissed her.

"Better?" Rob asked, sincere interest shining in his dark eyes.

"Oh, yes... better," she sighed, the words gliding out slowly as her mind spun with the surprise of his presence. "And you? Did you guys stay healthy?"

E. E. ORME   93

"Mila has a cough, but I think it's more allergy than viral."

Coco nodded, looking at the one-year-old who bounced on her father's knee.

"So, I have tickets to a show tonight. I was wondering if you're up to going?"

The sudden invitation startled Coco into her usual deer-in-headlights expression. Being with Rob would be heaven, but being out in the world in her current state might be hell. Rob's discerning eyes searched her worried face as she looked back at him, trying to gather her remaining shreds of confidence. Tia sat quietly looking at her coffee cup on the opposite couch, a purposefully vacant expression on her face.

"Tia?" Coco asked softly. She felt so small, so young that she wanted to ask permission, but she was afraid that if she did Rob might begin to put two and two together. "Do you think I'm up to it?" Tia raised her eyes off her steaming coffee. "Tia takes such good care of me," Coco added, turning a shy smile back on Rob.

"I think the theater would be okay, just go slowly and don't exert yourself."

"How much time do I have to get ready?" she asked, her beauty beginning to glow past her rumpled appearance as excitement flooded through her.

"About four hours so don't rush. If I took you as you are, you'd still be the most beautiful woman there."

Tia clicked her tongue disapprovingly, which made Rob laugh. "She does take good care of you," he joked, "and as for that, so will I." The playful warmth in his eyes sent even more color into Coco's pale cheeks.

The musical with its lavish sets, full orchestra, and costumes created an evening far beyond anything Coco had expected. Rob watched Coco more than he watched the production. The sight of her seemed to bring him more pleasure than the show. Coco couldn't help smiling each time she caught his eyes on her.

"Are you bored?" she whispered.

"I saw it in New York a few months ago. I take it this is the first time you have seen it? You look enthralled."

"I am."

"So am I... just not with the show." Rob grinned, enjoying the rapid blush that colored Coco's cheeks.

Afterward, as they walked down the aisle with the other theater goers crushing around them, Rob slid his arm around her waist pulling her close in the pressing crowd. Coco raised her eyes to his with a quiet look of inquiry. Leaning over he placed a kiss on top of her head.

"I'm not usually this forward," he whispered into her ear, "but you're as familiar to me as sunshine."

CHAPTER ELEVEN

"Tia?" Coco walked into the kitchen three months from the day of the musical. She found Tia and Bebe at the kitchen counter cutting out sugar cookies.

"Look, Mama." Bebe waived her hands high over her head when she saw Coco. "El-e-fant."

Coco smiled at the cookie elephant but winced at the name. It sounded so strange. "Why do you call me Mama now?"

"Well," Bebe replied in her improved baby talk, "Mila has Dada... Bebe don't... Bebe has Coco Mama and Mila don't... okay?" Coco never thought that Bebe would be jealous of Mila for having a real parent.

"I like it when you call me Coco," she pressed, but Bebe ignored her.

"What did you need?" Tia looked up, gently reminding Coco that she had had a question.

"Oh, I found this necklace in the bottom of one of Magdalena's boxes. Can you tell me what it means?" Coco held out a little gold cross with *Psalm IIII* etched horizontally across it.

"That's easy, Coco, it's not even written in Spanish," Tia laughed. "It's Psalm Four."

"What does that mean?" Coco lifted Bebe's elephant off the counter, placing it onto the cookie sheet.

"I eats it, I eats it all up, yum!" Bebe yelled, her hands thrown excitedly in the air.

"This is a Psalm of David; it's a prayer of protection, a request for God's presence in your life. The last stanza is my favorite. It says basically that no matter how much money or security you think you have, without God in your heart, fear and anger and the sheer craziness of life will find you. There is no rest outside the peace one finds in God's presence. I adore the Psalms," Tia continued, still smiling. "When I first found God, I turned to the Psalms, first because I was angry and I wanted justice; later I read them out of love and forgiveness."

"What did you have to forgive?"

Tia shook her head and looked away. "Maybe I'll tell you sometime," she answered evasively.

Coco had heard that before. Tia often alluded to her life and then answered any question Coco might have with, *Maybe I'll tell you sometime.*

"I'm going to put that on your tombstone," Coco teased. She lifted the cross off the counter. The chain was as thin as a silk thread. The little cross looked well-worn on the edges like a piece that had seen many people through their lives. The warmth of it attracted her. She liked its smooth lines and edges.

Coco couldn't remember putting it on, but in that first week she unconsciously formed the habit of running her fingers over the lettering anytime she felt nervous or distracted. Psalm IIII became engraved in her mind, though its true meaning still eluded her.

Admittance into Gilman's School of Fashion was not so much a question as a certainty. Tia's character letter described

Coco as "a young woman of such taste and beauty that she rivals her super model mother, Magdalena Rodriguez, in every way." Tia also asserted that any fashion house would be lucky to have such a celebrity attend their school.

The staff at Gilman's wasn't foolish. They thanked Coco by phone for her consideration and hoped that she and her family would tour the school soon. By family, Coco knew they meant Magdalena. Coco was forced to explain that Magdalena was believed to be modeling in Milan and that she and her sister were the only members of the Rodriguez family currently living in Chicago.

That was how Coco came to tour Gilman's with Bebe and Tia in tow. Bebe behaved perfectly, yet the toddler's insistence on calling Coco *Mama* raised a few eyebrows. Tia stood quietly back as Coco led Bebe through the halls, looking in the design studios and sewing rooms.

Bebe stood on the floor beside Coco, watching her big sister go over the admissions papers one last time. Bebe was silently attentive, moving only when she walked to Tia to be held.

"Your grandmother must adore you." The head of admissions directed her comment to Bebe. Bebe gave the woman a perplexed look; she was unfamiliar with the word grandmother. Tia lifted her into her arms, smoothing down her pink taffeta dress. "I'll bet Magdalena sends you things from all over the world."

Coco bit her lip but couldn't remain silent. "Bebe's my sister, not my daughter. Magdalena hasn't seen her since she was a baby. Bebe calls me Mama because I'm all the family she has."

"I'm sorry." The woman looked shocked. "I had no idea. I never meant to pry."

Coco smiled, shaking away the woman's apology. "Don't feel bad. The paparazzi hounds our mother so we value our privacy. It's better if no one knows too much about us."

"Your letter and this conversation will remain confidential. I'm so sorry. I just assumed…. "

"Mothers abandon kids every day, and drug addicted super models aren't any better." Coco left without another word.

"You're going to have to deal with that your entire life, Coco." Tia spoke so only Coco could hear her. "You should've let that woman keep her delusions about Magdalena."

"Why?" Coco turned to look at Tia. "That woman was prying into my life. Besides, I wouldn't have been forced into that conversation if *you* hadn't gone and told them I'm Magdalena's daughter. I can't feel any kind of fulfillment about getting into Gilman's because I'll always know it was the connection to Magdalena they want, not me. I hate that she's the reason I get to study there."

"You have an advantage. I thought you should use it."

Coco shrugged. "Just ask me the next time you want to tell someone. I don't like being associated with her."

CHAPTER TWELVE

Gilman's existed in its own parallel world apart from the busy city outside. From the moment Coco stepped past the green front door she left modern Chicago behind and entered into a place where time passed at a different pace. People moved with more grace and greater purpose inside Gilman's walls. Even the air Coco breathed smelled fragrant, as though the essence of high couture hung in the folds of fine fabrics, aged amid tweeds and silks before enveloping her with its refined sophistication.

Gilman's was a hundred-year-old establishment, run by a solid family of European tailors. As Chicago clothiers, they were renowned. The interior of the building exuded rich old-world decadence, from mahogany wood paneling to twelve-armed gold leaf and crystal chandeliers. Large columns of green marble held up the decorative ceiling while the base of the columns stood encased in gold leaf grape and vine plasterwork.

Standing alone on her first day of class, Coco studied her surroundings. The ceiling shocked her to stillness – a rotunda of massive scale rose above her, decorated with images that she could spend days studying. The subject was a family, frozen in an idealized moment as they ate, laughed, and walked among fountains of flowers. Grapes hung in large clusters from delicately drawn fingers in offering from a man who sat at the center of the mural. Coco moved around the central gallery glancing at the other students, some sitting on the elegant nineteenth century sofas, others staring about, amazed at the beauty of the room.

Grapes were a common motif as were wheat ears and several other types of vegetation that Coco didn't recognize. Plenty was the theme, and the founding family wanted the world to know that lack existed only in their memories; they had arrived at the mouth of the proverbial cornucopia and wouldn't be vacating it again. There was nothing mean or glaringly offensive about the opulence. Instead Coco felt a welcoming aura that gently said, "We've learned how to live, now let us show you how."

"Hi," a voice called. Coco turned to see a tiny redhead in a black tank top and leggings. Her exposed arms were decorated with colorful tattoos. The girl looked to be about twenty-four and probably thought she was addressing a peer.

"Hi." Coco's voice echoed in the large, still room.

"You here for class or a fitting?"

"Class."

"You look like a model. The graduating students got an extension for their final show so I thought maybe you were waiting to be fitted."

"No." Coco shook her head and tried not to look nervous. "I'm not a model."

"You could be," the girl persisted. "I mean, you'd do great."

"I would rather design…." The words came out on their own, laced with an inexplicable level of confidence. When had she given herself permission to dream so big?

"Carmen." The girl nodded her head to Coco by way of introduction. "I have to know someone or I'll go crazy; I hate the whole first day feeling."

Coco stared at the girl not sure she wanted to know Carmen. The feeling that Carmen wanted something troubled her. In her experience, friendly people usually wanted something.

"I'm Coco."

"Cool, now I know you. So how tall are you?"

"Six foot."

"I'm four-eleven," Carmen laughed, turning her attention back on the room. "This place is weird." Carmen indicated their surroundings. "I would tear all this old shit down if I were them."

Coco turned a curious look on the girl. "You don't think it's beautiful?"

"No, why should I? It's nothing to do with reality. It's a backdrop for a wealthy delusional!"

"I think it's beautiful," Coco countered.

"It makes a pretty picture but I like reality more."

"Reality's usually ugly."

"Yep." Carmen nodded, the silver gauges in her ears twinkling in the golden glow from the Victorian chandeliers. "Look at that guy for instance." She pointed up at the central figure in the mural. "He's got himself all painted up like his family loves him and he's so happy and they're so happy. Yet he was probably an abusive wife beater who stole from his employees and messed with his daughters. But because he had money he got to simply paint a picture that will outlive the reality of who he was. Instead of being remembered as a bastard, he'll always be seen as a loving man in the center of a family who adores him. Like most things, I'll bet it's a lie."

"It's not a lie," a voice said from behind them. "Levi Gilman was a philanthropist as well as a businessman. His wife had this mural painted after his death so that the family could remember all the people he helped."

Glancing over, Coco saw a thin twenty-something man with thick brown hair, dressed in an impeccably cut suit. One look into his dark brown eyes and Coco knew he was a Gilman.

"And you know this because…?" Carmen questioned.

"He was my great-grandfather."

"Hmmm." Carmen shrugged. She didn't blush; she seemed not to have noticed that she had insulted the man's family.

"I'm Jack Gilman." The young man offered his hand to Carmen who shook it without introducing herself. Jack turned to Coco. "And you're no doubt…."

"Coco… just call me Coco. And this is Carmen," she added, to distract the boy who was seconds away from connecting her with Magdalena.

Jack frowned, his eyes locked on Coco, obviously going over everything he had heard about Magdalena's daughter. After a moment, he nodded. "I'm pleased to meet you, Coco. I've heard a lot about you. We'll begin class shortly in the room to the left." He smiled again before moving away to gather the students.

Carmen rose up on tiptoes to whisper in Coco's ear. She managed to reach her shoulder. "I'm still right, the mural guy was probably a total narcissistic jackass."

Coco shrugged, feeling nervous as they walked into what would be their classroom for the next eighteen months. If she could keep her identity quiet, then maybe she would find some peace. If not then no doubt her days would be riddled with endless questions about Magdalena, the Argentinean fashion icon she had never really known.

Coco grew to like Carmen. She had a natural urban style that was both daringly hard yet feminine, a style Coco learned to love. Carmen paired leather with paisley-print, plum-colored silk, taffeta with hard-chromed metal findings like spikes, studs, and smooth-edged dagger tips pierced with small rings. All of Carmen's designs were new, original, and fantastically inventive. Coco felt at times so drawn to Carmen's hard yet sensual style that she sometimes lost track of her own.

Three weeks into the new term the graduating class could no longer extend their deadline and were forced to have their show. This was a huge treat for the first-termers, who were allowed a midday preview of that evening's event. Coco saw Turkish revival prints paired with stiletto heels, kimono-cut suits paired with heavy leather boots, and myriad other innovative and not so innovative concepts; yet nothing they saw compared with the few sketches and natural taste Carmen already had exhibited in class. As Coco watched her she felt how lucky she was to be Carmen's friend. Carmen never needed or wanted anything from her except her friendship and advice.

"What do you think?" was Carmen's trademark question, one she aimed at Coco a dozen times a day. Coco gave her honest opinions and Carmen took them, the good and the bad, without any effect on her natural confidence. Coco's own creations were strikingly different from her friend's. They were naturally soft and old world. Where Carmen might use Lycra or patent leather, Coco used roughed out suede or doeskin. Her affinity for natural fibers was expensive yet the finished products were beautiful.

For her first term project Coco submitted three color sketches of her own designs. The first was of a flowing mid-thigh sundress, totally sheer, with the illusion of orchids printed white on white over silk. The under bodice was ivory silk, sewn skin tight with matching low-rise micro-shorts. The look was finished with roughed-out beige thigh-high boots that left six inches of exposed thigh between boots and hem. All the textures were soft, natural, and almost colorless. Coco and Carmen looked at their sketches laid out on the sewing table. The sight made them smile.

"This is soooo... you," Carmen laughed. "I love your drawings; you have got style."

"You too," Coco smiled, so amazed by Carmen's brilliance she felt lost for words.

Carmen's sketch was of a black fur piece – a princess cut floor-length gown cut with a savagely angled slit from hem to mid-thigh, finished with an enormous pink leather belt with silver studs and knee-high black leather boots with a polished finish. The design left the shoulders exposed, the fur cut to fit snugly around the upper arm to meld into a bodice that cupped the breasts in black fur and exposed pink silk lining. The look was soft... soft... soft... but with a biting edge of sensuality.

Jack was a common face at Gilman's. He worked with the first-termers. He was no older than they were, but as he put it, he had "been born in fashion and he would always be in style." Teaching at Gilman's was as natural to him as breathing. His advice was never bad – he had a natural eye – and he loved Carmen practically from the moment they met. Carmen pretended not to see it, but Coco couldn't ignore it no matter how she tried. Jack's dark eyes lit up every time the pixie redhead walked into the room. No matter how brash or rude she was he always seemed more alive in her presence.

"So," Coco pried one day while they looked through fabric swatches, "what do you think of Jack?"

 106 MAGDALENA'S SHADOW

"Hmmm…?" Carmen's eyes didn't move from the cloth samples she held.

"Come on," Coco persisted with a giggle, her teenaged innocence showing through.

"Why would I think about Jack?" Carmen raised her eyes to Coco.

"Well, he's cute, and he likes *you?*" Coco's voice rose playfully on the last word.

"Please don't be a *twit,* Coco. I want to take my life seriously. Do you know what happens to girls who get men? *Men* are walking social diseases that destroy more lives than AIDS ever will."

"Oh…" Carmen's words hurt her in a subtle way she couldn't describe. "I thought he seemed like a nice guy."

"Coco, they're almost all nice guys, and they slowly bind you up with their love and their needs, their marriage papers and their children, until you're driving a minivan and gossiping with soccer moms. Is that what I want? No! Women have got to be selfish if they want independence. You have one fatherless child already; I would think you would have figured out that even sweet men are trouble."

Coco stared at Carmen in shock. She wanted to tell her she hadn't screwed up her life *yet,* that Bebe wasn't hers, that life was going along just fine, and that she had no plans of messing it up. Yet she couldn't deny the reality that Rob was always in her thoughts. The idea of being an independent, single woman terrified her. Looking up at Carmen she realized that no matter what she said or what the world thought, Bebe was hers and she was a young single mom.

"Point taken!" Coco set down the swatches and walked away.

108 MAGDALENA'S SHADOW

CHAPTER THIRTEEN

After school, Coco's only wish was to go to Rob's to talk, a habit she had fallen into in the months since they had attended the theater. She longed to sink into the easy friendship they had developed, to feel the flow of relaxed conversation, to forget Carmen's earlier ferocity. With Rob, there was never pretense, nothing felt strained, and she always left feeling recharged and happy. But today as she went to make her escape, Tia stopped her.

"You're spending too much time with that man. You go over there almost every afternoon."

"Only because Bebe and Mila play together." Coco met Tia's sharp gaze without blushing. "I'm simply going over there to pick up Bebe and see how his day was."

"I want you to tell him how old you are," Tia pressed for the hundredth time.

"Why does it matter, Tia?" Coco felt instantly angry. "I told you we're not dating. We're friends."

"You know why it matters. Promise me you'll tell him!"

"Only when I see a reason to," Coco shot back, closing the door on Tia.

When she entered #1, Coco found Rob sitting with Bebe

and Mila in front of the fireplace roasting marshmallows over two logs which snapped and crackled on the grate.

"Hello," he said with his usual cheerfulness.

"Hey," Coco smiled, watching him push a marshmallow onto a skewer for Mila. The child was much too young to be roasting marshmallows so Rob had to hold the stick out of the flames while Mila watched her marshmallow turn from white to golden brown with wonder.

"Mine go poof!" Bebe yelled, leaping up to greet her. "Poof! All gone."

"Just blue fire, huh, Bebe?" Rob laughed.

"Yep," the toddler answered.

Coco sat down cross-legged next to Rob. Bebe jumped into her lap grabbing a fistful of marshmallows and her skewer.

"Eats, eats!" Bebe handed everything to Coco in a jumble.

"So I see," Coco answered, trying to catch the marshmallows and the skewer as they were thrust on her.

"Like this," Bebe shoved two marshmallows onto the skewer Coco held and then shoved the end into the fire. The marshmallows quickly grew in size, turned brown, and caught fire. "No, no!" Bebe looked at Coco with alarm. "No poof, Mama."

"Hey, give me a break, I'm a beginner." Coco laughed and accepted the two new marshmallows Bebe gave her.

"How was Gilman's?"

"Strange! My drawings were all accepted and I've passed first term, but I have a lot to do to get ready for the next project."

"You are still having fun? You have to like what you're doing."

"Yeah, I love it. I just wonder how realistic it is for me to be thinking of a career and be a mother too. It feels selfish

 110   MAGDALENA'S SHADOW

to leave Bebe with Tia all day. I feel like I'm sacrificing her for a dream."

"We all make sacrifices. Karen does all the parenting when I'm working. I wish it could be different but that's life."

"I don't know what I would do without Tia."

"Nannies and housekeepers are a necessity when you're single. We're just lucky we can afford them. So, what made today strange?"

"Carmen," Coco said flatly. "She was in a mood. She called me a twit and then went on to say that we have to be selfish to have a career and stay in charge of our lives. The way she talks it's like she hates men."

"And you don't?" Rob looked up with interest.

The question took Coco by surprise. When had she ever given him reason to think that she did? Her eyes searched his; he wasn't joking.

"No poof, Mama!" Bebe pushed the marshmallow stick with her hand.

Coco refocused on the marshmallows, drawing them further from the flames

"I don't know why I should hate men. I've never had a reason to. Men are people, some are good and some aren't. I don't like the concept of hating any group as a whole." When she glanced at Rob again she found him studying her. "What?" she asked, puzzled by his sober expression.

"I look at you and Bebe and I wonder what kind of man could have left you. What kind of man leaves such a beautiful, kind-hearted woman alone with a baby?" He shook his head, his half smile turning slightly bitter.

In a way, Coco knew he was flirting, winning her by caring. He flirted the way some people worked or others gambled, with a blinding diligence as if winning her over were the best part of existence. How could a judge ever rule against him, how could a woman do anything except smile and melt? She shrugged and tried not to melt. They were friends for now, and that reality was her guiding principle whenever they were together. They were friends until her eighteenth birthday, friends until she was done with school, friends until she grew up enough to know who she was and what she wanted out of life. On no account could Rob ever know the real Coco, the stupid girl who lived in an apartment that terrified her, in a city she couldn't handle, with a child that wasn't hers.

"It's amazing how desolate this place feels when they're not filling it with noise." Rob stared down at the two sticky toddlers who had passed out on the carpet behind them. Coco tried not to hear the wind as it howled malevolently around the building, causing the flames to leap and dance in the grate. In the distance, Coco heard Tia leave for the night, her footfalls echoing into the silence of the large entryway. "I meant what I said earlier." Rob spoke with absolute sincerely. "Who leaves a woman as glorious as you alone with a baby? Why did he leave?"

Coco looked up at Rob thoughtfully, her brow creased. He wasn't teasing or flirting. He looked concerned. Coco would never lie to him. That much she knew for certain. But she wouldn't tell him the truth either.

"Why does anyone do anything?" She shrugged and looked away. "I never expected to be raising a child on my own. Nothing in life goes the way you think it will." She shook her head, remembering the callous nanny who had signed Bebe over to a stranger she had only spoken to on the phone. "What about you?" she added. "You're a nice guy with a great kid and your wife left. Does that make any sense?"

Rob looked away. "I am what I am," he smiled bitterly, "and I wasn't what she wanted."

"What happened?"

"She and I grew up together. Our entire social network was built around the law firm. Hell, Dad was the firm. Everyone in our circle knew I was his illegitimate son born to his illegal housekeeper yet all the firm families were forced to tolerate me because they worked for my dad. I never knew how much I was despised until Chloe and I eloped. She had lived in this sort of blind state of privileged adoration all her life. When she married me all that changed. Her loving family disowned her the moment they heard. She turned pretty quickly after that, siding with them as if I had tricked her into marrying me. When Mila was born with dark skin and hair Chloe couldn't cope. She left Mila and me for another son of the firm, one of the pretentious Allen schmucks. Her family took her back and she's getting *respectably* married next month. Now everyone can pretend that Mila and I never happened. With Dad dead, no one ever has to pretend otherwise."

Coco couldn't believe what she had just heard. Her eyes searched his in the firelight. No one could look at Rob and see what she saw in that moment. She saw the fierce self-reliant man she knew, trod on and betrayed by his father's people because he was of mixed race and illegitimate. Coco slid her arm through his, not knowing how to comfort him.

"The love we give is all that matters in life," she said, her words flowing from her heart. "Not everyone deserves our love, but what matters is that we gave it. I feel God when I feel love," Coco stared into the fire. "When Bebe came, I was immediately overwhelmed by this connection, like I could never love anything or anyone the way I loved her. It was so deep, so eternal. I think that kind of love is God working through us. It has to be."

"I don't know...." Rob turned away from Coco's open sincerity as if it pained him. "I remember loving my mother on a level like that, but I think that's hardwired into kids so they stay close."

"What about your wife? You must have loved her at one time."

Rob laughed bitterly. "I loved the idea of her. She was rich, beautiful, and an important member of our circle. I had this idea that if I had her I couldn't fail. But she was never sweet, she didn't like kids, and she wasn't loving. Not like you."

The last three words caught Coco off guard. "And they say men usually marry their mothers..." Coco added, remembering an article she had read in *Elle*.

"My mother was sweet and loving. No one could have asked for a better mother. No, I most definitely didn't marry my mother."

"Are you still close?" Coco asked with a touch of envy.

"Maria was just Dad's mistress – a powerless Venezuelan illegal. She and I lived here, hidden away until I was eleven. That was the year Dad's wife died. After the funeral, he decided to take me to New York and raise me with his daughter, Beverly. Bev hated me for her mother's sake and still does. Anyway, Dad wanted a son so he shipped Maria out of the country, shut up this apartment, and took me to New York where I was reformed in his image. I haven't seen my mother since."

"I'm sorry."

"Oh, it doesn't matter anymore." Rob shrugged, but Coco could see that it did, that it tore at him still. "Dad sent me to good schools, he gave me a career; it could've been much worse."

"No one should lose their mother."

"No, they shouldn't, but it happens."

Coco ran her hand down his back, soothing him the way she would sooth Bebe.

"You make me a better person," he sighed, his eyes finding hers. The smile he gave her melted her heart.

"You're already good." She turned back to the flames to avoid his gaze.

"I'm trying to be. Tell me about him. What was Bebe's father like?"

Coco couldn't meet his gaze. Tia was right. She needed to tell him the truth but the thought terrified her. *Not yet*, she thought, promising herself again that she would never lie to him, not on any point.

"I don't know the first thing about Bebe's father. There's nothing to tell."

Rob looked back at the fire, his brow creased.

He was speculating, Coco could tell, thinking over all the situations that could have created the fatherless Bebe: rape, one night stands, and easy sex with faceless strangers.

"Stop it," Coco blushed at the thoughts. She was a seventeen-year-old virgin. How could he not see that?

"What?"

"I'm not like that. I could see what you were thinking but you're wrong. You could try to guess forever, but you'd still get it wrong. I'm happy with my life and with Bebe, so please don't ask and don't think about it. We're good."

"You are, I know. I'm sorry for prying." Rob pushed another marshmallow onto his skewer and roasted it.

Coco watched him for a while before glancing at Bebe. "I should get her home."

"In a minute." Rob brought the marshmallow out of the fire, blowing the heat off the smoldering tip. The expression in his eyes had shifted from warmth to

E. E. ORME 115

something very different in the flickering light. "This night got pretty intense pretty quickly and you still haven't even had a marshmallow."

Rob held the marshmallow up to her lips. She opened her mouth slowly, sucking off the crunchy top, leaving the soft center on the skewer. A fleck of white marshmallow clung to the corner of her mouth. Rob watched her as he slid the remaining marshmallow into his mouth and placed the skewer down on the tile.

"You have got some right here." He indicated her upper lip, but before she could move her hand to brush it away, his lips met hers, nibbling at the sugary lip. She melted, leaning slowly into the kiss that was so light, so gentle at first it was hardly a kiss at all. She kissed him back, the pressure increasing until she could hardly breathe. His lips parted hers as she felt how totally vulnerable she was to him. His sugary sweet tongue flickered over her own as she hesitantly met the open kiss.

And then it was over the way it had begun, dizzyingly sweet with a hint of gentle surprise. When Coco finally opened her eyes, he was staring down at her, his expression questioning her look of complete surrender.

"Don't play with me, Rob." Coco blushed. "You'll ruin us if you're just playing." She sat up, suddenly aware of how she must look. "Just because you can doesn't mean you should. I'm not… worldly like you. I don't play around." She looked embarrassed and ashamed.

"Who's playing?" His brow creased as he looked at her. "Everything you are is new to me; I've never known a woman like you before, Coco." He kissed her again, gently, sliding his hand down the side of her face. Coco kept her eyes closed, her hands resting on his broad shoulders, loving how he explored her face and throat with his lips. When he drew away again, Coco couldn't look up. If she moved it would be to ask for more. She felt his hands move over her collarbone, coming to rest on the cross at her throat.

"Beautiful." He lifted the symbol up into the firelight. "It looks so worn."

"It was my mother's." Coco lifted the cross out of his hands remembering Tia's plea for honesty. The gold felt warm to the touch. "I think it's been in my family a long time."

Rob kissed her again, this time on the forehead as he got up.

"Come on, I'll carry Bebe home."

Coco shook her head. "You don't have to." She felt afraid of what more kissing could lead to inside #2. In that moment, she realized how easy it would be to sleep with him.

Rob walked her to the door, stopping her before she left.

"Sleep well, beautiful." Leaning over, he kissed her goodnight.

I'm only seventeen, Coco reminded herself as the early morning bus took her toward Gilman's. She felt nervous and excited at the same time. In four months she would be legal but until then she had to hold out... stay friends or stay away. The problem was she wasn't sure she could manage to do either.

Carmen was waiting for her in the rotunda in a green fifties-era dress and black high-heeled leather boots. On Carmen, as always, it worked.

"Vintage?" Coco pointed at the green organza.

"You know it. I picked this up in Seattle last year."

"Cool." And it was. Carmen exuded confidence in the same way Rob did. Everything he had done with her the night before he had done with graceful self-assurance. "You were right. Men are dangerous!"

"What happened?"

"Just a kiss. It could've been more but...."

"Is it that cute neighbor you're always talking about?" Carmen interrupted. "Was he nice or do I need to kick his ass?"

"He was wonderful. I just hadn't expected things to accelerate so quickly."

"Just be careful and stay in charge."

Coco fingered her cross while she thought. "Tia says God's in charge. She says He has a divine plan for us."

"Oh the hell he does!" Carmen laughed. "That's bullshit, Coco. God's just watching, waiting to see us fall. You're on your own, girl."

The thought made Coco feel small and insignificant. With a belief structure like that it was no wonder Carmen went through life like a battle-axe.

"You okay?" Carmen looked hard at Coco.

"Fine," Coco answered, feeling uneasy and confused.

Coco sat tapping her pencil on the table and stared out the window. It looked onto the busy North Western Avenue in Ravenswood. Carmen sat sewing at a table ahead of her, concentrating on her work. The sun sank low on that perfect late autumn day. The few leaves that held stubbornly to the trees thrashed like tethered balloons in the constant wind. Autumn always impressed Coco with its color and vibrancy. She wanted to capture it, to drape the season across her sewing table, to cut it, stitch it, and make it last. She felt the death of summer, its warmth sinking under the cold of winter in the same way she felt her platonic friendship with Rob melting and changed by the heat of their growing attachment. Loving him, being his would be deliciously complicated but was it a complication she was ready for?

A movement distracted her. Jack leaned over Carmen's table and whispered into her ear. A second later she heard Carmen laugh. Jack leaned closer, and kissed her before going. Carmen stopped her work, her eyes lifted to watch him leave the room. Coco hadn't meant to stare, but in that second Carmen turned and caught her gaze. The two women locked eyes.

Carmen sighed, "Coco, remember when I told you men were trouble? Well, the real trouble is that I never follow my own advice. Jack and I are dating. I'm sure you have got something to say. God knows you had plenty of opinions on this subject before. Are you happy now?"

"I have nothing to say on the subject. Remember? I'M... NOT... BEING... A... TWIT," Coco said, turning to smirk at her friend.

The sun was setting when Coco returned home feeling tired and worried. Class had run late and she had needed Tia to stay with Bebe, but Tia hadn't answered any of her calls. She walked up the front steps past the evening doorman to the elevator. Inside the elevator car, the mirrored walls reflected a tall girl with long wavy black hair, thigh high leather boots, and a tri-colored fur coat that almost completely covered her black micro shorts. Staring at her reflection, she couldn't help thinking that she looked like a hooker, home from a hard night's whoring.

The elevator reached the top floor, the doors sliding open with the usual *ding*, but the view that greeted her was far from usual. A note was taped on #2, and another on #1. Coco moved toward her door to read that letter first. "Took Bebe to Karen, had a family emergency, see you tomorrow. Tia."

Coco walked to #1 where the second note hung. "Mila sick, Mr. Banks working late, at the drug store for fever reducer. Karen."

Coco moved back toward #2, pulling the note down as she unlocked the door. The interior was its usual gloomy circa 2000 postmodern self, except for the brightly colored toys on the couch and floor.

"You need redecorating," Coco said to the empty room, knowing how fun it would be to add color and warmth to the white-on-white room.

"I don't think it looks bad." Rob answered, walking in the door behind her.

Coco turned in shock; she had not heard his door open let alone him entering the apartment.

"Hey." She didn't return his smile. "That's the second time you have crept up on me. Do it again and I'll make you wear bells."

"For you," he answered seductively, "anything." Coco melted when he smiled his crooked smile, reeling her in. "I had an awful day." He nuzzled her ear, and breathed her in, "so I thought I would end it with… something nice." Rob kissed her neck and pulled her close.

"Rob," Coco tried to catch her breath, his charm and heavenly scent overwhelming her, "sometimes I wonder if you're good for me."

He raised one eyebrow as if challenged and then grinned wickedly. "It's a wise woman who asks herself that question." As he looked at her serious expression his grin faded slightly.

"Well?" Coco looked him straight in the eye. "What exactly are your intentions? I need to know."

He shrugged, the grin creeping back to his lips. "I'll let you know when I figure them out." He moved to kiss her.

Coco ducked. "I like you a lot," she breathed, her heartrate soaring as she caught his hands before they could slip around her waist, "and if you kiss me I'll like you even more, but I've got priorities and you need to give me time. I can't fall for you right now."

Rob looked earnestly into her shy gaze, her eyelids flickering uncertainly over honey colored eyes. "What do you mean fall?" His words slid sweetly into her ear, the resonance in his deep voice sending shivers through her body. "I believe in your case it's *fell*. I'm quite certain you're in love with me, Coco."

He raised her hands to his lips, kissing each one gently on the palm before running the tips of his fingers up her arms, sending sparks coursing through her body. His mouth covered hers in a kiss that left her breathless. He drew back slowly, taking in the soft yielding expression on her face before he kissed her again. The second kiss was every bit as gentle as the first, as soft and loving yet more purposeful and passionate as he explored her lips with his own until he felt her body melt toward him, her legs no longer supporting her.

He ended the kiss to look seriously into her eyes. "Get some rest," he added, nuzzling her ear, gently nipping the lobe before turning to go.

Coco sagged onto the couch tired and annoyed. Why did he tease her? Why did he push all her buttons and then leave her alone? She hated wanting him and she hated that he *knew* she wanted him. *Why can't I control myself better? Why am I lost the moment he enters the room?*

"Rob... Rob... Rob," Coco sighed, knowing that just the sound of his name turned her on. Add in the sound of his voice, his confidence, his intoxicating scent, and she was at his mercy, a toy without a will of her own.

122   MAGDALENA'S SHADOW

CHAPTER FOURTEEN

Karen delivered an exhausted Bebe at a quarter to eight. Mila's temperature was high but Bebe's was higher.

"I brought you this." Karen pulled a bottle of fever reducer out of her shopping bag. "They're both sick and this stuff works like magic."

Coco thanked her and saw her to the door. At the same instant Bebe leaned over the side of the couch and vomited.

"Bebe's much worse." Coco stood with Karen an hour later in the atrium. "Her fever is so high that I've called a cab to take us to the hospital. Has Mila's temperature gone up?"

"No, not like Bebe's has." Karen looked with worry on the red-faced toddler. "Poor sweetie."

"I wish Tia were here. Did she tell you why she had to leave early?"

"No, only that she had to go. I hope everything's all right."

The taxi waited at the curb. Coco slid into the dingy interior with Bebe clutched to her chest. Coco had dressed the two-year-old warmly in quilted pants, a snow jacket, and a hat. Though it was only fall it was already dipping toward freezing outside. Coco shivered in her micro-shorts and fur. She hadn't had time to change and her feet were killing her in the stiletto boots she still wore. Lights flickered through the glass as the cab wound through the empty streets past the closed shops and low lit store fronts. Every beam of light that passed over Bebe's face brought Coco closer to panic. The distant city lights cast her sister's feverish features in long shadows, making Bebe look almost corpselike. The only sounds Coco heard when the cab pulled into the emergency entrance were Bebe's shallow breaths and the panicked beats of her own heart.

Coco scrambled out of the cab, tossing cash at the driver before turning to run on clattering heels up the sidewalk of the old hospital. Patients clogged the doorway, smoking and talking under the eaves of the building in an attempt to escape the cold north wind. Coco pushed through the gathering only to find that the lobby was as thick with people as the doorway had been.

Nurses conducted triage in the overcrowded waiting room while patients sat, stood, and lay everywhere. Coco froze, her breath caught in her chest as she wondered if coming to the hospital had been a mistake. The reality was that without help she couldn't bring Bebe's fever down.

Coco walked toward the Admissions sign on the ceiling, looking at the line that ran under it. It took her thirty seconds to spot the end and sixty more to move through the crowd to reach it. Her feet screamed as one, then two hours ticked by. Bebe slept on, peacefully unaware that she was anywhere but home.

"Next," the nurse called from behind bulletproof glass.

Coco staggered up to the admissions desk. "My daughter's sick." She turned so the nurse could see Bebe's flushed face and black ringed eyes.

The nurse shoved papers through a slot before telling Coco a triage nurse would be with her as soon as possible. Thirty more minutes ticked by before a chair became available. Coco sat down feeling the blood in her feet slowly begin to recirculate while trying not to imagine the blisters and swelling she would find when she got home.

Another hour ticked by before a nurse called Bebe's name. Coco jumped up, afraid that if she moved too slowly they would skip her and move on to the next patient.

The nurse took Bebe's temperature before hitting a button at the side of her desk. A single light blinked and less than five minutes later a blue clad male nurse appeared to take them to a room.

"You're lucky we're not busy," the nurse said, glancing quickly over Bebe's file.

"You're not busy?" Coco asked, incredulous.

"No, like I said, lucky for you."

He led them to a small room sectioned off by curtain partitions. Twenty minutes later a second nurse bustled in with an IV and a blood drawing kit.

"Hey, sweetie," she said to the unconscious Bebe, "I'm going to take some blood and give you some fluids." The nurse glanced up at Coco, who sat at Bebe's head, holding her hand. "There's a severe viral infection going around. Your daughter has the same look and symptoms as a little girl I treated an hour ago."

A young intern no more than twenty-six entered the room but stopped dead when he saw Coco sitting beside Bebe's bed. He stared at her smeared makeup, disheveled hair, and stylishly risqué clothing. After the awkward pause, he took Bebe's vitals and left the room.

Another hour passed and no one disturbed them. The constant noise of people and machines eventually faded to background static. Coco draped Bebe's little pink snow coat over her lap for warmth and lay her head on the bed next to her sister. Within minutes she was fast asleep. Her last thought was that whatever it was they were giving Bebe, it was making her better. The color in her cheeks looked closer to normal and she was no longer too hot to touch.

Coco awoke to a hand on her arm. When she looked up she saw a small woman in a green plaid dress with a clipboard.

"Hello," the woman smiled down at Coco. "I need to ask you a few questions before your daughter can be released from the hospital."

"Bebe was born in Argentina." Coco blurted the statement as her first line of defense, her sleep muddled mind adding, "In Miramar. She doesn't have a Social Security card *yet*. We're Argentinean but we've lived here all our lives. I can pay you for her care. Honestly, I'll give you cash. I have cash!" The woman listened quietly, but her serene composure made Coco even more nervous. She couldn't admit that Bebe wasn't hers. If she did she could lose custody of her. "I had Bebe... by myself... when I was... in Miramar. I have cash. We can skip insurance and I'll just pay you and go, okay?"

The woman set down her pencil and said nothing; after an uncomfortably long pause, she got up and left the room. Three minutes later she returned with Bebe's release papers.

"If you fill these out, Miss Rodriguez, Bebe might qualify for medical coupons. With the coupons, you can keep your income. It'd also be a good idea to have her naturalized as a citizen seeing as you have citizenship here."

"I do?" Coco asked before she could stop herself.

"You have a social security number? You wrote it down on the intake papers." The woman looked a little sad as she presented Coco with a flyer for drug addiction and another for streetwalkers, tucked discreetly between two sheets of plain white card. Coco stared at the flyer and almost laughed. But the woman's sober expression pulled the smile from her lips.

"Listen. I know you're a lot younger than you pretend to be. I know you have had it rough. You have a baby and you're on your own, but that doesn't mean you can't get a fresh start, Miss Rodriguez. There's always hope. Many women turn their lives around. Haven House," she pointed to the pamphlet for streetwalkers, "has helped a lot of girls reenter mainstream society."

"I'm not a prostitute," Coco protested. "I'm in fashion."

"I'm sure you are." The woman nodded, an understanding smile touching her lips.

Bebe was off the IV and grumbling loudly. She hated being woken up, touched, or moved. Coco didn't have an easy time getting her into her pink winter coat. Bebe was nearly dressed when Coco heard movement behind her. She turned to look and saw Rob standing beside the open curtain, a look of concern etched on his features.

"Oh God!" Coco lifted the grumbling Bebe up into her arms and turned toward him. "Is Mila here too?"

"No," Rob shook his head, "she's fine. I was worried about you. You didn't tell Karen which hospital you were going to, and you were gone before I knew there was a problem. I've been calling you but you didn't answer. I told a nurse that I was Bebe's father, and even then they didn't want to let me back."

"How did you manage it then?"

"Bribery and intimidation." He walked forward to look at Bebe, his face serious.

"Bebe's better now. They gave her an IV and ran some bloodwork. She has a bad flu virus."

"I'm just happy she's okay." Rob felt Bebe's forehead before turning a grave smile on Coco. "I wish I had found you sooner."

"Me too. I could have used the company." Coco walked toward him, lifting up on her sore feet to kiss his cheek.

Bebe fell asleep as they walked from the hospital room, the swaying motion of movement lulling her into slumber. Coco kissed her head where it rested on her shoulder feeling far more at ease now that Bebe was better and Rob was with them. She followed Rob through the crowded lobby, her hand held securely in his.

"By the way, Rob, there's hope for women like me." Coco held out the flyers to him when they reached his car.

Rob's expression grew serious. He looked at her with concern. "I don't get it."

"Apparently, I look like a ho," Coco laughed, watching his perplexed expression turn to one of incredulity.

"Who gave you these?"

"A very nice woman who thinks I'm a prostitute."

"Well," he grinned, his expression softening, "I had better get you home quick if you charge by the hour."

CHAPTER FIFTEEN

The word was "impressionable." Coco was "impressionable." Tia's tirade began over sliced ham but continued while she scrubbed potatoes viciously in the sink.

"You are so young and you have got to be careful who you associate with. Until you know who you are, you could easily take on the attributes of someone else. God teaches us to guard our hearts against sin. Sin sounds like such a big thing but it usually starts small."

Coco slumped at the table where Tia's lecture washed over her. "I'm not sinful," Coco interjected defensively.

"Of course you aren't. You're an innocent. Just remember, as you move through the world, take what you hear and ask, 'What would Jesus do?'"

Coco erupted into laughter. "Oh no, Tia, that's too much."

Tia frowned at her. "I know the Bible bangers have destroyed the phrase, but... what I'm offering you is a measuring stick to know when you're in danger. If you listen to a person but their words make you uneasy, then you can ask: do this person's words align themselves with what my God wants for me? These are important questions. Life isn't the buildings and the people. It's a complex mystery of good and bad elements continually colliding. You look at a person walking down the road and you see a person. On the surface it's a person, but much deeper lies the soul – the soul of a person who may have done terrible things. That person may smile, offer compliments, be your friend – but they may mean you harm for harm's sake. You are impressionable, and evil wears many faces."

"This is too much." Coco threw up her hands and walked out of the room. Tia talked down Bible bangers and then turned into one in the blink of an eye. Even with Coco in full retreat the old woman wasn't done talking. Her voice followed Coco down the hall.

"Coco, all I'm asking is that when people speak to you, don't take what they say as truth. Listen to your soul before you make any decisions. How *it* reacts to their words will tell you if they have your best interests at heart –"

Coco slammed her bedroom door thinking of Rob and Carmen. Tia was attacking them with her words, using God as a reason to separate her from people she trusted, people she loved. She should never have been so open with Tia. The fact that Carmen and Rob weren't Christians was a truth that Tia didn't need to know. She also didn't need to know that the woman at the hospital had thought Coco was a prostitute or that Rob had driven all over Chicago in search of her. It all had seemed funny when she had told her, but now she felt judged and uncomfortable.

When the evangelizing housekeeper left that night, Coco took Bebe to Rob's, looking for company that didn't grate on her the way Tia's often did.

"I miss my TV," Coco announced sulkily, before taking a place on the sofa. Her hands ached from drawing, cutting, and beading, while her damaged feet screamed from standing all day. Bebe sat down quietly on the floor pressing the keys on Mila's toy piano, making the music up as she went along. She was still sick but she was always up for a song.

Rob switched on the television before handing her the remote and a glass of wine. Coco eyed the wine with apprehension but was further surprised when Rob leaned over and pressed a kiss to her forehead. He looked exhausted. Coco put down the wine on a side table and examined the remote.

"You could always buy a new television." Rob sat down beside her with Mila cradled in his arms. "You could also get a cellphone with a battery that lasts. That would have been very helpful last night."

Coco frowned and turned the channel on the TV. She needed a new phone but the lack of reliability and constant shutdowns of the old one gave Coco an easy excuse for missed calls on late nights. If Tia knew Coco texted Rob all day as well as spent her evenings with him there would be no end of hell to pay so Coco dealt the broken phone card to Tia as often as possible.

"I need a new phone. I know I do, but I've been too busy to get one. I don't want a TV though; it's too time consuming and Bebe saw things she shouldn't have. I'm usually fine without one." As Coco flipped through the channels, she saw two horrendous traffic accidents, a bomb being tested, and a live surgery. Bebe stared up wide-eyed and observant. Coco flipped the thing off and set the remote down with a sigh.

"What's the matter?" Rob looked from the blank screen down at her.

Coco shrugged, "It was all the same stuff."

"So turn on the Fashion Channel."

"No, I'm fashioned out. You put on what you want." She picked up the remote and offered it to him.

He shook his head and fed Mila a spoonful of cold medicine. "I like the quiet. I was in court all day listening to immoral people defend impossible positions, and I need quiet."

Coco watched him with his daughter, remembering how gently he had brushed sand from her eyes the first day she had met them at the park. *Maybe that's when I fell in love with you*, Coco thought watching him wrap Mila in a blanket on the couch.

"How is it you're a lawyer in New York and here? I thought you had to stick to one state?"

"I'm consulting." He didn't look up as he spoke. "My firm represents a lot of multinational corporations. If our clients are in trouble we're involved."

"So what did today's client do?"

"Same crap, different day. Believe me, it's nothing worth discussing." Rob shook his head, his face taking on a sudden expression of distaste.

Coco watched him a little longer. He was never himself on the days he worked. He seemed somehow bitter and even a little cold.

Bebe was singing softly out of key, without melody, but with a soft smile spread across her face. The toy piano tinkled right along with her. Coco smiled when she finished her song.

"That was pretty, Bebe," Coco said. Bebe got slowly to her feet and climbed onto the couch were Mila lay. After a short while she fell fast asleep.

"If you're bored why don't you take a book from the study?" Rob rose slowly, careful not to disturb the girls. "Dad left dozens of classics in there; you're welcome to whatever you like."

"Thanks," Coco answered without much excitement. She rose reluctantly to follow him, her eyes fastening on the width of his strong shoulders. Each day it grew harder and harder to organize her thoughts and hide her feelings. She was in love with Robert Banks, and the more Tia pressed her to stay away, the more Coco wanted him close.

The study was furnished in the same masculine theme as the rest of the apartment: dark hardwood paneling, leather chairs, and green shaded lamps. Row upon row of books lined the walls.

"This one's strange but interesting." Rob handed her Cervantes' *Don Quixote*. Coco fingered the leather book thoughtfully. It was a large, heavy, old book filled with black and white etched illustrations. "It's about a delusional old man who thinks he's a knight. It's good. Kind of medieval." Coco slid the book into one hand and reached for a tiny green volume with the other. "That one's a collection of letters and poetry. It's funny you grabbed it," Rob smiled. "Veronica Franco was a prostitute." Then he winked at her with a teasing expression.

"Really?" Coco brightened when she thought of all the Bible banging Tia had done that day. She suddenly felt rebellious holding literature written by an enemy of purity. "Can I borrow them both?"

"Sure." Rob turned to walk back toward the living room. "They're both pretty heavy reading, though, lots of big words."

Coco glared at him as he turned to grin at her. "I think I can handle them."

"Oh, I'm sure you can. Years of *Vogue* and *Cosmo* can prepare a woman for any kind of literature."

Coco nearly threw the Cervantes at him. "Demean me and you demean yourself."

"How so?" Rob asked, still grinning. Coco glared back at him but couldn't answer. She wanted to say, *because we're the same, because you love me, because we're two halves.* Nothing she thought of could be said. In frustration she answered, "You know...."

Coco lifted the sleeping Bebe off the couch, cradling her to her side. Taking the books she walked out.

"Coco," Rob called, following her into the hallway.

"What?" She turned and glared at him.

He stood there staring at her. His expression said, *I know. I understand.* But the words seemed stuck in his throat. Coco set the books down on the entryway table, still holding Bebe close to her side.

"You okay?" Coco looked at him sideways.

Rob shrugged, but he looked relived to see her walking back. "I like that you didn't have a witty comeback. I'm so sick of witty jerks and smart-mouthed bastards firing off perfect comebacks. There are days when I really hate my job."

"I'm sorry."

"Me too. It was a bad day."

Rob slipped his arm around her waist, drawing her close as he looked into her eyes. "You are... wonderful. I shouldn't have teased you." His eyes gleamed with unspoken emotion. But before she could question him he kissed her.

The following evening Rob appeared on Coco's doorstep with Mila, roses, and a pair of tickets to the opera on the Saturday following.

"Italian opera is one of the great joys of living." Coco's face glowed with joy. She had never been to the opera or been given roses before.

"Who's Tosca?"

"She's Puccini's greatest heroine." Rob sat down on the sofa and looked up at her. "You will love her. She lives for her passions… a lot like you do," he added, making Coco smile. She sat down beside him, her eyes bright and happy.

"Thank you." She clutched her presents but her smile faded. "Rob, last night was…."

"I know. I've been complicating things. I'm sorry." The kiss had been the last thought on Coco's mind before she slept and the first thing she thought of when she woke. Rob bit his lip, his eyes trained on Mila, who sat quietly playing with Bebe's new doll.

"So, what do we do?"

"Get married and have a ton of kids."

"You know that's not what I want. I want us like this. Just Bebe and Mila and us. I'm not ready to complicate my life."

Rob took her face between his hands, kissing her forehead gently. "I was raised with very high Catholic morals when I lived here with my mother. I lost all that when I went to New York to live with my father. I wasn't a good man until Mila was born, and I'm struggling to remain good with you. It would be so easy to ruin this. So easy to coax you into giving more than you're ready to give. You add so much to our lives, Coco, and I'm terrified that I'm going to screw things up between us."

"You're naturally good, Rob. Whatever happened in New York is in the past. You're a good dad and a good friend and I want to be with you because I love you. We can't screw up what's already perfect."

Rob slid his arm around her waist, and buried his face in her hair.

CHAPTER SIXTEEN

Coco's love for Rob, and her building anxiety over telling him she was seventeen, filled her with a nervous energy that pulsed through her with such profound strength that at times she felt she would burst with it. No matter how many times she walked Bebe to the park, ran on her treadmill, or paced through #2, she couldn't subdue it.

Her restlessness reached fever pitch on the day of the opera, which was the day she had chosen to explain to Rob that she was young, too young, and they would have to wait to be together until she turned eighteen.

Tia didn't like the opera date. She threatened to have "the talk" with Rob, but Coco derailed her anxiety with a promise that they were just going to the opera house and then home again. This seemed to mollify the old lady a little.

The day felt strange, discordant and unbalanced. As evening approached, it brought with it the dreaded moment when she would have to tell Rob the truth. Yet each time she imagined his reaction her heart leapt in her chest and panic overtook her. Would he forgive her?

That evening Bebe put on her best dress. And just like Coco, she added lipstick and eye shadow only in huge caking swipes. Coco finished the look by twisting Bebe's hair up into a bun on top of her head.

Coco looked incredible. She wore a floor-length black Yves Saint Laurent gown with her hair hanging in loose curls down her back. A gorgeous black fur coat lay draped over her arm. Taking Bebe by the hand she walked with her sister toward #1.

Karen opened the door, letting them in with a bright smile when she saw Bebe all dressed up for an evening with Mila. "Mr. Banks isn't in yet." She showed Coco to the living room. "I'm afraid he's tied up in court."

Coco nodded, trying to hide her disappointment. She turned her attention instead on the great glass windows and the distant setting sun, ignoring the instant rush of vertigo that accompanied the view. Not one blind was drawn and Coco could find no shelter from the expanse of city that surrounded her. *Humans were never meant to see the world from this height*, she thought, as a yellow leaf blew up the glass before her.

Kissing Bebe and Mila goodnight, she retreated to the quiet sheltering darkness of #2.

Rob knocked on #2 thirty minutes later. Coco opened the door, greeting him with a tranquil, faraway look in her eyes. Rob leaned over and kissed her, his eyes reflected a quiet relief as if the very sight of her was somehow healing.

"I'm sorry I'm late. The judge deliberated all afternoon only to call court into session later than anyone expected. The sight of you standing here in this black dress is the best thing that's happened to me all day." He kissed her gently. "I love you." The words seemed to tumble from

 138 MAGDALENA'S SHADOW

his lips, as if his heart were overcome by the reality that life felt empty when she wasn't around. "I think you have saved me. After years of drowning *you are* sweet air and solid ground."

Coco laughed and returned his kiss, her hands caressing his face.

"I've always loved you, haven't I?" Rob looked almost serious. "The timeline won't ever make sense but I know I've always loved you."

"Yes… always." Coco laughed again "And I love it when you're poetic, even when you don't make sense."

140   MAGDALENA'S SHADOW

CHAPTER SEVENTEEN

The opera's finale drew to a close, ending with Tosca's climactic suicide. In no way could Coco cope with the desolation she had just witnessed. What had begun as perfect love had ended in what, to Coco's mind, was the worst kind of loss. Everything about Tosca's story left her in pieces. Over and over again Coco heard the simple libretto sung in a high lilting soprano: "*I lived for love, I lived for art... I never did harm to a living soul!*" The words filled Coco with a haunting grief because they epitomized her love for Rob and her family, her love of art and beauty, and the gentle way in which she approached life. Coco sat bleary eyed in her seat, her arm laced tightly through Rob's. She tried not to cry another tear. Never in her life had she heard such music, seen such sorrow, felt such passion.

Coco watched Tosca save her beloved Mario only to discover him dead, shot by the very man who had promised to spare him. Coco watched in awed horror as Tosca sang of love and loss, of the depths of her despair and the hopeless life of slavery that awaited her. Taking her life in her hands Tosca did the one thing she could do; she stepped from the lofted parapet and fell to her death. Coco alone *knew* how far she had fallen. Coco had fought that view, that *fall,* every day of her life. It was Chicago stretching on into the horizon; a hundred miles of jagged city watching a lonely isolated girl plummet to a thirty-story death.

The opera embodied every one of Coco's greatest fears. It was Bebe down the elevator shaft, it was the view from #2, and it was losing Rob, losing Bebe, and losing Magdalena in the same instant. It was loss and loneliness, pain and lamentation sung in Italian. *"I lived for art, I lived for love. I never did harm to a living soul...."*

The crowd rose, clapping enthusiastically, but Coco couldn't move. She sat frozen, her black satin gown clinging like an icy chill to her body.

"You didn't like it." Rob watched her with concern.

Her eyes moved slowly toward his, blinking back tears. "It was...." but she couldn't finish. It was beautiful, incredible, and debilitating. A drama too vivid for a girl who had lived her life in the shadow of loss.

"I'll take you home." Rob pressed his hand to her back, helping her to rise. "I always forget how delicate you are." He smiled his half smile but it was sad, without charm or flirtation.

Coco felt herself guided up the stairs through the clapping crowd, into the massive foyer, while the resurrected Tosca bowed and blew kisses to the crowd.

Only when they entered the lobby could Coco speak. "You were right. I can relate to her. I would do anything for the people I love. I would rather die than lose what she lost."

"Don't say that." Rob's brow creased. "I'll take you to *Falstaff* next time, or *The Magic Flute*. No more tragedies, I promise."

Coco smiled her first smile since the curtain went up. "I've never heard such music," she said wistfully, tears welling up in her eyes again. "Thank you."

"No thanks, please. I never meant to make you cry. It's the last thing in the world I wanted."

"I know." Coco blushed sweetly. "I'm sorry I spoiled it."

"You didn't spoil it." Rob kissed the top of her head. "I was going to take you to dinner," he looked into her eyes, "but I think maybe we should go home."

"I think you're right." Coco steadied herself on his arm, trying to shake off the feeling that had overtaken her. All the restlessness and anxiety she had felt before had drained to nothing in the wake of Tosca's desolation.

Coco felt utterly quiet, heartbroken, and dependent on Rob's love. As he led her from the building a new resolution settled in her breast: she wouldn't tell him her age until after her eighteenth birthday. How could she risk losing him over a simple formality? How could she ever have dreamed of endangering the precious love that existed between them when there were so many other realities to fear? When she had seen Mario die before the firing squad she'd known that it was too soon for the truth. They had this moment, they had each other, and that was enough.

A sharp wind attacked them the moment they left the opera house. It lifted the hem of Coco's heavy black fur and twisted her hair into savage knots. Rob held her close as they made their way toward his car. Together they crossed the street away from the crowd exiting the opera house.

A voice called loudly from the steps of a nearby club. A man approached them grinning.

"Rob, you bastard," his voice rose above the wind. The man met them once they had crossed the street. Coco felt Rob stiffen, felt his shoulder slip in front of her in a protective gesture.

"What the fuck are you doing? I thought you were going to party with us."

E. E. ORME 143

"No," Rob said. "I made other plans."

"So I see." The man looked Coco up and down with an appraising leer. "Nice, Rob, but you have always had good taste."

"This is Bill Foster, my ex-brother-in-law." Rob bit his lower lip and glared into the wind. "Bill, this is Coco."

Coco nodded and looked away.

"Beverly is going to be pissed if you skip out on her. The whole firm is here." Bill never once took his eyes off Coco.

Rob's arm tightened around her waist. He looked over his shoulder toward the Mercedes that sat a few feet away. "Bill, you know my sister hates me. The last thing she wants for her birthday is my company."

"Come in for a second. It won't kill you."

The *in* Bill referred to was a loud techno bar called Itzy's with black lights and blue neon. "We need to get home." Rob looked down at Coco who remained silent.

"You are in no position to piss anyone off," Bill argued, taking a step closer. "Bev may be your sister but she's also your boss. It's her birthday and we're celebrating Smith v. Navfourth."

Rob looked again at Coco, momentarily torn. He reached his decision in seconds. "Like I said, I'll make it up to Bev. Right now, we're going home."

"It's okay," Coco said nervously, hating to be the cause of friction. "You should say hi."

"Listen to the girl!" Bill countered while Rob glared at him. "It'll only take a minute to show your face, Rob, and that minute might save your job."

Itzy's front entrance was guarded by two bouncers. Coco hesitated, frightened that one of them might ask to see her ID. In truth, she had no reason to fear them.

Rob was on the guest list and she was with him. No one questioned either of them. Once in, Coco couldn't hear Rob or any of the other sophisticated white-collar people she was introduced to. As she looked around she saw strange, surreal looking people moving and talking in the constantly flickering light. In a corner a woman laughed, her back pressed up against the wall while a man nibbled at her throat playfully. When the woman laughed again, Coco was startled by the glow of her bleached teeth in the black light: sparkling, sharp, and animal like. It seemed everyone in the club had glowing bleached teeth and hauntingly sharp eyes. They seemed more like a pack than a firm.

A glass of something found its way into Coco's hand. She sipped the drink nervously, remembering the flavor from years before when she'd sampled Magdalena's wet bar. Now the taste seemed less bitter, and after several sips she felt the liquor take effect.

Rob showed her to a stool at the bar. "Bev's party would have to be here," he grumbled, glaring at the walls. "Give me a second, and I'll be right back." Coco watched his broad shoulders disappear into the melee, his white shirt glowing purple under the black light, his black curls standing in dark contrast against the collar. As he disappeared into the crowd, Coco couldn't help comparing him to Tosca's Mario with deep satisfaction.

The music drowned everything in pulsing beats while Coco sipped her drink and tried to blend with her surroundings. Slowly the alcohol removed the last of her nervous agitation, leaving her free to watch the well-groomed Caucasian couples who moved around her. The firm had rented the entire club for the night, creating the select segregation this particular set of people desired.

Coco felt relaxed and almost herself when a hand fell onto her shoulder. Certain to find Rob's steely dark eyes looking down on her, she turned but found hungry green irises framed in a tanning-bed-brown face. The contrast was unsettling.

"So, gorgeous, how many drinks will it take until you think I'm hot enough to go home with?"

Coco didn't smile. "There's not enough alcohol in the world."

Bill leaned in, lowered his eyes to hers, and sat on the stool next to her. "Let's test that theory. You look like a lightweight to me." Turning he flagged the bartender for another round.

"I'm not here to drink with you." She turned her eyes back on the crowd in search of Rob.

"Why not? You are much too fine for a fuck-up like Rob. Where'd he take you anyway?" Bill looked at her gown, her black fur, and the gold cross at her throat.

"Tosca." Coco gestured in the direction of the opera house.

"Who the fuck goes to the opera?" Bill laughed. "Poor Rob, still playing the dilettante, trying to prove that he has enough class to hang with our crowd. He is so old-school it's sad. No one else does opera and plays and the symphony, just him."

"I loved it." Coco turned even further away, trying to ignore Bill, who never took his eyes off her. After what seemed like the longest minute of Coco's life she heard him speak.

"I'm bored, *chica*. How about we have some fun?" In that second Bill slid his hands around her waist, turning her on the stool to face him.

Coco opened her mouth to tell him to back off but no sound escaped her lips as Bill clamped his mouth over hers, his tongue shooting in. Coco fought desperately to get away, her nails biting into his forearm. She pushed him back, nausea turning her stomach. The man's saliva was stringy and thick; he tasted foul and even his skin emitted an unpleasant greasy smell. He took hold of her arms, forcing her roughly back against the bar. She slammed her right heel down hard into his foot while she fought him off.

"Simmer down," Bill commanded. He glanced quickly around the bar, but no one was looking. Before Coco could move he pressed her back to the bar with more force, his nose tracing the curve of her ear. "Rob's always been good at sharing. He won't mind if I try you out a bit."

Coco freed her right hand, bringing her fist up hard under Bill's jaw, causing his perfect bleached teeth to clatter together. But instead of being angry he laughed. "I love you Latinas. You girls never stop fighting." He bit her neck but was suddenly jerked backwards, his shirtfront and coat coming up under his chin, unbalancing him as he was hauled off.

"You fucking leave her alone," Coco heard Rob growl. He threw Bill viciously into the room.

The crowd staggered, taking the man's weight before pushing him back. Coco felt her fur being dropped over her shoulders, felt Rob's arm around her waist, half lifting her off her feet. Rob slammed the door open and the wind hit her hard in the face.

They drove home in unbearable silence. Rob's rage was palpable. Coco didn't dare look at him. When the tower came to view Coco pulled her coat tighter around her shoulders, bracing herself for the cold walk to the building.

Only when the elevator doors slid open on the 30th floor did Rob pause to look at her.

Coco had never seen this side of him. His fierce strength awed and repelled her at the same time.

"It was a bad night," she said gently. "It wasn't supposed to be, but it was."

"Bad is an understatement. Bad doesn't even begin to describe seeing him on you, seeing you manhandled like one of his drunk-ass sorority chicks." Rob shook his head, his jaw clenched. "I still have to work with Bill. I still have to deal with him, and right now I want to drive down there and kill him."

"I'm sorry," Coco shrugged. "Try to forget about it."

Rob laughed but it was a harsh laugh, not his usual soft chuckle. "You should go in." He pressed his hand into the small of her back, guiding her toward her door.

Inside #2, Coco turned to see Rob standing at the threshold, a storm in his eyes. She wished again that she could comfort him, that she could make him let go of what happened.

Coco dropped her coat off her shoulders, turning from him to drape it over the sofa. She could feel Rob's eyes fasten on the curve of her hips, the small of her back, the definition of her shoulder blades as they moved beneath the straps of her black gown.

"Are you coming in?" Coco asked, her eyes fixed on a painting she didn't see. She sensed Rob stiffen when she kicked off her heels.

Glasses tinkled at the wet bar and a moment later Rob stood beside her with a glass of gin and a damp washcloth.

"Wash him off you, please." He offered her the cloth.

Coco looked at him, at the cloth, and then at her hand as it rose without protest to his. She felt the soft terry cloth glide over her bruised lips, carrying away all traces of Bill Foster.

"Drink this." Rob offered her the shot.

"No, I've already had enough tonight, and you're being very controlling." She turned from him and heard the glass clink on the sideboard followed by silence. "Rob...." Coco turned to the wet bar where he stood watching her, the now empty glass resting between his fingers.

"Come here, Coco." His voice sounded firm yet gentle. Again, Coco found herself doing as she was told; like a little girl she walked to him, trusting and innocent. Coco leaned her head against his chest, hearing his heartbeat. She felt his hand cup the back of her head, stroking her long hair while he held her close.

"I wish I could make you happy." Coco looked up into his face, her eyes searching his. "I hate seeing you this upset."

Rob brushed a curl off her shoulder but didn't speak. If she could have seen his hands she would have seen the way they shook. "Rob, what's this all about?" His eyes were like steel, all the warmth she loved gone. "I'm okay." She pressed her hands to both sides of his jaw, trying to get him to relax. "How can I make you okay, too?" She smiled, blinking up at him.

His expression softened from rage to anguish. "I'm going to go home now." He quietly kissed her forehead before moving past her to the door. "I'll check on you in the morning."

Coco grabbed his hand, holding onto him possessively. "Don't." Her eyes filled with tears. "I'm sorry for what happened. I should've left the moment he sat next to me. I fought...."

"What happened isn't your fault," Rob interrupted, his voice low with emotion. "My God, Coco. You can't believe I blame you, you're...." But he trailed off, his expression pained. He pulled his hand from hers and moved again for the door. "I'm not myself right now. I've got to go. You're not the first girl I've seen treated like that. I watched my own mother treated like a whore by Bill's father, and I wasn't able to protect her, either. I need time… I'll see you in the morning, Coco."

"Don't go," Coco half begged. Despite Rob's assurances that he would be back, she had the distinct feeling that he was leaving her for good. The feeling flooded her with icy terror. Coco could endure anything but being left. On tiptoes, she rose up to place a kiss on his lips, a tear already sliding down her cheek. "Please don't leave me, not ever, especially not like this. I can't be left…."

It was the kiss that broke him.

In an instant Rob lifted her up against his body, holding her to his heart as his emotions took over. He set her on the tall wet bar, her knees parting, his lips crushing hers in an almost savage kiss. Coco kissed him back with the same intensity, his face held lovingly between her hands. She wrapped her legs around his hips, pulling him even closer, her tears mingling with his as they devoured one another. The mixed intensity of love and fear overwhelmed Coco; she didn't notice when the black dress slid off her shoulders, past her hips, falling in a shimmering pile to the floor.

Rob's hands and lips moved fiercely over her body. He kissed her, descending lower with each passionate caress, his touch erasing every insult Bill Foster had placed there. Rob pressed her into the cold granite. "I should've protected you better," he murmured. His fingers ran down her back, his lips finding her breasts, causing Coco to shudder beneath his touch. In turn her fingers slid over his body, pressing him close as she felt her body shiver at his touch. When he drew back Coco unbuttoned his shirt, pushing the white linen off his shoulders to land on her dress. Her lips tasted his neck only to discover that he was both salty and sweet. She tried to slide off the wet bar to her feet but Rob stopped her, pressing his lips to her throat as his arm came around her waist, his free hand sliding up her inner thigh.

"You did what you could. Don't blame yourself." Coco tried to distract him. "Rob, sweetheart, look at me." His eyes, when he looked up, were luminous and dark, a mixed expression of passion and pain. He pressed her back against the stone, kissing her lips to silence, his fingers moving again up her inner thigh in a way that made Coco dizzy. Smoothly he removed her panties, his teeth nipping at one thigh then the other until his lips replaced his fingers and Coco forgot that she had ever wanted off the granite, that she had ever had any idea other than giving in. His eyes flickered over her face, taking in her pleasure as he guided one leg then the other over his shoulders. With eyes half closed, his mouth returned to her center, pressing further into her with the better angle. Coco shook with pleasure until she shuddered with her first ever orgasm, her fingers tangled in his hair.

Rob's hands slid up Coco's body, over her hips, ribs, and breasts then down again until he took hold of her hips, sliding her off the granite. With eyes closed Coco arched her back as he moved slowly into her. The dizzying sweet pressure grew in intensity moment by moment as he moved inside her, withdrawing slightly, then pressing deeper. He teased her with his movement, nuzzling her hair before kissing the place behind her ear.

Rob pressed one last time all the way, but in that second Coco tensed, her eyes flying open as she cried out in pain. Her hands grabbed at Rob's arms causing him to freeze. Their eyes met, his sharp with worry and concern and then shocked realization. No wonder Coco felt unlike any woman he had ever been with. He shook with the strain. In that moment Rob lost control. It'd been years since he had last made love, not since the many months before Mila's birth. The shock of his body's reaction hit him where he stood; but that shock was nothing compared to the reality that Coco had been a virgin.

Time stopped. Neither of them spoke. And then it was over.

Coco felt Rob pull away as he set her on her feet. She watched him put on his clothes and walk from the room while her hushed sobs shattered the heavy silence that followed. All along she had promised herself that she wasn't lying to him, that they were friends who loved each other and that someday soon she would tell him. But not like this, never like this. After what seemed like an eternity he returned, no more than a dark shadow in the doorway.

"How old are you?" Rob's voice echoed coldly from where he stood, his hands grasping the door jamb, his eyes fixed on the floor, unable to look at the girl he had just deflowered. Coco remained silent. "I've asked you this question before, Coco. Please answer me. How old are you?"

"Seventeen." Coco answered, the word quivered into the darkened room. "I'll be eighteen in a few months. I'm of the age of consent now, I'm just not *your* age."

Rob nodded, still looking at the floor before he sagged into a chair by the wet bar. "When were you planning on telling me, before or after Tia had me hauled into court? You know what we just did is indefensible." He sat with his elbows on his knees, his head in his hands. "I thought you were my age. I imagined once that you might be younger, maybe twenty-three, but never seventeen. I thought you were a single parent *my... own... age.*"

 152 MAGDALENA'S SHADOW

"I am," Coco gasped through waves of panic, "I'm a single mother. Rob, and I love you…." She blinked back tears and tried to steady herself.

"You are too young to know what love is. And you aren't a mother; you are quite obviously nobody's mother."

"Don't say that. You know Bebe's mine. You have seen us together. No one else wanted her and no one else wanted me. We live here alone and you're the only person who's ever noticed *us*," she added, now sobbing. "To the rest of the world we don't exist."

"I don't know *you* at all. You're a kid. You're probably still hung up on fairytales like love at first sight and all the other childish things little girls hang onto. Jesus, Coco, you're too young to know anything. I would never have done this if I had known." He wiped his mouth with the back of his hand, sitting hunched in the chair, eyes averted. "Why did you lie to me?" His voice dropped, heavy with regret.

"I didn't," Coco shot back. "I never lied."

"Omissions are the same as lies. You have kept me in the dark, and you have endangered my freedom, my career, and the custody of my daughter. If anyone ever found out about this I could be disbarred and worse. What do you think would happen to Mila? How could you do this to me? I was totally honest with you!"

"Rob, I'm of the age of consent and I'll be eighteen in a few months. Please… I'm sorry, no one will ever know about this, no one, I swear it."

"Consent is not always a legal defense. I'm eleven years older than you, Coco. Even if I was acquitted my reputation would be ruined. Besides all that, I know what we did was wrong," Rob added, "and I have to live with me. I've been living a clean life since Mila came. I thought you were different. I trusted you. I can't live with this and be a person she'll respect, a person I can respect."

Coco walked slowly toward him, taking her dress off the floor to cover her body. Rob kept his eyes low as she sank down beside his chair and took his hand.

"I'll never tell anyone. I love you too much to betray you. No one will ever know. My mother, Magdalena, left us here. No one even knows she has a grown daughter let alone a two-year-old. We don't exist. I'll be eighteen in no time. Please be patient and believe that I love you, not as a naïve child but as a woman who's suffered enough to know what love is when she finds it. Please, Rob."

"You know we can't be together." His voice was level and cold. "There is a lifetime of living between seventeen and twenty-eight." Rob shook his head when Coco tried to wrap her arms around him. "Coco, I'm in shock," he whispered, pushing her away. "Why didn't you tell me? I thought I knew you... I remembered you being here... when I lost my mother. You...." He couldn't finish.

"I didn't know you then...." Coco shook her head in confusion, remembering only the shadow of a boy who used to live in #1.

"Your mother... *she* lived here?" Rob asked looking up.

"Yes," Coco answered, but Rob shook his head as she reached for him a second time.

"Magdalena? I remember... now it makes sense... she would stand in the doorway and talk to me with a baby on her hip, a baby that looked just like Bebe...."

Coco froze, her hands clenching the gown that separated them. "What are you talking about?"

"When I first saw you, you were a memory I didn't understand. Now it makes sense why you were so instantly familiar."

"You remembered her?" Coco asked icily.

"I thought you were...."

"You thought I was Magdalena!"

"I couldn't separate you from the memory; I couldn't see that you're just a *kid*."

"Oh God!" Coco rose to her feet, blindly balancing on legs that no longer wanted to support her. "I should have known. All along it was her, not me." Her eyes locked onto his as tears rolled down her cheeks. In the brief silence she suddenly understood. "I remember you too. You came over to talk to her."

"I had just lost my mother. Magdalena...."

"You were the boy I remembered. The boy who came to see Mama."

"Coco...."

But Coco couldn't see him for the sudden rage. "It was always her, wasn't it? How could I have believed you loved me?" She turned away from Rob, feeling the years of pent up rage toward Magdalena crush down on her in that moment. "That baby she was holding... *I'm* that baby," Coco sobbed. "You just *fucked* that baby!" Coco moved to run from the room, but Rob rose quickly, catching her around the waist, pressing his face into her hair. "How could you love her?" Coco sobbed still louder, her voice rising to a scream. "How could you? She would have eaten you up and left you. She would have made you love her just so she could leave you crying for more. Don't think I don't know!" Coco pounded her hands against her forehead. "Of course you love Magdalena. Everyone loves Magdalena. How could I ever have dreamed that you could love me?"

"Coco, calm down; you don't understand. I was confused by how familiar you have always seemed. Please, honey, calm down."

But Coco couldn't hear him. The satin gown fluttered to the floor as she broke loose. Rob took hold of her wrist. She swung at him savagely, her free hand smacking him hard across the face. Coco ran for the bathroom and switched on the shower, determined to wash everything and everyone away.

Twenty minutes later Coco emerged from the bathroom to find the house empty. Rob was gone. She had expected nothing different. The revelation that it was Magdalena he had flirted with, Magdalena he had kissed, and Magdalena he had made love to ripped her heart into so many pieces she could hardly breathe.

Coco walked methodically through the house, taking down pictures of Magdalena wherever she found them. Framed *Vogue* covers, full size posters hidden in back rooms – wall after wall, all tastefully displaying the smiling face of the villainous homewrecker who always seemed to find a new way to hurt her daughter.

"*I hate you!*" Coco ripped yet another photo from its frame. "I wish to God you were dead."

The door clicked open behind her. Rob carried a sleeping Bebe in, laying her on the couch. Coco lifted the toddler up and carried her quickly to her room. When she returned, Rob stood in the doorway, his eyes leveled at the floor.

"You don't need to hang around." Coco shoved another of her mother's photos into the garbage can she had dragged into the living room. "I won't rat out your Magdalena fixation. No one will ever know you fucked her daughter."

"Coco, look at me." Rob reached for her.

"No," Coco sobbed. "Don't you dare touch me." Rob's eyes sparkled with grief. "I could've handled anything tonight." Coco's voice softened when she looked at him. "I could've even handled losing you if I thought I had a chance of winning you back, but to lose you to *her*, to the reality that you love my bitch mother? I can't bear it."

"Coco, stop it. That's not true. I never meant to hurt you." Rob's words reflected a deep bitterness. "This is all wrong. Neither of us is what the other expected."

Coco laughed and looked up at the ceiling, tears streaming down her face and throat. "You… you are exactly what I expected: beautiful, loving, good, kind. You are everything I want in this world. I'm the disappointment, not you." She bent suddenly over the garbage can to rifle through the trash.

"Here, take this. Something to remember us by." She walked to the door where he stood. She pressed a picture of Magdalena holding a two-year-old Coco into Rob's chest with such force that she pushed him over the threshold of #2. "And try to remember," she added, her free hand reaching to close the door, "that one of us actually loved you."

158   MAGDALENA'S SHADOW

CHAPTER EIGHTEEN

"What's happened, Bebe?" Tia looked around the room the following morning in shock. She lifted the two-year-old up from between a heaping pile of clothing and the overflowing garbage can.

"Mama fixing." Bebe surveyed the pile as something smashed in the guest room.

"Coco?" Tia called, walking around a pile of clothes mixed with shredded photos and broken glass.

Coco stood in the guest room, a pile of Magdalena's clothing growing at her feet. Without turning to look at Tia she ripped another piece from its hanger, hurling it to the floor.

"What's the matter, Coco?"

"I'm getting rid of stuff!"

"Why?"

"Because it's time. This is my home not hers."

"What're you going to do with it all?"

"I'm going to throw it away." Coco came out of the massive walk-in closet, her arms filled with couture.

"Let's talk, honey." Tia noted Coco's red eyes and disheveled appearance.

"No, not till I'm done."

"Please, you're making a mistake. What'll you wear if you get rid of all this? This is your wardrobe not hers."

"It was sent to her, not me. I don't want her hand-me-downs, not anymore." Coco threw the armload on the floor before returning for more. Her last words hung in the air with cold significance for that was how she now saw Rob, as a hand-me-down, just another thing that Magdalena had dropped into Coco's life. Robert Banks was another beautiful object that was never meant for her.

Tia looked at Bebe who watched the scene with concern.

"Would you like to play with Mila while Coco and I talk?" The toddler smiled and nodded.

"Tia," Coco called coming out of the closet, "they left this morning."

"What? Why?"

"The case he's been consulting on wrapped up yesterday; they flew to New York this morning."

Tia didn't speak for a long time; she glanced between Coco and the pile of clothing in the center of the floor.

"I get the feeling there is more to this. What else happened?"

Coco turned away, ignoring Tia's question.

Ten minutes later Bebe bounced on the sofa, jelly and toast crumbs clinging to both her cheeks.

"Mila, please," she sang, "go Mila's now."

"I'm sorry, Bebe." Tia wiped Bebe's face with a washcloth. "Mila can't play today; she had to go to New York with her dada."

"Why?" Bebe persisted.

"Because that's where they live. They had to go home."

Bebe squished up her face and thought. "I see Mila." She jumped off the couch and ran to the door. "I see Mila, okay?"

Tia opened the front door certain that if Bebe didn't knock on #1 she would never understand that her friend was gone. Bebe ran ahead through the hall, her hands clenched to fists in preparation. When no one answered her knock Bebe sat down outside the door, her legs crossed, her chin resting in her hands while she waited. The expression of anticipation that had lit up her face quickly turned to one of worry.

"Come on, Bebe, let's go. We can go to the park if you like."

"Mila," Bebe said quietly, "just Mila."

"I know, honey, I'm sorry." Tia scooped up Bebe, holding her close when the child began to cry.

"Oh, Bebe." Coco began to cry too when she saw her sister's tears. "I'm so sorry." She took Bebe from Tia and held her. "I'm so… so sorry, I'll miss Mila, too." Tears poured down Coco's cheeks. Together the two sisters sat and wept on the sofa while Tia watched and worried about them both.

At eleven o'clock Benny the doorman arrived with two janitors to haul away the "garbage." Tia insisted on rebagging the clothes, separating them from the rest of the things that Coco wanted tossed.

As afternoon approached Coco wore only a T-shirt and a pair of jeans, two items out of a handful that she had bought for herself.

"I wish you would be rational about this," Tia reprimanded. "Your allowance is nowhere large enough for you to afford clothing like this."

"No," Coco watched a janitor carry off the last bag, "I'm not my mother and I refuse to wear her clothes again." Tia shook her head and she turned back to Bebe who played quietly in the corner.

In the weeks that followed, Gilman's became a whole new experience for Coco, a refuge from #2 and the memories she couldn't face. Instead of focusing on the pain, she chose to pour her grief into her second term projects. The soft feminine look, the style that represented her, didn't change, but her cuts became more daring, her materials more refined and delicate.

During the first few weeks after Rob had left for New York, Coco's style of dress changed as well. Gilman's stopped being a place to be seen as fashionable and became just somewhere she went each day whether she wanted to or not. When she arrived the first day after Tosca wearing blue jeans and a T-shirt, everyone had assumed she was hung over. As the weeks passed and the wardrobe change continued, rumors of a breakup and worse began to circulate. Everyone noticed when the much-envied couture coats and boots disappeared, replaced by one oversized red quilted jacket and Converse shoes. Coco even considered chopping off her hair but decided that a simple braid was easier to manage. The illusion of maturity she had worked so hard to create had tricked a good man, a man she loved, into loving an ideal that didn't exist. Coco was a girl. She was not a woman and she was not her mother; never again would she resemble Magdalena, not in any way.

CHAPTER NINETEEN

"Hey," Carmen called, dropping her bag on her work table. Nearly a month had passed since Coco had arrived at Gilman's dressed down and depressed. Coco didn't like to talk anymore, and she flatly refused to answer questions regarding what had happened. As the weeks passed Carmen's worry didn't lessen. The speculation around the fashion school was that Coco had been hurt, maybe even raped, but no one knew the truth.

Coco glanced up from where she sat deftly stitching jet beads onto a silk scarf she had found at a thrift store the day before. "Hi," Coco answered before turning her eyes back on her work. Piles of material lay across Coco's table, each with a scribbled-on yellow sticky note that briefly described the part of the vision the item would create. The vision was a black satin evening gown with jet beads and a sheer, flowing, beaded overskirt. Carmen sat in her chair and swiveled it around to face Coco and her piles of black cloth. "So, how's it going?" she asked, leaning her elbows on Coco's table.

"How's what going?" Coco replied, not making eye contact.

"The dress, the project, life... You know, all the things

we used to discuss. I miss talking with you. How are you, and I don't want to hear *fine*."

"Then I guess I've nothing to say," Coco retorted still not looking up.

"Okay. How's the dress then?"

"Fine."

"Show me," Carmen insisted, rising from her chair to stand next to Coco, who had two sketches laid out on the table in front of her. The first showed the dress from the side: low backed with satin and taffeta material gathered just above the lower back. The second showed the front view where a panel of satin slid from the rear gather up to encircle the rib cage, breasts, and shoulders. Black-on-black beadwork encrusted the bodice and overskirt with branched flowers that scattered petals down the length of the skirt. Petals fell into dark piles at the hem.

"The flowers are dropping their petals. I like that but why black? Why not an autumn color?" Carmen asked. "Is the black to match your new mood?"

Coco smiled. "Yes, to match my new mood, and if I did it in any shade lighter it would look like a wedding dress. I like black. Besides I have all this material I need to use." Coco indicated the piles of black fabric folded along the edge of her table.

Carmen ran her fingers over the different materials but stopped when she touched a particularly fine piece of satin. Lifting the bundle up, she discovered a beautifully finished Yves Saint Laurent dress.

"Oh, Coco, you're not going to cut this up, are you? It's gorgeous." Coco stared at the dress, remembering the last time she had worn it. The black Yves Saint Laurent and the fur were the only two pieces of Magdalena's clothes she had kept.

 164   MAGDALENA'S SHADOW

"That's exactly what I'm going to do." Coco looked away from the dress. "I'll patchwork it into the skirt – satin for the branches of the rose tree, satin at the bust, and satin at the hemline to add depth and darkness to the fallen petals."

"It's vintage, isn't it?" Carmen asked, holding the dress up to her body. The skirt lay bulked on the floor, evidence that at least twelve inches would need to be hemmed off if Carmen were ever to wear it.

"Yes, it's vintage!" Coco answered, glancing back at the dress. The sight of it, crumpled on the floor at Carmen's feet, reminded her of the way it had fallen at her own feet, the way it had deserted her that night. "I'm cutting it up." Coco refocused her eyes on her beading. The used scarf she had found at a thrift store was also satin, and when the dress was done the scarf would be wound through the model's hair, black roses gleaming through a pile of black-brown hair.

That was the image Coco had created, an image she couldn't seem to let go of. The dress had come to her the night she had ripped Magdalena from her home. All that night she had cleaned and cried with *this* macabre black dress floating through her mind. Adding the black satin Yves Saint Laurent had been the last piece, a decision she had made moments before the doorman would have hauled it away with the rest of her mother's clothes.

"I love it." Carmen looked again at Coco's drawings. "It's... like your other pieces, Coco, soft, chic, and elegant."

"It's so me, right?" Coco's voice sounded dry, almost condescending.

Carmen looked at Coco closely. "Not quite. I would say it's sad. I don't usually think of you as sad."

"Sad?" Coco looked up at her friend, her eyes searching Carmen's.

"Sad," Carmen repeated. "Beautiful, fragile, and sad."

Coco stared at the dress in silence. Carmen was watching her with a focused expectant expression. "I've asked you this before and I'm asking you again. What happened to you, Coco? You're totally different. You went out to the opera with Rob and the very next day you came to school looking like a worn-out thrift store special. What happened to you?"

"Nothing," Coco said angrily. She snatched the Yves Saint Laurent from Carmen who still held it. "I woke up, I came to my senses, and I realized that I'm just fine on my own."

Carmen said nothing. Instead she watched Coco busily try to avoid her.

In the following weeks, Carmen ate lunch with Jack while Coco worked through all her breaks, not resting until the black dress hung on a form, complete in all its twisted wistfulness. Carmen was right: the dress was sad. Tosca could have worn it like a shroud floating tragically around her as she jumped to her death. A fitting image, Coco thought; she had worn bits of it in her own finale. Now the tattered remains of love and loss lay cut, coiled, and stitched into the most beautiful gown Coco had ever seen. Coco's eyes misted over and her chest tightened when she spread a protective sheet over her creation. Yet in that moment her heart felt less cold, her shoulders less heavy. When she walked home that night she knew she would see Bebe and Tia and she would be grateful that she was alive. Somehow the completion of the dress had helped her know that Rob would fade. With time, he would be another face in a crowd of faces lost to memory. She would always love him, but she felt no longer certain that he had ever loved her. The dress was the death shroud laid over their short-lived romance. It was pain twisted and reshaped into exquisite art. As she watched the dropcloth float down Coco knew that someday she really would be *fine*.

CHAPTER TWENTY

Gilman's was a riot of activity by week's end. Everywhere students scrambled to finish their eveningwear projects. Coco's gown was the only completed piece. It hung nobly against the far wall, a beacon of elegant sophistication amidst the crisis of the day.

Now a used and very oversized man's tweed jacket and '80s' thigh-length suede coat lay stretched out in pieces on the surface of Coco's work table. But instead of separating the last few seams, Coco watched Carmen and Jack argue. It was obvious that Jack wouldn't win with Carmen; the moment Coco reached this silent conclusion he turned and stalked away.

"Did ya get all that?" Carmen shot a glare at Coco who had been blatantly eavesdropping.

"Most of it." She plucked threads out of the tweed jacket's shoulder seam, her eyes refocused on her work.

"Just checking. I just wanted to be sure you weren't left out. I mean no one can know your troubles, but you sure as *hell* know everyone else's."

"I'm sorry, Carmen." Coco watched the jacket's insides fall open as the seam separated. "Sorry I haven't been a good friend lately." Coco could feel Carmen's eyes on her, but she still didn't look up.

"So, what do you think? Should I move in with him or not?"

"Well," Coco replied slowly, still not raising her eyes. "You'd get free rent in the big Gilman house, but you'd also be living with all his relatives under one roof...."

"Yes, all the *crazy* relatives. But that's not the problem, is it?"

"No." Coco's smile looked bitter. "The problem is men. They destroy your focus while they eat up your heart."

"Right!" Carmen stared coldly out the window. "I do like the free rent part. And being with the Gilman family would have its advantages. But...."

Coco didn't respond. She separated the old brown satin lining from the back of the wool sleeve.

Carmen also faded into silence, her eyes refocusing on her friend. Her own evening dress hung mostly finished on its form near the table. "So, if you're saying more than two syllables at a time now, are you planning on telling me what happened to you?"

"Maybe." Coco felt her hands begin to shake, her eyes becoming fixed on the table. "What do you want to know?"

"Did he hurt you?"

"No, not on purpose."

"So, why did Rob leave?"

Coco stiffened at the sound of his name. It took her a moment to reply. "He was unhappy with me; I was not what he had expected."

"How could *you* disappoint? You're a six-foot Glamazon goddess. He knew you had a kid. He knew you for almost a year. What possible surprise could there be?"

"It was my age that upset him." Coco still couldn't look up. Carmen remained silent. When Coco finally glanced up she found the tiny redhead surveying her critically.

"Explain," Carmen ordered.

"He felt like a pedophile when I told him I'm only seventeen."

Carmen looked instantly shocked. "You're shitting me! I would have never guessed you were that young. I knew you were young but... wow, you're young."

"Thanks, Carmen." Coco glared at her friend.

"So, how did he find out?"

"You don't want to know."

"Yes, I do. You know everything about me and dipshit over there. Come on, tell me."

"He was freaked out that I was a virgin. He realized that Bebe isn't mine, and he asked me my age. I should've told him right away, but I liked him –"

"Bebe's not yours?"

"She's my sister."

Carmen didn't speak for a long time. Coco tried to steady her shaking hands, while Carmen searched her face, looking for the girl she had somehow missed. "This is seriously messed up, Coco. I still can't see it. You look like at least twenty-two or more. I can't believe you're still a kid. You were careful, right?"

"What?"

"Protection and all – you were careful with him? If he thought you were a sophisticated woman he probably thought you were on the pill... had things under control. You were careful, weren't you?"

Coco shook her head, confused. "It all happened so fast. He said he loved me. That he would always love me. We were going to take things slow, but his friend kissed me at a club and...." Coco trailed off, lost in memory. "It was such a bad night. It just got worse."

"You don't want to be a baby mama for real, Coco."
Carmen watched her friend with concern. "Sister or not,
one tot around the house is enough."

"What?" Coco looked shocked, only just grasping
Carmen's meaning. "I'm… I'm not pregnant."

"Well, if you think you're fine, then you're fine."

But Coco was silent. Her heart ached whenever she
thought of Rob. She had put him and the experience out of
her mind, concentrating only on the present. The thought
that anything more could have come of that night had never
occurred to her.

"We were as close as two people can get." Her voice
broke. "I thought we'd spend our lives together. I never
dreamed he would leave." Coco's hands shook, her shoulders
bowing forward, the grief of that night overtaking her.

Carmen moved quickly around the table and grasped
Coco's hands. "Sit down. You're okay, just sit down,"
Carmen soothed seeing huge tears begin to slide down
Coco's face.

Taking a deep breath, Coco regained herself, wiping the
tears from her eyes. "I don't know why I'm crying. I thought
I was past this. It just hits me sometimes, and I can't stop
the tears."

"You're crying because your heart's been broken; that
kind of pain doesn't just go away. It lingers, honey."

"I miss him." Coco closed her eyes feeling fresh tears
slip down her cheeks. "I miss him so much it's unbearable."

CHAPTER TWENTY-ONE

Week ten after the breakup and Coco came down with a stomach flu she couldn't shake. No matter what she did she felt tired and sick. Tia watched her move through the house, concerned.

"Are you eating from street vendors?" Tia stood in the bathroom door as Coco vomited, her hair pulled back in the compulsory ponytail, her knuckles white where she gripped the toilet.

"God, no," Coco choked, feeling a second wave of nausea hit her. Just the idea of street-vendor food made her wretch. Those strange men with their carts of hot dogs and tacos going up and down the streets hawking to the business class.

"Tia," she moaned when another wave of nausea hit her. "I haven't eaten anything but what you made me."

Tia shook her head with worry. "Are you nervous about showing your dress next week?" She turned toward to the kitchen for water and Alka-Seltzer.

"No." Coco's reply was hardly audible. The next wave of nausea sent her deeper into the toilet.

"Hmmm…" Tia muttered, pouring warm water into a glass along with two fizzing tablets. In the kitchen Bebe sat in silence, her untouched breakfast ignored in her baby dish. Tia shook her head at her before heading back to the bathroom. "Drink this." She offered the glass to Coco, who sat on the tile floor looking pale and glassy-eyed. "You look terrible," she added, watching Coco sip the fizzing water. "You look terrible and you have lost weight again. Have you been skipping meals as well?"

"I've been eating. I swear. I'm not nervous or depressed or even body conscious. I'm sick, Tia, and I don't know why."

The color returned slowly to Coco's cheeks; with time she was able to stand.

"Go sit in the kitchen," Tia ordered. "I'll make you some eggs."

"No, please," Coco said quickly, "I could handle some crackers maybe and a Sprite, but no eggs."

"If you say so." Tia left Coco bleary eyed before the bathroom sink.

"You sick too?" Tia asked Bebe, who still hadn't eaten.

"Yep," Bebe answered, poking her eggs with her finger.

"How sick?" Tia examined the toddler. "Are you sick like Coco?"

"No, I not hungry." With that Bebe left the table to play.

When Coco finally wandered in Tia was prepared.

"Sit." She indicated Coco's place at the large kitchen table.

Coco didn't argue. Her strength was gone and she felt desperate to rest.

"I have something to ask you and you won't like it."

"Then don't ask, Tia, I'm not in the mood."

"Well, neither am I, but here it comes. Did you sleep with Rob?"

Coco froze, her mind flipping from rage to indignation to exhaustion. But when she finally looked at Tia she didn't see condemnation but sincere worry.

"Why?" Coco asked. "What does it matter if I did?"

"It matters a great deal if you're pregnant."

"I'm not pregnant." Coco looked away, unable to look Tia in the eye. "I'm tired and sick and I'm ending this conversation, Tia." Coco got up to go but her head spun and she had to sit down again.

"Are you late?" Tia persisted.

At first the question seemed meaningless – late for school, late for the bus…. "Late?" Coco asked, and then it hit her. The answer felt lost somewhere in the fog of the last two months, months she had spent hiding from every part of normal living.

"I can't remember." Coco shook her head vaguely. "I don't know… I can't remember what happened last month or the month before. I'm sorry, Tia, I can't have this conversation. Not now, not ever."

"Well, let's hope you don't have to."

Over the next four months Coco avoided having the conversation by avoiding Tia and her kitchen all together. She simply told Tia she was having breakfast with Carmen to prep for the day. Coco managed to avoid a lot of things by simply modifying her life as she modified her clothes.

The reality that she had screwed up her life irrevocably depressed Coco to the point of illogical denial. Even if she could face her situation, how would she ever face Tia? Tell Bebe? Let alone deal with Carmen, who would no doubt tear her to shreds.

By avoiding the subject completely Coco realized that she could go on living as if the worst possible outcome of her short-lived love affair was not a reality. To layered skirts, she added wrap sweaters, long scarves, and hobo bags. Unfortunately, the arrival of summer break made hiding impossible. Three months after her eighteenth birthday Coco became sickeningly aware that no matter how she dressed or how she sat, she could no longer hide the baby.

"I'm not sleepy," Bebe said, rubbing her eyes. The toddler sat obstinately on the living room sofa, her toy dog under one arm, a defensively placed pillow in the other. She was trying to wall herself into the sofa, stacking pillows like ramparts around her and her small collection of toys. "I'm not sleepy and I'm not sleeping!" her voice rose in defiance.

"You are sleepy and you are sleeping." Coco watched her sister patiently. "Please be a good girl, Bebe, it's time for bed."

"No!" Bebe yelled, throwing pillows at Coco, whose patience was quickly wearing thin.

"Now, Bebe!" Coco reached for her sister, who threw herself back against the couch kicking wildly. "Come on, Bebe, it's time for bed." Bebe kicked harder, thrashing and kicking with her eyes closed. No matter what angle Coco tried, she couldn't find a safe way to pick up the exhausted child without risking a kick. "Stop it this instant!" Coco scolded, at a loss as to how to handle her sister.

"You're a fat mean mama and I don't like you!" Bebe screamed while throwing more pillows at her sister. "You're a fat mean mama!"

Just then Tia walked in with a basket of laundry. "What on earth are you doing?" Tia yelled when she saw Bebe chuck yet another pillow at Coco. "You naughty little girl. You go to bed this instant."

Bebe glared at Coco, gathered up her toys, and crawled slowly off the couch.

Coco couldn't move; she stood frozen beside the couch watching Bebe run obediently to her room with Tia following quickly behind. In the midst of her temper tantrum Bebe had noted the one thing that Coco had worked so hard to hide. Slumping down on the couch, Coco hugged a pillow and tried to recover some shred of her dignity.

In the distance voices sounded, closet doors opened and closed, water ran, and teeth were brushed. The sounds of Bebe's nighttime rituals washed over her unnoticed until they suddenly stopped and Tia entered the living room.

"Are you ready to have that talk now?" Tia sat down in a leather chair to Coco's right. "You need to face this, Coco. You had me fooled for a while, but you can't hide it anymore."

Coco didn't say a word. The only sound that broke the ensuing silence seemed to come from somewhere outside of her. The first sob was barely a whisper but was quickly followed by another and another, until Coco had to acknowledge that the grief was hers. In that moment the wall of denial slipped away leaving Coco to face the miserable reality of an unwanted pregnancy.

CHAPTER TWENTY-TWO

The ultrasound was the needed magic that brought Coco peace. The baby had his father's thick hair, his long fingers, his chin – and those hauntingly huge dark eyes. Coco carried the picture with her at all times, looking at it each time the day grew too hectic or her fears became too jagged. Over and over she studied his features – her baby boy, James – as he slept contentedly in the black and white photo. In less than two months Coco would get to hold her son and he would look like his father. She could already see his black hair curling around his temple, the strength in his steely dark eyes, and the set of his chin when he made up his mind. *He will probably be a real handful*, she thought, tucking the picture back into her bag. Bebe was a handful and she didn't have Robert Banks' genes for an excuse. The quiet acceptance that washed over her the first time she saw him was strong and enduring. Now it felt like he had always been there, a part of her life... of their lives. Slowly, day to day and week to week, James Robertson Banks became a person and not just a frightening idea.

It's too hot to be this pregnant, Coco thought while she walked to the park with Bebe, the heat making mirages of the distant concrete. The constant wind that gave Chicago its nickname was mysteriously absent that day, and for once Coco missed it.

"Not too long, Bebe." Coco stopped her sister before she had a chance to run off. "I'm tired and it's hot."

Bebe made no reply. Instead she headed to the water to look for ducks. She still loved the ducks, but now instead of chasing them, she watched them, counted them, and named them. They were all her ducks, and the thing Bebe hated most in the world was when little kids chased them.

"That kid chased my duck!" Bebe would shriek at the nearby adults anytime a kid stepped out of line.

"They're Chicago city ducks," Coco would gently remind her. "You used to chase them, too."

Bebe never listened. She was now the protector of all park ducks, and she went each day to bring them treats and check on them. Her favorite was a giant, fat duck named Bob, who ate right out of her hand. If any little Chicagoan dared chase him Bebe would go into a screaming rage until, with time, all the kids learned to leave him alone. The best thing about Bob was his bad foot.

"Bob is broken," Bebe once proclaimed, pointing at his bad leg. "That's why he gets cookies."

Bob got cookies. He ate out of Bebe's hand and followed her looking for crumbs. Bob's handicap made him sociable; he grew fat on fish crackers and handouts while the other ducks watched from the water. Bob knew the families, he knew the park, and he knew Bebe.

"Good morning, Bob!" Bebe yelled, running toward the water.

Bob stood in the shallows, his head bobbing up and down as he began waddling toward her. Coco dreaded the day when Bob disappeared. She was sure it was a matter of time before he got roasted by the homeless. Yet month after month passed and Bob remained. The trick with Bob was that he knew his people. Show him a kid, a mom with a diaper bag, and he was eating out of your hand. A man alone sent him swimming out to safety.

While Coco considered Bob and his many attributes, Deborah, Carson's mom, walked up.

"Hey, Coco." She sat down next to her smiling.

Coco wore only a thin sundress and James stood out a mile under the white cotton.

"Hi." Coco gave her an uncomfortable smile. Though she had spoken with Tia and with her doctor about James, she had yet to discuss him with anyone else. She had spoken with Carmen on the phone since summer break had begun but had made excuses as to why they couldn't get together. The day Carmen learned about James was not a day Coco looked forward to. Carmen was not pro-kid – if anything she was overly pro-choice.

"Wow," Deb eyed her, "you're pregnant. I wouldn't have guessed it under all your winter clothes. How far along are you?"

"Seven months." Coco looked away, focusing on Bob and Bebe, who stood by the water. Carson had joined their group, and Bebe was already instructing him in proper Bob relations.

"Do you know what you're having?"

"A boy," Coco smiled, glancing momentarily at Deb.

"Wow, one of each, just like me. You'll love mothering a boy. It's an incredibly loving relationship. There's nothing quite like the mother-son bond."

"Do you have a daughter?" Coco had only ever seen Deborah with Carson.

"Yes. She's eighteen now. She lives with her dad in Virginia. I miss her all the time, but she likes it there. Good schools and green countryside."

"I had no idea." Coco eyed her friend who looked no more than thirty. "You must have been young."

"I was fifteen when I had her. It feels like a lifetime ago. I was so scared, but everything worked out. I raised her and she's turned out well. She moved south her sophomore year. She's in a good high school and she's happy." Having skipped high school, Coco couldn't relate but she understood scared. It lived with her.

"Motherhood is scary. I keep thinking I'll get past the scared but I don't. I look at Bebe and I think, wow, she'll have a little brother to chase around instead of just ducks, but I don't know when I'll ever be able to wrap my mind around this."

"You never will," Deborah answered. "I look at Carson or I think of Lilly and I still can hardly wrap my mind around the reality that they're mine. Disbelief is part of parenting."

Coco nodded and watched Bebe and Bob walk up.

"Bob's hungry, Mama." Bebe began rifling through her snack bag while Bob wagged his tail feathers and bobbed his head expectantly.

"He always is." Coco smiled, and watched Bebe feed him fish crackers before heading back to the lake.

"Is he going to help?" Deborah watched Coco quietly.

"Who?" Coco glanced up, wishing she could avoid the question. It was too hot and she wanted to go home. Besides, to admit that Rob was the father would be to betray their secret.

"I can't remember his name... Mila's dad, right?"

Coco shook her head no, unable to say his name or betray him. With time, Deborah's eyes shifted off Coco and together they sat in silence.

"I'm eighteen," Coco confessed quietly. "The father thought we were the same age. It horrified him. He doesn't know about the baby."

Coco felt Deborah's eyes on her. Coco waited for the ugly questions to follow, but Deborah didn't say a word. Instead she slid her arm through Coco's like an old friend who understood and had been there. A child was coming, a little boy, and he and his mother would both need support.

"You're a good mom, Coco. If you ever need help, I'm here for you."

During the last week of August, James grew strangely quiet. He stopped kicking and wriggling in the evenings. His lack of movement made Coco worry.

"It just means it won't be long now," Tia said while she helped Coco into bed. She didn't need to help Coco, but the old lady had lost all her edge in the past few months. Where once she had lectured now she soothed, and Coco loved this new Tia who tucked her in like the mother Coco wished she'd had. What would Magdalena have done in Tia's place? She would probably have caught the next plane to Paris.

Coco tried not to think of her mother as she heard the front door close. Tia had left for the night and the silence in the apartment felt heavy and oppressive. Not even the normally constant sound of wind came to break up the buzzing silence. Coco let her mind wander away from #2, away from Chicago to Rob in his New York apartment, and then further into her memories of the beach house in Miramar. Only after walking through the garden of her mother's Argentine home was she finally able to sleep.

"Tia!" Coco called, suddenly waking in pain only three hours later. The clock glared midnight and the old woman was gone. Bebe slept on in the other room, and Coco was alone in bed, the sheets wet and sticky around her. The phone sat on the nightstand, but when Coco reached for it a jagged pain ripped through her. She groaned, unable to breathe through the agony.

Bridging the three-foot distance between the phone and where she sat was the single most painful thing Coco had ever done. The phone glowed in the darkness as she scrolled through her contacts looking for her doctor's name, but the pain grew too intense. Coco dropped the phone into the bedding and screamed. In the other room, little feet hit the floor as Bebe ran to her sister.

"Coco Mama?" Bebe flipped on the light and stared. Coco couldn't answer, her bedding was not just wet; it was bloodied.

"Oh, my God!" Coco cried, the pain ebbing only slightly. Picking up the phone, she dialed 911.

"I'm bleeding," Coco whispered into the phone when the operator asked her to state her emergency. "I'm eight months pregnant and I'm bleeding." Bebe climbed onto the bed while Coco gathered the covers around her, shielding the child from the bloody sight. The voice of the operator faded in and out of hearing as yet another contraction hit. Coco tried not to scream while Bebe watched in worry. Taking Bebe's hand in hers, Coco focused on her breathing. Slowly the voice of the operator grew less and less clear; the world lost its substance, Bebe's face blurred and all sound and sight faded to black.

CHAPTER TWENTY-THREE

Coco woke in a noisy white room, alone and in pain. People bustled past the glass wall that separated her room from the busy hall. In the distance she heard machines beep and voices ring out instructions. Unconsciously Coco stroked her belly, comforting the child she was accustomed to feeling. But where James had been, there was only empty pain.

"No," Coco gasped, her heart rate jumping on the monitor that beeped next to her. "No, no, please. My baby. Where is he?" Coco cried until she could hardly breathe.

The door opened and a worn looking nurse hurried toward her. "Hold on, honey, you're okay," she soothed, coming to Coco's bedside. "Is he alive?" Coco cried.

"You're fine, honey, everything's fine. You just rest now." Coco watched the nurse inject a syringe into her IV. The world went fuzzy, and sleep became unavoidable as the memory of James, of his dark eyes and strong chin, receded and was lost.

Daylight and the sound of voices woke Coco the second time. Bebe stared silently out the window while Tia spoke in a hushed voice. Again, Coco touched her tummy, again she found it flat, again she cried. This time instead of drugs, she was given Bebe.

"We almost lost you." Tia's face was lined with worry. "I'm so sorry, I should've stayed. I should've been there with you."

Coco sobbed and held Bebe to her side. It hurt too much to move so she just held her sister and sobbed while she thought of her little boy.

"Coco." Tia held Coco's chin in her hand in order to make eye contact. The drugs hadn't worn off, and Coco's gaze was unfocused. "Coco, little James is okay. Look at me… he's in the NICU. He's a little sick with fever but he's okay. Can you hear me? We were just with him."

Coco blinked. Tears blurred her vision while her drugged mind tried to comprehend this new reality. Somewhere James was okay, and beside her Bebe was crying. The little girl cried because Coco cried, because she had seen blood, because she had talked to the emergency operator when Coco had dropped the phone, and she had ridden in an ambulance beside her unconscious sister. Coco knew none of this; she didn't know that Bebe had pushed a chair up to the top lock on the door to let the EMTs in and then pulled a blanket over her sister while she waited for help.

All Coco knew as her giddy mind tried to focus was that James was alive.

CHAPTER TWENTY-FOUR

That evening Coco held her son for the first time. Tia settled him into her arms, a tiny beautiful boy with eyes so dark they looked black. Little fingers curled into fists as those dark eyes stared up at Coco, memorizing her just as Bebe had only a few years before.

"He's so beautiful," Coco felt the tears stream down her cheeks. "He's so beautiful. I can't believe I'm holding him."

Tia sat next to the bed, her hands resting in her lap. When Coco looked up there were tears in the old lady's eyes. "I'm just happy," Tia explained, batting a hand at the tears that sparkled in the dim light.

"Me too." Coco smiled up at her.

A moment later James's eyes closed and he was fast asleep.

"You said he was sick with a fever." Coco lifted her eyes off her son to look back at Tia. "He looks perfect."

"There was an infection and so much blood loss that they were afraid he had gone without oxygen." Tia smiled down at the sleeping baby. "But so far he seems fine and all his blood counts are good."

"What infection? How could he lose oxygen?" Coco still knew nothing of the complicated route her pregnancy had taken.

"You lost a lot of blood, Coco. When things rupture, anything can happen."

"I don't understand. What happened?"

"You had a small uterine tear. Infection set in. You hemorrhaged and nearly died."

"Oh, my God. How long have I been here, Tia?

"Almost three days. They had to operate on you twice." Tia looked away, not wanting to say what she said next. "Coco, I'm so sorry. You won't be able to have another child." The shock of Tia's words left a heavy silence hanging over the room. "Maybe if I had stayed and taken better care of you, we could have caught the tear sooner."

"No, we couldn't have. I felt fine that night, a little tired but fine. No one could've prepared for this."

"I know, but we came so close to losing you both. I'm so grateful that God saw you through."

Coco felt lost for words. She didn't cry over the children she would never have. Instead she looked down at her sleeping son. They were alive and she was grateful, grateful beyond words.

The damage was irreversible. After the emergency cesarean, the doctors performed a risky emergency hysterectomy. Twelve days after escaping death, Coco remained in the hospital.

There was a knock at the door.

"Can I come in?" Carmen walked quietly into the small room where Coco lay in bed feeding her son. "So you're a real baby mama now," Carmen teased gently. She looked down at James for the first time, a soft sad smile touching her lips. Coco blushed and nodded looking down at the tan bedspread as embarrassment washed over her. "Tia told me you were here," Carmen added, looking up at

Coco. "I hadn't heard from you in so long that when you didn't come back to school I stopped by your place. You should've told me!"

"I couldn't even talk about him with Tia let alone tell you. Besides, I know how pro-choice you are." Coco glanced up momentarily at Carmen, who was still looking at the baby.

"Pro-choice isn't pro-abortion; it simply means you have a choice. I would never have tried to make you choose one way or the other." Coco looked from Carmen down to James as a long silence followed. "Does he look like him?" Carmen asked, breaking the silence.

"Completely." Coco smiled sadly.

"Well, Rob must have been one fine looking man because this child is gorgeous." Carmen smiled at Coco, their eyes meeting for a moment. Coco looked away, her cheeks flushed with a shame she was far from coming to terms with.

James was two weeks old when Coco left the hospital. Her movement was limited. She was allowed to walk from the bed to the bathroom, but she couldn't pick up anything heavier than James. Tia came and went on a later schedule, buying food and doing the housework and everything else that was needed. Coco spent her time mothering the children and found, as the days passed, more happiness than she would have believed possible under the circumstances. As fall edged toward winter her strength returned until with time she was able to resume her life as usual.

Winter quarter at Gilman's was difficult. Coco was behind, but with Carmen's help she wasn't totally lost. Despite slight stressors and petty inconveniences, life found its rhythm somewhere between fabric swatches and baby bottles – that was until the morning the phone lit up at six a.m.

Bebe lay asleep next to her sister. She'd had a nightmare just before two and James had woken up twice, so between the two kids, Coco had slept only three hours consecutively. Bleary-eyed she reached for the phone, wishing she could sleep for a week.

"Hello?"

"Coco!" Carmen's voice rang with urgency. "Are you okay?"

"Yes. What's the matter?"

"Have you seen the news? It's everywhere. I can't believe it."

"What are you talking about?" Coco felt too tired to hide her exasperation. "What news?"

"I'm coming up; I'll be there in five."

"Wait –" But the line went dead.

True to her word, Carmen reached #2 five minutes later.

"What's going on?" Coco asked, the moment Carmen walked in.

Carmen held a newspaper rolled up in her hands. She offered it to Coco. "Brace yourself. It's not good." She steered Coco to the sofa, sitting down beside her. Coco opened the paper slowly. On the front page a large color picture showed smoldering wreckage backdropped by green, leafy trees.

"What's this?" Coco glanced up at Carmen. "I don't understand." Her eyes, fuzzy from lack of sleep, had trouble focusing on the tiny caption below the picture. Carmen gently turned the folded paper over where a headline screamed in huge black letters: **Latin Supermodel Killed in Helicopter Crash.** Coco didn't read any more. The paper dissolved into a blur of black print. Magdalena was dead.

190   MAGDALENA'S SHADOW

"I…" But Coco couldn't finish her thought. She felt Carmen's hand on her back as the words on the headline blurred in and out of focus. Blinking several times, she read:

"Argentinean supermodel, Magdalena Rodriguez, died last night when her helicopter crashed into trees near her home. It's unknown whether the accident was due to mechanical or pilot error." Coco looked up slowly. "Carmen, how can she be dead?"

Carmen shook her head. "I know it's unbelievable. When I saw the news this morning I headed straight here. I'm so sorry, Coco."

"I don't know how to feel." Coco swallowed hard, her chest constricting. "I should cry but I don't feel like it. I'm not even sad. Is that right?" She looked at Carmen.

"If you're feeling it, it's right. She was far from the loving mother you are."

They sat studying the photo, neither of them knowing what to say or do.

"I just heard." Tia walked through the door five minutes later looking more shocked and grief stricken than either Coco or Carmen. She went quietly to the sofa, settling on Coco's other side to look at the photo.

"It's all over the TV," Tia added. "They're already whipping out retrospectives and photo montages. I can't believe how fast those people work."

Coco said nothing. She heard Bebe rustling sheets in the bedroom, doing her usual not-awake-not-asleep morning wiggle.

"She'll be up soon." Tia noted Bebe's movement in the same moment.

"Are you going to tell her? She was her mother too," Carmen added, distractedly running her finger over her jacket zipper.

"No, she wasn't." Coco spoke softly and without reproach. "As far as Bebe knows I'm it. Besides, how do you tell a small child about death? She's not ready for any of this. I want to act like nothing's happened." Coco folded the paper before sliding it into a drawer in the coffee table "Because nothing really has happened." She felt Tia's hand squeeze her shoulder as the old woman rose and walked to the kitchen to start breakfast.

"I'll leave." Carmen rose to her feet. "It'll just confuse things if I'm here."

"Why don't you stay for breakfast? Carmen, I would like it if you stayed. I think I need you to stay."

Carmen nodded and sat down again. Coco sat beside her lost in thought. She couldn't help but wonder if some part of her was broken. After all the years of grief and longing, Magdalena was dead, and she couldn't feel anything.

"Carmen." Bebe walked into the living room rubbing her eyes, her hair rumpled into messy flattened ringlets.

"Hi ya, girly," Carmen beamed at the three-year-old, who looked at her critically. Bebe stared for a moment longer before turning to the kitchen to find Tia.

In the weeks following Magdalena's death Coco could find no sanctuary from the memory of her mother. Sympathy poured in with each step Coco took. She nodded, smiled, and thanked everyone for their concern, their support, and their condolences. In all their caring consideration, not one of them allowed her the one thing she wanted most: to forget Magdalena had ever existed.

Sadly, not even Benny the doorman missed saying how sorry he was that such a brilliantly beautiful woman was dead.

"I remember her so well," he sniffed, more distraught than Coco, "coming in and out with you when you were only so high." He held his hand just above the floor.

And that would have been around the same time she left me and didn't look back. The thought crossed Coco's mind while she stared at the height the doorman indicated, the height of a child only a few inches taller than Bebe. Coco held her silence only because the man was clearly suffering.

The worst blow fell when Coco returned home from Gilman's to find a box of white lilies in the atrium with a note from Rob. This was the gesture that nearly broke her. After a year of silence, he sent flowers because Magdalena was dead. Not because she had almost died having his son or because he had broken her heart in a million tiny pieces, but because Magdalena had flown into a tree. "*Bitch,*" Coco muttered, her eyes skimming over the briefly stated sympathies Rob offered her. Coco left the flowers in the hall. They stunk of death and betrayal, creating that sickly floral scent Coco now associated with funerals and false promises. Clutching the note to her chest she unlocked #2. Once in her room she laid the card containing Rob's strong handwriting in her jewelry box next to a lock of Bebe's hair and James' hospital bracelet. Then, taking a deep breath, she willed herself to forget she had ever seen it.

194   MAGDALENA'S SHADOW

CHAPTER TWENTY-FIVE

Three days after the accident that killed Magdalena Rodriguez, the lawyers began to prowl. They started first with Tia because she was the sole caretaker of the apartment.

"I take care of Miss Rodriguez and her children," Tia replied repeatedly, explaining to each lawyer who called that Magdalena did have a daughter – no, two daughters– and that she had worked for them for almost three years.

"They have no record of you." Tia turned to Coco after ending a particularly unsettling conversation. "We have to get your name into Magdalena's probate case. If you are not represented, you'll get nothing."

Coco spoke to the next lawyer who called, explaining repeatedly that she was Magdalena's daughter. He sounded incredulous even after she had given him her social security number and date of birth. The attorney called again the following day, insisting that her social security number belonged to a Nicole Valentina Rodriguez, not a Coco, and as far as everyone in the world was concerned Magdalena had no children.

"Well, then who the hell am I?" Coco yelled into the phone before slamming it down. "You don't suppose I'm some orphan she picked up on a whim somewhere and just decided to mother for a while, do you?" Coco turned to Tia, who waited anxiously nearby. "I mean, my God, the way these people talk it's like I'm some freeloader messing with their heads."

"I told you we need a lawyer." Tia looked at Coco with renewed determination.

"I know, Tia, I know. We'll get this sorted out. A simple blood test would fix everything."

"They would just need to look at you to see that you're her daughter," Tia added, her face lined with worry.

The next stage in the invasion came with the arrival of men to inventory the furniture, appraisers to value the art, and real estate agents to assess the apartment's current market value. None of them got past the chain that Tia kept perpetually across the door.

Coco's lawyer was a small man, no more than forty, with sandy blond hair and small round glasses set in wire frames. He sat at the kitchen table with his briefcase and a smile.

"An international probate settlement can be lengthy and expensive, but the court has assigned an executor to oversee how all the money is managed in the interim. I don't want you to worry. We'll work with the executor to keep things running smoothly. Please don't worry," he assured them repeatedly – and yet they worried. Papers where signed and statements were taken all in the knowledge that there would be no immediate resolution. Worse still, the money on which they depended was cut to less than an eighth of what they were accustomed to despite the letters and calls made to the executor. The housekeeping account was reduced to only what would cover the dusting required in an "empty penthouse." Coco's personal account was frozen

196   MAGDALENA'S SHADOW

pending identity verification. The worst day came when the agency called Tia to work at another house. Coco instantly called her lawyer demanding that the executor pay her housekeeper's salary during the probate process.

"You and the kids can't live on one quarter of your housekeeping money alone," Tia told Coco while going over the household expenses. "I've stretched it as well as I can, but Bebe needs clothes, and there is hardly enough money for food let alone diapers and tuition."

Coco sat quietly across the table. They were becoming prisoners of the situation, never leaving the apartment empty in case someone got in – even remaining with Gilman's was looking like less and less of a possibility.

"I'll look for work." Coco raised her eyes to Tia's. "Maybe I could take in some alterations or make someone a dress?"

"Hmm…" Tia shook her head. "I think you should talk with the school. If you explain the situation they might be willing to cover your tuition. You are a bit of a celebrity. And…." Tia paused for a moment. "You could consider asking Rob for help. As I've said before, he should be paying child support."

"Yes, but first I would have to tell him he has a child, wouldn't I? And you know how I feel about that."

"He has a right to know."

"No one has a right to my son. Tia, if you tell him I'll never forgive you."

"James needs a father," Tia insisted, but Coco didn't reply.

They'd had the argument before. Each time Tia begged Coco to be reasonable and each time Coco assured her that she was being completely reasonable. Sharing her son with his father wasn't something she was willing to do.

E. E. ORME 197

"If I had material I could make Bebe some clothes. I'll look around and see what I can come up with."

Tia looked suddenly uncomfortable, shifting ever so slightly in her chair.

"What?" Coco looked up at the old lady who was looking at the floor. "I promise not to cut up anything you like, okay?"

"Um…" Tia mumbled before she folded her hands looking thoughtful. After a moment's hesitation, she glanced up at Coco, that same look of discomfort on her face. "I never threw your clothes out. I couldn't. They're all in the basement. I kept thinking you'd come to your senses so I've been storing them. You could sell some?"

Coco didn't speak for a long time. When she did it was to ask, "Do you ever do as you're told?"

Tia flared up with indignation, but Coco was laughing, teasing the old woman.

"I'm only dictated to by my own God-given good sense, child," Tia snapped. "When you gain some common sense then I might consider listening to you."

"You're a wonder, Mrs. Brown," Coco laughed. "So, will you show me where you have hidden the bags, or do I have to ask Benny?"

Coco sorted the stowed-away clothing into what could be sold and what could be used to make Bebe's new wardrobe. By the end of the week little Bebe had a gray wool pinafore embroidered with black silk thread that she wore with a black long-sleeve, crew-neck blouse Coco had found at the thrift store for a dollar. Each week, Coco made Bebe a new outfit, each one more creative and fun than the last. Overalls, skirts, dresses, and shorts embroidered with flowers, vines, and colorful bugs hung in Bebe's closet. But even with Bebe's wardrobe problem solved, they still needed more money.

Gilman's wasn't interested in coming to any sort of agreement. Either Coco paid her tuition or she left the school. As fourth term came to a close, Coco gathered her materials and said goodbye. Carmen took the news the hardest, persecuting Jack relentlessly for not having the power to do anything.

"I could give up my apartment, move into one of the guest bedrooms and pay you rent," Tia said that night while they sat in the kitchen going over the Rodriguez's absence of fortune on a yellow legal pad.

"And after that you could start paying me to work here," Coco added sarcastically. "Besides, where would your family live?"

"Luciana moved out last month. I've been living alone ever since."

Coco didn't reply. That moment marked the first time Tia had ever mentioned a member of her family by name. Even after everything they had been through together Tia hadn't mixed her home life with work.

"Well, you should live here then. Living alone is awful." Coco wondered quietly what Luciana looked like and where she had moved to.

"It does take some getting used to," Tia admitted. "I like having people around me."

"So do I." Coco rose slowly to her feet. "And I'm done worrying about money for tonight." She walked toward the hall to the bedrooms to check on the kids.

Bebe slept peacefully in the first room, a stuffed animal clutched under her chin, quietly unaware that her big sister was watching her.

Next Coco checked on James who lay in his crib at the foot of her bed, a tiny hint of a smile on his sleeping lips. His dark hair curled at his temple exactly the way Coco had imagined it would all those months before he was born. In reality, he was far more beautiful than the baby she had imagined. Gently she pressed her finger into his open hand, delighting in the way his sleeping fingers grasped it, sending a flood of warmth through her heart.

From the hallway, she heard Tia gathering her things for the night.

"I'll walk you out." Coco joined Tia by the door.

The old woman wore her purse slung across her shoulder over a tightly buttoned raincoat, a hat pulled resolutely down over her brow. Her chrome wheeled basket leaned by her side. This was the image Coco would always have of her: Tia prepared for the elements and whatever else came her way. And yet the image was somehow sad and solitary – Tia was an elderly woman with no one to go home to.

"I hate sending you out into the night like this. I would love it if you came here to live."

Tia smiled and shrugged. "If you insist."

"I do." Coco opened the front door to #2 and walked with Tia to the elevator. "I'm glad that's settled." They stood together in a comfortable silence until the car arrived and the doors slid open. "See you in the morning, Tia." Coco smiled and hugged her goodnight.

Coco lingered in the hallway long after the elevator doors closed, long after Tia had reached the paved sidewalk thirty stories below. She sat on the little used atrium sofa where Bebe had once been unceremoniously dumped and studied the transitory place that had been the stage for some of the biggest moments in her life. Here she had first seen Rob when she had been a baby on Magdalena's hip. Here she had retreated when the Keeper had mistreated her, in the days and #2 had felt like a prison. Here she had found the boxes from far off destinations like New York, Rome, and Paris all filled with clothes, and here, she thought with a pang, she had seen Rob again, standing in the storage room doorway and... and again on the night she had shoved a cracked picture frame into his chest while she pushed him out of her life.

This last memory was a wound that didn't heal; yet it was also the moment that had redefined her, the first and only time in her life when she had fought back. *Sadly, it should have been Magdalena I slapped, not him.*

"Poor Rob," Coco whispered to no one. She rose from the sofa to return to her apartment. "Poor Rob and poor me."

Instead of walking directly home she passed by #1, tracing the doorknob with her fingers before pressing her forehead to the dark hardwood door, in the same way she had once walked to Rob and pressed her forehead to his chest. She missed the way he had wrapped her in his strong arms, and they had stood like that, lost in each other for a moment. "Good night," Coco whispered to the grainy wood door before she kissed it and turned to leave.

The dim atrium light cast shadows off the furniture, turning the room into a pattern of light and dark. Saddened by her many regrets, Coco almost missed seeing a package half hidden in shadow behind the partially open storage room door. After Magdalena's death, the boxes had stopped coming. Now to Coco's surprise, she found a small red envelope addressed to N.V. (Coco) Rodriguez stashed just inside. Coco pushed open the door, watching the little package flop over as the door knocked it sideways. Who had sent it? Who but Rob knew she was here? The thought tied her stomach in knots.

Carrying the package into #2, Coco studied it carefully, looking for Rob's name on the label. There was no return name or address. Coco's heart leaped in her chest when she saw the New York City postmark. Carefully she opened the red packaging with a pair of Bebe's baby scissors, which were about as effective as a teaspoon. After two minutes and one curse the package opened. It contained a letter and around a dozen photos.

Hi, Coco.

I wasn't sure if you go by Nicole now or if you still go by the nickname, but then you'll always be Coco to me. It's funny how things stick. I used to tease Mag about how dark you were, like a bar of chocolate. Anyway, I thought you'd like these photos. I was so upset to hear about your mother's death that I thought I would give these to you. If I can help you in any way, please don't hesitate to call.
Yours sincerely,
Ryan Blackwell

Coco read and reread the letter, shocked by the thought that the name Coco was her nickname. If Ryan Blackwell was to be believed, then her name was Nicole. Coco slid thoughtfully down onto the sofa. For eighteen years, she had not known her own name. Tears rose in her eyes. Even her son's birth certificate listed her as Coco. She had never seen her own birth certificate. She had wondered once if, like Bebe's, it simply read Baby Rodriguez. The pictures sat in her lap, their weight reminding her that there had been more in the package than the enlightening letter.

The first photo was of Magdalena, taken when she must have been no more than sixteen. Her face wasn't airbrushed, her hair was imperfect. She looked real, like a real girl captured in a snapshot on a real day. Coco had only known the dream, the airbrushed perfected image, so beautiful it bordered on angelic. The back of the photo read: *Magdalena's first shoot as a Blackwell girl, age 14.* In the next photo, Coco saw Magdalena in a little yellow two-piece, her head tilted back as a hot sun rained down on her. This photo was far more professional than the first.

Each photo was a progression of Magdalena's teen years. In the third-to-last picture Magdalena sat with a group of friends, her features as young and lovely as in the first photo, yet Coco couldn't help noticing that she looked pregnant. Coco flipped over the photo: *Magdalena, Me, Jim, and Alex, Chicago, three months before you were born.* In all those years of sadness, of loss, and of anger Coco had never once seen Magdalena as anything other than a beautiful, missed, and sometimes hated *woman*. As Coco stared at the photo she saw the girl who had given birth to her, a teen mother younger than she had been when James was born. For the first time in Coco's life she felt a sad empathy for Magdalena, the exploited child in the yellow bikini.

Coco flipped to the next photo, taken in a hospital, of Magdalena and a newborn baby. In the next photo, Coco was a toddler in sunglasses on her mother's lap. And then the pictures stopped.

Coco knew how the story ended. The teen mom left her child with competent employees while she became one of the most successful fashion models in history. And the child grew up alone only to become a teen mom herself. *Funny*, Coco thought, her fingers flipping through the photos a second time, *funny how I unknowingly repeated my mother's mistake.* Yet somehow in this new light, all of Magdalena's transgressions seemed less terrible. Coco knew how hard it was to be a mom, let alone a young mom, and she had never had to work because her mother had. Now when she looked at the grandeur of #2, at the art and the fine furniture, she felt a spark of gratitude for the life she had been given. Still, she thought, Magdalena could have visited, could have answered her letters. Other than the handful of trips to the beach house, they were total and complete strangers.

Coco went to put the photos into a box in her closet when she remembered that the lawyer on the phone had said her social security number belonged to a Nicole Valentina, not a Coco Rodriguez. Coco laughed. She was Magdalena's daughter. She had a name, a photographed history, and a real hope of winning her mother's estate in court. When Coco went to bed that night she made a mental note to call her lawyer in the morning.

CHAPTER TWENTY-SIX

"Ryan Blackwell of Blackwell Modeling." Tia read a business card to Coco the next morning. "Is this yours?" Tia handed Coco the card that must have dropped unnoticed from the package the night before. Coco looked it over. The card was pressed on quality paper with the silhouette of a woman who looked remarkably like her mother. Over breakfast Coco told Tia all about the package, the photos, and the name.

"I'm dark like chocolate," Tia teased, "you're hardly even cinnamon colored."

Coco flipped through the pictures until she reached the one where she sat in her mother's lap.

"Look how dark I was compared to her, though." Coco studied the photo before handing it to Tia. There was no mistaking Magdalena in the photo; and Coco was Coco, even with the sunglasses on.

Tia smiled at the photo. "So, your name is Nicole."

"It feels so strange to find out I have a different name after all these years."

"I don't doubt it. This Ryan knew your mother. Have you thought about calling him? He may be able to tell you who your father is."

Around lunchtime Coco disappeared into her room with Ryan Blackwell's card and didn't return for over an hour. When she did emerge, her feet hardly touched the ground.

"I have a job!" Coco said, throwing her arms around Tia's neck, taking the old woman by surprise. "He wants me to model for him. We've been talking for the past hour; he knew my mom and he wants to send me some work, he wants to help us –"

"Coco," Tia said soberly. "We don't know the first thing about this man. He may not be a good person. Please calm down and think. He has never even seen you, but he's sure you'll make a model? If something sounds too good to be true, then it is!"

Coco looked hurt. "He knew my mom and he knew me when I was little," Coco replied. "He offered me work when we need money so badly. I'll do some shoots and then I'll come home."

"You have no idea what type of modeling he has in mind. Please slow down. This man might not be doing legitimate work anymore – he may never have. He could want to photograph you naked, for heaven's sake."

Coco laughed suddenly at Tia's look of concern. "He can photograph me any way he likes if it means I can buy food for my kids and pay the electric bill."

"Coco, don't you dare say such a thing! You have no idea where that road leads. It sounds so easy but being put in degrading situations eats at your soul."

"Oh no." Coco shook her head. "No talk of souls, please. Besides how do you know? You have never posed naked."

"How would you know?" Tia turned angrily from the room.

Coco prepared as best she could for her meeting with Ryan Blackwell. She even sewed a new outfit for the occasion. When she pushed open the door to the restaurant, she wore a hip-length ivory trench coat with a plunging neckline over a beige silk skirt cut three inches longer than the fitted coat. These she coupled with beige stilettos and a strand of crystal beads wrapped twice around her neck. Her hair hung loose in shining waves down her back.

"You are a picture of perfection," she heard a feminine sounding male voice call from somewhere behind her. "OMG, honey, you're completely Mag's daughter."

When Coco turned, she saw a small man standing behind her in designer jeans and a fitted tee.

"Mr. Blackwell." Coco walked toward him, her hand extended.

"Call me Ryan, please," he drawled, "but no, I'm not Blackwell. He's my partner. I'm Ryan Craig. Oh, honey, you just work it and you aren't even trying." He smiled, his eyes sweeping over Coco from top to bottom for the third time.

Coco gave a shy little laugh as Ryan Craig or Little Ryan, for that's how she would always think of him now, took her by the arm and led her to a small private room in the back. The room was lit with expansive crystal chandeliers and matching wall sconces. In the center stood a large, perfectly round mahogany table where a girl, an older man, and a boy so beautiful he had to be a model were seated.

"Look who I found," little Ryan giggled, parading Coco forward only to spin her at the end of his arm. The effect looked awkward since he was a foot shorter. "Isn't she divine?"

E. E. ORME 207

Coco blinked and smiled shyly at the people who, except for the girl, had risen on her entrance. The moment felt fraudulently preplanned.

"Hello," Coco murmured, suddenly too shy to move.

Thankfully she didn't have to; in seconds the older man was beside her, taking her hand in his.

"You look just like her. I can't believe it. You look just like Magdalena. But the crazy thing is, you are actually more beautiful. Look at her, Tom." The man turned to the beautiful boy, who on further inspection was closer to Rob in age, around twenty-eight. "Isn't she even more beautiful than Magdalena?"

Coco bristled. Somehow, in some way, it felt disrespectful and wrong to make the comparison; to diminish Magdalena in death felt cruel. Besides, what did the woman ever have besides her beauty? All of Coco's shyness fled. She set her jaw, turning from the man she instinctively disliked.

"This is Tom, Coco." Mr. Blackwell led her trophy-like to the table. "And Clara, and of course you have already met Ryan, my partner." Mr. Blackwell didn't elaborate on whether he meant for business or pleasure. "And here we are... all together... in Chicago... excited to make new friends." The statements were strange and again Coco felt the instinctive bristle. *Do people like this really exist?*

The meeting felt shamefully contrived with little Ryan insisting on being everyone's new best friend and Mr. Blackwell smiling on as the three young people became "acquainted." No mention was made of modeling, shoots, fees, or schedules in this schmooze-fest where Coco was the main dish. In fact she slowly realized that Tom and Clara knew each other, had known each other for years, and yet it was made to seem as if everyone at the table was newly acquainted and joyful to be instant friends. *Why all the*

subterfuge? Coco thought while she smiled, nodded, and answered questions.

Only after the waiter had gone, and Coco found she held a glass of wine, did anyone bring up modeling.

"Clara just did the most amazing shoot for *Elle*," Little Ryan drawled in his falsetto voice. "Clara, you're a goddess... truly dear a god-*dess*."

Intrigued by a mention of the business that had created the meeting, Coco pushed her glass of wine to the right of her plate and asked, "Will it be in next month's issue? I love *Elle*; it's such a classy magazine."

"Oh, yes," Clara said in drawn out lazy syllables, "but you won't be able to see me, I'm a giant pair of legs behind a white plumed fan. It's totally art."

Coco smiled, nodding as if she understood.

"So, dear, are you ready to dust off the soot of this little town and come to the CITY with us?" Ryan giggled, his odd intonation adding a vulgarly comedic element to the luncheon.

"And do what exactly?" Coco looked seriously around the table. "I need to know your expectations and my compensation before I commit to anything."

"Do what?" little Ryan exclaimed, throwing his hands in the air. "Do everything! Become famous! Luncheon with Valentino, meet with Prada, get to know Dolce and Gabbana. And she asks *DO WHAT*?"

The passion embroidered into the little speech alarmed Coco.

Mr. Blackwell set a calming hand on his mini-counterpart before turning soft, almost concerned eyes on Coco. "Coco, dear, what my partner here is trying to say is that you have the look and the face and the name to do anything in this world that you want to. Women who sign on as Blackwell girls see the world, they party with the rich, and they are famous. If you choose to put your faith in us we'll see to it that you become a rising star, that every door is open to you, that any and every opportunity is yours to take or refuse."

Coco nodded quietly, her eyes glancing around the table into the seemingly earnest eyes that focused on her. Yet even these words created just another pretty speech with no real meat behind it. Pretty speeches wouldn't induce her to leave James and Bebe, not even for a few days. Taking a deep breath, she invoked her very best Carmen-like attitude. "I'm sorry, but until you have tangible work for me, I won't be 'dusting off' Chicago. I'll happily go to New York City for a booked shoot, but partying with the rich and famous doesn't interest me. Work interests me. Book something and we'll talk." She was reaching a shaking hand for her ivory clutch when Tom suddenly stood up beside her.

"I'll walk you out," he smiled brightly. He was so beautiful it hurt to look at him.

"Thanks." Coco was surprised by how in a hurry he was to help her escape.

"Wait, wait, please," Mr. Blackwell said, rising to his feet. "I haven't been at all clear. Yes, of course there will be work, but you are, as of yet, an unknown. People must meet you, must see you, must hear your story; otherwise how do you propose to get your name out? When I talk about parties and dinners I am discussing your career. Please, Coco, for your mother's sake, sit down. I'm so sorry I wasn't clear." Ryan Blackwell spoke in an earnest tone that belied the calculating glint in his eye.

"Why for my mother's sake? Why for Magdalena? What does she have to do with this?"

"I think she would have wanted this life for you. The freedom, the style, money, travel, parties, and more fun than you can imagine. I built her career brick by brick; I can do the same for you."

A new kind of bristling anger spread up Coco's back, turning her cheeks pink. She watched the man in silence, her face giving away nothing. *Are those the things Magdalena turned to when she turned from me and motherhood?* Coco wondered while she surveyed the people who looked back at her.

"Perhaps it should be me who is sorry for not being clear," she shook her head, glancing down at the floor, her bag clenched tightly in her shaking fingers. When she lifted her eyes again to Mr. Blackwell's face she knew how Carmen would answer. "It's important," she said with slow command, "that you understand that I have commitments. I will need a streamlined schedule detailing what you want me to do and when – I can't be away from Chicago for more than a few days at a time. Chicago is my home and I have commitments."

"Now *I* don't understand, Coco," Mr. Blackwell looked both hurt and confused, his aged and sun damaged face filled with controlled emotion. "You sounded so committed on the phone. We flew here to meet you. Do you think we do this for every pretty face?"

And there it was: the needling guilt, the blatant manipulation that worked so instantly on Coco's resolve.

"Do you have any idea how many girls beg to sign on with me every day? Do you have any idea what my time is worth? And here you are, with everything I have to offer thrown at your feet, and you narrow the door, limiting my generosity?" He shook his head, sliding back into his chair in a display of dejection.

The act was good, it was very good. Coco almost fell for it.

"On the phone," Coco countered, pulling together her last shreds of courage, "you talked about work and money and a career. I've no time to waste on pretty words and fancy parties. You either have work for me or you don't. If you have all the connections, then this shouldn't be hard."

"And it's not. It's not hard at all. Come to New York next week and I'll have work for you." Coco stared at him, trying to see if he was sincere. "I will have work for you," he repeated with greater resolve.

Coco nodded, prompting a huge smile to spread across Blackwell's face.

"I'll come but at your expense. You send me the plane ticket and you book the hotel."

And with that Coco left the room. By the time she reached the street she was shaking all over. She had stayed firm, hadn't she? Everything was on her terms, wasn't it? Or was she doing exactly what they had wanted anyway? None of it made sense. A feeling of foreboding settled over her as she walked down the block to catch the bus. If she had looked over her shoulder in that moment she would have seen Mr. Blackwell standing silently under the restaurant's awning, watching her go.

Coco had nothing to say when she got home that afternoon. Tia didn't press her. Lunch had been so strange, all the pretty words with no real purpose. Coco felt tired, rude, and confused after the unnaturally forceful way she had spoken with Blackwell. Once she had changed back into her uniform of sweats and a hoodie she took James out of his swing and settled down on the sofa. Her baby's weight felt solid and reassuring against her chest. She tried not to think of the money she needed or the trip to New York the following week. Right here, right now, this was what she wanted: James in her arms, Tia in the kitchen rattling pans and dishes, and Bebe singing to her dolly on the living room floor. Coco closed her eyes and breathed in the scent of her son's hair while she listened to Bebe's song, making a memory she could take with her. Slowly she felt her body relax with the knowledge that this was all she needed.

214   MAGDALENA'S SHADOW

CHAPTER TWENTY-SEVEN

The ticket arrived, the hotel was booked, and Coco flew to New York, smiling as best she could when she kissed her kids goodbye. The trip would be short; she would make money and return home again to buy groceries, kiss James, and play with Bebe. This was her quietly whispered mantra as she gripped the armrests on her aisle seat and tried not to cry. She felt the plane shoot into the air, felt the force of the acceleration pressing her into the cushioned seat, and tried not to imagine the earth disappearing from under her. Once in New York she would smile, shake hands, make pleasant conversation, and kick ass if things didn't go her way. Now, in the quiet anonymity of the plane, she allowed herself to feel the subtle tremor that touched her fingers, the voice in her head crying out at her vulnerable stupidity. Fear lived with her, whispering its unwanted advice at the worst moments. It told her: *You should have stayed small and quiet. You should have stayed home. Who are you to dream so big?* Fear was a stalker she couldn't shake. A thing she blocked out while she went on dreaming and hoping and working toward something more. Taking a deep breath Coco shook out her fingers, closed her eyes, and searched for the peace she felt when she held her son or watched Bebe play. She remembered riding the bus with James snuggled to her chest and Bebe looking out the window. She saw the streets slipping past, felt the weight of her son in her arms while Chicago, the only world she understood, slipped by.

Coco stepped out of the cab feeling lost in the brown stone maze that surrounded her. She shivered nervously in the gray wool slacks, black heeled boots, and black beaded tank she wore with a hip-length silver fox fur. The cabby dropped her suitcase at her side, took the money she offered, and left her standing dumbstruck and alone in the middle of New York City. The hotel she'd been driven to wasn't a hotel; in fact, there were no hotels or homes anywhere in sight. Coco surveyed the building that matched the address Blackwell had given her with apprehension.

If little Ryan hadn't walked out of a large brownstone building to her right, Coco would have cried; his sudden appearance saved her from showing how out of her element she truly felt. The moment she saw him she grabbed her suitcase and walked straight at him.

"I hope I'm not late." She smiled brightly when she handed him her suitcase and walked confidently inside.

On entering the building Coco quickly realized that she had been dropped at some type of disorganized youth hostel. Inside she found what had once been the spacious old-world lobby of a hotel or boarding house. Just inside the door sat an enormous mahogany entry table covered in fashion magazines. To her right stood a mahogany console built into the wall with old brass hooks and a row of pigeonholes like those once used for a hotel registrar's desk. Old sofas in every color, style, and state of disrepair lined the walls. Here and there among the used furnishings, dirty dishes, and dog-eared magazines sat dozens and dozens of girls her age. A willowy blonde gave her a sour look as she walked to meet her.

"You'll be staying with La La tonight." Little Ryan cheerfully indicated the blonde.

"I have to share a room?" Coco looked down on the little man with concern.

"Yes. I'm afraid we're full up."

La La glared at Ryan whose cheerful smile didn't fade. "If my mother knew what a shithole this place was and how much debt I've incurred staying here she would have me back in Los Angeles by now," La La said.

"Language, La La. You have housing in New York City and a brilliant career ahead of you. Please take Coco to the ninth floor and make her feel welcome."

La La sauntered off, leaving Coco to follow.

The ninth floor was no better than the first. Dust lined the hallway in thick layers. Flip-flops sat abandoned outside each door in an attempt not to walk the filth into the bedrooms.

"This is my room." La La indicated the door but kept walking. "This is your room." The door swung in on an empty, dust coated room filled with boxes, old furniture, and late fall sunshine.

"But there's no bed?"

"No matter what that toad says, *I don't share*. There's a spare bed in the next room and a dresser you can use. I'll have someone bring them in. As for sheets, blankets, and pillows, I suggest you go shopping." Without another word La La turned and walked away.

Coco looked through large dirty windows at the view outside. From where she stood in the doorway she could see brown brick buildings, green puffs of distant trees, and small birds flitting in and out of a nook in the weatherworn window casement.

I'm in New York. The sudden reality that she was living one of her greatest dreams hit her all at once. *I'm in New York!* Coco smiled before taking a step toward the window. In three strides she was across the room, grasping the heavy old molding around the window to steady herself against the view. But vertigo had lost its grip. She was only nine stories up and she was in *New York*. "I'm in New York." The words tumbled out in a half-breathed sigh. The sun peaked between office buildings and warehouses while sirens blared and horns honked. If she closed her eyes she could hear the soundtrack from every New York movie she had ever seen, performed live right down to the "Hey, buddy" and "What the fuck?!"

Coco kept her eyes closed and listened to the city, not caring that this room didn't have a dresser let alone a bed yet. The moment La La had opened the door Coco had known this was where she wanted to wake up and fall asleep for the next several days. The best part was that without the howling Chicago wind and the thirty-story height, the view wasn't scary. Usually anything over five stories triggered her vertigo but not here. Slowly Coco realized that the building felt solid. The tower where she had spent her life seemed to move like a tall tree, swaying ever so slightly in the constant wind but not this place. Maybe it was its years of solid service, but the building felt real beneath her, strong and immovable.

Letting go of the molding Coco stood unsupported before the view, her arms raised over her head. She started to laugh. "I'm in New York," she giggled, spinning in a sudden big circle. And then she did something she hadn't done in all

 218 MAGDALENA'S SHADOW

her years of high-rise living: she jumped for joy. It took only seconds before someone below her yelled, "Knock it off!"

"Sorry!" Coco yelled back, still laughing. But she wasn't sorry; she was in New York and *she wasn't afraid*.

Coco found the spare bed but not the dresser. Instead, she stole a packing crate from the end of the hall to set her suitcase on. With these two items in place her little room felt strangely cozy. Coco sat cross-legged on the edge of the mattress and watched the lights go on in the neighboring buildings. Closing her eyes, she felt the hum of the city, its pulsing life force washing over her.

"Coco," a voice called from somewhere down the hall. The door was open and a moment later Tom stood in her doorway looking just as beautiful as he had at the restaurant. "What're you doing?" A half smile touched his perfect lips.

"I'm watching the city." Coco turned her eyes back to the window.

"When you're done watching the city I want to take you to dinner." Tom laughed and leaned up against the doorjamb to watch her. "Just you and me."

"Okay." Coco smiled up at him. "Just you and me."

Tom was far older than she could have guessed. He was thirty-four, which made him even older than Rob. He was also shrewd in a way Rob had failed to be.

"You look like you're about eighteen, am I right?"

"Yes," Coco nodded, while they walked together past store fronts and restaurants.

"That's old to start modeling. You're lucky your mom was a super model."

"How old are models usually?"

"They'll say they're fifteen, sixteen but some lie. Some are as young as twelve or thirteen."

"That's way too young."

"That's the business. You have never been to New York before have you?"

"How can you tell?" Coco laughed.

"It's the way you keep looking at everything. It's different, isn't it? The city, I mean. I came here from Ohio. I had been to Chicago a dozen times, but when I came to New York I knew I would never want to live anywhere else."

"I'm feeling that way right now." They had just walked into a Vietnamese restaurant and the scent of hot soup was heavenly. "So, what else can you tell about me?" Coco asked, happy with the booth they picked because it gave her a view of the street.

"Well," Tom gave her a shrewd look, his eyes narrowing theatrically. "You sew your own clothes, you have good taste, and you have been violently in love."

"No, that's not fair," Coco laughed, caught by the absurdity of the insight. "The first is obvious, the second is just flattery, and the last is cliché. Every eighteen-year-old has been violently in love, it goes with the territory. Try again."

"Not in love like you have been. No… I'm right." He grinned smugly and then lifted his eyebrows, daring her to disagree a second time.

Coco shrugged. "Okay, I admit it. I though he was the one. We were going to make a life together. I guess most teenagers don't usually think along those lines."

"Your turn." Tom looked at Coco with a more serious expression.

"What?"

"Come on, tell me about me in one glance. No one ever can. I'm a mystery."

"And I'm easy!" Coco made the statement with a playful pout.

"Oh, are you? It's nice to know these things up front. It saves a man a lot of time and money."

"Yeah, ha ha," she laughed. "I mean, how did you know I had been in love?"

"Sizing people up is my gift." Tom spoke with complete confidence.

Coco shrugged but decided to see if she could discern anything about him. His eyes were gray and large and very calculating. He had an aquiline nose and blond curly hair. She decided to go with the most obvious guess first.

"Mediterranean," she stated.

"Easy, go on."

"You're naturally… bitter," she guessed. He didn't tell her she was wrong. "I can see it in the way you look at things," she added. "You like people more to study than to interact with them," Coco played this guess off what he had already told her about himself, "and even when you're in a crowd you are still alone. You're not a joiner."

"Very good," he grinned, "very, very good. I've been too busy to have my heart broken, and I spend more time collecting people to watch than I do actually interacting with them. Even when I'm talking with them I don't pay them any attention because they've usually already disappointed me."

"How do they disappoint?"

"They're whiny or they sell out or they're just cheap and *easy*. You interest me, though. You're the first person I've seen who did *not* fall all over herself to get on Blackwell's good side. I don't think you'll disappoint. God, I loved the way you talked to him at the restaurant. Thank you."

"Anytime."

"So, what are your *obligations*? Do they walk on two feet or four?"

"That's an odd question." Coco drew back, feeling suddenly uncomfortable.

"Well, people these days think as much of their dogs as they do their kids."

"No comment," Coco answered firmly.

Tom watched her for a moment, his eyes studying every inch of her face. "Okay, have it your way. But if I were to guess I would say two."

"Guess away," Coco retorted before she picked up her menu and ignored him.

"I'm shooting you tomorrow," he said after a momentary silence, his eyes coming over the top of her menu.

"What with?" She met his eyes and laughed.

"A Canon," he grinned back, enjoying the old joke.

"Ouch!" Coco cutely pouted.

"It'll only hurt if you fall off the set."

"So, you're the photographer as well as the talent wrangler?"

"Yes, and an agent, spokesperson, and sometimes model; you name it, I do it. Once you sign with Blackwell, he owns you. You will learn every inch of the business, and he'll work you till you drop."

Coco studied Tom in silence before glancing back at her menu. She didn't want to sign with anyone, not when she was seeing the field for the first time. Besides, there was that certain something about Ryan Blackwell that she instinctively disliked. Just thinking about him gave her the shivers.

CHAPTER TWENTY-EIGHT

The shoot the following day had only one purpose –
to build a portfolio that Blackwell could begin showing
to potential clients. After sitting for the makeup artist and
hairdresser Coco walked onto the dreaded set and earnestly
prayed she wouldn't fall.

"Steady now," Tom called, watching her. "No falling."

"Quiet down you," Coco teased, standing before him in
skin-tight black leather pants, stacked stilettos, and a push-
up bra, her hair piled in a bouffant on top of her head.

There were twenty wardrobe changes that day and
no catering at all. By late afternoon Coco was starved and
exhausted.

"I'm worn out. I think I'll get some takeout and go
home," Coco looked up at Tom, who wore a green fitted
T-shirt with his leather satchel slung across his chiseled
chest.

"Can't. There's a party tonight. I have to take you out
and show you off."

"No," Coco whined, but his glare silenced her.

"Be a good model or you won't get your face in any
of those glossy magazines," he warned in a surprisingly
effeminate way.

"You're gay, aren't you?" Coco spoke before she could catch herself.

"Sometimes," he winked, and then running his hand all the way down her backside, he added, "and sometimes... I'm not."

Coco swatted at his hand and laughed.

At that evening's party, Coco was introduced as N.V. Rodriguez. It was Blackwell's idea. He liked the way N.V. sounded like *envy,* and he wanted everyone to envy him for finding her first. Coco walked into the party towering a foot above Tom in her stilettos and a black tutu of a cocktail dress that was really just a bustier and a frilly micro skirt that didn't even reach mid-thigh. Coco felt ridiculous, but the outfit was also Blackwell's idea, so Coco wore it along with that morning's painfully backcombed bouffant hairstyle.

"If I sit down in this," she whispered to Tom, with a perfect smile plastered across her lips, "my bottom will be in direct contact with the upholstery."

"Umm... yes," he sighed happily, "and then every man in this room will be rushing to sit exactly where you sat. It'll be the closest any of them can ever hope to get to that most desirable of locations."

"OMG!" Coco giggled, feeling every bit a seven-foot-tall drag queen when she mimicked little Ryan's favorite exclamation.

But to Coco's horror she found it was true. Only they weren't content to just sit were she sat; they also wanted to stand where she stood, sometimes when she was still standing there. Well, to be fair, most of the people were very well-behaved with the exception of three very odd businessmen who repeatedly gave her their cards and couldn't be coaxed to move more than four feet from her.

"Why do those men keep giving me their cards?" Coco asked.

"Well, you're the new dish, Coco, and everyone wants a taste. Some models are what you might call courtesans. They sell their look but also their feel. When Ryan said your possibilities were endless he wasn't lying. You could make a fortune as a professional girlfriend."

"Interesting." Coco continued smiling but made a mental note to toss the numbers as soon as she got home. "Parties and prostitution? Is this normal for a Blackwell girl?"

Tom seemed not to hear her – instead he offered her more champagne.

Early the next morning the first contract arrived. It was a boldly obligatory document brought to her room by little Ryan. Like Blackwell, he desperately wanted to see Coco sign as a Blackwell girl. But this first contract asked for too long a commitment. The second draft arrived after lunch. The length of the time commitment was less but it contained a much higher agent fee than the first draft. Each new contract brought up new concerns and all of them demanded that she lose ten pounds off her already thin frame and maintain that specified weight throughout her career. The longer Coco remained under Blackwell's roof, the more she wanted to leave.

Coco might have signed the third contract if it weren't for Tom's careful advice. Without his help she wouldn't have known that she had a right to continue negotiations.

The days passed in a flurry of champagne luncheons where the champagne was lunch and champagne dinners with light low-fat appetizers. Before Coco knew it the first week was over and she was five pounds lighter. She had promised Tia she would eat well and only be gone a week, but every time she asked Blackwell about work he was evasive.

"I don't want to waste you on little labels. We need to be patient. More importantly you need to sign with me before I can represent you." So Coco continued to go to parties, shake hands, sip champagne to fill her empty stomach, and make small talk between reviewing each new draft of Blackwell's binding contract.

"I'll tell you what Blackwell is thinking," Tom explained one evening, trying to soothe Coco's growing agitation. "Your mother left a big hole in this industry when she died; under a strong contract Blackwell is hoping he'll be able to slip you into that hole."

Coco went still beside him, her face losing its mask of gaiety. She stood on a yacht in New York Harbor; music played in the background while people danced and drank under a darkly clouded night sky. Coco could feel the late fall wind cutting her to the bone, bringing back memories of the night she had lost Rob. She would never forget the way the wind had torn at her, grasping and cruel. She tried not to think about Rob when she tightly clutched the same floor-length black fur she had worn that night over the white cocktail gown she now wore.

Turning to Tom she asked, "What do you mean, slip me into my mother's hole?"

Tom began to laugh at the lewd joke he thought Coco was making but stopped when he saw her face. "Coco, it's an instant *in*."

His words were meant to erase the anger from her eyes but they had no effect. "I'm not riding my mother's coattails. I either do this on my own or not at all."

"You don't have a choice if you want to work in fashion," Tom said frankly. "You are *her* daughter. She was *their* icon."

"I don't want this." Coco grabbed the icy railing and gazed out on the sparkling city. *It all looks so beautiful*, she thought, looking out on the picture-perfect skyline. "I don't want this, Tom. I should be home; I would never have left if it weren't for the money. Yet here I am –"

"Yet, here you are, on a yacht in New York Harbor with one hell of a future. What do you have to complain about? With the right contract, you're set for life."

"I told you I have other obligations," Coco shot back, heartsick at the mess she had gotten herself into. She was N.V. now, not Coco. She already had met with one journalist whose prying questions had upset her. Once her story went global, all her peaceful privacy would disappear along with her sole guardianship of James. His birth was a matter of public record, and she knew Rob wasn't the sort of man to stay away from a child once he found out he had one.

"I have commitments that most girls don't have," Coco confided. "You can't understand how hard it is for me to be here. If life had been different, I would be overjoyed... but I'm not going to make the same mistake my mom made."

"Which is?"

"I'm not going to leave my children for all this." Coco swept her arm at the city. "I'm not going to sell them out so I can live everyone else's idea of the perfect life. I was happy before she died, before probate and poverty."

Tom stared off thoughtfully, his arm leaning elegantly on the railing. A couple danced quietly behind the glass wall of the cabin moments before the music ended.

"Two legs – I was right!" Tom laughed after a while. "Are these the kids of the violent love affair?"

"My little son, James," Coco nodded. "He's his son, but Rob doesn't know about him. Bebe calls me Mama, but she's actually my sister; I'm the only mother she knows."

"Your sister?" Tom asked with sudden interest.

"Yes," Coco laughed, "she's Magdalena's too. Neither of us has a father we can name. I didn't even know she was my sister till she was almost a year old. Before that she was just a baby dropped at my door."

Tom was quiet for a long time. When he did speak his voice was low but comforting.

"Don't sign with Blackwell. He's an abusive fuck and he'll work you till you drop. You won't have a hope in hell of seeing those kids for more than a few days at a time if you're his. He'll work you and he'll starve you and when you get too hungry he'll tell you to shoot heroin between your toes so you don't notice the pain."

"Oh, my God, I had no idea he did stuff like that!"

"There's a lot you don't know." Tom stared out at the water, a bitter expression marring his perfect features.

"Tom," Coco broke the silence, "I need money. I have no way of knowing the state of Magdalena's finances. She could be leaving me nothing but debt. I need to earn money and I need it soon or my kids will starve."

"Try not to worry. I know people. You don't need Blackwell, not if you'll trust me. I can do what he does, only on a non-soul-owning level."

"Tom, you're the closest thing I have to a friend in this business. If I can't trust you then I've already lost. Just remember, I need money and I need it soon."

CHAPTER TWENTY-NINE

When they returned to Blackwell's building a few hours before dawn Coco was surprised to see Ryan Blackwell sitting in the lobby, a crystal glass in one hand, the *Wall Street Journal* in the other.

"Coco," he called waving her over, "just the girl I wanted to see." Coco walked to where he sat, taking the faded leather chair he offered. Her fur slid open to reveal the little white cocktail gown she wore. "Thanks, Tom, for keeping an eye on our Coco," Blackwell nodded in a way that dismissed Tom from their conversation.

Coco was suddenly glad she had told Tom everything. If Blackwell pressed her for a commitment she could answer him with a confident *no*. As Tom walked off down the hall, Coco turned to face her host.

"This is an awfully late hour for you." Coco offered Blackwell her sweetest smile.

The calculating glint in Blackwell's eyes did not soften. In the low lighting, he looked almost sinister. "I couldn't sleep," he said. "Not when I'm being taken advantage of. I've housed you and sheltered you, offered you my connections, flown you here, and never asked for anything but your trust. Even with all I've done, you still flatly refuse to sign my contracts. Why, Coco, when I've been so generous? Why do you refuse to sign? A contract is standard, without one we cannot do business."

"I can't see that much business has been done as it is. I've gone to your parties, met people, shaken hands, and sipped champagne. You said you'd provide work and money yet the only photo shoot I've done was with Tom?"

"I told you, I can't represent you without a contract."

"And I told you I need paying work, scheduled shoots, and a contract that doesn't make me your slave. You ask for years of my life, you want to own my name, my image, and you demand outrageous representation fees. It's your fault not mine that we haven't come to an agreement. I was clear with you when we first met. I have commitments and because of your inability to compromise I'm in no way closer to having a career that will pay the bills."

"That goes to show you how very little you know about this business; I've already devoted myself to setting a stage for your great unveiling. Most of what I do is behind the scenes. All I've asked of you is that you go out, make a good presentation, and sign a contract that will allow me to represent you. That's my job. I represent models."

"Your contracts are too binding. I'm not ready to make the level of commitment you're asking for. Come up with something that's flexible and we'll talk."

"I've been about as flexible as I can afford to be," Blackwell countered. "Do you think this building pays for itself?"

"I'm not interested in your finances," Coco interrupted. "As I've said, come up with a contract that allows me more freedom and we'll talk." Coco rose to leave but Blackwell was suddenly there, looming over her.

 230   MAGDALENA'S SHADOW

"I don't think you're aware of who you're dealing with. No one turns down one of my contracts. There will be no new terms, not if you want me to represent you."

"Well, I guess I'll be looking elsewhere for representation." When she rose to stand a second time, her heel was kicked out from under her and she fell to the marble floor.

"Oh, pardon me," Mr. Blackwell said smoothly. He bent over Coco, took her by the arm, and pulled her to her feet. "These old stone floors can be so slippery."

His hand dug into her arm as a large red welt bloomed across her right cheekbone where her face had struck the floor. Her body convulsed in panic, her breathing reduced to short gasps. Blackwell stared quietly down at her, his fingers crushing where he gripped her.

"It's funny how quickly these accidents happen. Your poor pretty face. Oh well, we'll just have to wait until you are all healed up before you can go out again."

Coco felt herself recoil when her strength returned. She fought against his grip. He freed her instantly, but as she turned to run he kicked her feet out from under her again. Coco stumbled, tried to catch herself in her stilettos, but landed knees first on the stone floor. Behind Blackwell the door opened and two models walked in.

"Are you okay?" Blackwell asked with feigned concern.

Coco staggered quickly to her feet, feeling Blackwell grasp her around the waist, lifting her from the floor.

"Fight me and I'll kill you." His words were no more than a hiss as he guided her to the elevator.

When the doors began to close, Coco lunged away from him. She made it two feet through the doors before he caught her. The doors closed as Blackwell smashed the unblemished side of her face into the mahogany wall until Coco went still.

"I haven't had to do this in ages. With the way the market runs I generally have my pick of the girls. They'll do literally anything to sign with me – and I mean *anything*. But not you. We'd have made a fortune together. Now I'm afraid your pretty looks are all spoiled. No one will pay to look at you now, Coco – maybe in a month or two but not now."

The elevator continued up, rising further than Coco had ever taken it. The doors opened onto the snow-covered rooftop patio.

"I'll just leave you here," Blackwell said, ripping Coco's fur coat off her shoulders, "while you take some time to think. And remember, you owe me as much as your goddamned mother owed me. I made her career and I'll make yours, even if I have to torture you, your kids, and your beloved old housekeeper to do it. And don't think I'll overlook that cradle robbing lawyer who knocked you up. No one you love is safe, little girl. You will sign with me or I'll rain hell down on Robert Banks and everyone you love."

Only when the doors slid closed did the shock wear off. Coco hit the elevator button several times but the car didn't return for her. A harsh northern wind tore at her thin, blood stained dress while white flurries swirled around her feet. The world blurred and contorted, hardly visible through puffy, tear-stung eyes. The wind picked up to a frigid screeching gale.

"Oh, my God. Oh, my God!" Coco cried.

Taking a step, her legs gave out and she landed in the snow on hands and knees. "Please help me, someone, please help me!" Her hair fell forward around her shoulders, long black tendrils glistening with white flakes. In that instant, the gold cross she wore tickled her chin. "Someone!" Coco screamed, her hand moving unconsciously to grasp her mother's necklace. "God help me! God, I'm here. Someone please help me!" she screamed, watching the snow continue to fall. Coco prayed aloud, her eyes searching the rooftop for another way out.

When her skin turned blue and she stopped shaking, Coco knew she was going to die. Blackwell hadn't come back for her and the sun hadn't yet risen. As she gave into the cold she stopped thinking about how badly death hurt. She stopped fearing the darkness and forgot about the amount of snow that had gathered around her. She listened only to the city, to distant noises now more easily heard in the stillness of the abating storm. Soon the sun would rise. Soon she would be dead. Soon she would never need to worry about anything ever again. Each noise that echoed through the city brought with it a memory: Bebe with her ducks, James with his rattle, Tia with her chrome handcart trundling down the hall with a bushel of vegetables. When her eyes closed on the world Coco felt a powerful love swell in her chest. It was the same love she had once felt for her mother. It was a warm healing love that swelled each time she looked at James or heard Bebe's voice. This love had guided her through life, through loss, and through every tragedy and every joy she had ever experienced. Now it filled her with soothing warmth, her heart rate slowing until she fell unconscious.

"Get up," a voice commanded loudly. Coco snapped awake; she felt as if electricity had passed through her. She tried to lift her head but found she couldn't. "Get up now, Coco." The voice was not coming from any one place; it was all around her – in the snow, in the ensuing silence, everywhere and nowhere like an echo. "Get up, NOW!" It spoke with such authority that Coco couldn't help but obey.

Coco staggered to her feet, her legs feeling like dead wood underneath her. She was alone on the expansive rooftop, the white snow adding an ethereal light to the scene. "Come here," the voice ordered. Again, the sound came from everywhere at once. Coco took a tentative step forward, looking first right then left. To her shock, a shadow stood at the northwest corner of the building, a hand extended, waving her forward.

Slowly and with great difficulty, Coco stumbled forward, the snow drifts coming up over the top of her shoes while her hair hung in frozen ropes around her. *I'm dead*, Coco thought, staggering still closer to where the shadow waited. *I'm dead and this is my angel.* Even her afterlife was a cruel joke. No tunnel of light came to lift her from her misery. *Oh no, that would be too easy.* When the thought crossed her mind she almost laughed like the lost soul she was. As punishment, she envisioned a hundred years of solitary wandering, a hundred years of waiting for God to notice her. *I should've been a better person*, she lamented silently when she reached the northwest corner. The shadow was gone but the voice returned, everywhere at once. "Go down," it ordered with the same authority.

Coco looked out over the edge at the tiny world below. No, she wouldn't just have to walk the world for God to notice her; she would also have to scale large buildings. As her bitterness rose, she leaned over the side of the building, and noticed a thin metal ladder coated in snow. Again the humor of the situation struck her. "Go down," she repeated to herself though her lips could hardly form the words. Lowering one foot and then the other, she stepped onto the ladder, her toes feeling for each rung as she went. The funny thing about being dead, Coco thought as she lowered herself hand over hand down the side of the building, was that she stopped bothering to be scared. *Too bad I didn't do that a long time ago*, she thought, passing the first of nine sets of windows.

 234   MAGDALENA'S SHADOW

She was long past the place where her fingers should have stopped working. Far past having legs that could support her, and yet she moved on slowly and solidly, down the side of the building simply because her angel had told her to. She imagined all the other places she would wander in her hundred years of solitude, never stopping for rest. No sooner did exhaustion take her than the voice would call her back into motion. "Okay, okay," Coco said, lowering herself down another rung "You keep talking and I'll keep walking."

She lost track of how long she had been climbing when the ladder suddenly ended. She hung there, her foot feeling for a rail that didn't exist. The ladder should have slid to ground level but it was frozen in place. No voice echoed through the gloom to guide her. When she looked down she saw the shadow standing on the ground some fifteen feet below her. But Coco knew what she had to do. She had to let go.

Hitting the ground was like landing on a dozen feather beds. It should have hurt, she knew, but nothing hurt now, absolutely nothing. She laughed as she staggered to her feet, the shadow never wavering in its stark contrast of dark against white snow. Coco smiled at her angel, wondering if it would lead her to heaven or somewhere else completely. Suddenly it didn't matter so much. Nothing mattered except when she thought of Bebe or James, Tia… or Rob. But the shadow moved on, down the alley, always six feet ahead or more so that Coco had to hurry to keep up with it. Every time Coco stopped to rest or lost sight of the guiding apparition she would hear the hollow voice say, "Walk," and Coco walked.

"I'm tired," Coco called but it never slowed the pace, never said, "Rest, we have all eternity." Coco wished it would. If she could sleep for a little while she knew she would be able to follow this thing wherever it called. When she fell against a strange low slung tunnel wall, so heavy with darkness she could see nothing, the need for sleep became too great. Her knees buckled and she began the slow slide down the stone to the pavement below.

As her eyes closed, the voice said, "Get up," and she did.

The tunnel was an endless expanse of blackness that ended in a treed, snow-white wasteland filled with the frost covered remains of an ancient cemetery. The scene made sense; this was where she would rest. Hallowed ground was the sanctuary of the spirits, the place where you rested when you were dead. But the shadow didn't stop. It crossed the bracken filled, stone laden yard at the same swift pace, stopping only when it reached the wrought iron fence that marked the boundary. As Coco approached the figure she was struck by an odd feeling. Somehow, she knew this person. Now just five feet from the form, Coco tried to make out the face, so familiar yet so strange.

"We've met before!" Coco whispered.

"Keep walking. You're there."

Coco gave a slight nod, stumbling past the figure toward the only thing that lay on the other side, an old white granite building with just a few lights on inside. The moon hung full overhead when Coco stopped and turned back toward the cemetery. There in the gateway, on the perimeter that marked the place between life and death, stood Magdalena, her heavy dark hair framing her face and shoulders, her eyes alive with a light Coco had once known.

"Oh, Mama," Coco whispered, wanting so desperately not to lose her again. But the voice sounded all around her, everywhere at once, "Keep walking," and Coco walked.

CHAPTER THIRTY

Coco remembered Rob as a dream. He was one of the four people who had made her life good. In the dream, he took off his jacket and wrapped her in it. Gently, he pulled her wet frozen hair away from her body and laid her on the atrium sofa with such loving care that somewhere inside, her heart broke all over again. The first sob was hardly more than a shiver, the second rattled her chest, making her convulse with pain. Rob kissed her forehead, holding her to his chest as they waited for the ambulance to come.

"Rob," Coco whispered through cracked lips.

"Yes?" Rob leaned over her, peering down into her disfigured face.

"I found you." She tried to smile, her swollen lip cracking with the effort, a sliver of red blood filling the crack. Slowly her eyes slid closed and she went still.

"Coco!" Rob yelled, shaking her. "Don't go to sleep."

Coco's eyes flew open suddenly. She smiled what reassurance she could offer. "I'm okay." She looked into his worried eyes. "I'm okay."

Rob nodded, tears sliding down his cheeks as Coco went still again.

Hazy memories of fluorescent lights and numbing pain created the surreal experience that made up Coco's hospital stay. She could have sworn she had seen her mother. She remembered Magdalena leading her to Rob's law firm. She remembered Rob sitting beside her bed, sometimes talking to her in a whisper, sometimes quiet, but always there. Now when she woke it was Tom sitting by her bed, Tom who talked, and Tom who never left her side. Now when he looked at her his eyes filled with tears. Coco smoothed the hair from his forehead, yet even this small action exhausted her.

Tia arrived in a flutter of anxious tears to sit with Coco. She arrived alone, having left Bebe and James in Chicago with Deborah.

"Why are we doing this again?" Coco spoke quietly one afternoon when she felt well enough to talk. "It hasn't even been a year since the last time you had to sit by my bedside. I need to stop all this drama; it's turning into a habit."

Tia tut-tutted, petted, and reprimanded her until she felt loved and cared for in every possible way. But Tia wasn't her only visitor. Police officers arrived to question her. She told them everything she could remember, but some of the memories were too strange to recount. In the end, she chose not to mention the fact that her dead mother Magdalena was the one who had led her off the building.

In the second week a young lawyer in a perfectly cut gray suit sat beside her bed and quietly informed her that on top of criminal charges, Coco had every right to a civil suit against Blackwell. The man read the proposed suit aloud. The wording bothered Coco in a way she couldn't understand. There was something poignantly familiar in the language. When the lawyer finished, Coco signed her name, never reading the law firm's letterhead which read Foster, Robinson, Allen, and Banks.

After three weeks Coco felt well enough to fly back to Chicago, no richer but far wiser than she had been before her brief modeling career. When the plane taxied down the runway, Coco had a sudden thought. "Who called you, Tia, how did you know I was in the hospital?"

"Rob called me. He called me the same night he found you."

Coco leaned her head against the plane's window feeling two realities collide. The dream wasn't a delusion. Rob had found her in the snow. Of all the millions of people in New York City, why Rob? The answer was simple. Coco's guiding angel was no stranger to the dramas of her life. Magdalena had led Coco to Rob because he was the only person in the city Coco both loved and trusted.

Coco lay in bed and tried to ignore the pain. Her back and both legs had been badly injured when she had jumped from the ladder. Her right ankle had sustained several hairline fractures, while her right leg had not only broken but had also twisted, its tendons and ligaments tearing with the spiral break. Even after seven weeks of rest, the joints remained stiff, swollen, and painful.

James lay in her arms, his little face closed in sleep while Bebe played quietly at the foot of the bed, flatly refusing to leave Coco's side. If Coco moved to the sofa, Bebe and her dolls were only steps behind.

"How are you feeling?" Tia lifted James out of her arms, placing the infant in his crib.

"Like I was beaten and left for dead." Coco closed her eyes remembering every punch Blackwell had thrown. She felt Tia's arm slide under her pillows lifting her to a sitting position. A tray of pills and food were set across her lap.

Two large white pills were the only thing that helped with the pain. Two massive pills every five hours made moving possible. The breaks and fractures had healed, yet the damage to muscle and tendon screamed through her body every time she tried to do more than lie still.

The one activity she could manage with little pain was to draw in her sketch book. She drew a new dress for Bebe and an evening gown that quickly led to a whole new line of women's wear. Sometimes when she was feeling less depressed she would sketch a dress for herself while she waited for the day when she could sit at her machine and sew again.

When she was feeling very weak and alone she thought of Rob. His voice echoed through her memory telling her to stay awake. Without him she would have fallen into a heavy sleep and never woken again. She wanted to thank him, to apologize for the past, for everything that had happened. Again and again her mind recalled the moments of brief consciousness in the hospital when he had sat beside her and held her hand.

At around three in the afternoon, Coco sat in her white bathrobe on the sofa listening to James laugh as Bebe bounced a toy giraffe before him. Coco loved watching them play, loved the fact that her son and her sister were already so close. Tia was out grocery shopping when the intercom buzzed, the lit button on the side of the phone indicating a first-floor lobby call. Coco rose slowly off the couch, walking like a broken spider toward the intercom, her stiff legs hardly able to carry her.

"Hey, Benny."

"You have a guest, Miss Rodriguez," Benny said. "Her name is Angie Thompson. Shall I send her up?"

"Put her on the phone first, Benny."

"Hi, Coco, this is Angie Thompson. We met at the Ford party in New York City last month. I heard about your accident and I was wondering if you're up for a quick chat."

Coco riffled through her memory, trying to remember one face and name out of the dozens of new acquaintances she had made in New York.

"Okay," Coco tried to sound confident. "I'll buzz you up." She had decided she would remember the woman when she saw her. Coco opened the door to #2 before she hobbled back to the sofa.

"Come in," Coco said when she heard Angie's footsteps in the hall. When the petite woman walked in, Coco instantly recognized her. Angie Thompson was the journalist who had covered the Ford party. In a panic Coco looked from Bebe to James, quietly realizing there was no way to hide either of them.

"Mama, there's a lady in my house!" Bebe shouted, pointing a finger at Angie. The toddler ran to Coco, jumping heavily into her lap. Pain shot through Coco's legs. She moved Bebe quickly to her side and tried to catch her breath. Slowly the pain lessened.

"It's okay," Coco soothed, "she's a friend."

"I can't believe what happened to you." Angie smiled while sitting down on the sofa next to Coco. "How are you?"

"Mama's taxi crashed." Bebe said, parroting the lie she had been told. Coco glanced down at Bebe and then back at the journalist.

"Taxis are so dangerous. You have to be very careful." Angie smiled at Bebe who continued to watch her with apprehension. James, feeling suddenly ignored, began to holler from his swing.

"Why don't you go keep James company while Mama and Angie talk, okay, Bebe?" Coco coaxed the toddler off the sofa. Angie watched Bebe walk toward the swing, smiling when Bebe picked up the giraffe that made James laugh.

"You have a gorgeous family. You must have been very young when you had her."

"She's Magdalena's daughter. Bebe is my sister."

Angie's eyes sparkled in the way Coco had expected.

"Listen, I imagine you'd like to write a story about all this, and I wish you wouldn't. Please understand that my family's privacy is very important to me. I don't suppose there is any way I could talk you out of this?"

Angie smiled bitterly. "I know this isn't fun for you, but Ryan Blackwell is going down in flames and everyone wants to know about the girl who's taking him down. Your story is so sensational that I'm shocked you let me in."

"So am I." Coco shook her drug addled head. "How did you know where to find me?"

"I told Tom I was a friend of yours."

"He knows you're a journalist. He knows we're not friends."

"I promised him two hundred thousand for those photos he took of you. My publisher will pay you three if you will give me an interview. Your story will be on the cover of every tabloid in America whether you like it or not so it's best you get the truth out now."

"I'm not allowed to talk about what happened that night. My lawyers have asked me not to."

"That's okay. We can talk about you – your love of fashion, your mother, and your kids. We'll keep it sweet and personal. Besides, I've already read the police report and the charges. The allegations are world news. This is about *you* not Blackwell. I promise to make this painless, N.V."

Coco shrank from the sound of the name Blackwell had given her; it was another reminder of his manipulation. "My name is Nicole Valentina but I go by Coco. Please call me Coco."

Angie set a small silver digital recorder on the couch between them and smiled. "Thank you, I would like that. I'm recording. I hope that's okay."

"Only if you promise you'll never mention my son. You can write about me and about Bebe. I'll even tell you why she calls me Mama, but never ever tell anyone about my son. I'm trusting you, okay?"

"Okay," Angie nodded, "you have my word. Tell me what it was like being Magdalena's daughter. Do you miss your mother?"

Coco thought for a moment, her eyes suddenly stung with tears. The vision of Magdalena standing at the cemetery threshold was still so clear. "I used to think I hated her. She left me when I was very little. Now I just…." Her voice trailed off. "I've learned that the part of me that loved her is stronger than the anger. I miss her every day." The words hurt as she spoke them, their utter truthfulness sending a stab of sadness through her. "I miss her more than I can say."

CHAPTER THIRTY-ONE

Angie kept her promise; the interview was painless as was the article that ran the following week in over forty different publications worldwide accompanied by the dozens of photos Tom had supplied. Coco felt a spark of pride when Tia returned home from the grocery store with several different magazines, all with Coco's face on the cover. But by far the best part of the interview was the $300,000 that Angie's publisher wired to Coco's account; as mercenary as it felt, Coco noticed a change in her health the moment money stopped being a terrifying worry.

"Thank you for selling me out, Tom," Coco whispered into the phone several weeks later. She held James who was still only contemplating sleep. She walked the baby in gentle circles around the room, her phone held under her chin, her loose hair hanging down to her waist.

"My pleasure," Tom laughed. "It was the most profitable thing I've done in years."

"It's the most profitable thing I've done in my whole life." Coco laughed softly, watching James' eyes begin to close.

"How well are you getting around now?"

"Pretty well. I'm still taking pain killers, but I can walk almost normally."

"Well, I think it's time you got back to work. I've got a friend in Rome who wants you in his show next Friday. It'd be an amazing experience. Also, I've been in contact with some fairly large designers. Every time I say your name they ask to meet you."

"Tom! I'm a single parent whose mother just died in a helicopter crash. I've been beat up and left for dead and I need time to heal."

She laid James in his crib. There was no sympathy in the ensuing silence.

"In a better, kinder world that would be a good plan. However, you are hot right now and you need to get back to work." Tom spoke with a worrying level of conviction.

"No. I'm not going back out there."

"Yes, you are. You're front page right now, Coco. That won't last unless you make it last."

"I have money, Tom; I don't need to do a thing."

"And how long do you think that money will last? Think about the expense of a penthouse apartment like yours. Think of the expense of two little kids and a housekeeper. How are you going to support them when it runs out? You'll be in your twenties, which in this business makes you ancient. You do this now and your career is set, no more money worries, not ever."

Coco couldn't argue with his reasoning. But she felt instantly tired and depressed. "I get time off in between shoots to see my kids."

"Deal."

CHAPTER THIRTY-TWO

When the plane lifted out of Chicago the second time Coco didn't white-knuckle the arm rests. The many fears she had lived with had dissolved the night she had descended the Blackwell building under the mistaken assumption that she was dead. Even when the plane hit turbulence she felt only annoyance when her ginger ale splashed on the two white pills she had only just set on the tray. Somehow flying thousands of miles over the earth, cresting the North Pole, and landing in a foreign country wasn't the least bit scary. *Maybe it's the drugs*, Coco thought. She popped the last pill, closed her eyes, and waited for the pain to dissolve. She felt emotionally numb. Even leaving home this time hadn't upset her, not the way it had when she had left for New York. Coco lay her hand over her eyes, crowding out the light that only intensified her headache. She felt raw, as if all the pain of the last two years had scarred her so deeply that she had stopped hurting and gone numb. *Or maybe it's the drugs*, Coco thought again, but a moment later she was crying and she couldn't stop.

Hours later the plane landed smoothly on the black tarmac outside of Rome. People rose in their seats, gathering their belongings while Coco sat staring out the window. She had watched the whole landing, felt the plane descend, watched the wings change as the plane slowed and dropped back toward earth. They hit the ground at what felt like two hundred miles an hour, the brakes screaming as the plane charged down the runway, decelerating at such a speed that the whole plane shook. She knew she should be terrified. Any other time in her life this scene would have sent her over the edge but not now, not today.

The plane taxied quickly to its gate, coming to a silent stop. Coco watched the people organize their carry-ons. A long line of passengers filled the aisle, waiting for the door to open. Coco put on her Chanel sunglasses, pushing them into her dark hair, and watched the passengers begin to stream by. Only when the last one passed did Coco shoulder her bag, straighten her black pencil skirt, and walk off the plane into the busy terminal.

Her body still hurt, but her mind was calm. She joined the stream of travelers who walked slowly past security and observed several happy reunions: a mother welcomed by her children, a wife embracing her husband. As she moved through the crowd, she didn't see the group of men standing to her right.

"N.V.!" a voice called, stopping her in her tracks. Coco smiled mechanically and turned to see who had called, but was blinded by camera flashes. Half a dozen men called her name with various accents while they snapped her photo. Coco turned quickly away but the men followed. The bystanders, who only moments earlier had allowed her to melt into their quiet flow, turned and stared as Coco stumbled away from the paparazzi, moving through the main terminal toward the front entrance.

 248   MAGDALENA'S SHADOW

"Stop!" one of them called with a distinctly British accent. Coco had no idea where she was going.

"Just give us a minute of your time and we'll leave you alone!"

Coco's hands shook. Slowly she turned to face the men.

"Take the glasses off!"

Coco's eyes flashed over their faces. Behind the paparazzi, stood a crowd of inquisitive people. How had this happened? How had they known she would be here?

"Take off the fucking glasses!"

Coco didn't move; she felt frozen as she watched them watch her. Like a cornered deer with no fight left she waited for the attack. Airport security came only seconds later, breaking up the crowd. The uniformed Italians escorted Coco to a waiting Mercedes. The paparazzi dispersed into different cars. They fell in behind the Mercedes, passing other cars when traffic would allow and pulled up alongside her car. Coco lay down on the back seat, her bag clutched to her chest, and sobbed quietly to the sound of harsh voices calling N.V. through the city noise.

Tom met her in her room with a bone shattering hug.

"Tom, did you sell me out again?"

"Publicity is part of fame. It was good exposure. You have no idea how badly people want you. You should see the blogs I read last night. All your mother's fans are out in force wanting to get a look at you."

"A little warning would have been nice." Coco sat on the bed, taking off her heels.

"You knew what it would be like, and you know you didn't have to come." His smile was beautifully teasing, his huge eyes innocently blinking in the golden light.

"No, I had no idea that I would be hounded out of the

airport or sworn at or chased. Nothing could have prepared me for that."

Tom had once said that Blackwell would work her until she dropped; it didn't take long for Coco to realize that working with Tom would be a similar experience. He didn't beat her, a definite improvement, but the schedule he set bordered on torturous. Coco wanted to rest on the day after her arrival in Rome, but she was already scheduled for fittings, beauty treatments, and parties that went on well into the next morning. In between these appointments and scheduled frivolities lurked the paparazzi, mysteriously present at every location. They called her by name, snapping her picture with unrelenting zeal and swore at her when she didn't do what they asked. By the fourth day Coco felt so tired she was seeing double. Her body ached, and she needed rest.

"I've never walked a catwalk." Coco reminded Tom of this vital fact the morning they watched the first section of runway being secured to a stage in preparation for the Friday show.

"Just don't pull a Naomi and you'll be fine."

"Pull a Naomi?"

"Don't you remember when she fell off the stage and landed in the audience? Like I said, don't fall off and you'll do fine."

"You're so much help." Coco glared at him before turning to find the designer.

Coco arrived Friday morning feeling prepared for her very first fashion show. The designer's assistant had shown Coco how to move, how to look, and when to turn. She was also assigned an assistant of her own to help her change quickly and find her place in the lineup. She knew what was expected of her, but as she stood backstage in a floor-length black and white diagonally striped evening gown she felt choked by fear.

"Drink this." Her assistant pressed a thin glass of champagne into her hand.

Coco's nerves were visibly strained. All the other models watched her quietly, making her feel like an animal in the zoo. *Will life ever be any different?* Coco wondered while she sipped the champagne, willing herself not to bolt down the whole glass.

Like the painkillers, the alcohol worked quickly on her thin frame, easing the tension in her neck and shoulders as its warmth spread through her. *I'm not scared*, Coco thought as she listened to the chaos around her. On the other side of the wall hundreds of people were taking their seats. *I'm not scared*, Coco thought again when the music began to swell with the low vibrating pulse of bass followed by a throbbing metallic sound Coco could describe only as European techno. Clearing her face of all emotion Coco stepped up to the curtain as the designer adjusted the fold of her gown, sending her out with a simple, "Go."

Afterward, Coco remembered what happened as a sort of dream. She had walked out into the light, her long legs solidly under her while the room fell to a hush except for the pulsing music. Sweeping her hips right she swung the train of fabric behind her and took that first step down the catwalk, her face a mask of emotionless beauty, her stride over a foot longer than normal as she moved to the end of the walk and turned, her hand rising to her hip as again she swung the long train of fabric back behind her. Applause filled the air accompanied by snatches of murmured conversation. "She's Magdalena's daughter," Coco heard one woman say. "She looks just like her mother." Other voices welled up through the music, fading into noise while Coco moved toward the safety of backstage and the next piece she would wear in the collection.

It's amazing how short fashion shows are, Coco thought. Though the design team spent months in preparation the show itself was little more than twenty minutes long. Coco moved back out into the light for the fifth time, this time in a black and white floor-length sarong cut from geometric fabric, her hair piled high on her head with solid silver chopsticks. Coco prepared to walk out alone, but the designer stepped forward and took her hand. Like a precious bird, Coco, the last model of the evening, was led out into the light with the designer who bowed and blew kisses to a standing ovation. Cameras flashed and someone called out N.V., but the quiet passive mask she had mastered never slipped from her face.

Away from the applauding crowd, through camera flashes and reflected light, Coco moved back to the well-lit security of the changing area where half-naked models walked, stripped, and dressed in clusters around her, their own clothes rediscovered in preparation for the after party. Silent as a shadow, the assistant was there beside her, unclasping the back of the sarong, sliding it from around her neck before helping Coco step naked from the gown. Before she could raise her eyes to the silent man, she found herself alone in a crowded room, the assistant disappearing with the gown while her own clothes lay closeted somewhere near the place where the stylist had done her hair and makeup.

"You didn't fall off," she heard Tom say. Coco turned to where he stood beside a beautiful man, whose silver and

252   MAGDALENA'S SHADOW

black hair sparkled in the light. The man appraised her with the eye of an expert, unembarrassed by her body, clothed only in the nude colored thong and stacked clear plastic heels.

"Tom, I would like to dress before I meet your friend." Coco turned to hide her embarrassment. She walked to the place where she had last seen her clothes. Tom ignored her, talking instead about how vibrant the show was.

Coco found the small black A-line dress she had worn that evening, slipping it quickly but carefully over the silver chopsticks in her hair. When her fingers felt for the zipper, the stranger stepped forward and slid the tiny zipper up her back, sparking a pleasant shiver of surprise through her. She caught his eye, her placid expression giving away none of her curiosity.

"This is Paolo," Tom said, once Coco was dressed. "He owns several big labels here in Europe. He has wanted to meet you for some time."

"And now he has." Coco offered her hand, but instead of the customary shake he took her hand in his, holding it as Rob had the first time they'd met.

The gesture possessed the same confident grace exhibited in his appraising glance and the management of her zipper. He knew his attractions, knew that a girl could get lost in the quiet depth of his dark eyes – Italian-brown, so rich and beautiful that only a self-assured man could possess them. Coco broke from his gaze, turning a smile on Tom before she took Paolo's arm and led him through the doors to the reception area. She had no plan, just a sudden desire to leave Tom behind. The moment she entered the hall she was hit by the flashing lights of dozens of photographers.

"Isn't this a bore?" Paolo said, his hand coming supportively between her shoulder blades while he smiled for the photographers. Coco felt momentarily panicked, her

E. E. ORME 253

eyes scanning her surroundings for the door to the reception room. There was no escape. The crowd was too thick. Coco was forced to stand and smile.

No sooner had Coco adjusted to the scene than she felt Paolo leading her from the cameras, through the crowd, and into the chandelier-lit party room. Paolo's presence comforted Coco in a way she could not describe. Just when she began to feel truly comfortable Tom resurfaced at the far end of the room, moving toward them with three flutes of champagne. Coco's heart sank the moment she saw him. The glint in his eye told her the night was just beginning, and it would be all about business. Smiling brightly Tom took Coco's arm, drawing her politely away from Paolo into the party, introducing her to everyone who mattered. The crowd thickened and Paolo disappeared.

CHAPTER THIRTY-THREE

Two pills lay in Coco's hand. She rolled the pills toward her fingers, watching their white coated sides roll smoothly back and forth across her palm. She hadn't felt pain in three days, yet today she was shaken, tired, and scheduled for a lingerie shoot she didn't want to do. The pills were such a comfort. She liked the way they numbed her fears, dulled her hunger, and softened the world. She stared at them, studied their shape, aware that she no longer physically needed them, but that she wanted them more than she wanted to go home. They were rest and comfort wrapped up in shiny white coats.

"Time to go." Tom walked into her bedroom.

"I know," Coco sighed, popping the pills into her mouth. She opened her water bottle and drank them down.

"This is Maria. She'll be handling your wardrobe." Tom indicated a short plump Italian girl standing next to a rack of hangers, each hung with a tiny bit of black material. Coco prayed for courage. She imagined all the places the ribbon-like undergarments would go. After hair and makeup Coco slipped into the first piece, a tiny black pair of minimalist panties decorated with pin sized white polka dots. No bra accessorized the panties. Pulling her hair over her shoulders, Coco hid her breasts as best she could before slipping onto the set.

The photographer was a small Frenchman with bloodshot eyes who barked quick orders at the Italian staff in French. After several moments he noticed Coco standing silently before his camera. The little man didn't smile.

"You look like a frightened little girl." he yelled, his heavy French accent warping his English.

"How would you like me to look?" Coco asked.

"I like frightened little girls." He adjusted the hair that fell over her right breast before returning to his camera. His instructions were concise and easy to follow: cross your arms, pout a little, drop your chin to the right. Coco followed his every direction, and he seemed satisfied with her, until he gave her a direction she couldn't follow. "Now look like you just had sex," he said while adjusting his lens, his eye watching her through the viewfinder.

Coco stood still for a moment, at a loss. She tried to think back to the one time she'd had sex and her face grew sad.

"No! No!" the little man yelled. "I said sexy, not sad."

"I'm only eighteen," Coco interrupted, but her excuse made him laugh.

"If you were a French girl you would know what I mean."

After several more attempts at "sexy," he threw his hands in the air and disappeared through a side door, returning minutes later with a boy in a black Speedo. The boy stepped onto the set smiling. Coco stepped quickly off the other side.

"No! No! No!" The Frenchman yelled. "Back up on the stage now."

256   MAGDALENA'S SHADOW

Coco stepped back onto the set, standing as far from the dark haired male model as she could. He was beautiful; he was young, Italian, and he was thoroughly enjoying her embarrassed confusion.

"Come here," he laughed and held out a hand.

"Why would I do that?" Coco asked sharply, turning her resentment on the photographer. "No one mentioned this."

"Are you a model?" The Frenchman yelled the question. "If you are, then model as you're told. If you aren't, then put on some clothes and get the *fuck* out!"

Coco's eyes widened while the boy laughed.

"Come on. We'll have fun," he coaxed.

Coco took a slight step toward him. "You'll have fun," she corrected and took his hand, coming to stand next to him. She felt like Eve, ashamed in her nakedness. The only difference was that Adam was having a great time, and they both needed more fig leaves. Before she could attempt a second protest the boy wrapped his arm around her waist pulling her gently to him.

"You're okay," he whispered when she stiffened, his lips brushing the back of her neck, his fingers running down the sides of her waist to rest on her ribbon-clad hips.

"Yes, good," the Frenchman barked. Lights were adjusted. A fan switched on blowing Coco's hair free from her shoulders.

Slowly Coco relaxed and began to move with this unknown man, directed by the photographer's constant commands. But when Coco turned to face the camera he yelled. "No! No! No! You are too sober. You need to look drunk on sex, like you just had sex, please."

The boy kissed her neck, tracing her waist and hips with his fingers before pressing his lips to her jaw. He ran his hands down the side seams of her panties again before turning her toward him, leaving her back to the camera. The first kiss was gentle, asking if a second would be okay. When Coco didn't protest, he kissed her again, careful not to smudge her makeup or frighten her. A subtle wave of peace passed through her. Cautiously, she breathed in his scent, felt his fingers teasing her body. Slowly, he turned her toward the camera, her eyes unfocused, her lips parted.

"Yes," the photographer called, happily snapping away. "This American is not made of ice after all."

Six wardrobe changes later Coco was alone again on stage and attired in nude-colored doe skin panties and a push-up bra, her hair piled on top of her head with only a few tendrils curling around her face. When Jean the photographer asked her to "look like sex," she instantly softened into the mask of sensuality he wanted without any help.

"You don't look as golden as I would like." Jean stared at her thoughtfully. "Add more gold bronzer." He motioned the makeup artist forward. With a bronzing pencil the artist gilded Coco's eyes. Yet still the look wasn't what the photographer wanted.

"Dust her in gold and paint a copper toned tattoo on her left arm."

The makeup artist shrugged. "What of?"

"N.V.," Tom suggested, wandering in from another room where he had been lounging.

Jean nodded slowly, signaling the artist with a wave of his hand. Several minutes later Coco had a copper colored oil pencil tattoo on her upper arm. Her own initials branded on her body in gold dusted Romanesque lettering.

"Take down her hair," Jean waved in the stylist, "and mess it up."

Minutes later he was back behind his camera with Coco crouched on the floor, her hair carefully thrown around her, the copper tattoo dusted with gold powder, glimmering through the wayward strands that shrouded her. The look was fierce yet fragile, creating an image that spoke to the heart of sensuous love, golden sunshine, and exotic pleasures that only Coco understood. Slowly, imperceptibly, as the shoot wrapped for the night, Coco, the supermodel's daughter, became N.V. the icon.

"That went well." Tom got into a taxi an hour later with Coco sliding in beside him. She felt too tired and hungry to reply. "So," he scrolled through his digital calendar, "a light dinner and then a party about an hour outside of Rome. I've got the directions in here. We'll GPS them," he added happily. Coco watched him, his features awash in digital light.

"I'm so tired, Tom. Can't we skip the party?"

"It's Paolo's party on his country estate. You remember Paolo, don't you? You should. Everything you have modeled since you came here has been his."

"Yes. I remember Paolo." Coco's response lacked enthusiasm.

"So cheer up and stop whining. You don't want to disappoint him, now do you?"

After the light dinner Coco changed into a little silver dress and slipped into a silver fur to wait for Tom in the hotel lobby. The drive to the estate took well over an hour. Coco fell asleep as the car wound its way out of the city toward the hillside. When the car stopped, Tom woke her by opening the door. The moment Coco moved to get up, a jagged pain shot through her legs, the result of standing in stilettos for hours in a body that was still healing.

Tom watched her quietly before turning to his bag. He rifled through the contents until he found a small bottle of something and poured a shot into the cap. "This will wake you up and take the pain away."

"I can't mix alcohol with my painkillers." Coco looked away from the offered shot.

"It's juice." Tom pressed the shot into her hand.

"And what else?" Coco looked suspicious.

"Mmm… nothing that'll hurt you." Tom smiled sweetly, coaxing the shot to her lips.

Coco sipped the juice, finding mango and orange mixed with a hint of something more tropical, maybe pineapple.

"Just good old vitamin C," Tom laughed, shaking his head at her. The grin that followed was not altogether reassuring.

Several minutes later Coco felt refreshed but in an ethereal, hyper-alert way. Tom escorted her toward the enormous stone house that loomed above them. She leaned heavily on Tom's arm as they walked carefully up the steps into the crowded interior.

"I have to go see someone but I'll be back in a bit." Tom spoke loudly over the music, his lips close to her ear. Coco couldn't hear him. She was no longer herself. A heightened color painted her cheeks. Her eyes glowed luminously bright. Tom smiled as he looked at her. "I'll go tell Paolo you are here."

"Was there a painkiller in the juice, Tom?" But he was already gone. Coco became suddenly distracted by lingering traces of movement that followed her fingers.

Tom didn't return and Paolo was nowhere to be found. Coco stood alone in the crush of unfamiliar people who drank and chatted in the dizzying thump of discordant music. Moment by moment the painkillers mixed further with Tom's drug. An unsteady feeling took over Coco's limbs. Her heart felt heavy in her chest triggering a desperate need for fresh air and open space. Her entire body felt wired with life. The room shifted and undulated, creating things that couldn't possibly be there. Every time the bass thumped the chandelier shot sparkling bits of light out into the room. *Like fireworks,* Coco thought and smiled, trying to catch them.

She walked from the house into the less populated winter courtyard where a fountain stood in the center. The heavy silver fur she had worn during their journey lay forgotten on the couch inside. Everything in the courtyard looked vivid with life. The water in the fountain splashed mercury colored droplets, which glistened in the moonlight. Coco leaned over the stone edge, catching the metallic tears in her hand. She felt suddenly happy in a way she hadn't felt since she'd… she quickly pushed Rob far from her mind.

A man approached and watched her dip her hand wrist deep into the fountain, raising it slowly as the mercury-like water ran thickly down her fingers, dripping slowly, sensuously off her long natural nails.

"This is my favorite part of the garden," he smiled, continuing to watch her childish delight.

Coco smiled up at him before rubbing the water between her fingertips. It felt cool, the way water should, but it still looked like molten silver. Slowly, as the water dried away in the winter chill, Coco was able to see that it was Paolo who had come to join her. He was older than she remembered, maybe forty-five, with thick black hair sprinkled with silver. His skin was a lovely shade of olive, his features strong-lined and masculine. His height and masculinity reminded her of Rob. Coco looked away from Paolo, suddenly embarrassed.

"I've never been anywhere so beautiful." She gestured to her surroundings.

"And I've never seen anyone so beautiful."

Coco shook the water from her fingers over the fountain, a soft smile touching upon her lips. Rob had flirted with her in the same way. He had been fooled by her beauty. He had suffered. "You shouldn't be taken in by my looks, Paolo." She shook her head, her expression growing serious. "I'm not a woman at all. I'm really just a little girl." She swayed suddenly where she sat, her eyes cast back on the water.

Paolo caught her shoulder, steadying her, his expression shifting from interest to concern.

"Little girls grow up." He watched her slender fingers dip back toward the fountain. His hand followed hers, holding her fingers from the frigid water. Slowly he helped her to stand. "I think that you'll spend the evening with me. I think it's no good allowing the prettiest little girl in Rome to wander alone in the garden without her coat on."

They walked out of the quiet courtyard toward the glowing party inside. Coco didn't feel the cold late winter breeze that blew dead leaves in circles around her feet, nor did she feel the exhaustion that had gripped her body on arrival. She felt light and free: all her burdens, all her guilt, lifted as if by a miracle.

Together they entered a room hung with golden chandeliers and renaissance tapestries. People stood chatting everywhere. Tuxedoed waiters moved elegantly through the crowd with crystal champagne glasses held high on silver trays. The room pulsed with energy, music, and movement.

Coco passed through the scene feeling as if she were walking through an old-world movie. Paolo held her hand securely in his. Before them several logs burned in a massive fireplace. But the crowd grew too thick and Coco lost hold of him. She froze in the press of bodies, her addled mind not knowing what to do.

Paolo quickly found her again, his soft eyes searching hers before he again led her toward the warming fire. "Come and see my painting," he said gently in her ear, his nose grazing the dark curls of hair Coco wore pinned like a crown on her head.

The scent of his skin, the brush of his lips, and the gentle tone of his voice reassured her. Coco followed him slowly to the far side of the room where the painting of a willowy black-haired girl hung in an ancient golden frame over the fire.

"Familiar?" He smiled at Coco, his eyes sparkling in the light. The girl in the painting looked like a mixed image of Magdalena and herself.

"It's incredible," Coco laughed. "Who is she? She looks like a Rodriguez."

"She's one of my ancestors. But I'll tell everyone that it's you, and tonight they will believe me." He smiled and lifted the hand he still held to his lips, kissing the palm.

Coco felt awkward dancing with Paolo for the first time. When he took her in his arms before the fire she hadn't known what to expect. Now their two bodies moved slowly to a languid Italian love song, while Paolo's hand slid to the small of Coco's back.

"You haven't danced like this before?" he asked. "I know how little Americans dance together. I think it's good for you to dance with me now… and if you like dancing, maybe you'll like other things, too."

Coco laughed at his direct way of talking. "I imagine I will," she smiled, glancing away from his soft dark eyes.

"Good, then maybe we should skip dancing and go straight to kissing? But not until after this song, it's one of my favorites."

Coco had to admit she liked it, too.

There was something childlike and sweet about the way Paolo D'Ambrosia kissed her openly in the warmth by the hearth, and later on the sofa with all his guests milling around. For a girl who had never had a childhood sweetheart to practice with, it was refreshing to play innocently with a man; and she found that the world gained a drunken luster when Paolo nibbled her ear in between chatting with his friends about politics or soccer. She liked the way he played with the ends of her hair and slid his fingers along her arm, asking her if she would like some chocolate made that day in Belgium or perhaps another glass of wine. His honeyed voice slipped musically between beautiful Italian and fluent English. He seemed to enjoy talking with Coco, asking her questions about Chicago, a town he knew well.

By three a.m. the party had dispersed and Tom was nowhere to be found.

"I've had a lovely evening, Paolo," Coco felt the effects of the wine and the drugs still coursing through her body, "but I should go back to my hotel tonight." She smiled and tried to stand, worried that if she stayed things would get out of hand.

"I have dozens of empty rooms here." Paolo indicated the vast house around them, catching her hand in his. "You sleep here, and maybe in the morning when you're rested we'll make love, but not tonight. I'm too tired and you're too beautiful. Things would be over too quickly."

264   MAGDALENA'S SHADOW

Coco couldn't help smiling at his self-assurance. "Well, we wouldn't want that, would we?" she teased. "But I think it's too soon for sex, even in the morning."

"Coco?" Paolo lifted her chin in his hand. "Americans have sex. Italians make love. I can show you the difference."

A blush spread slowly across Coco's cheeks. This time when Paolo kissed her it was long and sweet, his lips nibbling, softly playing over hers with tender kindness. Coco melted into the kiss, her lips parting as she pressed her body to his and their tongues met for a brief moment, sending a thrilling shiver through her body.

"But not now." Paolo let her go. "Good night, Coco." He smiled and turned to go.

Coco didn't look at the plush room his servant left her in. She didn't see the fine paintings on every wall or the texture of the bedspread embroidered with silk thread. All she was aware of was the softness of the pillow and the way the bed enveloped her nearly-naked body in perfect comfort. In the morning she would worry about how not to have sex with Paolo. In the morning she would find her way back to Rome.

266   MAGDALENA'S SHADOW

CHAPTER THIRTY-FOUR

Only when Coco awoke did the beauty of her surroundings captivate her. Only then did she see the card on her dresser on top of a plush white robe. It said, "I hope you feel rested. Meet me in the sunroom." To Coco's dismay the dress she had left on the floor the night before was gone. She would have to wear the robe.

"Paolo?" Coco found him in the giant, glassed in sunroom complete with citrus trees and a pool. "My clothes are gone. I hope you didn't take them."

"Of course I did. They'll be fresh and clean and hanging in your closet in about an hour, I would guess. In the meantime, I suggest you try this." He held up an enormous strawberry dipped in dark chocolate. "I never like a morning so much as when I eat strawberries for breakfast."

Coco took the fruit from his hand and bit into it, the flavor erupting on her taste buds like heaven. "Perfection," she smiled happily. "Like everything here, Paolo… perfection."

"Yes. That's the only word for it." He took her hand in his and kissed her fingers. Ever so slowly he pulled her down beside him.

The sun shone down through the orange trees as morning progressed slowly into afternoon. It was strange to have been forgotten. Coco wondered what had happened to her wayward agent and his friend. But instead of worrying, she ate strawberries and drank champagne, ignoring the hours that slipped by. Anytime she mentioned her pressing schedule or the work she had been doing, Paolo scowled dramatically and fed her another strawberry.

"You work for me now. I saw the proofs from your shoot yesterday, and I'm satisfied that you deserve a rest. I say no work for you today, just champagne, pleasure, good food, and good company." He smiled and indicated himself.

"Well," Coco sighed with a laugh, "that's exactly what I need." She closed her eyes and listened to the winter wind that tore at the other side of the glass. All around her orange blossoms bloomed, filling the air with their sweet perfume.

One didn't stay at Paolo's estate and not end up in bed with him. This was a fact Coco learned later that day after a foot rub that ended in Coco's first ever massage, which all took place in the sunroom. Paolo began massaging her legs, sliding her inch by inch out of the white robe. Slowly he pressed her gently onto her stomach, massaging scented oil into her shoulders and back. The pleasurable feeling removed the last of Coco's reserves so completely that when he slid her panties off she didn't complain.

Over the last few days Coco's idea of what was right and wrong had somehow entered a state of gray confusion – so much so that when she felt Paolo's weight on her back and his hands between her legs she only enjoyed the feeling, never once thinking to protest. She enjoyed the way he bit her neck and kissed her half-hidden face; she even liked the way he moved into her body, taking her from behind with such expert grace that she felt only pleasure, his hand sliding under her, teasing her to a climax long before he came.

268   MAGDALENA'S SHADOW

"My darling," he laughed as he pulled her happily into his arms. "I told you that a morning started with strawberries and chocolate is a wonderful morning. I cannot think of one thing that would make this day any more perfect. Strawberries and Coco: what man on earth is as lucky as I?"

Coco smiled, resting her head on his shoulder, her eyes tracing his body. Some of his chest hairs were silver, and he had a scar on his ribcage more than three inches long. His heart beat against her ear with a beautiful thrumming. Without knowing why, Coco felt a sudden overpowering grief. She felt Paolo's arms around her, his heart beating with her own, and remembered sitting with Rob, her head resting against his chest hearing the music of his heart. She had memorized his heartbeat, the rumble of his laughter, the tonality and rhythm of his conversation. A cruel loneliness found Coco in that moment; it brought with it the naked realization that she was, in her heart, still afraid of the world and in desperate need of shelter.

Paolo talked on happily, his voice bringing small comfort. She didn't question why she had chosen to have sex with Paolo. She didn't recall how it had happened, but she found that what was done once was more easily accomplished the second time. The third time they made love the grief slipped further from her, replaced by the short-lived intoxication of easy pleasure.

Coco watched Paolo sleep, ensconced in his massive medieval bed, its four black pillars the size of tree trunks. She felt rested and content to watch the sun rise over the estate, its gardens blushing with pink light, masking the grey-green winter drabness in gold and rose colored hues. Slipping silently from bed Coco put on the now familiar white robe and unlocked the double door to the balcony, feeling the instant chill of the wet gray morning the moment she stepped out.

I can breathe here, she thought, her hands coming to rest on the old stone railing while the chilly breeze played in her hair removing the intoxication of the last two days. Standing on the balcony she tried to picture Bebe running in the garden, her little pink feet chilled by the winter dew, a mischievous smile on her face. She envisioned James sitting on the rich Turkish carpets, grasping onto the sides of the massive bed as he learned to stand. It felt good to remember them, to draw them near if only in her mind. *This would be the most beautiful place to raise them*, she thought, knowing that life would be so easy if Paolo would keep them.

Her attention was quickly diverted when the door opened quietly behind her and Paolo walked out wearing his matching white robe. He kissed her throat, his arms coming around her waist, pulling her to him. With eyes closed Coco turned and kissed him good morning, but a moment later they were back in bed, their robes forgotten on the floor, their arms and legs entwined as they began to make love again. Paolo caressed every inch of her with loving care, kissing her and nibbling her until his mouth reached her inner thigh.

"Not that." Coco sat up to stop him, a sudden sad look crossing her face.

"Whatever you like, Coco." He rose up to kiss her lips, his hands sliding her body down the bed until her hips rested in his lap.

"Oh God!" Coco's back arched as they suddenly merged, her body instantly reacting to the intensity of this new position, her arms clasped tightly around Paolo's neck as he held her hips to his, forcing her to move against him. But no matter how hard she tried, Coco couldn't push Rob from her mind. He had touched her and tasted her in that same way, his kisses running up her thigh. Tears streamed down Coco's cheeks. She held Paolo close, returning his kisses again and again, her body pressing ever closer to his. A ragged sob escaped her the moment she felt him finish inside her.

When Coco opened her eyes, Paolo was looking at her, noting the tears that coursed down her face.

"Are you okay?"

"Yes," Coco smiled, "I'm fine."

"Pain?"

"No."

"Then what's the matter?"

"I'm fine. There is nothing wrong. I promise."

"I think you must be the first woman I've ever met who doesn't like to be kissed down there," he laughed, stroking her hair away from her face. "Why don't you like it?"

"I like it." Coco turned her face from his as fresh tears filled her eyes. "But I can't take it."

"Why?" Paolo persisted. When she looked back at him, Paolo was still watching her, his eyes soft with concern.

"I had a friend… a lover… he did that once and then he left me."

"What a fool." Paolo shook his head.

"I loved him," Coco admitted sadly. "I was a fool too."

"How did you get the scar?" Paolo's hand moved to her stomach, his fingers tracing the white line that ran down from her belly button.

"Well," Coco laughed bitterly, "I had his baby nine months after he left. My life seems to be running a touch on the dramatic side. I try to make good decisions, be a good person, but I make so many mistakes."

"Was he your first?"

Coco nodded.

"And since then?"

"Just you." Coco frowned. "I don't do this often if that's what you mean."

"That's not what I meant. In all honesty, I've never met with such a sweet and innocent girl in my life. You are practically a virgin." His expression faded to a look of dismay. "And your baby?" Paolo asked after a long pause. "Where is it now?"

"Home. He's at home with a friend."

Paolo nodded slowly. "You are so young, Coco. Most girls your age care only about clothes and the next party. You are a mother. You talk with me like a woman, and you make love with such fresh innocence that I'm left in awe of you. Most girls I take to bed smile and simper, but they aren't sincere. They like my money or my cars or my big houses, but not me. You don't even seem to notice that I'm old and gray."

"Because you're not." Coco pushed him playfully. "Don't say that. I think you are beautiful." But his mention of other girls stung her. After a long silence Coco couldn't help asking, "Do you do this a lot? Bring girls home for sex and strawberries."

Paolo didn't answer at first. He seemed to be choosing his words carefully. "It's become a game, I guess. Sex is another way to fill up the days. My wife is a good Catholic. She won't give me a divorce and she won't be my wife, so I live this sort of half-life, married but alone, lonely but not free to find anything more. It... how do you Americans say?"

"Sucks?"

"Yes. It sucks," Paolo agreed, his lips twisting in a bitter smile.

"Then why don't you find a permanent girlfriend?" Coco ran her hand down his chest.

"I've tried, but again they aren't sincere. I'm a vain man; I need to be loved for me and not my possessions."

"When men look at me they just see this," Coco looked down at her long, slim, cinnamon colored body. "I don't get a chance either."

Paolo laughed. He leaned over and kissed her. "You are the most charming girl I've ever met. I see you beyond your debilitating perfection."

"And I see you beyond your big houses and fancy cars."

CHAPTER THIRTY-FIVE

"I'm leaving for Milan on Monday." Paolo traced Coco's collarbone with the tip of his finger as they lay in the sunroom three days later.

"Don't." Coco buried her face into his neck and hugged him.

"I must. I have businesses there that I can't put off."

"How long will you be gone?"

"A week."

"I'll be back in Chicago by the time you return."

Neither of them spoke for a long time. When Coco rolled onto her back she noticed a butterfly with giant green wings land on an orange blossom near where they lay.

"We don't have butterflies like that in Illinois." Coco watched the insect flit from one flower to another.

"Nor in Rome. I bring them in from South America – from Brazil and Argentina."

Above the glass, storm clouds filled the sky blown by a fierce wind; yet inside, a foreign butterfly, as fragile as ash, as beautiful as a rope of emeralds, floated safely from blossom to blossom.

"You could keep me like that butterfly," Coco said softly. "I'm South American and beautiful and rare."

Paolo laughed but when he looked at her she was serious. "Would you want to be kept, Coco?"

"Sometimes it sounds very nice. Sometimes I'm so afraid. The idea of having a safe place to land seems very comforting." They watched the butterfly in silence for a long time.

"I'll keep you if you'll let me, but you may not want me to."

"Why not?" Coco rose up on her elbow, her long hair falling around her face as she looked into his eyes. He lay on his back looking troubled.

"Because I arranged this week with your agent well over a month ago. I am paying Tom twenty-five thousand euros for your time."

Coco didn't know what to say or how to feel. "Why are you telling me this?"

"Because this can't be allowed to happen again; you need protecting. You need a good man, someone who will take care of you. Tom sold you and you need help."

"Who from? You?" Coco glared down at him in anger.

"Yes... me. Or someone like me. Someone who cares what happens to you."

"I can't bear this. I'm not a whore. No one has the right to buy and sell my time."

"I know that now," Paolo said quietly. "I thought you were a professional at first, but I quickly realized you were here because you wanted to be. I'm so sorry," he added, trying to comfort her.

"Tom sold me to you?" she asked looking into his eyes, "and you thought I was a *professional*?"

"Yes..." Paolo saw the anger in her eyes when she rose to find her robe.

When Coco reached her room, she found her clothes hanging exactly where he had said they would be five days earlier. She pulled them from the hangers and headed to the bathroom for a shower. When she reemerged Paolo was sitting quietly on the bed watching her.

"I'm sorry," he said again. "I never meant to hurt you."

The words burned through Coco like a hot iron. "Funny," she gathered her things in a fury, "that's exactly what Rob said to me the last time I saw him. That night he broke my heart and left me pregnant."

A car and driver waited outside the door. Coco slid into the black Rolls without a second look. As the car pulled out of the driveway she felt Paolo's eyes on her, willing her to look back; she knew then that when she saw him again those eyes would call to her as they did now. He was a rich womanizer, but a sincere one, and she liked him.

An hour and a half later the Rolls slid through Rome, passing men every bit as beautiful as the one she had just left. *Rome is a fountain of masculine perfection*, she thought, fishing distractedly in her bag for lip gloss and a tissue. The car stopped. The driver opened her door. Taking her hand, he helped her out onto the tricky cobblestones, her heels sliding at odd angles on the uneven ground.

"For you, Signorina." The man handed her a black package. Coco took it, letting it fall to the bottom of her bag before she walked into the hotel to find Tom.

"You're back," Tom beamed, coming to kiss her when she entered his room.

Coco noticed the beautiful boy from Paolo's party lounging in a chair near the fire. Coco turned to look at the boy who smiled up at her sweetly.

"So, Tom, was he a good fuck? I hope you didn't pay too much for the pleasure." She walked over to the boy, surveying him like a purse she was thinking of buying.

"He gave it freely." Tom grinned cheerfully and poured himself a drink. "And just so you know he doesn't speak a word of English."

"You pimped me out! You whored me out and you didn't even have the decency to tell me!"

"Like you'd have gone if you knew," he laughed.

"Why did you do it? We were making plenty of money. Why?"

"It wasn't about the money, Coco. You needed a good lay and you needed it badly. Don't you remember the way you shied away from that model at the shoot last week? Coco, you needed breaking in and Paolo was the perfect choice. Besides, if you land his label we'll be set for years."

"So, I was also sleeping with Paolo for the contracts? That's an amazing second twist."

"That's the way a lot of contracts are made, Coco. What happened is nothing compared to what some girls go through to get signed." Tom shrugged and drank his whiskey in one gulp. Something in the way he held the empty crystal glass reminded Coco of Blackwell. Blackwell had held his empty glass in that same way the night he had beaten her for not signing.

"Tom..." Coco spoke in a low controlled voice, her mind reaching sudden undeniable conclusions. "You knew Blackwell beat his girls, didn't you?"

"Yeah. Sometimes, but never badly enough to mess them up permanently."

Coco listened, her eyes caught by the fire in the hearth. "Then why did he leave me in the snow to die?"

Tom didn't answer. He looked suddenly pale. When she asked him a second time he shook his head and poured himself another drink.

"You were supposed to come and get me, weren't you? I was too valuable to die. I was supposed to be scared enough to sign, nothing more."

"You were already gone when I got there!"

"Why did you wait so long?"

"Remember, publicity is part of fame. I would never have let you die. Besides, he had so much dirt on you. If I had brought you in and patched you up the way I did with all the others, he would have just blackmailed you until you signed. He knew about Rob and James so I needed you in a hospital. It's that simple. With the media and the lawyers, you were instantly cover page material."

"How did he know about Rob and James?"

"He's been watching you for years."

"Why? Why would he do that?"

"Think about it, Coco. He found your mother in an Argentine ghetto, yet when she got pregnant, he didn't kick her to the curb? He kept all those baby pictures of you, too. Why do you think that was? Don't tell me you never wondered."

"Blackwell is nothing to me."

"Believe it, honey. I heard him say it himself. You are his *daughter*."

"I don't have a father. Now tell me why did you wait so long to come for me, Tom? I nearly died."

"I just told you. If you got the cops involved and there was a conviction, then Blackwell would go down."

"But why me?"

"Because I was tired of cleaning up after him, tired of comforting his victims, and tired of him. I loved the fact that you didn't worship him from day one. You were different because you had balls and *commitments*, because you're Magdalena's daughter, and the world gives a shit whether you live or die."

"And because you wanted the publicity, the celebrity, and the chance to represent me if I survived. And let's not forget the fact that you thought you could make millions selling my ass. I can't believe I ever thought you were my friend."

Tom stared at her and then laughed, dismissing her accusations with a wave of his hand. "Let's not forget, it's my contract you signed, not Blackwell's. I own that ass, honey, and as sweet as it is, I will sell it when necessary."

"The contract is finished, Tom. It was void when you let Blackwell beat me."

"You hadn't even signed with me then. Besides, only a crazy person would walk away now. I will get you work with all of Paolo's labels – and I'm talking with Prada, one of Magdalena's key labels."

"It's over, Tom." Coco picked up her bag and walked out of the room.

Tom reached her in seconds. "It sure would be sad if Rob found out he has a son he doesn't know about. Imagine how he would feel if he knew what a whore you are."

Coco turned on him. "And imagine how you would feel if the New York P.D. found out that Blackwell had an accomplice. I don't think Prada would be as likely to take your calls if they knew you were a murdering pimp."

Tom stopped where he stood and watched Coco disappear into the gray day.

Coco hailed a taxi, directed it to the airport, and slumped back in her seat feeling empty and exhausted. When, she wondered, would life stop sucking? Somehow, in some way, she had to find a rhythm that made sense, a place of peace where all the crap of living couldn't touch her.

Closing her eyes, Coco prayed for the first time since she had knelt on the roof in the snow. "God, if you're listening, I need help. I've been tossed around for years now, and I'm so tired. Please give me a safe place to land and the will and ability to make good choices. Please guide me and forgive me."

In the front seat, the cab driver watched her as often as he watched the road, but she didn't care. Rome rushed past in a blur of cars, people, shops, Vespas, and buildings. Coco prayed the whole way, desperately trying to still the nervous grief that filled her chest, constricting her breath. "God, I need help…" At that moment a phone rang. The sound came from her bag, a plaintive electronic ringtone played from a phone Coco didn't own. Peering into her bag she found the sound came from the black package Paolo's driver had given her. Opening the package, she found a check for twenty-five thousand euros and a flat square box containing a diamond necklace, matching earrings, and a slim smartphone.

"Hello?" Coco answered the phone.

"I'm too old to hurt this badly," Paolo sighed, his voice hushed with grief.

"And I'm too young." Tears sparkled in her eyes.

"Can you forgive me?"

"No." Coco wiped away the tears with the back of her hand.

"I'm coming to Chicago in two months. Please let me see you."

"If you must."

"Have a good flight home."

"Tell me something first?"

"Anything, sweet girl."

"You have been in this industry for a long time. You

knew my mother. Did you know my father? Is Blackwell my father?"

"There were rumors."

CHAPTER THIRTY-SIX

Tia met Coco in the lobby with James on her hip. Bebe ran to Coco, her hands outstretched.

"Bebe!" Coco swept the little girl into her arms. Tears filled her eyes. "I missed you so much." James babbled in Tia's arms, his face lit with a smile the moment he saw his mother. Setting Bebe down Coco took James from Tia, kissing her son. Together they walked toward the elevator and home.

"You are on the cover of all the gossip magazines." Tia handed Coco a cup of tea and indicated a stack of magazines on the kitchen table. Coco flipped through the magazines, reading the outrageously fabricated headlines.

"Well, at least they haven't made me a post-op transsexual Martian with a drug problem," Coco laughed, flipping through the glossy pages. Tia walked back to the table, slipped the *Star* out of the pile, and flipped it open. Under Coco's picture read the caption: *Magdalena's lost daughter addicted to prescription drugs and prostitution.*

Coco read the article carefully, stopping when she was sure it didn't mention her son. So far Tom hadn't made good on his threat.

"Are you still taking the painkillers?" Tia drew Coco's attention from the paper.

Coco nodded slowly, knowing that she should have stopped taking them weeks ago.

"Do you need them or just want them?" Tia asked, sitting down across from Coco, her eyes fixed on her.

"Both," Coco answered truthfully.

"You have lost a lot of weight. Have you been starving yourself?"

"No, they don't cater the shoots so I had to find food when I could. Honest, Tia, I'm not starving myself anymore."

"The article says you were openly stoned at a party. Is that true too?"

"No… Yes." Coco looked away, not wanting to see the look on Tia's face. "Tom gave me something. I had no idea it would affect me like that."

"What about the prostitution?"

"That's not true at all," Coco laughed, the check for twenty-five thousand euros feeling red hot where it was tucked into the bodice of her dress. Tia didn't find humor in the moment.

She looked at the new jewelry Coco wore, her face lined with grief. "Who gave you the diamonds, Coco?"

"A friend."

"And did you have sex with this friend?" Tia's eyes sparkled with unspilled tears.

Coco shrugged, looking into the living room to where the kids played: James in his swing, Bebe on the floor.

"And here I thought you had some sense."

"I like him. He's kind and mature and rich and he adores me."

"Of course he adores you. Bad men make you feel like you're the only woman in the world. Just how *mature* though? Mature like Rob or older?"

"He's forty-five, I think." Coco pulled the tea bag out

of her mug. "You'll meet him when he visits in a couple of months."

"Good God, Coco, he could be your grandfather!"

"No, he couldn't. He wasn't even thirty when I was born – definitely not old enough to be my grandfather."

Tia glared at her. "He's probably a pedophile." She turned her back on Coco, too upset to go on.

As the weeks passed their relationship didn't improve. Coco tried to explain that she hadn't done anything terrible, but Tia couldn't hear her. The old Christian's ideas on right and wrong were strict and inflexible. Things would have continued to deteriorate between them if not for a phone call from Coco's probate lawyer.

"We've found a will tucked behind a portrait of you in Argentina. It was in the Miramar beach house. Your mother left everything to you. The other parties may still contest it, but this is a huge gain for us. If everything goes smoothly you could be in possession in just a few weeks."

"What other parties?"

"The other parties that are seeking to inherit. There's a business partner and an old friend who are challenging you at present. After this they may back down."

"Who's the business partner?"

"Delilah Ramirez, she runs Magdalena's label."

Coco found Tia in the kitchen preparing lunch. Her stern silence filled the room. Coco poured herself some tea, sitting down next to Bebe, who was eating apple slices.

"They found a will." Coco watched Tia, who stood with her back to Coco.

The old woman stopped working and turned slowly toward her. "What does it say?"

"It says I get everything."

"Thank God." Tia sank into a kitchen chair, genuine relief on her face. "Thank God. I hope this means no more modeling?" Tia turned to look at Coco.

"No, I'll do as I please. I love you, but you're not going to tell me how to live my life. I've told you I didn't do anything wrong in Rome, and it's true but you still judge...."

"And love and care, nurse, feed, and worry about you. How do you think it feels watching you go out into the world? It's like sending a hamster into a snake pit."

"I'm the hamster?" Coco laughed. So did Bebe, chunks of apple flying out of her little mouth. James laughed from his highchair, banana dripping from his fingers while Tia looked from one face to the other, her sharp eyes softening. A slow sad smile spread across her tired lips while large tears formed in her eyes.

"It's too much, Coco. I love this fragile little family. You have been hurt already, almost killed. You have got to take better care of yourself, for their sake if not your own. Without you there is no us. Without you, everyone gets broken apart." Tia spoke so only Coco could hear.

"I know." Coco put her arms around Tia, pulling her into a hug. "I'm sorry."

"No more drugs, Coco."

"No more, Tia. I promise."

"You okay?" Bebe asked, a look of worry on her face.

"We're fine," Coco smiled, "don't worry, Bebe, everything's fine. I think we should celebrate the end of probate." Coco lifted James out of his highchair. "Let's go to the zoo. We'll eat junk food and look at animals."

Bebe shot out of her chair bouncing happily in circles around them. Tia sat quietly, too tired and relieved to do anything but blink back tears. Coco looked at her little family with new eyes. For the first time, she could see the

delicate threads of love that kept them bound together –
how many times had they been strained to breaking point?
For years they'd been quietly inconspicuous just to stay
together. Now their lives were public and nothing would
ever be the same.

288   MAGDALENA'S SHADOW

CHAPTER THIRTY-SEVEN

Paolo called Coco every morning; he said he liked the sound of Coco's voice when she had just woken up. He began each conversation with *Good morning, my darling, you'll never guess what marvelous thing just happened.* He would then launch into a fantastical story of luxury, travel, and style that awoke Coco's deepest longings for love, pleasure, and the adventure that came with living a full life. After each call, Coco felt herself more emotionally reliant on Paolo than ever before. It wasn't that he made her any solid, lasting promises; it was more that he shined a light on the drab grey tones of her world while painting his own luxurious life in splashes of wild drunken color. The stories he told her of Italy, of Europe, of parties, friends, and travel were enough to turn the most solidly rational woman's head.

"I miss you, Paolo." Coco felt her jagged loneliness lift each time he called. The first calls had been strained, but by the third call he had won a renewal of her trust and affection, both of which she was grateful to give.

"I miss you, too, my darling. In two weeks I'll be in Chicago. Then I'll kiss you and make love to you and we'll be happy again."

Coco laughed, loving the way he always voiced his thoughts with absolute honesty. They talked about everything. She told him about the kids, about Tia, Rob, and Magdalena's will. He knew everything there was to know about the lawsuit against Blackwell, the beating, and how Magdalena had led her through the snow to Rob's law office. In turn Paolo talked about his estates, Italy, business, and pleasure. Coco liked their conversational simplicity. She liked the solid way their chats floated between the deeply personal to a broader world experience with ease.

CHAPTER THIRTY-EIGHT

"Blackwell has declared bankruptcy," Coco said. Carmen was driving her to the doctor because her ankle had swollen again.

"How do you know? Did your lawyer call you?"

"Yes. I may get nothing out of this but more legal bills. I have to fly to New York to meet with the law firm who's representing me." Coco didn't tell Carmen that it was Rob's law firm or that she'd signed on with them when she was too medicated to notice his name in the letterhead and too sick to think of using her own lawyer. Instead, Coco stared out the window trying not to think about Rob or Blackwell's bankruptcy or the rumor that Ryan Blackwell was her father. She was down to one painkiller every four hours, but one didn't fight the pain or stop the anxiety. She felt emotionally strained by her legal troubles. She and her lawyers were working to extract her from Tom's contract, while settling her mother's estate and overseeing the suit against Blackwell. Without the numbing effects of the drug she wasn't sure how much longer she would last.

In two days they would read Magdalena's will, but there might be only debts and mortgages to inherit and now Blackwell was filing for bankruptcy. The thought sent her reeling. Coco had a lawyer for everything, but no money coming in save Paolo's check that she still hadn't cashed. If she took the money it would make her a whore. If she didn't she might also be filing for bankruptcy. Instead of worrying, she let her mind wander to the house in Miramar and the memory of her mother.

"Carmen?"

"Hmm?" Carmen pulled into the medical center's shadowy parking garage.

"There's something I've never told you, and you'll probably think I'm nuts. I can't tell Tia or she'll freak."

"If it's about your ancient Italian lover, I already know. So does Tia. She called me before you got home. There were pictures in *Vogue*, you and him at a fashion show. She was totally unhinged."

"No wonder she grilled me so hard." Coco frowned, remembering how Tia had called Paolo a pedophile. "But it's not about that. When I was left in the snow I saw something. I thought it was a hallucination for a long time, but now I'm starting to believe it was real."

"What did you see?" They were deep in the parking garage, cars passing like blurs of color. "I saw my mom. I didn't know it was her for the longest time. She was a shadow by my side, but she kept telling me to get up and keep walking. I would have lain down and died if it weren't for her. I could never have willed myself to live through that." Carmen didn't say anything at first. When she did speak, her words were startling.

"That is complete bullshit, Coco!" Carmen said angrily, "You're the toughest cat I know. You come off all sweet and shit, but you kick ass when necessary. You kicked your own ass that time. You thank yourself for that – not that bitch supermodel. Don't you dare give her credit, Coco; she wasn't there for you when she was alive so I can't see her dragging her ass out of hell on a snowy night just to keep you from dying." Carmen rammed the car into a spot, hitting the brakes so hard they screeched. Before Coco knew what was happening Carmen got out, leaving her behind.

"What're you doing?" Coco stepped out of the car, watching Carmen walk toward the elevator.

"I'm walking," Carmen snapped.

"What did I say?"

"What did you say?" Carmen turned on her, her eyes flashing. "How about *I would have lain down and died if it weren't for her*? How the hell can you say that when you know it's not true? You lived. You lived because you are tough and because your kids need you – because we all need you – not because Magdalena Rodriguez decided to give a shit." Coco took a step forward, but Carmen waved her off. "It's our job to survive, no matter what. We keep fighting, we survive, and we fucking thrive. There are no other options."

"I'm sorry. I didn't...."

"Knock it off. Stop being so damned nice all the time. Stop apologizing, and stop giving everyone else credit for how amazing you are. The idea of you suffering like that just rips my heart out, and then for you to give credit for your survival to that... that bitch, just rips me up all over."

Carmen stomped to the elevator leaving Coco behind.

Tia, her face dark with unspoken anger, met Coco at the door of #2.

"If you're going to rip into me, save it. Carmen just took my head off, and I'm not in the mood."

"*Il mio amore,*" a voice called from the sofa.

Coco turned, her heart leaping in her chest, a smile touching her lips when she saw him sitting on the sofa. "Paolo!" Coco walked to hug him, kissing him sweetly on each cheek.

"You are happy now, my love?" Paolo held her face lovingly between his hands.

"Completely, now that you're here," Coco kissed him again. Somewhere behind her Tia sniffed and left the room.

"Your Tia is very opinionated. I think you have let her get out of hand. She sat here glaring at me for the last half hour."

"I'm sorry about her, but you know very well that she's more than a servant. She's family."

Paolo shrugged and kissed her again. "She's like a Sicilian grandmother only without the black widow's clothes – angry at anyone who dares to be happy?"

Coco couldn't help laughing. "That's exactly how she's been behaving lately. She thinks I became a sinner in Rome. She thinks you led me astray. You will have to be *very* charming to win her over."

"But, Coco, I'm always *very* charming."

Tia returned in that moment with Bebe and James, plopping the still sleeping baby down in Coco's lap before disappearing again, this time into the kitchen.

Paolo winked at Coco. "Is she now reminding you of your past follies and current obligations?"

"Right again," Coco sighed and kissed James.

"Mama?" Bebe pointed sternly at Paolo. "There is a man in my house."

Paolo burst out laughing, eying the sleepy little girl with her rumpled hair and pink princess pajamas. "Hello, Bebe." He extended his hand to shake. She eyed him suspiciously before running to Tia.

294   MAGDALENA'S SHADOW

"I think your women want to run me off?" Paolo laughed.

Coco returned the still sleeping James to his crib, but when she moved back down the hall toward the living room she found Paolo standing in the doorway watching her. For a fraction of a second Coco saw Rob. He had stood there that last night, his hands on the doorframe, his face a mask of anger and regret. Coco looked at the small wet bar to her right, her face flushed with the memory.

"You could have come with me." Coco stared at Paolo, wanting him anywhere but in that spot. She glanced at the chair where Rob had sat, too grief-stricken to look at her in the moments before she had pushed him from her life.

"I think your Tia will hit me with her rolling pin if I follow you to your room." Paolo laughed into the silent room.

Coco walked toward him, altering the scene to kill the memory. "Where do you want to go tonight?" She kissed his jaw, pulling his hand off Rob's molding. Just imagining Paolo's prints over Rob's made her feel unsettled and sick. Her reaction shocked her: why was she thinking of Rob again? There had to be something she could do to break the hold he still had on her.

"I thought we could have dinner and then... whatever." Paolo's eyes sparkled chocolaty warmth in the dim light.

"Let's do *whatever* first." Coco held his gaze, her body moving against his with seductive grace. Sadly, the kiss that followed only intensified her memories. Coco compared it to Rob's and the difference in passion and connection saddened her. "Besides, I'm not even hungry," she added with quietly concealed frustration. *What if it had been the drugs that made Paolo so appealing?* She found it suddenly hard to look at him.

Paolo's face was alight with anticipated pleasure. "Yes, that's a much better plan." He kissed her ear. "Two months without making love has been like torture."

"Paolo," Coco looked up surprised. "You haven't been faithful, have you?"

"Coco, don't be cruel. Of course I have. I've tasted perfection. How could I ever again settle for the mediocre?"

Coco laughed, shaking her head as she reached up to kiss his cheek. "I have something for you." She took his check and the diamonds from her pocket.

Paolo looked with surprise at the gifts he had given her. "Those were for you, Coco."

"If I'm with you, it's because I want to be, not because you paid me." Coco tore the check in two, pressing the halves along with the diamonds into his hands.

Paolo looked struck, his expression soft and sad. "Keep the diamonds, Coco. Please, for me?"

Coco watched him for a moment, and then nodded slowly before allowing him to slip the jewels around her neck.

"Always, these were for you, my love, just for you." He kissed her throat, letting the necklace fall against her skin.

Paolo waited in the living room while Coco dressed for dinner. Tia slammed pots in the kitchen, peering into the living room occasionally to glare at Paolo.

"I'm going out." Coco entered the living room, catching Tia mid glare. "Have a good night." Tia gave her a withering look before turning back to the kitchen. "I won't be late," Coco added, but Tia didn't respond.

"You will like this room." The motion of their entrance into Paolo's hotel room triggered every light in the suite. The room was massive. Large art nouveau wall sconces lit

296   MAGDALENA'S SHADOW

up early twentieth century furniture. The sofa, chairs, and pillows were all upholstered in soft pink and pale green silk. Coco walked slowly across the creamy marble floor, her heels clicking musically as she slid her silver fur from her shoulders, allowing it to fall slowly to the floor. The peach colored gown she wore revealed her bare back, small waist, and slender hips. Her body pulsed with anticipation. Slowly she looked around the room for the perfect place to enact her fantasy. The sofa with its lush cushions and broad seat reminded her of the couch in Paolo's sunroom, sheltered beneath orange blossoms.

Gracefully she sat down, feeling the silk pillows beneath her. *Perfect*, she thought, and stretched out on her side to turn an invitingly sweet smile on Paolo.

"Come here, Paolo." Her eyes fastened to his. She rolled slowly to her stomach, her peach gown clinging to every curve of her body; her glorious bottom, like two round cantaloupes, rose deliciously below the sweep of her back. Paolo stared, her beauty seeming to have overpowered him. Coco laughed, pushing herself up on her elbows, her head tilting slightly to the right. Carefully she pulled a pin from her hair, allowing the dark mass to fall down around her. Paolo stepped slowly to the edge of the sofa, coming to his knees beside her, his hand grazing her shoulder blades, running down her spine to rest on the curve of her bottom.

"You paralyze me. You are more beautiful than any woman alive." He kissed her cheek, nuzzling her dark hair while his other hand slid down her bare arm to where her fingertips rested on the silk carpet. "Come to my bed, darling," he whispered, taking her hand in his. At the same time, he lifted the hem of her gown, sliding his free hand up her long thigh to rest once again on her bottom.

"Yes. Later... I want you here first."

Paolo needed no more instruction. Sliding her gown off her shoulders he kissed her throat, freeing her inch by inch from the peach dress. Coco turned her face to his, kissing his lips, her hands roaming over his body as she undid his buttons, biting and kissing the exposed skin. Moments later her dress lay at her feet, her panties pulled slowly past her hips as Paolo's weight came down on her back, his breath hot in her ear as he bit her neck and pulled her hips up to his. This was what she wanted, what she had fantasized about for two months, sex like they'd had that first morning in the sunroom, hard wild sex with no smiling or sweet conversations. In that moment, Coco knew she didn't want to see him; she just wanted to feel him as he pushed into her, his right hand under her pelvis, his fingers moving in time with his hips. Coco closed her eyes, no longer afraid of what she would see. She gave into the intoxication of sex, setting her body free to react as it would. Her mind took her far into the past, to the only man she had ever loved.

Coco felt her climax like a welcomed summer rain. She greeted it mouth open, eyes shut, her body melting into the delicious warmth of the moment. All the hot need that had built up over the last two months faded from her. Yet Paolo was far from finished. Pulling from her he rolled her onto her back, sliding her down the sofa into his lap. He pressed back into her, holding her hips firmly against his. Again she felt the familiar tightening as her body shuddered with pleasure, her limbs shaking as she cried out. But when she closed her eyes, again it was Rob she thought of. Instinctively Coco grabbed onto Paolo, thrusting her hips against his, intensifying the motion until she felt him bloom inside her in the last moments before he came. But it was Rob's name on her lips, lips that she bit into silence.

298   MAGDALENA'S SHADOW

With her eyes open, she held fast to the reality that Rob had left her and Paolo was with her now.

The reflection that greeted Coco in the bathroom mirror several hours later was that of a skinny, vulnerable harlot: poor and naked under smeared makeup and costly diamonds. Her features, though still beautiful, were cast with the shadow of weary regret. Already Coco could see the woman Tia feared, the woman who sold herself for a smile, a kind remark, or the pleasantness of feeling loved, even for only a moment. Paolo lay quietly in bed, happily satisfied with life while his lover hid behind the closed door, safe to face herself and this ugly reality. *No matter what he says or promises, I'm still unprotected and alone.* She stared steadily at her reflection, feeling the old panic twist through her body.

She didn't cry. Instead her face became peacefully void of emotion, masked with a calm she couldn't feel. *I'm a liar and a user and I hate who I have become.* She mouthed the words silently at herself feeling every part of this revelation wash coldly through her. She had never meant to hurt Rob yet her lie had killed everything they were. Now she was lying to Paolo, pretending to love him when she was incapable of doing so. Innately she knew Paolo's love for her was far different than Rob's had ever been. If she told him she thought of her ex-boyfriend when they made love, he would probably shrug and smile because he used her for sex and friendship in the same way she was so blatantly using him. In her heart, Coco knew she wasn't the type who could survive on flagrant sex and secondhand pleasures. She needed... what? Whatever *it* was, was a thing she had yet to discover – an empty slice of herself, torn from her in the days before she had words to name it.

Coco walked back into the bedroom. "Paolo."

He turned his head slowly to her, smiling as he watched her nestle down beside him. "Yes?" He reached for her hand, pulling her close, nuzzling her breasts as she curled into him.

"Do you think about your wife when we are together?"

Paolo laid his head back on the pillow thoughtfully. "I think of her in the morning. We'd drink espresso together before the family woke. Sometimes we'd make love but most of the time we just talked. I miss our mornings."

"What happened?" Coco slid her ear to his chest, listening to his heartbeat.

"I cheated on her with a girl who worked for me. Cristina found out, and she has shut me out of her life ever since. She lives in her family's house in Rome, and I live everywhere else. We share the children and the business. She's my partner but no longer my wife or even my friend." Coco listened, quietly running her fingers over his chest. "It was the stupidest thing I have ever done – to lose my beautiful wife over an insincere little girl. My wife knew how to love a man; that girl was empty." He shook his head, still visibly angry with himself.

"Have you tried to win her back?" Coco closed her eyes, trying to imagine what Cristina would look like. "If you regret your actions and you still love her. Do you think you'd cheat on her a second time?"

"No, but I know her; she's as hard as ice when she's angry. I don't think she can forgive me."

"You have a smile that melts ice. I think you should go and see her, at least ask her to forgive you if nothing else."

They fell into a long silence.

"Are you breaking up with me, Coco?" Paolo stared silently at the ceiling, his features strained.

"I don't know." Coco looked away from him, her eyes stinging with tears she wouldn't shed.

The clock on the wall read one-thirty a.m. when Coco returned home. She headed for the fridge, finding a package of cold spiced chicken. She wrapped the meat in a lettuce leaf and sat at the table to eat. Wrapped only in her fur, she felt the cool weight of the diamonds from where they hung heavily at her throat and ears. When she knotted her tangled hair into a ponytail, her earrings caught the light, refracting prisms across the immaculate kitchen cabinets.

After their talk, Paolo had remained kind. He had walked her to his chauffeured car and kissed her goodnight. She had watched him disappear from view, his face lit with a steady smile. There was patience in that smile: patience, perseverance, and a seemingly endless amount of open kindness.

She had told him that she loved him, and she had meant it. There were many kinds of love, and the love she felt for him was one of friendship. Worse than the lack of deep love, were the dozen *if only's* that lived in the empty places in her heart. *If only* he were young and free, *if only* she had never known Rob, *if only* life had been different. None of that mattered now. Coco could feel her life organizing around her while she waited, like a wayward traveler, to see where it would lead.

From his crib in her darkened room, James began crying. His small voice rose to where she sat in a plaintive whimper. Coco knew the cry. Setting down her lettuce wrap, she walked to her son, who sat in the middle of his crib, his silver flecked eyes peering through the darkness in search of her.

"You're okay." Coco lifted him into her arms and kissed him. She heard a noise behind her, the shuffle of stiff feet as Tia opened the door.

"I didn't hear you come in," Tia said. The two women stared at each other for a moment: one at the beginning of her life, already burdened by her mistakes, the other at the end, filled with knowledge and advice that fell on deaf ears.

"Good night." Coco turned away, her attention focused on her son.

"No, it isn't." Tia's voice rose in grief. "You smell like sex, like that man. How can you let him use you like this?"

"Paolo's not using me, Tia." Coco gently put James down before switching on his mobile. It lit up softly in the dim light and began to play a lullaby. "He's kind to me and loving and I like him. He makes me happy."

"Of course he makes you happy."

The old woman spoke with bitter sadness, gone was the usually acidic condemnation. Tears glimmered in the corners of Tia's eyes yet her voice was firm. "He makes you feel loved and special, showers you with gifts while he gains your trust. Then he'll slowly lure you away from the people who love you until it's just you and him."

"Paolo's not trying to lure me, Tia."

"No? He's already talking trash about me; next it'll be your friends and then your kids. He doesn't want a girl with two babies, Coco. He wants a supermodel lover with no strings attached. He'll plant dissatisfaction in your heart while he offers you the moon. He doesn't consider the consequences, because it'll be you who pays the heaviest price."

"Stop it, Tia. What makes you so twisted? For God's sake, he's just a nice guy who likes me."

"If I'm twisted it's because of men like him. I know him, Coco. I know his type."

 302   MAGDALENA'S SHADOW

"No, you don't." Coco shook her head wearily, wanting peace, a shower, and some rest. Besides, James was still awake cooing and rustling in his blankets and he didn't need to hear them fight. Coco walked past Tia into the hall, but the old woman followed her.

"Paolo's charming, anyone can see that, but he's a manipulative businessman first and foremost. He sees a good investment and a lot of pleasure when he looks at you."

"Well, that figures. You already think I'm a whore, why not believe Paolo's a pimp if that's what makes you happy?"

"I'm not happy, Coco. Not about any of this. He is what I believe him to be, and he's using you and degrading you slowly. He'll break you down bit by bit because he wants to own you. Please believe me."

"Why should I? Oh, because you know the type? A good little Christian in your prim little nightdress knows the type?"

"I wasn't born a Christian, Coco. God saved me when I needed him most – when I needed freedom and hope and a future free of men like your Paolo. You look at me and you judge me, but you have no idea what my life has been."

"No, I don't, because you never tell me anything. You keep your little secrets, dropping cryptic hints here and there. When I ask you any questions, you say, *Oh, maybe I'll tell you some time.* I'm sick of it, Tia. You don't own me, and you don't know what it's like to be me. You think I'm a whore but I'm not. I'm just a girl trying to raise her family and find a little love."

"What do you think a whore is, Coco?" Tia stared at her while the question rang in the room. "Do you think a whore never comes home tired and hungry and smelling of sex, just to kiss her baby and try to scrape together some food for the night? Do you think a whore never wants to be loved, to be cared for, to be safe? You look at me and you see a sweet little old Christian lady, but I was a whore, Coco. For thirty years I lived on a pleasure yacht, coasting up and down the Gulf of Mexico and through the Caribbean Sea. I was eight years old when I was sold and thirty-eight when they threw me overboard because I was too old and used up to be profitable. Thank God I could swim. Some of the girls couldn't. You should've heard their screams." Tia turned to leave, but Coco stopped her.

"You're lying. You have to be."

"What does it matter now?"

"It matters because you're using this story to control me."

Tia met Coco's accusation without anger. When she spoke her voice was strong.

"Remember I told you I used to hide in a house my mother worked in so I could spy on the rich family who lived there? I was so poor and they were so rich. Everything they had, everything they were was so beautiful. One day the father found me. He kissed me and fed me sweets and then he fed me laudanum. It was just enough to keep me quiet. I was completely conscious when he raped me. I could hear his children playing in the garden. I was eight years old, and I never saw my mother after that day. Some of the men on the pleasure yacht gave me sweets and toys just like he did. Some said they were my daddy. They made me trust them and love them. They promised all sorts of things before they did what they did. Trust is the tool those types of men use most. It's the first step to seduction. Few men want to feel like rapists so they give gifts, offer safety, and promise love. A girl goes willingly when she trusts no matter how young or how innocent she is. I have known a thousand

 304   MAGDALENA'S SHADOW

Paolos, Coco, a thousand beautiful wealthy men who have promised me the moon." Tia stood like stone, but Coco had to lean against the wall behind her, her mind filling with visions she didn't want to believe.

"Where did you swim to when they threw you over?"

"To Haiti. I had seen so many girls go over. I made one of the sailors teach me to swim in exchange for sex. We weren't supposed to sleep with the crew. I swam to Haiti, and I worked the streets until Reverend Brown found me. I worked in his ministry for twenty years and then here in Chicago at one of his halfway houses. I've been helping girls get off the streets for so long now I can't even remember all their names. I call them my daughters, and they call me their Tia. Coco, there are millions of whores in the world; there are millions of good and loving women who have been used and broken, drugged or degraded, and I've had to watch you slide slowly among their numbers."

Tears slid down Coco's face. She couldn't look away from Tia's soft sad eyes. A heavy silence hung in the still darkened hall.

"That girl who lived with you was one of the girls you helped? You never had children of your own?"

"I had two babies on that yacht, Coco, but the sea held them before I did."

Coco took Tia's hand as a slow sob overtook her. She saw Tia's babies thrown into the Gulf, their little faces appearing for a moment above the water, struggling before they sank from view.

"How do you bear it?" Coco could hardly speak through her stifling tears. "How do you get from one day to the next? How could anyone survive that?"

"By believing in a loving God and by helping others so they never have to suffer the way I have. But I can only do

E. E. ORME 305

so much, Coco. Please believe me when I tell you that Paolo isn't your friend and never will be."

"He would never hurt me the way those men hurt you. You have to believe me, Tia. I trust him."

Tia let go of Coco's hand and turned without another word toward her room.

CHAPTER THIRTY-NINE

Coco wore black to the reading of Magdalena's will. She sat alone with her lawyer while Magdalena's attorney read the document in a loud monotone voice. Everything happened as her lawyer had said it would. The will wasn't complicated. It directed all of Magdalena's estate to be put in trust for her daughter, Nicole Valentina, until her eighteenth birthday. Being already of age, Coco was able to take immediate possession of her mother's bank accounts, her perfume line, #2, the beach house in Miramar, Argentina, and the label, La Sangre, a small fashion house with no real base.

"How much money is in the bank account?" Coco asked Magdalena's lawyer after the will had been read.

The man riffled through his papers, pulling up the assets sheet. "Five hundred thousand."

"That's all?" Coco asked in surprise.

"Miss Rodriguez spent as much as she made." Her lawyer spoke candidly. "I encouraged her to save, but she had no interest in investing."

"Did you know her well?" Coco sized up the fat middle-aged man.

"I was her lawyer." The statement meant that either he

knew everything or nothing.

Later that day Coco met Paolo for lunch at a European style cafe that Paolo swore served the best food in Chicago, but as he later lamented, couldn't hold a candle to the worst dive in Rome. Afterward they returned to his room. No part of Coco was ready to see Paolo as the monster Tia painted him to be.

"So, you have five hundred grand, a Chicago penthouse, a beach house, and La Sangre?" Paolo slipped her out of her dress and kissed her shoulder.

"And her perfume line," Coco added, unbuttoning his shirt. "That's got to bring in some revenue?"

Paolo shrugged. "Maybe. It will certainly need work. Magdalena never took care of her projects. She started things and then left them to other people to manage. If the people were competent then things went well – if not, disaster."

Coco closed her eyes and remembered the Keeper. "That's what happened to me. Magdalena hired people to raise me, and then never checked to see if they were doing a good job."

Paolo nodded sadly. "Suffering makes us stronger." He leaned in and kissed her.

"What do you know about Mama's La Sangre label?" They slipped lazily into bed.

"I know Delilah Ramirez runs it. She's a very hard working woman and cheap. She buys poor grade material at huge discounts. She uses Chinese labor from unmonitored factories. All her designers are contractual; if she likes their work she buys the rights to the single item. If not, they worked for nothing on an item they will have to hawk to someone else. She keeps no staff, no office; everything is done through her computer."

"Sweat shops?" Coco's mind stuck on the one key point. Paolo had been kissing her throat, his hand sliding down her hip, but he stopped to look at her.

"Don't sound surprised, Coco. Half the clothes in your closet where sewn in substandard conditions by adults and children who were paid next to nothing. I use Italian workers, but my clothing is very expensive – too expensive for your large American department stores. Also, my designers are salaried; they're free to be creative without worrying about starving to death."

"Do you make a large profit?"

"For now, but as things change it's harder to see the future. We do more online sales, but people want everything cheap. It's good, it's bad, and it is business." He smiled, suddenly bored with the topic. "Let's not think about it." He rolled Coco onto her side, his hips pressed against her bottom. "Let's just think about how well we fit together." He ran a finger down her spine to the tip of her tailbone. "Let the rest of the world fall apart. All my factories can burn, China can rise up, and fashion can go to hell." He sighed with deep satisfaction before rolling her onto her back.

"I told you no!" Coco swatted at his head when he kissed her panties, sliding them slowly off her hips.

"And I say yes," he grinned, pinning her hand to her hip.

"Paolo!" Coco felt his kiss enter her body. "You know why I don't like it!"

"You do like it. I know you do, but it makes you think of him…." His voice faded, his mouth playing over her core. She felt her eyes slide closed and remembered cold granite and a black dress, violently shredded.

The sex that followed contained its own violence, the emotions so intense that when it was over Coco lay next to

Paolo and quietly cried. She thought of Rob. She thought of Tia and her thirty years of hell, and felt herself degraded.

"Why?" she implored after a prolonged silence.

"How could I leave his memory on your body? Now when we make love you'll think only of me." His answer brimmed with self-satisfaction. Brushing back her hair, he lifted her chin in his hands to look in her eyes. "He is your son's father, but I am your lover. I am glad he was such a fool as to lose you. You are better off without him."

"He wasn't a fool," Coco sobbed.

"Yes, he was, my love."

"No, he was a good man. He was my friend."

"And he left you alone and pregnant. You said so yourself. He left you alone with no one to care for you. You should wish him to hell. I would never have hurt you the way he did. Never."

The words gutted Coco. She began to cry harder when she recalled Tia's words from the night before. Even with Tia's warning in her ear, she had fallen into Paolo's bed again. When he attacked Rob without ever having known him, he inadvertently weakened her trust in him.

"It hurts me, Paolo, when you talk like that about someone I loved. You seem to forget that you are still married. What can you offer me but sex and empty promises?"

"You know what my wife is."

"Yes… I do," Coco answered through bitter tears. "She is a good Catholic woman who loved you and you broke her heart, just as Rob was a good man I lied to."

Paolo lay back on his pillow and closed his eyes, letting the truth of Coco's words wash over him. She felt an almost instant regret for the way she had spoken to him, and yet she was right to hurt him. He needed to be hurt. He had hurt her with his play at ownership. He had attempted to prejudice her memories while he conquered her body. He had done something she had told him never to do, and he had done it smiling.

"What then? Are we too bad to ever again be happy? Have I nothing to offer you if I cannot offer marriage?"

"I don't know." Coco pushed him away, leaving the bed to find her clothes. "What I do know is that no one will have any peace until we make things right. James needs a father, Paolo. His father. Rob needs to know he has a son, and Cristina deserves a husband she can trust. I shouldn't have done this again. I told you before, go home and ask your wife to forgive you. Go on your knees if you have to. God knows some humility would do you good."

312   MAGDALENA'S SHADOW

CHAPTER FORTY

The three weeks that followed passed in a haze of frustration and uncertainty. Coco felt lost between what felt right and what felt wrong, what she could accomplish, and what seemed too terrifying even to contemplate. How could she ever find an easy way to tell Rob about James? Hiring someone else to tell him would be cruel and writing to him felt the same, but telling him in person was more than she could cope with. She couldn't bear to look him in the eye and tell him he had a son. Nor could she bear to witness the pain she knew he would feel.

Her one consolation was that Paolo was back in Italy, and Tia had chosen to stick to subjects pertaining to the kids and #2. She no longer mentioned Paolo or Rob or how far Coco had sunk into sin. Coco considered all of these things and more when she stepped into the hall she shared with #1 to collect the mail.

To her horror, the door to Rob's apartment was wide open, voices rising and falling musically as several people spoke in turn.

"And it comes fully furnished?" a man's voice rang loudly. Coco remembered the decidedly male decor, its dark rich colors a perfect backdrop for everything masculine.

"But we can redecorate," a woman's voice chimed in hopefully, the long silence that followed indicating a coming storm.

"The penthouse is well below market value," a second woman added breaking the silence, "a steal even in this market, and I'll be more than happy to connect you with a decorator here in the area, someone who can work with both your needs...."

Coco grabbed the mail, her heart in her throat. *He can't sell #1*, she thought, before bolting into her own apartment. She slammed the door bringing Tia from the kitchen to see what was wrong.

"Are you okay?" Tia was surprised by how pale Coco looked.

"Rob's selling his apartment," Coco gasped. "Why would he do that?"

"Because he doesn't live there," Tia stated flatly. "Did you honestly think he would come back?"

"Of course I did." Coco sank to the couch with her mail forgotten in her hand. In Coco's mind he was always coming back. All her fantasies depended upon him coming back: back home, back to her, back to everything. When he returned there would be explanations, apologies, forgiveness, and he would hold her and life would return to the normal state of happiness it had been. Mila and Bebe would once more live like sisters and she and Rob would talk quietly with James sleeping in his crib nearby. But Rob was selling #1which meant he would never come back, not to her, not to James, and not to his home.

"N.V., you must know that La Sangre was always meant to be yours someday; that's why your mother chose the name. It means *The Blood*, the tie between mother and daughter," Delilah Ramirez smiled a hard-chiseled smile as she spoke. "I'm so pleased to have a chance to meet you in person." The look on her face reflected the opposite. "This is exactly what Magdalena envisioned: a family-run company. I hope you will see me as a sort of auntie, someone you can trust to run everything for you."

"Thank you." Coco tried not to dwell on the reality that Delilah had tried to inherit Magdalena's estate or be distracted by the noise and bustle of the busy restaurant where they met. La Sangre was a floating company with no offices, no employees, and no meeting rooms where they could talk quietly.

"I would like to begin by discussing production. I'm concerned with the price you're paying for labor." Coco indicated the spreadsheet that lay neatly before her in a prettily bound pink folder.

"I'm renegotiating the labor contract right now. La Sangre will have better labor and lower prices than any other U.S. fashion house. I don't want you to worry; my connections with the Chinese labor markets are second to none."

"That's not what Coco means," Carmen countered. "Coco wants her workers paid well. Chinese labor is fine. It's these unregulated, substandard factories they work in that we object to. These are slave labor prices you're paying. Furthermore, I've gone over your garments, Miss Ramirez. Your cloth is very poor; in fact, all your materials are substandard. We worked with better material in design school than those you use. Nothing is well made. The seams are weak and the clothing practically self-destructs."

"Who are you, may I ask? And who's this Coco you refer to?" Delilah turned a vicious look on Carmen.

"N.V. goes by Coco." Carmen indicated Coco where she sat at the table. "N.V. is her modeling name. I'm Carmen, your new head of design. Coco and I don't want slave labor associated with La Sangre or the Rodriguez name and we don't want to be associated with clothing so poorly made that the discount stores don't want it. Magdalena's name shouldn't be the only thing selling the La Sangre line. The clothes should sell themselves in quality, cut, and style. It's time La Sangre stood for something other than cheaply made crap."

Coco glanced between the two women. Confrontation always made her uncomfortable. Everything Carmen said was true, but she spoke in such an offensive way that any chance of negotiation or compromise was quickly becoming impossible.

"Well, Madam Design Head, please tell me, if my life's work is all cheap knockoffs and poorly made crap, where do *I* fit into this new vision for La Sangre?" Delilah's sharp retort matched Carmen's insolence. "I'll remind you that I'm under contract to lead this company for another three years."

"We hope you'll want to stay on with the label. It's our hope that you will embrace the changes we are attempting," Coco spoke softly, doing her best to save the moment. Delilah looked from one face to the other. Around them people chattered, kids laughed, and food was delivered; yet at their little table a mini-empire was being fought over.

"Neither of you have any real-world experience, do you? You're straight out of fashion school and ready to take on the industry?"

"We have a thorough understanding of design and construction. We're counting on you to help us learn the business side of the industry." Coco smiled warmly while Carmen continued to look on Delilah with contempt.

"Well, I'm the last person to leave a sinking ship." Delilah's smile turned vicious. "I'm going to enjoy watching *you* run this small label without cheap labor, using expensive material, and a dead spokesmodel. I'm going to relish every moment of this while I collect my annual three hundred grand salary. And please don't think for one moment I'll renegotiate my contract to aid this little endeavor of yours." She leaned back in her chair looking from one to the other. "What fun," she added after the pause. "This is going to be as entertaining as a hanging."

"I hate meeting at restaurants," Carmen complained while they walked to her car. "No swearing and sure as hell no ass kicking allowed. What're we going to do with her?"

"Pull a Tom."

"What's that?" Carmen glanced up at Coco when they reached the car.

"Work her half to death and then sell her ass the moment she's too tired to notice."

Carmen burst out laughing. "That's a rocking plan, and just another reason why you're my favorite little ho."

"Thank you." Coco slid into Carmen's car, her bitter smile fading in light of the fact that Delilah was right: they didn't have a hope in hell, not with the cost of labor, materials, and everything else. They would have to change everything about La Sangre in order to save it. Go smaller, pricier, and forget the mass market. Coco recalled Delilah's comment about sinking ships. Yet it was their ship to sink, and they would go down with style.

"So, what's next?" Carmen paged through the little pink folder Delilah had given them at the lunch meeting. It outlined La Sangre's inventory and retailers. Jack sat beside Carmen on the plush couch inside #2.

E. E. ORME 317

"First," Coco began, "I think we should design an entirely fresh new line. Then we need to find textile houses that sell quality cloth at a price we can afford. After that we line up a fair-trade manufacturer. Then we find stores that will sell the line at a price that keeps us from going bankrupt or we contemplate bringing in investors and opening up our own boutiques." Coco looked at Jack who nodded slowly.

"Okay," Carmen looked up from the folder, "do we know anyone who knows how to network with textile mills and manufacturers?"

"Just Jack, and he'll have to learn as he goes. We're stuck with Delilah so he'll need to work hand in hand with her on the purchasing and manufacturing. You and I'll do the design, cut the patterns, create the mockups, and make the lookbook."

"Well, Asshole *is* used to dealing with difficult women," Carmen said seriously. Jack only smiled. "He'll work well with Delilah. You should meet some of his aunts. They make Delilah look like a fluffy little kitten."

"Have you been permanently demoted to Asshole?" Coco looked at Jack sympathetically.

"I get my name back when my dirty clothes make it to the hamper for one month straight," Jack replied. "The nickname is Carmen's charming little way of training me to be more helpful at home."

"Cleanliness is a virtue and only the virtues get to keep their names." Carmen patted his knee. "Besides it's better I swear at him than flush his dirty undies down the toilet again."

Coco tried to fathom a man like Jack. He was always so easygoing that not even Carmen's vengeful and controlling nature seemed to ruffle him.

 318   MAGDALENA'S SHADOW

"It's a good thing you're used to dealing with difficult women." Coco turned an accusing look on Carmen who pretended not to notice.

The business of running La Sangre began with a budget, followed by a representative series of drawings created to outline La Sangre's newly redeveloped line. When this was accomplished Carmen began sampling fabric at the best prices she could find. In the meantime, Coco met with Magdalena's perfume people, praying that the product would bring in enough revenue to cover the expenses they would incur while improving the clothing line.

"Will you want to keep Magdalena as your spokesmodel?" Rolf Van Clisen, the perfume's marketing director, asked from where he sat across from Coco in the firm's lavish conference hall.

"Yes, of course." Coco felt surprised that he would even ask such a question. "She's why they buy the perfume. It's her scent."

"The firm believes that with her passing it might be appropriate to infuse the campaign with a new element."

"Like what?"

"Like you." Van Clisen gestured casually toward Coco. "We have hundreds of stock photographs of Magdalena, enough to take us into the next century, but icons fade. It's desirable to create a bridge between the past and the present. By incorporating your image with hers, we'll have a campaign that both new and returning customers can identify with."

"That's fine as long as Magdalena is included; I don't want my mother cut from the campaign, not ever. It's her perfume." Coco felt surprised by how much this one point mattered to her.

"No, of course not. This new direction we're proposing would place more emphasis on the Rodriguez name while still maintaining Magdalena as the founding icon. Incorporating you into the campaign, N.V., would only serve to help her image live on. Your image in the marketing will add a youthful vitality that will attract a broader range of customers. Perhaps when she's older, Bebe will also be interested in representing the fragrance?"

Coco felt instantly protective; there was no way she ever wanted Bebe objectified before a camera, subjected to little French photographers or men like Tom and Blackwell. As the thought washed over her it turned from anger to sadness. Coco suddenly knew how Tia felt. In the end, Bebe would be free to live and do as she chose. If Coco ever asked her not to model, she would probably use Coco's own words against her, saying, "I'll do as I please."

"Yes, she probably will," Coco admitted. "Let's work on branding the Rodriguez name. Schedule a shoot soon and I'll be there. I'm flying to New York on the thirty-first." Coco rose quickly. She grabbed her bag and left the conference room, horrified by the idea that Bebe might someday walk in her shoes.

Only days before Coco was to fly to New York, Rolf Van Clisen and his staff sat at a large table opposite Coco, the proofs taken at the shoot spread out before them. During the initial shoot Coco had wondered at the many ways they made her stand and move. Each pose had seemed bizarre. Now that she saw the result it all made perfect sense. The first photo sent a stab of grief through her heart. Coco stood facing Magdalena. Her right arm embraced Magdalena's shoulder, holding her so close that their foreheads touched. With chins tilted in and eyes downcast, mother and daughter stood locked in a loving embrace that never occurred in real life.

Coco couldn't stop the tears; they flowed unchecked down her face. She pulled the second sheet of proofs from the pile. Here she stood, hand in hand with her mother in identical black dresses, a vivid green landscape spreading out behind them. A passing breeze caught their skirts as they stood cheek to cheek staring at the camera. Neither smiling nor unhappy, they existed peacefully in an imagined moment. Coco sobbed silently, her fingers flipping through photo after photo. The room thinned out until she sat alone with Van Clisen.

"I'm sorry for your loss," he said, gathering the proofs Coco could no longer bear to look at. "Words are insufficient in moments like these."

"Thank you." Coco twisted a tissue in her hands. "Will you send me a copy of this picture?" She indicated the photo where Coco and Magdalena stood bare shouldered in a black and white embrace.

"Of course. It would be my pleasure." He separated the proof from the pile.

The next day a parcel arrived at #2. When she opened it, it was the photo, framed beautifully in a blackened steel frame. She placed it next to a photo of Bebe in an old gold frame. She looked at all the pictures that lined her mantelpiece: Tia, James, and Bebe; Jack and Carmen; herself and Magdalena.

There was a decidedly empty place to the right that desperately needed to be filled, a place for Rob and Mila.

322   MAGDALENA'S SHADOW

CHAPTER FORTY-ONE

The law offices of Foster, Robinson, Allen, and Banks were housed in a large old-world granite building that shone white in the spring sunshine. Coco vaguely recalled the building's wide ornate metal double doors, its cornices and large picture windows. When she walked around the corner of the building she could see the cemetery, now transformed by springtime into a green natural haven for squirrels and wild flowers. Coco had left Chicago that morning, flying into New York on the pretense of discussing her suit against Ryan Blackwell, but in truth she hoped to see Rob.

She stood some moments staring at the cemetery gate where Magdalena once had stood, wishing she could see her mother again in this life. Would she ever stop missing her? Quietly, almost imperceptibly, a door to her left opened revealing a small blonde woman, painfully thin with strange gray and silver eyes. Coco immediately recognized the silver fire, strength of will, and steady self-assurance sparkling in their depths.

"You must be Rob's sister, Bev." Coco offered her hand. "He told me all about you. And your dad." Coco smiled sympathetically, her eyes cast toward the cemetery where he lay buried.

Bev's face blanched slightly while her icy silver eyes sparkled in the spring light. She shook Coco's hand quickly, letting it go as soon as she could. "I saw you admiring the view, and I'm pleased you could spare time to go over your case, Miss Rodriguez. Shall we go up to my office?"

Coco nodded. "Rob told me the firm used to be the Banks family home. It's beautiful."

"My great-great-grandfather built this house," Beverly replied crisply. "He was an English admiral who came to New York to consolidate our family's shipping interests in the eighteenth century. Much of the estate was developed generations ago, but I keep this bit of green to remember my family's history and to protect the cemetery."

Coco looked from Beverly to the cemetery. "Rob loves this house very much. I'm glad he gets to work here even if it's no longer a family home." Coco turned toward Beverly who stood watching her.

"I'm an only child, Miss Rodriguez, and I'm afraid that Mr. Robert Banks no longer works here." Beverly's smile faded. The silver glint in her eyes intensified giving her features a look of quiet satisfaction.

Coco felt an initial shock. It was quickly replaced by a deep sense of dislike because she knew instinctively that this woman saw a wetback when she looked at Rob and an illegal when she saw Coco. Family pride made Beverly Banks an elitist. She was money-spoiled, bigoted, and closed minded; an old world American aristocrat, all DAR and WASP to her bitter scrawny little core.

"I'll be happy to go over your case with you myself, Miss Rodriguez. I see a lot of room for negotiation. Even though Mr. Blackwell has declared bankruptcy, we should be able to move forward with our suit." Coco nodded, feeling a shiver run down her spine; Rob was selling the Chicago penthouse, and he no longer worked for his dad's law firm. How was he supporting himself and Mila? Coco followed Bev reluctantly inside the Banks family mansion, no longer impressed by the grandeur around her. The house was stuffy, cold, and strongly imbued with a feeling of exclusivity.

Coco sat down in Beverly's office and tried to relax. "Do you have a number where I can reach Rob?"

"I'm sorry but I'm not at liberty to give out private numbers." Bev spoke apologetically, yet her expression told Coco she wasn't sorry, not in the least.

Beverly gave Coco a quick overview of the lawsuit, showing her the different directions they could still take the case. Coco felt cold and sad as Beverly's icy voice washed into background noise. Once the meeting was over, Coco rose mechanically to go.

"Well, thank you." Again, Coco offered Beverly Banks her hand. Beverly took it, shook and let Coco go with a smile that said *don't let the door hit you in the ass,* before returning to her desk. "If you see Rob, tell him to call me, okay?"

Beverly shook her head at Coco in feigned confusion. "As I told you before, Mr. Banks no longer works here. I don't know how to help you, Ms. Rodriguez."

Like hell you don't. Coco walked from the room fighting to conceal her deep disappointment.

Coco passed dozens of portraits of long dead Banks family members and partners. Only when she reached the stair to the first floor, did Coco have an idea. Turning into the next office she asked where she could find Bill Foster. Two doors further down she found him sitting at his desk, his computer playing seventies groove music.

"Bill," Coco peered at him from around the door. "May I come in?" The moment she saw his green eyes, her old hatred rose up inside her. This man was part of the reason she and Rob had lost control that night.

"Miss Rodriguez!" Bill rose to greet her, his eyes taking her in slowly.

"I see you have some manners." Coco noted his polite greeting but waved away his proffered hand before looking over the room. "I suppose your country club upbringing gave you that much," Coco added. She walked past him toward the massive window that mirrored Bev's own view.

"Just enough to get me in the door; after that... well, you know," he trailed off shrugging his shoulders while they both remembered the way he had manhandled her at the club.

Turning toward him, Coco saw a leering intensity in his eyes, and something else she couldn't put her finger on... maybe suspicion. "So, tell me, why did they fire Rob?" She tried her assumption on him to see where it might lead.

"You tell me," he snorted before sagging back into his chair like the lounge lizard she knew him to be. Yet his reply confused her.

"You first," she smiled, hoping he would say more.

Bill shook his head, but when he looked back at her a sly smile lit up the right side of his face. Rob's half smile, only on Bill it looked cruel. "You couldn't have made me work your case for free, no matter how sweet the rewards. Unlike Rob, I wouldn't have risked my job or the firm's reputation for your tight little ass."

Coco stared, too shocked to do anything else. But suddenly it all made sense: Rob had never charged her. With all the other lawyer's fees, she had not noticed. This reality gave Bev the excuse she had been looking for to get rid of her half-brother. Now Coco, the Latin whore, was handed the blame.

"Ya got me." She smiled her most dazzlingly guilty smile. "But I was wondering if you could do me one little favor," she added, blinking sweetly. "I need to tie up some things with Rob. You don't happen to have his number, do you?"

Bill laughed and shook his head at her. "Haven't you caused him enough pain?"

Coco studied him quietly before leaning slowly toward him. "Ah, Bill...." Coco looked directly into his greedy eyes. "Rob *never* gets tired of the kind of pain I offer." Her words hit Bill like an avalanche of sexual possibilities, his eyes taking on a soft lusty drunkenness as he stared at her.

"You know, I may be able to help you after all."

When Coco walked out of Bill Foster's office he was ready to lick her shoes. Coco now understood history's hatred of sexually powerful women. The right move, the right word, and money changed hands, marriages ended, as did careers, even lives. Tia once said that John the Baptist had lost his head because some slut wanted it on a plate. Coco caught her reflection in one of the huge gilt rococo mirrors that lined the entrance hall. This reflection was why Coco had Rob's email address, written on a sheet of legal paper. It was also why Bill had given her his private number and the address to his penthouse apartment in the city, a comfortable distance from the conventional suffocations of his upstate wife and child. Without hesitation, she threw Bill's number and penthouse address into the next available trash can.

328   MAGDALENA'S SHADOW

CHAPTER FORTY-TWO

Coco didn't want to use Paolo's phone to email Rob, but her old phone was dead and she'd come to rely on Paolo's high end smartphone for everything. Coco opened her email and typed in Rob's address. She clicked into the subject line, and wrote... nothing. After ten minutes, she settled on "Coco Says Hi." Infantile but far better than "Forgive Me, I'm Legal," or any of the other repulsive subject headings that ran through her mind.

I hate this, Coco thought, before clicking into the mammoth white expanse where she was supposed to write something sensible.

Rob... Bebe and I miss you and Mila. We'd love to see you both again. I stopped by your office but Bev said you'd quit. I have a small business now, and we could probably use a good corporate lawyer considering how naive I am and how mouthy Carmen is. We're not getting sued yet but it's just a matter of time. Anyway, I hope you're well, and give our love to Mila. I never finished Don Quixote, but I liked the Franco poems. Thanks. Veronica was amazing. I miss talking with you, and I miss having you close in #1. It's sad that you're selling. You know my landline number

so don't be a stranger.
  Hope you are well.
  Love, Coco.

Coco hit send before her nerves broke and she closed the page completely. A split second later the email was in Rob's inbox.

When the phone rang that night she grabbed it, bolting at full speed to her bedroom. James crawled down the hall behind her while Bebe bounced on the bed beside her. Coco sat on her bed and put her finger to her lips before she hit the answer button.

"Hello?" Her voice wavered.

"Hello, Miss Rodriguez," Beverly Banks' voice echoed into the still room. "We have some excellent news for you. Mr. Blackwell's bankruptcy lawyer has informed me that he's willing to sign over the New York City building he formerly occupied. Are you familiar with the building?"

"Yes," Coco answered flatly, wishing a house would fall on Beverly and her nasally well-bred voice.

"If you will accept these terms then we can go ahead and move to settle."

"How much of the building do I get?"

"All nine floors. Your suit's for over one hundred million. The building's value is estimated at less than the number indicated in your suit so you would be taking a loss."

"I didn't think I'd get anything after Blackwell declared bankruptcy. Honestly, this settlement sounds fine. I'll be in touch."

When Coco hung up the phone she felt sad. The only joy she felt lay in the enormous sum Rob had stipulated for her near loss of life. It showed how very much he still valued her.

"Who was that?" Bebe asked still bouncing on the bed.

"A business lady. You wouldn't like her," Coco said, wrinkling up her nose. A moment later the blanket began sliding off the bed. Bebe peered over the edge, giggling as baby James peered up at her.

Rob didn't call the next night either. On the fourth day after she had sent the email, Coco took her family to the library to check out books. While Bebe collected books from various shelves, Coco checked her email for the hundredth time. There was nothing but spam.

So that's it, Coco thought, and closed her phone. Rob was finished with her. She had done what she could, and he hadn't responded.

The library was full that day: children filled the kids' section, some read while others stacked books on the small colorful tables. At a large table just outside the kids' section, four teenage girls sat looking at fashion magazines. Coco remembered how at one point in her life the arrival of a new *Vogue* or *Bazaar* had felt something akin to the joy other kids felt at Christmas. Glancing casually over their magazines she saw a perfume ad – *her* perfume ad with Magdalena. In the same moment a girl glanced up, her eyes showing no sign of recognition before she looked back again at her magazine. Coco smiled; without makeup and airbrushing she was not N.V. the fashion model; she was just a mom hanging out with her kids.

Good, she thought, remembering how Tom's paparazzi had dogged her in Italy. *Maybe this is how my life will be. Maybe I've found the balance I've been looking for: single but capable, famous but anonymous.*

E. E. ORME 331

James woke, his eyes looking up at her from where he lay in his front carrier.

"Hello sweet boy," Coco said. She smiled and kissed him on the nose.

CHAPTER FORTY-THREE

New York City never loses its appeal, Coco thought. She stood with Carmen and Jack on the steps of the Blackwell building, a damp spring wind pulling at their clothes in the shadow of the nine-story red brick building. The inside of the building had been sacked. All the furnishings were gone along with the large mahogany entry table, so mammoth in size that Coco could not image how they had managed to get it through the doors. In the dim light, the large mahogany console that once had served as a hotel registrar's desk had also come under attack; a criminal with a crowbar had cracked the old wood in an attempt to rip the piece from the wall.

Coco ran her fingers over the damaged carved flowers wishing there were a way to repair them. Behind her, Carmen and Jack moved quietly over polished red brick, looking at the massive support columns that studded the room. Slowly the three made their way up the first flight of stairs, exploring room after room until they reached the ninth floor.

Coco bypassed the other rooms, moving to the room that had been hers. When she opened the door, she was surprised to find everything exactly as she had left it: a pair of socks in the corner, her makeshift bed pushed under the window, gray light pouring in on rumpled sheets. Inside the closet her clothes still hung on their hangers – handmade skirts with rip-cut tees, her corduroy patchwork jacket hanging alone on the closet wall. Coco slipped it off the hanger, pulling it over the black angora turtleneck she wore before turning toward the view she loved. Nine stories, she remembered thinking, is perfect: you can look out on the world but you're not so high up that you can't see the people below you.

"Your jacket…" Carmen walked up behind her looking confused.

"It was in the closet. They took everything but the bed and my handmade clothes. I'm trying not to feel hurt."

Carmen came to stand beside her, looking out at the view. Sunlight poured in between the surrounding buildings, lighting up the room where they stood. "We should move here." Carmen slipped her arm through Coco's. "We should run La Sangre from here, Coco. It's amazing."

"That's how I felt the first time I came here. I loved New York the way I loved this room the moment I saw it."

"Would you be okay leaving Chicago?"

"I think I would." But Coco felt a knot form in her stomach at the idea of leaving #2. The real question was how would Bebe and James take the move?

Back on the first floor they found a large old kitchen that opened onto what must have once been a dining room.

"Wow." Carmen ran her eyes over the heavy crown molding that still lined the windows and doors.

"It needs a lot of remodeling," Jack said quietly. "If we're going to work here we'll need to open up the second and third floors for offices and conference rooms."

"Some of the rooms are already big enough for conference rooms. Why can't everyone just use a bedroom for an office?" Carmen looked worried. "We can't be wasting time on remodeling."

"We need large spaces to lay out the proofs and the designs. We need a space where we can all work together," Jack said, looking at Coco.

"Well, there's no money for renovations," Coco said, "so we take it as is or sell it and find something else. It would be smart to sell it and find something smaller."

"Or rent the extra space and make money," Carmen added, giving Coco a nudge.

336　MAGDALENA'S SHADOW

CHAPTER FORTY-FOUR

On Coco's return to Chicago she found a message from the reporter Angie Thompson requesting a follow-up interview. Coco called her that night.

"I've been hired by *Vogue* to do a follow-up interview with you. We'd like to do an article on how your mother's death transformed your life. *Vogue*'s readers want to know how you are adjusting to being the heiress to Magdalena's vast estate."

"I would love to be featured in *Vogue*." Coco felt more than pleased with the idea of being in her favorite magazine again. In her first run she had been a blip on the runway scene, just a photo lost in the back half of the magazine. "So, this will be a big article?" Coco asked, hopeful.

"They want a full shoot and article. You'll get the cover, Coco."

"Oh, my God, Angie, this is amazing!"

"You could say no," Angie teased. "Honestly, if you don't want to be on the cover of *Vogue* you could refuse."

"I want it. I want it!" Coco practically bounced off the couch she was so happy. "I don't want to talk about James, though, remember? You have to stick to our agreement."

"No problem. I'll see you next week."

The shoot was executed with more professionalism than Coco had ever experienced. No little Frenchman yelled at confused Italians, and no one told Coco to look like she had just had sex. The entire shoot was magical, as were the garments they gave her to wear. Coco wore a thigh-length kimono in red and yellow silk. The silk felt cold when she first slid naked into it. She liked how the fabric warmed instantly to her, its soft panels enfolding her body like a second skin. She sat perched on a gold ottoman, her dark hair tumbling around her, one knee drawn up under her chin, and stared at the camera. She felt a languid pleasure in the warmth of the set lights and the attention of the photographer. *This is it.* The thought filled her with warm, soothing happiness. *This is all my dreams and all my fantasies colliding into reality right now.* Though her lips never smiled, her eyes filled with joy.

When the feature ran the following month, the storeroom filled with boxes from around the world. Now, instead of Magdalena's name on their labels, N.V. Rodriguez took her place. As Coco carried the first box inside #2 her heart beat strangely in her chest. Magdalena was dead, Coco was on the cover of *Vogue*, and the boxes were addressed to her. She remembered the frightened child she had been, a girl so different from the confident woman she had become. So much had changed and continued to change. Her life had made a complete revolution from stagnation and loss to confidence and freedom.

Only one month after listing #2, it sold with #1. A man from Florida bought them both with the idea that he would knock down the adjoining wall making one gigantic penthouse suite. Coco packed quickly, arranging the move with all the courage she could muster. Tia puttered, trying to maintain the status quo for the children. When specialty movers came to take and store the art, Bebe became hysterical.

"It's okay," Coco soothed the four-year-old, "they're still our paintings; these men are going to keep them safe for us until we're settled in our new home."

"No new home!" Bebe spluttered between sobs. "This is home!" Giant tears streamed down both cheeks.

Tia sat on the sofa next to them. "We'll be closer to a park." She rubbed Bebe's back comforting the child with Coco.

"Will Bob be there?" Bebe asked.

Tia and Coco looked at each other. No one had thought about Bob.

"We can't take…." Coco began but Bebe was already running from the room.

340 MAGDALENA'S SHADOW

CHAPTER FORTY-FIVE

Life in New York was very different from life in Chicago. There was no kitchen except the one on the first floor, and baby proofing the old building was impossible. Tia said little, but Coco felt the strain building up in her little family. Bebe was hit the worst by the move. She had never been the same after losing Mila. Now with the loss of Bob and #2 she seemed almost depressed. Coco did what she could, including the four-year-old in her daily business and enrolling her in a local preschool, but after the first month Tia confronted her in the hall, well away from where the children played.

"There is no stability here, Coco. You need to create a home for her. A home with a kitchen and living room – and she needs a pet."

"Are you serious? A pet?"

"Yes, a pet and a home. We're living in a collection of bedrooms with no center."

"Well, what do you suggest we do? I'm trying to run a business here. We can't afford an apartment."

"I think we should move down from the ninth to the fourth floor. I want to be closer to the kitchen."

"I need the lower floors for the business, the middle floors are rented out and Jack and Carmen are already living below us. Besides, this floor gets the most sunlight and has the best views. This is our floor until I make up my mind about keeping the building."

"Coco, if you're set on living here then you need to renovate this floor into a proper apartment. I want to try to recreate the floor plan we had at #2. It would help Bebe if she felt at home, and I'm too old to be without a kitchen in easy reach. You have money, Coco, you're just afraid to spend it."

"I'm not set on living here. We may have to sell. Right now, I'm living day to day. I know this hasn't been easy on anyone, but I need you to make do with what we have." Tia looked inflexible. "Tia," Coco begged. "Every cent I have has been invested into the label. We have to live carefully on what money is left. If this label goes bankrupt so do we. I cannot borrow money. More debt is the last thing we need."

"I've moved here without complaining, but when I see Bebe suffering I'll speak up. It's our job to create a home for her, Coco. She needs a proper *home*."

"I know you're right. It's not like I'm enjoying seeing Bebe suffer, but remodeling is out. I'll consider selling but you have to give me time. I'll figure something out, Tia."

When Coco reached her office on the second floor her desk was already stacked with documents and post-its.

Carmen poked her head around the doorframe. "Come and see this."

"What?" Coco rose to follow. Carmen worked in the room next to hers. An open box overflowing with colored cloth sat in the center of her desk.

"Look at these swatches!" An ecstatic smile lit up Carmen's face.

Coco lifted the pile of colored squares out of the box. The colors were all in nature tones, from pale taupe to vermilion red surrounded by lavender and dusky rose, sandstone beige and avocado.

"This is silk!" Coco looked up, impressed.

"And look what they're going to charge us." Carmen handed Coco the invoice. "It's so cheap we can actually afford it."

"No, we can't," Coco snorted. "We can't afford anything. Only order enough for the mockups. We'll bulk order after they're completed."

"Sounds good." Carmen happily spread all the colors across her desk. "I can't believe we found one fabric merchant with the right colors and the right price. I'm in heaven."

"What are you two so giddy about?" Delilah Ramirez stepped into Carmen's office. She looked over the array of swatches, her eyes landing on the invoice. "That's about six times what I pay for good American cotton," she smirked, shaking her head.

"I think you mean Indian cotton. You never once bought American," Carmen spat back. "And besides, this is silk, Ramirez, but I don't expect you know how to tell the difference."

"Whatever you say, Madam Design Head." Delilah waved her hand through the air. "I thought you'd like to know that Kansas Distribution's contract with us is up for renegotiation, but if you're using silk then you have already moved out of their market."

"They are La Sangre's Midwest distributor." Carmen spoke in answer to Coco's confused expression. "They bought Delilah's cheap crap to stock their warehouse stores."

"Let's not word it quite like that," Coco glared at Carmen before turning to address Delilah, "I don't want to cut the whole Midwest out of our clientele. Let's try not to lose them."

Delilah smiled like a cat on a mouse. "At these prices for materials alone, you have already lost them. Let's call this the first knot in your noose, shall we?"

"I hate her," Carmen said before Delilah was even out of earshot.

"Behave." Coco glared at Carmen. "You need to use diplomacy with her. It's your job."

"You can't use diplomacy with Satan. Evil doesn't negotiate and neither do I."

"Thanks for making an effort." Coco turned toward the door.

"Wait, Coco. I want to order this silk, but the contract has to be drawn up by a lawyer. We'll be ordering tons of material if the mockups work out; what do I do?"

"Have we settled on a manufacturer?"

"The silk people make it." Carmen looked confused. "They dye and weave the silk at their factory."

"I mean, who's making the silk into clothing? You can't order cloth until you know where you're sending it. Did Jack and Delilah come up with anyone?"

"No." Carmen looked dejected.

"Well, I guess you better go talk to her. I imagine it'll be a fun conversation after your last remark."

Coco closed the door to her office. The single bulb hanging from the ceiling gave off little light and the sun in her window glowed gray and hazy. Tia was right. There was no stability here. It was neither a home nor an office. Coco slumped down in her chair, flipping open the design book Carmen had given her that morning. Inside were all the sketches they had created for the new line. Everything the modern woman would want, or so Carmen said.

Coco flipped through pages of blouses, skirts, dresses, and pants. Everything was fresh and sophisticated. Coco was halfway through the book when her phone rang.

"My darling." Paolo's voice poured into the room, but Coco hesitated to reply when she remembered how their last conversation had gone. She had pushed him away after he had broken her trust. Even with this memory on her mind, the sound of his voice filled her, soothed her, and created that certain kind of dizzy allure that made him so desirable.

"Oh, Paolo, tell me Cristina has given you a divorce and you're calling to take me away from all this," she laughed.

"My love, if God and the Pope would allow me two wives, I would be on a plane already."

"Oh well, for a moment I had hope."

"You don't need hope, my love, not when you are the only woman in my life. I adore you and all is well. Now tell me, what's wrong?"

"Business is wrong."

"This is only your first month. It's not supposed to be easy; besides, I really am calling to take you away from it all. Come back to Rome for the spring show. I'll pay you well and we can book several shoots while you are here. Your face and my clothing are synonymous these days. Come to Rome. We'll behave like old friends all day and make love all night. You will be happy then."

"Book the ticket and I'll be there, Paolo – but I'm not going to bed with you. I'm done with men until I get my head on straight."

When she hung up the phone Coco felt a little better, until she remembered that she was supposed to create a stable home for Bebe, which made flying to Rome a bad idea. Sadly, stability would have to wait. They needed the money. Coco would go to Rome.

CHAPTER FORTY-SIX

Rome was a much needed and very pleasant break from the worries of New York City. Paolo's driver met Coco at the terminal's main gate, carrying her bags to the car. With Tom out of the picture Coco entered a relaxed flow completely devoid of paparazzi. Stepping from her elegant hotel into the plush interior of Paolo's new Maserati became a smooth and effortless dance: fittings to shows, shows to shoots, everything accomplished without the stress, anxiety, starvation, and exhaustion she had experienced before. Coco mingled with designers and models, photographers and journalists in an easy state of contentment while Paolo dropped in and out of her days with his usual charm and grace. She had managed not to sleep with him, though he behaved as if their love affair had never ended. Paolo existed in a state of perfected opulence, living as if everything he wanted already belonged to him. It wasn't in his nature to be angry or petty. In his dealings with Coco, he chose to be patient, loving, and very available should she change her mind.

"My love." He kissed her cheeks as he took her hand, leading Coco off set at the end of the final shoot. "I'm throwing a party tonight, and you must wear this gown."

He indicated the green and gold beaded dress she still wore. "Everyone will want it once they have seen you in it."

"Paolo, of course I'll wear it if you want me to. Where's the party?"

"Very near here. I don't think you have seen our house in Rome."

"You mean your palace," Coco corrected with a smile. She had heard about the ancient *palazzo* Paolo referred to as a house.

"A palace is for royalty," he smiled. "I'm a common Roman. A palace is just a big house without its queen. But with you there it'll be a palace once more."

Coco smiled, shaking her head at him. "All right, but I'm still not sleeping with you. Will Cristina be there?"

"Yes. I'll introduce you." He smiled wickedly.

"Does she know about us?"

"But of course, her spies are everywhere."

The party began at eleven that night. As usual, the driver picked Coco up promptly, weaving the sleek Italian car through the chaos of Rome with his usual skill. When the car stopped it stood before a massive rococo mansion. Every window in the magnificent building glowed with light, and colorful lanterns lit up the walkways and gardens of the D'Ambrosia house.

The driver stood quietly beside Coco's door, waiting for a signal that she was ready to exit. Gathering her wrap around her shoulders, Coco watched him open the door. She had begun the long walk through the garden when a man in livery spoke her name into a headset. A moment later Paolo stepped into the garden to meet her.

"Did they radio you that I was here? Is your party that organized, Paolo?"

"They radioed my assistant who informed me. I would never wear one of those silly headsets, Coco. Can you imagine being all wired up like that? No, I'm too old for such nonsense."

"So, it's better to leave the wires to the hired help, is it?"

"Exactly! How are you, my darling? It feels like days since I last saw you."

"And yet it's only been a few hours. Whatever will you do when I fly back to New York?"

"Go crazy with missing you." He leaned over and kissed her. The kiss was sweet; it melted her heart and her resolve in one gentle motion. "I adore you, Coco."

"And I adore you, Paolo, and I'm still not sleeping with you." Paolo only smiled. Together they stepped into the *palazzo's* great hall, its expansive ceiling painted with fat cherubs and gold leaf rococo flourishes.

"I love your parties," Coco smiled, dazzled by the room and the way the crowd parted to admire her. Many of the faces in the room were now familiar. Coco recognized the designer she had worked with on her first runway show. The little woman stepped forward, kissing both cheeks as she greeted her. Models and journalists embraced her as did rich patrons, celebrities, and a few fellow fashion devotees Coco had come to know.

"And this, my friend, is my beautiful Cristina."

Coco turned, her eyes falling on the tall slender woman with her long black hair worn in a twist at the nape of her neck. She was beautiful, with large almond shaped brown eyes and a long thin aquiline nose.

"I'm so pleased to meet you." Coco said, feeling shy and at a loss as to how to greet her lover's wife. It felt wrong to shake her hand or to kiss her in the Italian style.

Cristina was silent for a long moment while she looked

Coco over. Her look was appraising and formidable. In an instant Coco understood why Paolo lived in awe of her. Coco felt her cheeks begin to glow with embarrassment.

"You are just a little girl." Cristina's voice held sadness not scorn. "Your models, Paolo, are always so young."

Raising her eyes, Coco observed Cristina openly. Her beauty flowed naturally around her, a beauty no camera could ever capture, because it was the power in her voice and the way she stood in complete mastery of her surroundings that made her beautiful. Her gown was simple, tastefully cut to fit her body exactly. It was more than evident that no second gown had ever been thought of in the making of this one perfect piece.

Cristina's eyes locked on Coco's, holding her in her power. "Such a little child." Cristina glanced sadly at Paolo before turning her back on Coco.

Paolo chuckled quietly before leaning in to whisper in Coco's ear. "Now you see why she has always frightened me."

"And thrilled you," Coco said, her eyes scanning Cristina's perfect shoulders. "Your palace has its queen, Paolo."

"And its dragon," Paolo added soberly, his eyes locked on his magnificent wife. Coco felt Paolo move from her side. She felt him leave her for this woman who so dominated the room that it was impossible to see anyone or anything but her. Coco watched her move through the crowd with absolute grace. Cristina was Paolo's perfect match: an imperious Roman woman for a loving Roman man, reining him in with her sexuality only to let him out just enough to keep him wanting.

"Signorina Rodriguez," a voice said close to Coco's ear, drawing her attention away from Paolo's wife. "You are even more beautiful in person." The man speaking was

350 MAGDALENA'S SHADOW

young, no more than twenty, and amazingly beautiful. "I'm Alessandro," he smiled, "come and dance with me."

Alessandro wasn't as confident as most of the Italian men Coco knew, but his shy sweetness disarmed her and after one dance she found herself sitting on the sofa talking and drinking with him.

The music swelled around them, moving to a faster beat than either of them wished to dance to. Without even considering her actions, Coco gently twisted one of his thick black curls around her finger, releasing it to bounce back in line with the others around his temple.

"You are very good-looking," Coco stated candidly, letting her fingers trace the line of his cheekbone and jaw.

"I'm glad you think so, because I think that you are perfect. Your scent," he nuzzled her neck, "your beauty," his fingers grazed her collarbone, "everything about you is beyond desirable."

Coco pushed him playfully away and laughed, but she felt someone watching her. Cristina stood on the other side of the room, a look of concern freezing her perfect features. Their eyes met as Alessandro turned to see what Coco looked at.

"I think she must hate me."

"Why should she?" Alessandro asked in surprise.

Coco looked at Paolo, who stood by the window talking and remembered all the ways they had made love, all the hours they'd spent touching and exploring each other's bodies.

"I have no idea," Coco lied. "Jealousy, perhaps?"

"No." Alessandro shook his head. "I have never before seen Mama jealous of any woman. If she does hate you there must be another reason."

"Mama?" Coco looked at Alessandro with surprise.

"Yes, I'm afraid so," Alessandro laughed, leaning back on the couch while Coco stared at him.

"So, Paolo is Papa?" Coco recognized the familiar features of the father in the son.

"I should hope so," Alessandro answered, his face set in confusion, which then burst into a smile. "Who else?"

A photographer walked up to them. "Signorina Rodriguez, may I take your photo?"

"Yes," Coco leaned into Alessandro and smiled for the photographer.

"And who is your friend, Signorina?" the photographer asked when the picture was taken.

"This is Alessandro D'Ambrosia." Coco turned to smile at the boy.

Alessandro laughed, kissing her suddenly on the mouth as the photographer snapped another photo. Coco didn't kiss him back. Her heart felt heavy, and the moment Alessandro released her she saw Paolo watching them.

Coco slept in till noon the next day, waking only a few hours before her plane left. She dressed slowly, trying not to think of the boy at the party or the fact that he was Paolo's son. It had never occurred to her that Paolo and Cristina's children were her own age. In her mind, they had been children only a little older than Bebe and Mila. She hadn't dreamed that they might have a son her age. Everyone knew Paolo was old enough to be her father, but she had managed to ignore that fact until the moment she had met Alessandro.

The car arrived to take her to the airport one hour before her plane was scheduled to depart. The driver took her bags, escorting her into the warm, beautiful interior. As she slid inside she found Paolo waiting for her behind the darkly tinted glass.

"Paolo?"

"How did you sleep?" Paolo eyed her suspiciously.

"By myself, if that's what you are asking."

"You cannot blame me for being suspicious. You did meet my son last night. From what I saw, it seemed you liked him very well."

"I met your son, Paolo, but he is just a boy." Coco couldn't meet his eye.

"Yes, but a very charming boy. Very like his father."

"Yes, very." Coco scowled and bit her lip.

"It's funny, but I remember you saying you were done with men."

"I am." Coco turned from him, wishing to God he would leave her in peace.

"So, you have moved onto boys?"

"No, Alessandro did what he did without my permission."

"Well, it upset poor Cristina –"

"There is nothing *poor* about that woman," Coco interrupted, her eyes flashing dangerously. "She hates me on principle."

"Perhaps, but you have had her husband, and you may at any time you please have her son, so you see she has every reason to hate you. However, Cristina isn't the reason I'm here, Coco. I came to see you off, to wish you a good trip, and to tell you I want to see your spring line before anyone else."

"Why?" Coco asked. "La Sangre is a struggling label with sketches instead of finished products. I don't know if we'll stay alive long enough to make the clothes let alone shoot a lookbook."

"But you must," Paolo insisted. "You must succeed at this, Coco; it will be good for you. Just let me see your lookbook before anyone else."

"Why do you want to see it?"

"I have my reasons."

Paolo tapped the glass, at which point the driver entered the car and started the engine.

CHAPTER FORTY-SEVEN

Carmen met Coco at JFK, her little car a startling contrast to the Maserati Coco had become accustomed to. A part of her didn't want to get in, didn't want New York City and stress when she could have Rome, pleasure, and luxury.

"Hey, Carmen." Coco slid in beside Carmen, who gave her a weak smile that spoke of hells yet to be traversed.

"Is it Jack?" Coco asked going for the less stressful conclusion.

"No, he's fine. It's Delilah. She's come up with an old contract that says we can't change manufacturers for another three years. Also, she's axed the silk. She contacted the company and destroyed any hope we had of working with them."

Coco nodded but didn't reply for a long time. "Paolo wants to see our lookbook. He made me promise to make one and show it to him first. Why do you think he wants to see it so badly?"

"I don't know." Carmen stared at the road before them. "I don't know anything anymore."

Tia smacked a gossip magazine down on the entryway table in the first floor lobby. "I thought we'd come to an understanding. I though you understood that your promiscuity hurts everyone who loves you." Coco staggered back, shocked at the energy eighty pounds of angry old woman could wield.

"What now?" Coco looked down at the paper. On the cover was a photo of herself cheek to cheek with Alessandro, an inset photo showed them kissing. The terrible part was the headline that read: *Father of N.V.'s love child revealed.*

Coco opened the paper, spreading it across the lobby table where Tia had dropped it, flipping until she found the article. Every inch of the story was pure fabrication, but the photos were real: pictures of Coco and James at the park, the zoo, and even one taken walking out of the Blackwell building with both kids in tow. Above the family photos lay an earlier photo of her with Paolo along with that week's photo of Alessandro kissing her. In the captions below, Coco read Alessandro and Paolo's names, each referenced as the possible father of her son. There was even a comparison between the baby's features and the D'Ambrosia men. *As if James looks a thing like either of them*, Coco thought, staring at the photo.

"What do you want me to do?" Coco looked sadly up at Tia. "There's nothing I can do."

"You could stop giving them fresh material for one thing. How long had you known this boy before you decided to start a relationship with him?"

"A playful kiss isn't starting a relationship." Coco quickly lost her calm.

"It was in my day," Tia retorted.

"Yeah, well, just have me stoned to death then. I think that was the common cure for harlots *in your day*. And of course, there is always crucifixion. But you save that for the people you really like, right?"

"Shame on you," Tia hissed. "Rob will see this." She held up the paper. "That will be God's punishment, and then you'll have to start dealing with this mess you have made."

"Shame... on... me?" Coco asked slowly. "Once again, Mrs. Brown, you step out of line. No one talks to me like that. Are we clear? Your idea of propriety and my idea of propriety are very different. Don't you ever judge me or my life again. I'm no one's whore or victim; do you understand?"

The look on Tia's face said she clearly didn't. No part of Tia could understand a girl kissing a gorgeous boy at a party just because he was gorgeous and they were at a party. The two women locked eyes, each glaring defiantly at the other.

"Oh dear, this kind of confrontation isn't conducive to a healthy workplace environment," Delilah sighed dramatically as she stepped around the corner. "In fact, I find this level of workplace aggression rather upsetting. Let's try to keep our personal lives out of the office, shall we?"

Coco leveled her glare on Delilah, but the joyful sparkle in the other woman's eyes stopped her. Delilah wanted Coco angry. She wanted a scene, because she wanted something she could use.

"Thank you, Delilah, I'll keep your suggestions in mind," Coco answered coolly before turning away to find her kids.

"She's Satan," Carmen whined. "No one can deal with that devil. Everything I do she destroys, every move I make, every thought I think is sabotaged by her. I can't do this, Coco."

"Yes, you can. You have to because I have to. Everything I own is riding on this label. Let's concentrate on what we have. We have drawings, we have a few bolts of sample material, and we have the ability to sew. Let's just make the clothes and shoot the lookbook. At least we will have done that much. There is no way she can screw that up."

"She'll find a way."

"You're the fighter here, Carmen, so fight. Don't let her get to you."

"I don't think you get it, Coco. She got to me weeks ago. My mind's a mess."

"Well, straighten it out." Coco picked up the design book from her desk. "Just start making the clothes, okay? I'll make Delilah work on something else to keep her occupied. Just focus. Okay? You're a brilliant designer, just design and sew, and let Jack and I worry about the rest of it."

"Okay." Carmen turned from the room to hide in her office.

The following weeks slid by in a blur of frustration and quiet rage. Only when Coco persuaded Delilah to visit several Mexican manufacturers did they find their much-needed peace. Delilah was gone for three weeks on long drawn-out tours of four different factories, each tour in a different city with a different resort and separate social engagements all paid for by the prospective manufacturers. The ensuing peace was the one glimpse they got of what life at La Sangre would have been like without her. It was Gilman's all over again: Jack flirting with Carmen, Carmen chatting with Coco while beautifully tailored clothing came together piece by piece on their sewing table.

"Who's going to model these?" Carmen asked one night while they cut an apricot sundress.

"Me silly! Everything's been cut to my measurements." Coco looked up at her friend with surprise. "It's my label. I'll work the shoot."

"You're under contract to work for Paolo. Are you allowed to model your own label too?"

"It's not an exclusive contract. Besides, if it was he wouldn't care, I'm sure…."

"No, you're not, you better ask him first. Just because he's your *friend* doesn't mean that business isn't still business."

"I hate all these contracts. If it weren't for contracts, we could have fired Delilah months ago."

"If we had a lawyer we could probably get rid of her now. There's always a loophole."

"Probably," Coco sighed, thinking of Rob while she put away her thread.

She had come to the conclusion that he was out of the country, probably in Europe with Mila. With some minor investigation, Coco discovered that his New York apartment had been sold and his cellphone number now belonged to someone else. Wherever he was, he was offline, off the grid, and out of reach.

Just the day before, Coco had passed a man on the street. He had looked average but his scent had been a bittersweet memory that stopped her in her tracks; he wore Rob's cologne. The fragrance filled her with a sudden dreadful longing, making her miss his laugh, the sparkle in his eyes, the way he flirted and kissed. No one kissed like Rob. Not Paolo and definitely not Alessandro. They were lovely men, but they both lacked the passion and intensity Coco had felt with Rob. No one touched her the way he had touched her, no kiss compared to his. The intensity he held in a single glance was enough to make her lose control. She missed him, she needed him, and she wanted more from life than the constant grind of another day.

When Coco went to bed that night her heart felt heavy. James was growing up before her eyes and she felt a thousand years old. The long hours in her office and the hectic schedule meant she was missing the most important parts of James' life and her own. Where had she been when he had first sat up? What had she been doing when he had learned to walk? Where had she been when he had spoken his first word? He was already eighteen months old and he was growing up without her – and without his father, a man who would have loved his son completely. When Coco closed her eyes that night she prayed. She prayed that Rob and Mila were all right; she prayed that they were somewhere close by. She prayed that someday soon she would be able to tell them about James.

CHAPTER FORTY-EIGHT

Coco and Carmen sat in the sewing room threading small silver beads to a silver A-line dress, its thigh-length hem stretched between them as they added beaded star bursts. Bebe flipped through her book quietly in a chair while James emptied and filled a basket of fabric scraps they let him to play with. Each time he emptied the basket he laughed, each time he filled it he laughed harder.

"What are you doing, happy boy?" Carmen playfully tickled the baby who giggled more.

"Silly baby." Bebe grinned at him before setting her book down. She slid off her chair and walked to James, placing a scrap of red silk on his head. James froze where he sat, a confused look on his face. Dropping the remaining scraps he reached for the red silk, pulling it down off his head. Bebe smiled as she watched him examine the material that had appeared so magically on his head.

"Beeee!" he squealed at Bebe, shaking the red cloth at her before bringing it back down to examine it.

"Did you hear that, Mama?" Bebe ran to Coco. "James said Bee!"

Coco smiled, kissing Bebe on the head while she watched James play. "He'll be talking more and more now," she told

Bebe as they watched him.

A moment later he stood up, carrying his basket of scraps on unsteady feet toward Coco. "Um… um." He lifted the basket up to her.

"Thank you, James." Coco took the basket from her son, watching him turn around and sit back on the floor to play.

There was a knock at the door, and a moment later a young girl entered nervously, carrying a note for Coco. The girl was one of Jack's new interns, a fashion student who worked for free. The interns got experience while La Sangre got manpower at no extra expense. The one problem they had found was that the interns were so star struck that none of them could act normally around Coco. As this particular intern approached, her gaze lost its focus and her face turned red. She set down the note and bolted from the room.

"Run, little rabbit," Carmen called after the departing intern.

Coco laughed and picked up the note. She hadn't finished it when they were interrupted again.

"That girl is useless." Alessandro walked in wearing a perfectly tailored Prada suit and shoes. "I sent her to get you, but she is so slow I decided to come myself."

"Alessandro." Coco stared at him in surprise. "You are the last person I expected to see here today. What are you doing in New York City?"

"I came to see you, my beauty." He walked toward Coco with complete confidence and tried to kiss her.

Coco recoiled from him, moving awkwardly away. "You should have told me you were coming." She looked quickly from him to Carmen and then toward the kids. Bebe was watching, a look of concern on her face.

"And here is the little fellow I read about." Alessandro moved toward the baby, who was busy examining his toes.

"This is James." Coco moved protectively to where he sat.

Alessandro looked thoughtful. "I know...." He turned unsmiling eyes on her. "He is the other reason I came. My whole family is very unhappy about him. That article has raised many questions."

"Why?" Coco reached for James, lifting him in her arms before she turned to confront Alessandro. "You know they never print the truth in those gossip magazines."

"I know he's not my son, N.V., but he looks so like me... like us," Alessandro added, his eyes locking on Coco.

"I don't know what you mean." Coco looked down at James' black curly hair and large brown eyes – so like Rob – but in a way also like Paolo and his son.

Alessandro sat down in Bebe's chair staring at James. "Mama says that Papa and you are lovers. She saw the photos of the baby and refuses to speak to him. She believes that this is his son. Is it true? Are you lovers? Is that baby my brother?"

"Carmen, please take the kids to Tia." Coco quickly handed James to her friend.

Bebe stood up, looking from the strange man to Coco, obviously upset. "James is *my* brother, not yours," Bebe stated with absolute firmness.

"He is your nephew," Alessandro corrected, looking at the four-year-old sharply, "not your brother. You do not have a brother."

Bebe burst into tears, hardly noticing when Carmen took her by the hand. Coco heard her sobbing all the way down the hall.

"What are you doing?" Coco hissed the moment the kids were out of the room. "Don't you ever talk like that in front of my children. Don't you dare come in here spreading your insinuations. James isn't Paolo's son. He was born months before Paolo and I met. Any fool could do the math."

"Are you lovers?" Alessandro asked again, his voice calm and direct.

"Not at the moment."

"Good, I could never share a woman with him." He lifted a hand, running it down Coco's arm. "You are, as I once told you, delicious in every way. I'm sorry if I upset you. I was jealous, that's all."

"Get out!" Coco moved toward the door.

He didn't move for a long time. Instead he casually watched the rage play out on her features. Slowly he rose to his feet, moving toward her. The look on his face was still possessive, but soft as if he meant to be kind. Coco felt his hand slide into her hair. He moved to tilt her head back, his lips coming toward hers in an unwelcome kiss. Coco slapped him hard and pushed him from the room.

"Get out and don't ever think you have any right to touch me again. If you feel I led you on at the party, then that's your mistake. I was having fun, nothing more. Don't ever come here again, Alessandro."

Looking alarmed, Jack arrived in the hall with Carmen behind him. Together they watched Alessandro walk toward the stairs. He stopped before the first step, turning toward Coco. He didn't speak; he just looked at her and then turned away.

Bebe had stopped crying when Coco found her sitting with Tia on her little pink bed. James lay asleep in his crib, his eyes shut tight, his breathing deep and rhythmic.

"Are you okay?" Coco lifted Bebe into her arms and sat down next to Tia.

"Why did that man say that James isn't my brother?" Bebe's face clouded over with new grief.

"Because he doesn't understand us." Coco kissed Bebe, rocking her gently in her lap while Tia patted the little girl's back and smoothed the hair from her face. They sat together in silence while Coco tried to find words to describe their unique situation. "You know how I told you that I'm your sister and your mama. It's like that with James too. He is your nephew but he's like a brother too."

"What's a nephew?"

"A nephew is your sister's son."

Bebe nodded her head, laying her cheek on Coco's shoulder. "If you are my sister then who is my mama? Is she in Europe like Mila's?"

"No, honey. Your mama is in heaven with God. She couldn't take care of you so she sent you to me."

"Then I'm glad I'm with you, Coco." Bebe hadn't called Coco by her name in years.

"You can always call me Mama, Bebe." Coco hugged Bebe close.

Tia stroked the child's back, her eyes reflecting a sadness no words could express. They sat quietly together in the ensuing silence.

"That's okay." Bebe shook her head before looking seriously up at them. "I had a mama already."

Coco's eyes filled with tears as her heart ached for Bebe. "I love you more than any mama ever loved her baby." She lifted Bebe's chin in her hand until the child looked at her. "You are my baby girl and I love you."

Bebe nodded slowly and closed her eyes.

Coco couldn't reach Paolo for several days. When she did hear from him the phone connection was so bad that his voice was garbled and the call dropped.

"Where are you?" Coco asked when he called her from a different number several hours later.

"You would never guess," Paolo laughed. "I am skiing. I have left Rome and business and I'm having an adventure. How is the work on my lookbook coming along?"

"*My* lookbook is scheduled to be shot next week. That's one of the reasons I wanted to talk to you. I'll be modeling the clothes. That won't violate our contract, will it?"

"Not at all. You should be the one modeling La Sangre's new line. What was the other matter you wanted to discuss?"

"Your son was here, and he was very rude to me and my children."

"I am sorry," Paolo sighed. "I imagine he told you that Cristina believes I am James' father?"

"Yes. It was very upsetting. I thought you said her spies were everywhere. If she's so well-informed how can she think such a thing?"

"I don't know. She's jealous and angry and being very unreasonable. We have been separated for years. It is probably more the idea that I *can* still start a new family that is infuriated her. I am sorry you have been caught in the middle of my family vendetta. I will make it up to you, I promise. Just be patient and keep working on the spring line."

"I never stop working. It's all I ever seem to do. What are you planning, Paolo? Why is this line so important to you?"

"I am not planning anything, my darling. As I told you, right now I am skiing; later I may plan something. Who knows?"

"All right, you keep your secrets."

Shooting the lookbook for La Sangre's new line took seven days, far longer than any of them expected. Each piece required a different look, setting, lighting, and feel. The stylist they hired altered Coco's hairstyle and accessories with every wardrobe change, and by the end of the shoot Coco felt she had been brushed, cinched, and sculpted in so many ways that she just wanted to be done. The resulting proofs were visually spectacular. Carmen and Coco sat up late into the next morning selecting the proofs that would go into the final pages: four shots of Coco wearing each piece, with a description beside it.

"Why are we doing this?" Carmen asked. "Oh that's right. It's our swan song." She laughed without humor, her eyes skimming over a photo of Coco in a green gingham dress. Coco knew it broke her heart that they couldn't afford the materials they had used in the collection for a real ready-to-wear line.

"Something good will happen," Coco reassured her. "I'm putting the building up for sale. If it sells we'll have the money we need to manufacture the line."

"And if the line fails you'll go bankrupt. We don't even know what we're doing, Coco. Delilah was right. We have no real-world experience. You shouldn't take such a risk."

"Don't think like that. We've learned more on the job than we ever could sitting in Gilman's classroom. We may not know what we're doing, but at least we keep trying. If I don't invest more money in La Sangre it really will die, and I don't want that. This is a beautiful collection. It's truly amazing. The world needs to see your work."

"And yours." Carmen turned sad eyes on Coco. "Many of these designs are yours, Coco. Don't ever forget that you are not just the pretty face," she added with a half-smile before turning back to the proofs. "You know, I would still be living with the Gilmans in Chicago if you hadn't taken this risk. I just wish we could get the clothes out there for everyone to see."

"We still can if we lower our standards." Coco bit her lip. "Of course, none of it would look the same because the quality would be gone: plastic instead of silk, linen, or cotton, poor stitching instead of quality. No tailoring at all." Coco shook her head. *No, it's better this way*, she thought. They sorted through the last photos highlighting the ones they wanted on the computer before dragging them onto the lookbook.

"What do you think Paolo's up to?" Carmen asked.

"I don't know. He's skiing. There is no telling what he'll do after that." Coco watched Carmen match the last four photos with their blurbs, dragging and dropping each item into its own section. The lookbook was done. They ordered only three hard copies – one for Coco, one for Carmen, and one for Jack. Paolo would get his copy through email. Coco imagined him viewing it through his smartphone while standing on some alpine slope in between runs. She felt a sudden pang of anxiety as they reached the end of the project. They had gone over every page, arranging photos, correcting misspellings and typos until she was certain the lookbook was perfect – and yet when Carmen went to hit send Coco hesitated.

"Are we ready?" Coco turned to Carmen.

"We're ready." Carmen smiled at Coco before she moved the cursor over the send button. A second later it was gone, just data in the web, their dreams shooting formlessly out into the world.

CHAPTER FORTY-NINE

Spring sunshine poured into the ninth floor windows of the Blackwell building. James sat in the light on a sheepskin rug, his fingers buried deep in the wool. With rapt attention, he examined the effect of the light on the white strands of fleece. Everything was new to the baby: the dust in the sunbeams swirling and dancing around his head, the glow of light on color, the splendor of sunshine refracted and reflected on the walls and floor around him.

Coco sat silently beside him, watching him catch sunshine in his hands, enjoying his laughter and the way his black curls shone in the brilliant afternoon light. The moment felt beautiful and miraculous all at once. *I'm here right now*, she thought, *I haven't missed this moment*. No part of Coco's new life brought her greater joy than when she had the chance to watch James watch the world.

Coco didn't hear Tia at the door when she returned from the park with Bebe; she didn't hear the mail rustle when Tia set it on the table by the door. It was James who saw Tia and Bebe enter. He rose to his feet, pressing his palms into the floor while he pushed himself up. Coco smiled at the sight of dimpled arms and dimpled knees working together. After a momentary struggle, he was standing, running to where Bebe stood.

Coco rose slowly, not ready to let go of the moment. She was sorting through the stack of mail when the phone rang. "Miss N.V., there's a man here to see you," Lidia, the shyest of the new interns, informed her.

"Okay, show him to my office, I'll be down soon." Coco turned tired eyes on her little family. The time of sunbeams and silence had ended; it existed now only in her memory. Leaning over, Coco kissed Bebe on top of her head. Before she left she hugged Tia who looked happily surprised.

"I have to meet someone but then I'll be up. We can eat lunch together." Coco took a green pashmina wrap off a hook by the door, throwing it over the black tank she wore with jeans.

Coco passed Lidia on her way down the hall to her office. She passed Carmen and Jack as they argued, and Delilah as she played solitaire on her computer. Five steps from her office, Coco took a deep breath, smoothed her face, and prepared to meet whoever was waiting. Quite suddenly, she caught a familiar scent. Her heart leapt in her chest. Before she had seen him or heard his voice, Coco knew that Rob waited for her inside.

He stood by her desk, his shoulders framed in a perfectly tailored Armani suit. He held his briefcase tucked under his arm, his eyes fixed on the window in the far wall. Coco froze. The subtle scent of his cologne made her heart thump erratically while the sight of him struck her as powerfully as it had the first time they had met. Coco watched him turn toward her, his face ready with a slight smile that faded the moment he saw her.

"Coco?" he asked with confusion, his eyes softening, almost sad.

They stared at each other, neither of them knowing what to say or do. After a moment, Coco walked toward him, slid

370   MAGDALENA'S SHADOW

her arms through his, and held him. He stood frozen for only a moment before she felt his arms on her back. She could have stood like that forever, so grateful to see him, so happy to hear his heartbeat against her ear again. Sadly, she felt him withdraw from her. When she opened her eyes, he had stepped back to look at her.

"What are you doing here?" Rob looked into her face with concern.

"I live here," Coco smiled gently up at him.

Rob stared at her and then laughed. "Do you know that's the first thing you ever said to me? When I first met you in Chicago you said, *I live here.* You were standing in the storage room, remember?" He smiled, watched her close the door and draw up a chair.

Coco took his hand in hers after they sat down. "I didn't think I would see you again." Tears sparkled in her eyes. "You disappeared. You must have seen my email."

Rob shook his head as he looked at her. "No, I didn't. I've been…disconnected for a while. Mila and I live in South America, in Venezuela. You emailed me?"

Coco nodded. She looked at his hand where it rested in hers. A thousand questions, coupled with a sudden fear ran through her mind. "Then how did you know I was here, Rob?"

Rob looked away, confused. "I didn't. I'm as surprised as you are. I'm supposed to meet someone called N.V. Rodriguez. I stopped in to make an appointment but the girl downstairs said N.V. could see me."

Coco nodded slowly. "Well, you're lucky I'm even here. I'm so busy I can't usually fit anyone in on short notice. We just finished our spring line so I'm getting a short break. You came at exactly the right time."

Rob said nothing. He seemed to be waiting for something.

Then Coco understood. "I'm N.V.," she added, looking away. "It's my modeling name and my legal name. Magdalena called me Coco, but I was christened Nicole Valentina."

Rob didn't answer; his face had lost all its earlier warmth. "So, Coco's not even your real name?"

"Are you here on business?" Coco interrupted before he could list out all the lies that lay between them.

"Yes."

Rob's answer made Coco's blood run cold. Slowly she let go of his hand, stood, and walked around the desk. When she sat down again, the desk stood between them. She felt a blush rising under her clothes; she felt humiliated and hurt, but her well-trained features betrayed nothing.

"How's Mila?"

"She's good… big. You'd hardly recognize her."

The words stung. Coco knew it was true. Over two years had passed since she had seen the little girl. "Bebe's big too. She looks like me. She's already very tall."

They fell into another uncomfortably long silence. Coco glanced at Rob's briefcase reminding him without words that there was a reason why he had come.

"I'm here to present you with an offer." He slid smoothly into his legal talk, setting a white folder on the desk between them. "A Milan fashion house is offering to buy an eighty-five percent share in La Sangre." Rob opened the folder.

The paperwork swam before Coco's eyes. She stared at the pages, shock still rippling through her. "Why?" Coco asked absentmindedly. "Why do they want my label?"

"The offer outlines everything." He slid the document toward her.

Coco blinked back tears. She stared at his hand where it rested on the desk. How could she possibly remain level-headed enough to talk over an offer when her self-control was beginning to slip? "Maybe this *isn't* a good time." Coco said, and stood up to look out the window. With her back turned toward Rob, she could hide her eyes. "I couldn't finish *Don Quixote*," she added, her voice breaking. "It was absolutely unreadable, kind of like the average legal contract. Rob, you can't expect me to read a document right now. You can't appear out of nowhere and expect me to be able to keep myself together enough to act like I haven't been missing you for over two years."

Coco stood beautifully silhouetted against the window, her dark hair mingling with the green silk wrap.

"I can read it through with you so it makes sense," Rob spoke softly, trying to coax her back to her chair. "This doesn't have to be painful. We'll read through it and then you can decide if you are even interested. If you are not interested, then I'll tell my client you have declined, and this will all be over."

"I know how it works. I'm not a stupid little girl anymore. What I am is tired and very, very confused."

Coco turned to glance at the document, her eyes slowly lifting to Rob's. He looked, if anything, resigned to the misery of the moment. "You can have tomorrow, Rob, but not today. I can't do this today."

Rob nodded, rising to his feet to place the offer back in his briefcase. When he moved to go, Coco turned back toward the window, unable to watch him leave the room. "I'll see you at nine o'clock." The sound of her voice stopped him where he stood.

"Nine." He moved again for the door.

"Rob," Coco said. "It's good to see you."

"You too, Coco." And then he was gone.

When she heard his footfalls fade, Coco closed her office door and sat in silence.

There was a soft knock at the door. Carmen walked in. "You okay?"

Coco nodded. The worst of it was over. She had seen him, spoken to him, and it was plain that he had come *on business. But why?* Coco wondered, feeling the pain of their history wash over her. *Why couldn't Rob have come to see her for her sake? Why had it been business that brought him back into her life?* She had dreamed that when she found him they would fall into each other's arms, kissing and apologizing, and never leave each other again. But instead of kisses she had been given documents, polite conversation, and... what?

Coco returned to the ninth floor to find Bebe riding her trike down the hall with James running behind her. The moment James saw his mother he lifted his arms wanting to be held. Coco lifted him, cradling him to her chest. A fresh stream of tears ran freely down her checks. Her throat felt choked with subdued sobs. She slid silently into her room, moving into the unobstructed spring sunshine that filtered in. It felt good to close her eyes and breathe in James' scent, his baby smell lingering in his black curls.

When she opened her eyes, she saw Rob, standing on the far sidewalk looking up at the building. Coco didn't try to hide their son; she stood frozen in the light, her green wrap a beacon in the brown brick facade. She swore he saw her, but after a moment Rob turned and walked down the street like a man facing a strong wind, though not a leaf stirred in the early spring heat.

Later at dinner, Coco didn't tell Tia that she had seen him. This pain went beyond anything Coco could describe. God had given her the only thing she had prayed for since surviving the snow; and the prayer was answered without love, without passion, and without even the friendly familiarity she craved. Coco would have settled for friendship if she absolutely had to; she could live without Rob's love if she could see him smile, hear him laugh, or talk with him. But this… businesslike politeness? Fighting would be preferable.

Coco woke early the next morning, taking time to look her best. If she had to face him and remain professional she would do it with all her defenses in place. He had been shocked but pleased to see her. That first moment of recognition had been sincere even if the rest of their meeting had been a sham. Coco clung to the smile of surprise he had offered her while she hot-rolled her hair, remembering how deeply and completely they had once loved each other. One lie and one night had destroyed everything. And now there was James. Once Rob knew she had hidden his son from him he would hate her. Coco stared at herself in the mirror, fresh tears rolling down her cheeks. "Stupid, so stupid." She shook her head at her reflection. Her vision became blurred by the tears that stung her eyes. He would sue her for custody and they would end up fighting in court.

Coco's hand shook as she set the last roller. *Today I'll need waterproof makeup and a black dress,* she thought, feeling as if she were dressing for her own funeral. She chose soft sandstone colored lipstick and a copper colored eye pencil that she followed with waterproof copper mascara. *Less is best,* she thought, while staring into her reflection, *especially when I'll probably end the day crying.*

Coco sat at her desk at nine o'clock, her hair set in a pile of flattened ringlets high on her head. Only a few dark curls fell in corkscrews around her face and throat. The black dress she had chosen had a scalloped neck and very short sleeves. She wore small gold hoop earrings and her mother's cross. This was her armor against the day. *Feel like a lady and I might just survive*, she thought, and waited for Rob to arrive.

At ten minutes after nine Rob walked into the room. He wore a gray silk suit with his usual perfect grooming, but he lacked the healthful glow she had seen the day before. His eyes looked tired.

"Good morning." Coco watched him walk toward her.

"Good morning," he responded, setting the hated briefcase down between them.

Coco held her coffee mug between her hands; the heat comforted her while she studied the wood grain of the desk. "Coffee?" she asked glancing up. He set the offer on the desk before her and sat down.

"Thanks." He didn't look up.

Coco rose slowly; in the hall she found an intern who returned minutes later with a fresh cup.

Then they were alone again.

"I googled you last night." Rob looked slowly up at her. "It's funny, when I ran Coco Rodriguez I found nothing, but run N.V. and it explodes."

"I've been busy." Coco reached again for her cup. "I hope you didn't believe any of the articles. No one ever prints the truth about me." Rob didn't respond. Coco glanced up, suddenly worried. He was looking at the offer, his eyes silver flecks, his jaw set. "None of it's true," Coco repeated.

"So you said," Rob answered, his tone biting.

Coco shrugged. "Believe what you like," she said, wishing to God they could just talk like they used to.

"Coco, you can ask for a different lawyer to go over this with you. We don't have to do this."

"Yesterday you said you'd help me through this and today you're quitting on me? I told you none of those articles are true, Rob. You don't need to tuck tail and run because a few tabloids dragged my name through the mud. And even if I did misbehave, you have no right to judge me."

Rob's cold eyes held hers without flinching. "What you do with your life is your business."

"I'm glad you have finally figured that out." They stared at each other as a long pause ensued.

After a while, Coco decided to change topics. "Rob, I never got to thank you for helping me that night." She watched him watch her. "I would have died in the snow if you hadn't helped me. Thank you."

But Rob only scowled more. "That...." he couldn't finish. "Don't thank me, I...." After a long pause, he reached for the offer.

"And I never got to tell you how sorry I am for lying to you." She placed her hand over the document before he could open it. "And for pushing you out of my life. I should have been honest with you. I'm sorry. I made a lot of mistakes."

"You are not the only one." He looked at her hand as it rested on the offer. "It's in the past." He took the offer gently from her. "I'm going to request that a new lawyer make you this offer." His voice was soft now. "I don't see how we can get through this." He stood up and placed the offer back in his briefcase.

Coco stood quickly. "We need to talk. Business can wait. I have something I have to tell you."

"No, Coco. I think we've done all the talking we need to do." He moved for the door.

"Fine, run away again."

"Me? Don't blame me. I didn't run away, you pushed me out, remember?"

"You ran away. We could have worked things out if you had had the balls to stick around. Instead you flew to New York without a word."

"I had committed statutory rape, and you were a screaming, sobbing wreck. I didn't know what else to do. I couldn't comfort you; I couldn't talk to you…."

"You and your damned labels. Don't you call what we did *that* ever again! I was of the age of consent. So what if you are eleven years older. I loved you and I loved being with you. We didn't do anything wrong. You make it wrong when you call it something it never was."

"What we did was wrong. We have laws to protect little fools like you from rotting old men like me. Christ, Coco, you don't even –"

"Old men?" she interrupted. "You're thirty. Knock it off with the *old* crap. You got scared that your pretty little friends and your nice law firm would find out because you cared more about your reputation than you did about me."

"And don't forget the pretty little court trial if anyone *had* found out. Do you have any idea how hellish statutory rape cases can be? Even if you testified as my consensual girlfriend you were *seventeen*. I would still have had to prove my innocence. There would have been no surviving that kind of humiliation. I could have lost Mila and my career, everything. I still ended up losing my place at the firm."

"You cheated your firm out of the fees. I would have paid you. You lost your job on your own."

"Like I would have charged you after what happened?"

"Everything that's happened to *us* is because of you and your ego and your self-loathing, and your lack of trust in me and your –"

"DON'T YOU DARE BLAME ME!" Rob's voice rose for the first time. "DON'T." He sat down suddenly, his elbows on his knees, his face in his hands.

There was a knock at the door and Carmen peeked in.

"We're okay." Coco snapped, waving Carmen off before sinking down into the second guest chair beside Rob. She watched him for a long time. When he finally raised his eyes he looked exhausted.

"Rob, I'll never get over you. I've tried, but you are it for me."

"That's ridiculous. I'm too old for you and you're too damned young...."

"*Stop it*. You are the kindest man I have ever known. I loved watching you with Mila. You are a good dad, a good friend, and I love you."

"You have no basis for comparison, Coco. Look at the scum you have been subjected to."

"For a whole year you hardly made a move on me. We were friends and I loved that. I miss the way we talked and the way our girls lived like sisters. I miss us!"

"I was the only man you ever knew, that's the reality. And I wanted you from the moment I met you, so don't think my intentions were ever pure."

"I wanted you too. I wanted you in every possible way and I liked the attention."

"That's how girls are. They like attention. They feed on it and I dished it to you. You're, what, twenty now? Wow, such a big girl...."

"Who are you, Rob?" Coco stared at him, tears glistening in her eyes. She shook her head in disbelief. "There were times when I felt so completely loved by you, and yet now you act like you never once cared for me. All along you told me you went bad when your father took you; maybe that was your only moment of honesty." She stared at him for a long time, her eyes seeking some truth while he turned to stare fixedly on the wall behind her. "Was it all a game then? Love… marriage? Was that a game to get me in bed?" Her heart broke with her words.

"We never made it to bed. *Remember*?" His eyes remained fixed in the distance.

Coco wanted to strike him more in that moment than even on the night he had confused her with her mother. Her hand rose impulsively.

Rob's fingers closed around her wrist, his eyes locking onto hers. "Never strike me again."

He didn't hurt her; he just held her there while the memory of the last time she had struck him passed between them. All of Coco's reserve broke when she looked into those dark steely eyes. Tears ran down her face when she saw him, saw the man she loved distorted by pain and grief. Had she ever really known him or had she fallen in love with the idea of him? Slowly her other hand rose to his face, tracing the hard line of his cheekbone down to the inflexibly set jaw.

"After you left I believed that you never loved me. I've spent the last two years convincing myself that I was wrong."

Rob suddenly released her, his expression softening. "It's better like this. You'll…."

Coco silenced him before he could finish. She moved forward, her lips coming to his. The kiss was light, like a child's kiss before bedtime.

"It's not better, not better…." She stared into his eyes. "Goodbye, Rob." She stood slowly and walked to the door. She felt Rob watching her as a lifetime of regrets passed between them.

"Coco?" Rob's anguished voice broke the silence. But no sooner had he broken down and called her name than there was a knock at the door and Paolo walked in.

"Hello, my darling. How do you like my present?" Paolo didn't see Rob sitting in the chair.

Coco felt unable to smile through yet another shock, tears still streaming down her cheeks.

"What's the matter? You don't like it? It's a good present."

"I don't understand. What are you doing here?" Coco froze as Paolo reached to kiss her. Before his lips touched hers, she heard Rob shift behind her. "Paolo," Coco drew back, "please don't."

"Did you sign?" Paolo turned, his eyes catching Rob's movement. Rob looked away, his face an expressionless mask, his eyes still fixed on the window.

"What?" Coco looked at Paolo in confusion.

"My gift... my offer to buy this troublesome label of yours for an outrageously large price! After this, all you will have to do, my love, is design, model, go to parties, and be happy. It's a good present!"

"You're trying to buy La Sangre?"

"Yes, of course. My name is in the contract." Paolo moved from her to Rob. "I was told the offer arrived yesterday."

"And was asking Rob to present the offer another part of the gift?" Coco looked at Paolo with contempt.

"No, he's your business, my darling, and as I have warned you before, it is best not to look to the past."

"But here he is," Coco raised her hand in Rob's direction, "working for *you*, in my office. Please don't try to tell me this is a coincidence, Paolo."

"I would not if I had an answer. I didn't hire him, Coco. I promise. The offer went through our corporate lawyers before it was faxed to a firm we work with here in New York. I don't know what he is doing with it." Paolo looked at Rob with guarded suspicion. The two men locked eyes for a moment. Paolo was the first to look away. "It doesn't matter, my love. This man is your past. I am your future and the offer is a good offer no matter which paper pusher presents it. Sign it, Coco, so we can eat." He turned from the room to knock on Carmen's door.

Coco shrugged sadly and walked to the desk, her eyes tired from crying, her spirit broken.

Rob watched her stare at the document.

"Don't sign it."

"I have no intention of signing it until I have gone over it. I'm not stupid, and I'm not going to be pushed around by either of you."

"Good, because you need to read it. You need to read it and you need to have your lawyer go over it with you."

Coco stared at him for a moment. "I'm in between lawyers at the moment. Besides I trust Paolo. He's my friend. Now you tell me why I shouldn't trust him when he says it's a good offer."

"You shouldn't because he's trying to take you for everything you have and everything you are! I've read this thing and you shouldn't sign it, not without one hell of a lot of amendments. Read it, and you'll see what I mean."

"Okay, and then what? You'll help me write a counter offer? I'm tired, Rob, and I'm heartbroken and I don't want to fight with you anymore. Besides, aren't you here working for him?"

"That bastard can fend for himself. If you give me time to help you understand what this offer really asks for, I promise there will be no fighting."

"You'll help me?"

"For as long as you need me."

When she looked at him his face was soft, all the earlier ferocity gone.

"We had a baby." The words slipped out before she knew what she was saying, fresh tears streaming down her face. "Rob, we had a baby."

"I know." Rob's eyes were unable to meet hers. "I saw the photos last night. I thought you'd find a good man, but instead you found Paolo. How could you have a child with a man like that?"

"Come, Coco," Paolo's voice broke through the room. He stood in the doorway having overheard Rob's words.

"Not now, Paolo!" Coco watched Paolo look at her before walking away. When she turned back to Rob he wouldn't meet her gaze.

"You can't think that Paolo...."

"I don't think anything, Coco. I'm here to do a job not to judge you, remember. I don't have the right to."

"Yet you are judging me. You're judging me because you stayed up all night reading internet trash and looking at paparazzi photos. Did you even try to find the email I sent you? Did you even look at the pictures of our son?"

Rob ignored her words. Instead he took the offer and locked it in his briefcase. "Don't tell him you didn't sign it. Go and have lunch with him. Talk to him about your son. God knows that baby ties you to that man in a way that can't be undone. I'll be here when you get back."

Stunned into silence Coco watched Rob walk from the room.

Lunch passed in a flurry of one-sided conversation. Paolo spoke and Coco listened. She had always loved his conversations – how he made her see what he had seen, taste what he had tasted. Even in her current mood, Coco couldn't help smiling when he talked of skiing, the Alps, and all the people he had met.

"I'll take you, my love. We'll ski and drink wine and be happy."

"I would like that." Coco smiled when he took her hand.

"Yes, there is so much to see, so much to do. You shouldn't stay here shut up with business and children, Coco, you should see the world."

Coco's small joy fostered by his company faded. She didn't feel confined by her children. The realization that he wanted to separate her from them caused her fresh pain. Tia was right on every level. Paolo's one goal was to separate her from the world she knew in order to sweep her into his own.

Paolo remained oblivious to her sudden grief. "Do you remember when we made love and talked of butterflies?" he continued softly, his eyes brighter than she had ever seen them.

"Of course, I never forget a single minute with you."

"I want to offer you everything I have, Coco. Be my butterfly; let me keep you all your life. Let me love you and care for you, surround you with beauty, luxury, and pleasure. As my queen, everything you want will be yours."

At first Coco didn't reply because she didn't know what to say. "Paolo." Coco squeezed his fingers affectionately after a long silence. "You take my breath away. You are too kind."

"Then you'll come." He laughed with confidence, never doubting his power over her.

"No." Coco shook her head. "I do love you, and once being your kept woman would have been wonderful but…."

"Why would you say no? I've offered you the world. Think about designing in Italy, of modeling, of me and all the love I can give you. Think of the worlds I can show you. I know I can never be your husband but –"

384   MAGDALENA'S SHADOW

"Paolo, I can't," Coco interrupted. "Not now. I don't know what I want. What I do know is that James and Bebe come first. I don't want to be with them only when I'm not with you. I don't want to hurt you, not ever, so I'm telling you now what I told you before: this won't work. You have raised your children. Now I need to raise mine."

When lunch ended, Paolo took her back to her building, kissing her lightly as he said goodbye. He had regained his free and joyful mood. In that moment, Coco knew he hadn't given up, that he never gave up on what he wanted. But Coco knew she would never again allow herself to be isolated from the world the way she had been isolated in #2 under the strict management of the Keeper. No single person or situation would ever again manage her life for her. She was her own person now and she would die independent.

In that moment, she envied Paolo his light heart and the careless way he passed through life, one adventure moving happily onto the next. She would sign his contract, free herself from the label and her poverty, and maybe she would find that same kind of carefree joy or at least something like it.

When Coco turned toward the Blackwell building she felt weighed down by what she faced. Rob hated Paolo because he knew they had been lovers. He hated him because he believed that Paolo was James's father and that she would never escape him. He had already pitted himself against Paolo, and now he would work on her loyalties in the guise of protection, making one final stand for her honor before he left her alone again.

When Coco entered the building, she found Rob in the atrium on his cellphone, his face still wearing its professional mask. She went up the stairs to her office to wait. Five minutes later he was there, looking as polished and efficient as he had before their fight. Coco felt disheveled and weak, her broken heart hanging on her torn sleeve.

Rob slipped into the chair opposite her. He flipped the offer open and began outlining the document in clear, easy to understand terms. After half an hour Coco understood that his fears were real.

"Paolo wants," Coco slowly organized Paolo's demands on her fingers, "eighty-five percent of the label which is to be relocated to Italy, the rights to Magdalena's image, this building, a fifteen-year fully exclusive modeling contract that restricts me from doing work for anyone but him, and my relocation to Italy as a contributing designer?" Rob nodded. "Yet the amount of money he offers doesn't even cover the current value of this building." Coco shook her head. "Why would he do this to a friend?"

"His wife filed for a permanent separation. She'll take half of everything. With this contract, he could keep you close while he kept himself rich. Your label may be struggling but your image isn't. With backing and know-how, you and Magdalena are an empire, Coco. You are a very valuable empire."

"When did you find out about the separation?"

"I didn't just read tabloids and gossip blogs last night, Coco."

"Thank you." Coco looked up at Rob.

"No thanks. Please."

"He just asked me to go back to Italy with him."

"Are you going?"

"No." Coco looked down at her hands where they lay in her lap. "He wants me, not my family. I'll never leave my children. Besides I would fall into his lifestyle, and that's not what I want, not when I know I could never trust him."

 386   MAGDALENA'S SHADOW

"You have always known your own mind. That's one of the things I admire about you."

"Well, this makes four times that you have helped me when I needed you." Coco looked up, a sad smile framing her lips.

"Two," Rob answered, watching her, "now and in the snow."

"And at Bev's party when Bill manhandled me, and when Bebe ran away."

Rob shook his head, a cloud passing over his face. "Coco, if I had protected you properly three of those four would never have happened."

Coco didn't know how to answer. For a moment it had felt like old times, just easy conversation and trust. Now his face was tense again and he was angry, but not at her.

"You take too much on yourself, Rob. Life is for living. I never once asked you to keep me safe."

"But if I hadn't left you alone you would never have been manhandled by Bill, or beaten by Blackwell, or nearly sold to Paolo D'Ambrosia. If I had stayed you wouldn't be alone now with another fatherless child."

"I like my fatherless children and I like my life. What I don't like is being treated like a glass ornament to be loved or abandoned or sold on a whim."

Rob watched her quietly, his face filled with unspoken emotions. After a pause, he looked down at the contract.

"Well, if Paolo will accept a counteroffer, then you will be independent. You'll have time and money to spend how you like, as well as a knowledgeable man to run the Rodriguez image and label. You'll be free to model and still have time for your kids. If D'Ambrosia is one thing, he's a brilliant businessman." Rob took out his laptop while he avoided meeting her eyes.

The counter offer agreed to Paolo's terms but on a far more limited basis. Paolo would get a 65% share of La Sangre, as well as Coco as his spokesmodel – but not exclusively – and he would also get the Blackwell building. Coco would retain 35% of the label and keep a say in how it was run, but she wouldn't need to relocate. Furthermore, Carman and Jack would retain their positions as design leads. Paolo would get all this if he agreed to pay over twice the offered price.

"There is someone I want you to meet." Coco drew her arm through Rob's. "Come upstairs and meet James."

Rob hesitated, drawing gently away, his expression unreadable. "I have to get this to Paolo before I catch my plane tonight. I have to go, Coco. I'm sorry. I wish things were different."

His answer hurt her. "You can't be leaving already?"

"I need to get back to Venezuela. My mother is very ill and Mila needs me. This was supposed to be a quick bit of contract work. I had no idea what I was walking into."

"Who hired you?"

"Cristina D'Ambrosia." Rob watched Coco's reaction. "It seemed strange at the time, a wealthy Italian woman calling Venezuela looking for an ex-pat New York lawyer to negotiate a contract. Now I know why she did it. She was very explicit in her request. She asked me to present the offer to you and to explain your rights. She told me to act on your behalf. She said you were a young and naïve model who needed help."

"I thought she hated me."

"She was protecting you, Coco. When Paolo married her she was an A-list socialite and heiress to her father's fashion house – a fashion icon with a label. Sound familiar? Paolo's played this game before."

388   MAGDALENA'S SHADOW

"I judged her so harshly. Poor Cristina."

"She must have known what Paolo was planning. He said he ran the offer through their corporate lawyers. All she would need to do was intercept it and send it to me, thinking I would help you see how Paolo was using you. She is probably having him tracked, phone calls and all."

"He said she has spies everywhere. And I always use one of his cellphones to call him. I told him all about you."

"Well, there's one mystery solved. Stay safe, okay? Don't be so trusting." He moved to go.

"Rob, I have something I have to tell you."

"I can't do this, Coco. I'm worn out and I have to go."

"At least forgive me before you leave. I need that more than anything."

"Forgive you?" Rob asked, looking both surprised and saddened. "Coco, there is nothing to forgive. Please let go of what happened. All I want, all I have ever wanted for you, is that you live your life on your terms. Be happy, okay?"

There was a hesitation in his movement, a lonely expression of grief in his gaze. He looked like a man who was looking, for the last time, at someone he loved. Quietly he kissed her. A second later he was gone.

390 MAGDALENA'S SHADOW

CHAPTER FIFTY

Three months passed. Rob didn't come back and he didn't call. It seemed that the offer that saved her label from an early death was the final act in her love affair with Robert Jameson Banks. She still loved him and he still didn't know that James was his son. Coco thought of him while she watched the last of her furniture being packed into a semi to be stored indefinitely. The mover sealed the doors, handing Coco the clipboard for the final signature. Ten feet from where she stood a taxi waited. Coco watched the moving van drive away before she locked the Blackwell building for the last time.

Life is definitely strange, Coco thought, gazing up at the ninth floor, to the ladder she had used to climb down the building on that snowy night when she had followed her mother's shadow. Coco shook her head before turning toward the taxi that would take her to the hotel she now called home. She had survived the last abandonment – watched Rob walk away one last time – and yet the pain had been minimal. She loved him and always would, but she knew she could survive losing him; now she could go on with a thicker skin to face whatever life threw at her. Rob had left for a third time and she had survived. She was okay.

For the next week Coco, Tia, and the kids lived as New Yorkers: going to shows and museums, eating out every meal. Coco enjoyed the city, something she hadn't had time to do in the long months at La Sangre. Yet even with such pleasures before her, she felt older than she had felt before Rob's return. Seeing him and losing him a third time had matured her. She had learned to be wary, to be careful, and to live her life on her terms even when that meant living it on her own.

"I'm hungry, okay?" Bebe yelled, "But no China food," she added, taking her sister by the hand and pulling her to her feet. "They eat DUCKS!"

Coco laughed but Bebe turned on her in shock.

"Okay, okay, no China food, Bebe," Coco laughed again, turning to wait for Tia, who appeared in a nice new lavender dress and pearls. "You're steppin' out, girl," Coco teased admiringly.

"Thank you… I think." Tia smiled while James bounced around her.

Whenever they went out, Coco was admired and watched, yet it no longer bothered her. Even when the paparazzi caught up with them outside a restaurant, she wasn't fazed. Instead she held James up and told him to wave.

That last week in New York was one of her happiest of her life, but when they boarded the plane on the following Monday she was ready to go.

Ever since Magdalena's death Coco had planned to make this trip. And now, as James neared his second birthday, it was time. The plane shot down the runway, Bebe and James looked out the window and clapped as the wheels lifted off the tarmac, and the plane headed south toward Argentina.

CHAPTER FIFTY-ONE

The beach house faced northeast on a bluff overlooking the sea. Everything about it looked as she remembered it, from the tall square windows painted white to the purple flowering wisteria that hung in garlands of vine across the pergola-draped patio. Coco walked around the house with James asleep in her arms. Lights flickered on inside. On the other side of the glass Tia followed the housekeeper through the living room with a sleepy looking Bebe in tow. Coco hadn't entered the house. She was looking for something, something she remembered but had yet to find. All of her childhood memories of Magdalena's beach house were hazy and distant except for this one place in the garden. Coco didn't know why, but she felt that before she entered the house and confronted the many rooms filled with her mother's things, she had to find the one place where she had felt most at home.

In the distance the waves crashed and seagulls screeched over the high wind. Miramar, Argentina was cold in July – cold and windy and gorgeous. The scent of the winter garden mingled with the ocean winds triggered a memory of the footpath she followed. Turning around the northeastern corner of the house she found what she had been looking for. Hidden behind the house and looking out over the sea sat a turban shaped little summerhouse built in the Turkish style. Coco remembered long afternoons spent on plush pillows below the yellow and cream dome with its round canvas walls. This had been her playhouse, her quiet place, the place where she and Magdalena once had sat together and watched the sea. Stepping onto the blue and white tile floor, Coco unlaced the heavy canvas curtains and stepped inside the yurt. The interior remained unchanged. Curved overstuffed sofas and cushions rested along the walls, meticulously cleaned and cared for by Magdalena's housekeeper. In the center of the room sat a large circular table with sitting cushions placed at its edge. Over the table hung a Turkish chandelier made of bronze and cut glass. Blue and yellow beads hung in many layers from its six arms.

Everything was exactly as Coco remembered it. The only thing missing was Magdalena. Coco sat on a sofa overlooking the sea while James slept, nestled in his many blankets. Closing her eyes, she let the sound of the sea fill her senses, her mind drifting back to the memory of brown eyes and a soft chiming voice. In that instant Magdalena was with her again in this quiet place, holding her daughter in a love more lasting than the love she had ever given in life. Coco opened her eyes to the coming light and watched the sun lift out of the Atlantic.

July passed into August and no matter how chilly the wind, Coco never missed a chance to rest with James in the summerhouse. Her body and spirit were renewed by the tranquility of the place. Wrapped in blankets they watched the waves crash against the shore while sea birds flew overhead.

394   MAGDALENA'S SHADOW

Out in the distance, Bebe and Tia walked along the beach, gathering rocks and shells, the wind pulling at their hats and coats. The sun shone high, already sinking west of midday. Coco memorized the solitary beach, her mind drifting from James to Bebe, their upcoming trip to Italy, and how happy she would be when they returned home to Argentina. Never in her life had she felt more at home than she did here. The stillness, the quiet, the natural perfection of the place satisfied every craving, every need she had ever felt for home and peace.

In the distance Bebe and Tia examined a tide pool while another child ran to join them. Bebe seemed to know her as the two girls hugged repeatedly, bouncing hand in hand at the edge of the surf. Coco remembered examining the same tide pools with other neighbor children the way Bebe did now. She thought often of her mother and of her old life, but where grief had been there was now only gratitude. She could see the chain of events that made up her life, the many choices that had brought her to this moment, this quiet place of peace. The chain was stronger now and her memories clear. She held no regrets, only a prayer that someday her family would grow. She wanted to feel the love and friendship she had felt when Rob had still loved her, and yet even with this longing she found contentment with her life and with herself. If life had given her anything it was a strong self-reliance and the ability to move on come what may.

Her attention wandered further down the beach to where Bebe played, hearing her laughter through the crashing surf. A second sound joined the others, the sound of someone in the garden. Looking around she saw only the plants, green and lush in their subtropical winter colors. The rustle came again, followed by the movement of a man in blue jeans and a gray cable knit sweater.

"Rob?" Coco stared in disbelief.

He saw her then, a soft almost shy smile framing his lips. "Hi, Coco." His voice barely reached her through the heavy wind.

"That's Mila, isn't it? She's down with Bebe...." Coco felt suddenly overcome with emotion, tears rising in her eyes. "You brought Mila! You brought Mila and she's with Bebe! How did you find us?"

"I tracked down Carmen in Italy, she said you were here."

"I'm glad. I'm so glad." She shook her head, reaching out her hand to touch him, to see if he were real. She felt his hand close over hers, warm and strong. She shook her head again, too happy to speak. "I can't believe you're here. I thought you were in Venezuela." Coco blinked back tears, trying to regain her composure.

Rob shrugged, smiling a sad version of his half smile. "I was in Venezuela with my mother. She passed last month."

"I'm sorry." Coco looked away to hide her tears, feeling totally unable to meet the soft grief that lingered in his eyes. The first time they had met he had just lost his dad. Now his mother was dead as well.

"She was sick for a long time," Rob said slowly. "After... you and I parted," he hesitated, "... I started looking for her. I found her in time – in time to say goodbye. That's why I had to leave New York so quickly. I got the call that she had collapsed while you were at lunch. I'm sorry for the way I left you so abruptly. It wasn't what I wanted, but I have never been good with grief. Seeing you again and losing her at the same time was more than I could deal with."

"I knew you were unhappy. I just thought it was because of me." Coco smiled sadly, still unable to believe that he was there with her.

James slept on quietly beside her, lost under the blankets, his little body pressed against hers. When he eventually woke, Coco thought, Rob would learn the truth; he would see his own eyes mirrored back at him and he would know that James wasn't Paolo's son.

"I'm going to New York at the end of the week," Rob broke gently into her thoughts. "I wanted to see you before I left."

"Look how happy the girls are." Coco shook her head at him. "You can't separate them so soon."

Rob smiled, watching the girls before turning his eyes on Coco, her hair blowing around her face. They fell into another long silence.

"Coco," Rob began slowly, "I...." He paused, collecting his thoughts, the sound of waves crashing in the distance. "I've been doing a lot of thinking, trying to wrap my mind around everything. What happened between us was...." He trailed off in memory. "I'm sorry. If I could take back that night, all my mistakes, I would."

Coco shook her head. "It doesn't matter now. I could say that I should have been honest with you, but if I had none of it would have happened... and I'm glad it did."

"I wish I could look at it like that." Rob looked surprised. He studied her face, trying to read the placid expression he found there.

"Rob, I just meant that every second with you has been precious to me. I don't have any regrets except one. I shouldn't have pushed you out. You have no idea how much I have regretted that."

"Yes I do. Our regrets are the same. Coco, if I could have one wish it would be to go back to what we had; I miss you and I miss Bebe." Looking away, he cast his gaze out over the sea. "If I had a second chance, I wouldn't treat you like a glass ornament. I just want to come home. Wherever you are is home to me, Coco."

Coco watched him quietly, too shocked to speak.

"I… I can deal with Paolo… in a mature way," Rob continued after the silence. "I'll even be polite for your sake and for the baby's. I know he's part of your life forever now, I just don't want to live without you."

"Rob, you never have to. Don't go back to New York. Don't leave again. Stay with me."

Coco ran her fingers along the line of his jaw, leading him into a kiss. Coco felt his lips touch hers with a gentle passion that built until her lips parted to his. He kissed her like a man thirsting for water after days in the desert, savoring her and the moment with complete rapture. When the kiss ended, his eyes were different, soft in a way she had never seen. Taking his hand in hers she prepared herself to do what was right.

"Rob, there's something you need to know." Coco's fingers brushed Rob's cheek, bringing his eyes to meet hers. "Rob, Paolo has no claim on me other than through work. I told you not to believe what you read on the internet. James isn't Paolo's son." Rob looked at her with concern. "I tried to find you," Coco added gently, "I wrote to you when you sold the apartment. I should have tried a long time before that, but I was angry and hurt and stupid."

"What are you saying?"

"I'm saying that you were right. I was still a little girl when you left and I'm so sorry. I should have told you."

"I don't understand." Rob looked both hurt and confused.

"I named James after his father, middle name first. His name is James Robertson Banks. You are his father."

The look on Rob's face melted from confusion to anguish. He looked from her to the ocean. "Why… why,

Coco? Why didn't you call me? I would have come back. I had a right to…." but he couldn't finish.

"I was alone and scared and you were a world away. I always dreamed you would come back, but you sold your apartment. That's when I knew I had lost you."

"I don't know what to say, Coco." Rob spoke without looking at her.

"I've done the best I can. I've made mistakes, but at the time I thought I was doing the right thing in leaving you to live your life while I tried to go on with mine. None of this has been easy."

Rob stared out at the ocean. In that moment, James woke up, his black curls peeking out from under the blankets.

"Beee." James pointed out at Bebe and Mila where they played.

"Do you see Bebe playing?" Coco watched James pull the blankets away, his eyes fixed on the coastline.

Rob turned then, seeing his son for the first time. All the pain melted from his face when he saw James' silver flecked brown eyes, long lashes, and black curling hair.

"You see. He looks just like you, Rob."

James looked from Bebe and Mila to Rob, who sat beside his mother.

"James." Rob knelt down on the blue and white tiles in front of his son.

James looked at Rob, examining his black curls and tan complexion, his face breaking into a wide smile.

"You had him alone, Coco." Rob turned to look at her, his eyes filled with grief. "You didn't need to have him alone."

"Yes I did," Coco answered with gentle resolution. "You said we broke the law. He's the proof. You left saying that I had endangered everything you were because of my age, and I was too heartbroken and depressed to cope with losing you, let alone being pregnant."

Rob slowly lifted the baby into his arms and sat down again beside Coco. James smiled, his eyes turning back to where Bebe played. "I'm so sorry, Coco. If I had known, I would have come back."

"I wasn't sure." Fresh tears filled Coco's eyes. She closed them and remembered James' traumatic birth. "There's one more thing you need to know. I can't have any more children. I almost died having him, and I can't have any more."

At that moment Bebe and Mila ran up the walk, leaving Tia on the beach.

"I can't believe you're here!" Bebe squealed, throwing her arms around Rob's neck.

"I missed you too, little one." He kissed the top of her head, tears sparkling in his eyes. "Look how big you are."

"Did you see James?" Bebe grabbed Mila's hand, pulling her in front of the baby. "This is silly little James. He's my brother." Bebe kissed James, squishing his little cheeks between her hands before she turned to lead Mila into the house.

For a long time the garden was hushed in silence. Rob held Coco's hand, tracing her fingers with his thumb while he looked at his son.

"I don't know what to say," Rob said finally.

"Just say you understand and that you forgive me for not telling you."

"I understand. I wish things had been different, but I understand. Still, you shouldn't have had to have him alone. It must have been terrible."

"Losing you was terrible. Having James was the best thing that's ever happened to me."

"Coco, most girls wouldn't have gone through with the pregnancy."

"That was never a thought."

"Thank you." Rob looked down at his son.

Coco couldn't see his face. He kept it from her, but she could hear the gratitude mixed with grief in his voice.

"Thank you, Coco."

James looked up, reaching a small hand to his father's face.

COMING FEBRUARY 2018

A PLACE AMONG THE THISTLES

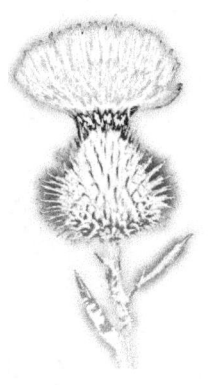

A PLACE AMONG THE THISTLES

E. E. ORME

SPRING
1961

GIDRA

I'm trapped in a black and white film. The leading man is missing, and the role of heroine has been usurped by Mama. Her Grace Kelly hair and Rita Hayward figure draw the attention of every man on this antiquated steamer, while I'm left to glide in her shadow looking small and childlike by comparison. We've run away again, fled from the nameless thing which moved us from Austria to London, London to New York. After New York, we'll travel to Virginia. After Virginia, only God knows where we will land.

I miss London. I miss my lovers: those fine old gentlemen who showered me with money and gifts in exchange for kindness and kisses. I miss my routine and the small but lavish apartment where I knew peace. Imprisoned on this ship, I watch my autonomy fade to a memory. Here, I am Mama's possession, a moving, serving ornamentation: obedient, cheerful, and attentive to her every whim.

She won't tell me what prompted this new flight, so I must try to imagine the thing she's done in the few hours I have to myself. Precious are those small sections of time in which she leaves me alone, allowing me space to rest the way I did in my apartment. In those moments I am calm, safe, and free to let down my guard and erase the fraudulent smile that corrupts my lips in every other waking moment. I liked London. I liked Vienna more. Would I like Virginia? I've watched the slow down-sweep in our fortunes. Noting, in my singular way, how every flight brings us closer and

E. E. ORME

closer to poverty and degradation.

At least John Stuart is kind. He dances with me, chats with me and fills my silence with his soft southern comforts. He is forever describing the beauty of his family home in Virginia, the vastness of its lands and the quality of its horses. He knows my weakness for horses, for open spaces, for peace. I drink in his promises, resting my hope on the colorful pictures he paints. John Stuart, whom we call J.S., is Mama's lover, but he is my friend, has always been my friend, ever since the night I brought him home to sleep with Mama.

But even J.S.'s friendship comes at a price. My new life in America will include his son Parker, a quiet, private school boy of sixteen in need of company and maybe a little more. I laugh when J.S. describes how the uptight boy needs a lesson in pleasure before he is consigned to the monotony of a sallow and shallow protestant wife. What I think J.S. really wants is to see his perfect son brought down a little. Parker seems to embody every virtue his father lacks. It's no wonder J.S. is so eager to introduce us; what true sinner ever could love a saint?

I'm bored sick with bitterness, trapped on all sides by an endless expanse of icy black water, while my dance card fills with the name of my first American client, a boy of sixteen. It fills, the way it always has, with men, with sex, with the work we do to keep our bellies full, our wardrobe up to date, and our jewelry boxes overflowing with valuable tokens of false affection. Every hard-won gem that crosses our palm is a sad half promise of love coupled with the vague notion that there is a future in what we do. With every mention of Parker, I grow more resentful, more worn by the grief I mask behind a playful flirtatious smile.

Where do old courtesans go to die? This seven-word

 2   A PLACE AMONG THE THISTLES

question dogs my days in a never-ending repetition of fear and loneliness. *Where do old courtesans and worn out prostitutes go to rest their heads when the game's played out and the music's died away? Maybe to America?*

We stand in a cold gray fog on the main deck; Mama flirts with a fellow passenger while J.S. looks bored, and I hope against hope for a glimpse of the Statue of Liberty. When the fog thins, I see Lady Liberty for a brief moment, her strong features glowing in the morning light. People call and point and move down the railing hoping for a clear glimpse. *Give me your tired, your poor, your huddled masses yearning to breathe free...* the words, taken from her tablet, play through my head while tears fill my eyes, because maybe just maybe there will be a place here in this new country where a tired little wanton can make a home. *Bring us your shamed, your degraded, your broken painted ladies,* I add, praying against hope that here there is peace and freedom enough for one more.

4   A PLACE AMONG THE THISTLES

PARKER

STRATHMORE HOUSE
LOUDOUN COUNTY, VIRGINIA

I want to rip it down. I want its existence to fade from memory. I want to bulldoze its cavernous hallway and release this overpowering scent of dust and damp decay. I want a bonfire of the vanities, a bleeding out of old blood and of bad blood until this toxic patrimony comes to an end. I want to watch Strathmore House fall.

The many faces of my dead relations hang upon velvet paper and richly lacquered wood paneled walls. Their portraits, mounted like trophy heads, stare out on the world with glassy sightless eyes. In every room their dead eyes find me, smothering my small rebellion into bitter submission.

I have no home but this, a fact that is as real as the clockwork appearance of a house maid just after the first stroke of the fifth hour. She will come as her forbearers came, to draw the curtains and block the late afternoon light.

"*Home*." The word is no more than a bitter sigh, yet it echoes through the lofted hall like a pledge of fidelity to this place. In the distance the great hall clock ticks on noisily, its mechanical sound marking the minutes while it breaks up the silence.

In stillness I watch the shadows recede, forced into hiding by the bright afternoon sun that washes in through the western windows. The room is bathed in golden light and glittering dust particles that rain down through many fingered sunbeams. I reach to catch the sunbeams in my hands the way I once had, but I'm stopped by an ingrained propriety that reminds me I'm sixteen and almost a man.

I need a change, the kind of change that brings hope and freedom from this iron clad routine that is all duty and service to others' notions of what it is to live. I want to open the windows and feel the rush of fresh air as it pours over the stone sills. Yet even as I open the window, feeling the first rush of air, the great hall clock strikes its first of five notes bringing the house maid on silent feet to darken the stagnant room.

"Mr. Parker." Doreen, the dark-skinned maid nods to me, her voice a whispered acknowledgment that I exist. I nod in return and watch routine prevail. The window is closed. The curtains are drawn, the room darkened in obedience to a long dead ancestor's living wish. The heavy curtains sway with the residual murmurs of motion while the maid leaves as silently as she came. Having cut the last sunbeam short, the curtains go still, creating an automated evening or mechanical night that merges seamlessly with the pervasive silence–a thing broken only by the clock's tick tock.

GIDRA

No one comes to greet the ship when we dock in New York Harbor. I imagine what it must have been like in the 30's when a steamer this size pulled into port. I imagine tickertape flying in long white ribbons, confetti filling the air as hands wave to excited onlookers. Scenes from old movies play through my head of beautiful blondes bundled in white fur coats, their elegantly quaffed hair gleaming under small cloche hats. Looking right I see a heroine, an idealized beauty just as perfect as any Hollywood actress, but my mother, Sophia, is no black and white film star, and her fans, *all male*, only visit her in secret.

Mama stands at the railing, her eyes fixed on the city, her thoughtful expression hidden behind the soft smile that always touches her painted lips. The wind picks up, freeing a wisp of silver blonde hair. She lifts a gloved hand to her forehead to catch the stray strand, her eyes shifting to mine when she sees me watching her.

"*Schastliv?*" *Happy?* she asks, her eyes meet mine before dropping to make certain that my dress and fur are immaculate. Mama's smile brightens when her eyes again find mine. She is *happy* which means *I will be happy* too. I wonder why she bothered to ask. *Schastliv?* This word and its meaning are strangers to me, because we're about to disembark through customs with false passports and a yellow valise filled with thousands of dollars in jewelry, and she thinks to ask me if I'm *happy?* I am frightened!

Frightened of being caught, imprisoned, and shipped back to what? There is no country that will claim us. Yet Mama is *happy* and that *happy* must suffice for both of us.

A steward waits with our luggage, including the yellow valise, loaded neatly on a trolley. I eye the steward, my suspicion of everyone rising because a *faux joie de vivre* coupled with sheer desperation are all we have to turn this trick. We walk down the gang plank through a gathering ocean fog. It chills the air and obscures our view. The luggage trolley rattles down behind us, its reassuring clatter giving me courage as we enter the customs office.

The moment the door closes Mama laughs a high and chiming laugh that brings all eyes toward her. I would blush if I weren't so terrified. Mama takes J.S.'s arm and kisses his cheek, pretending that he's the most amusing man in the room. Glancing around, I count five open stations. Behind each station stands one uniformed immigration and customs clerk. Three are old, their faces lined with care and officious hostility. The other two are young but one is married, his cheap ring barely visible on his fat finger. *So where is the mark, the easy play?* I look over the room again. The last man is young, but before I have time to assess him, Mama guides us toward his station.

"Gidra, my love?" Mama's English comes in a thick mixture of Russian and German accents to fall like warm syrup in my ear. These three words dispel my terror as they remind me to be fearless in the game.

I move up before her, greeting the uniformed clerk with my warmest smile while Mama and J.S. stand behind me like the Berlin Wall. I place our two fake passports on the work surface before glancing around at all the other clerks and passengers.

"What an awful lot of work you must have to do?" I

A PLACE AMONG THE THISTLES

ask with soft concern. "Are there always this many people?"

The clerk takes up my passport, his eyes sliding from my photo to my face, our eyes catching.

"No, ma'am, it's only busy when a ship comes in."

"Oh, I am glad. Just look at all these people." I look around the room again, inspecting our luggage trolley for Mama's yellow valise before refocusing on the clerk. "It would be terribly hard on you if it were always this busy."

"Yes, ma'am, that would be rough." His smile is shy. A soft blush touches his pale cheeks.

"Do you have to stamp every passport?" The government stamps glint in a basket to my right, their chrome with red and black wooden accents make them look important.

"Every one," he nods, looking at the stamps.

"Now what does this one do?" I ask, tapping the top of the closest one.

"Oh, now that... Well, you shouldn't touch that. It's official." He sets down my passport to lift the stamp.

"I'm so sorry." I smile up at him, looking both apologetic and playfully abashed.

"Oh, that's all right. Now, if you don't mind my asking, what brings you to the U.S.?"

J.S. answers with an impressive air of authority. "We'll be spending the summer on my estate in Virginia," He sets his authentic passport over mine and Mama's. Red and black stamps litter its pages, bright in their official ink. J.S. has been everywhere. But what catches the young clerk's attention are the words *Diplomatic Passport* embossed in silver lettering across the front. The inside pages are littered with visas and other important looking government stamps.

I watch the clerk take it up. His eyes moving from the passport to J.S.'s face and then back again. His brow knits before he sets it down. To my surprise he stamps each passport before returning them.

"Enjoy your summer, Captain Strathmore. It's been a pleasure serving you, sir."

I watch J.S. take all three passports, depositing them into the breast pocket of his *Jermyn Street* tailored jacket. My features would reflect suspicion if they weren't trained to show only naivety and amusement. How has J.S. acquired a diplomatic passport? Why was I told to distract the clerk if J.S. already had the ace in his pocket?

I follow Mama and J.S. through the customs house and out onto the sidewalk. J.S. tips the steward, but the depressed look on the boy's face tells me it's a meager tip. Mama wastes no time. Before the boy is even out of sight she's retrieved her precious yellow valise, leaving the trolley looking somehow shabby without it.

I must admit that despite all obstacles, we have arrived. Once again we have tempted fate and won. No one has arrested us *yet*, which means the game can commence with its usual vigor. If our game had rules the first and only rule would be, "All's fair in love and war," because in our game, the wars never end and love is just a fanciful state of mind.

PARKER

I wake each morning at six o'clock to the sound of the third-floor clock gonging in unison with the great hall clock below. My door is opened on the hour by a maid named Althea. With tired eyes I watch her draw the curtains and set my egg and toast on the breakfast table. Althea is the honey colored maid I like, the one with the fine hips and slim waist. She is pretty and paler than a house maid should be. I want to call her to me. I want to talk to her. I want to make her smile before I draw her close and touch that fine rich skin. There is such sweetness in her face, such innocence in her eyes that I am both tempted by and ashamed of, the wicked track my mind has taken. I watch her leave without a word.

Walking to the breakfast table I know from past experience that this is the usual Tuesday breakfast, and that tomorrow I can expect bacon, potato, and a biscuit. This is my grandfather The Judge's menu, still repeated six years after his death. Either way, I like Tuesday's breakfast best because plain as the meal is, it reminds me of the townhouse with lace curtains and yellow walls.

The smell of scrambled eggs and hot toast mingle in my mind with the remembered aromas of Lily's Turkish coffee and rose water perfume. This rich mixture of scents calls forth a memory of home more vivid with color than any photo. With fork in hand I close my eyes, letting the first bite make everything clear again. Her face, the dust on the window casing, the way the old table wobbled when we ate.

I miss her smile and the way she'd tell me to hurry up and eat. I liked that best of all. "Parker, hurry up and eat," Lily would say, grabbing a scarf off a kitchen knob as she passed through the room, looking for yet another lost item in the piles of lost and misplaced things that decorated our living room. Lily never wore a watch or looked at a clock; she existed in a state of perpetual lateness, which characterized our lives in the townhouse.

I always called her Lily. She was small and young, and I'd tried calling her Mother once, but the name wouldn't stick. It was like calling a cat a dog. Lily wasn't a mother, and I have never been a son. We were just Parker and Lily in the days before she was taken and life gave way to a yearlong cycle between boarding school and this great tomb. God, I hate this damned house. What would Lily say if she knew…? But I stop myself before I finish the question. I should never have allowed it to begin with. Instead I imagine Lily by her kitchen window eating toast with a cat at her feet. She smiles, pushes back her long brown hair, and tells me to *Hurry up and eat.*

GIDRA

The fighting has begun in earnest. Mama wants to see New York, but J.S. either won't or can't fund the trip so we are forced to move on. I'm glad to skip New York. Glad to slip unnoticed into the back seat of J.S.'s battered old Benz, glad to disappear into the comfort of my silence. Mama is enraged. She switches between soft whimpering protests to overt accusations and outright attacks.

J.S. revs the engine too high, his anger at Mama and his situation spilling out on the car. I know J.S. would love to show Mama off in this great city the same way I know Mama would love to be seen out in her gowns and furs, but a city of this caliber is not kind to the impoverished, and J.S.'s funds ran out months ago. I do not speculate on Mama's funds. She won't spend a cent of our fortune. Not while J.S. is still around to foot the bill.

I've never seen a dime of the money I've earned. The only rewards for my work I'm allowed to keep are the jewels I've received that are more decorative than valuable. Everything of real value goes into Mama's yellow valise to be counted and clutched close against that dreaded day when we can no longer earn our keep.

The skyscrapers loom large over head as the car moves past the docks and out into the city. A waterfront fog precedes us, clouding over the top tiers of the office buildings, casting everything in dark gray shadow. New York is amazingly modern. I've never seen a city with such megalithic skyscrapers. London has its tall buildings and modern sections but nothing it has can compare to what I'm seeing now. Still, all this grandeur makes me feel small, too small to follow Mama and J.S. through these dark streets pretending we belong when in truth it's much easier to tuck tail in our poverty and run.

It's nice to close my eyes in this gray darkness. It's nice to nestle amongst my things and rest against the worn upholstery of this old car. It's nice to fade into nothing and just forget myself for a minute. Sleep dances close but never comes. I could sleep now; I could sleep forever if only Mama would be quiet. I'm eighteen years old or some age close to that. I'll never know my true age, but eighteen sounds good right now. It fits the way I feel, young enough to curl up and sleep, old enough to understand the weary heaviness that has overpowered my mind.

I know I'm sad, sad for all I've lost and for all I've never known. I would like to have a real birthday and a last name, a home with a house cat and maybe even a horse again. I'd like friends and normal clothing. I'd like to be allowed to wear pants instead of skirts and dresses.

I'm so sick of dressing up and stripping down that I'd like to just go free. I'd like to kick off these infernal heels, throw away my gloves, and let myself go. I'm tired of this shadow life. I'm tired of playing the perfect little doll so pretty and youthful on the exterior that men can't help themselves when they see me. I'm not a doll. I'm not a toy. Somewhere underneath the dresses and the smiles, the pretty jewels and dazzling makeup, is a woman I would respect if I could find her.

Closing my eyes hard and then closing them hard again, I play a little game with myself, one I started many years ago. When the light behind my eyelids turns red and black with intense blinking I imagine him as he looked the last time I saw him, his eyes dark brown like warm chocolate. I remember the lines of his face, too thin with illness but beautiful all the same. I remember the sound of his voice, my name on his lips calling me close. I feel his arm around my waist pulling me to the bed. I hear the sound of his voice when he asks me to bring something to ease the pain.

Lying here with the tumult in the car filling my ears, I remember Albert until he is all around me. His spirit fills the empty spaces, his eyes look into mine, and our lips meet for one earth shattering moment. I hold him close, keeping him safe from the cold in the same way I kept him from death. Only when I feel his presence do I feel my body relax. Only in his company can I be myself, young, happy and innocent of all the sins that have been visited on me since God took him. Now with this trick of the soul I'm at peace. Wherever Albert is, is home because he is the only home I've ever known.

16   A PLACE AMONG THE THISTLES

PARKER

Strathmore House does not wake with the happy noise of family; if it has a pulse or heartbeat it is in the busy work of Alma the housekeeper and the maids who pace the floor in a never ceasing repetition of service. In this moment one maid, the curtain maid named Doreen, kneels near where I sit on the stone floor with my copy of a Tolkien book spread across my lap. I watch Doreen oiling the wooden banister while her sister, Althea, the one with honey gold skin and golden brown eyes, stands high above us on a ladder cleaning the chandelier. She glows with light, a sponge in one hand, her face and features illuminated by the shimmer of electrified crystal. I like Althea. She is always kind to me. All my life she's been here to welcome me home like an old friend at the close of every school year. Her smiles offer me a kind of warmth I find nowhere else. If anyone lived year-round in Strathmore House, she wouldn't work there. Light skinned girls don't work as maids, especially not pretty ones, and she is pretty in her monochromatic uniform.

Light dazzles off her wet sudsy hands and arms, her fine figure outlined where she stands. I am distracted from this artistic play of light on beauty by the crunch sound of movement on the gravel drive. All activity comes to a sudden stop. We freeze, observant in our places, our ears detecting what our eyes cannot yet see.

Scrunched childlike under the entryway table I watch first one maid then the other straighten and peer through the window; their colorful forms, one honey, one ebony, clothed in long black skirts with white aprons set a beautiful contrast against the yellow gold wallpaper and cream crown molding. Suds slip unnoticed from sponges, slide down crystal teardrops to fall to the stone floor leaving each bubble to lie like a glistening rainbow where it lands in the pensive room.

Action replaces stillness; bubbles are burst, blown by the passing swish of skirts and a folding ladder. The last trace of the moment is removed when rag in hand Althea, polishes the damp tile, killing the last bubble before disappearing at the click of the front door. The hall is as desolate as if no life had ever touched it. I do not shift from my hiding spot on the floor. Instead I fade into the heavy silence which precedes hurried motion. I remain, legs crossed, book on bent knees, and watch the two mahogany doors.

The left door opens, bringing sharp afternoon light and heat to fall across the floor in the shape of an unexpected someone, all narrow angles and stilted shadow. Golden light frames abundant curls and long skirted legs, stretched and lengthened by the afternoon light until this being is no more human than the Naiad or Tree Sprite, its heavy curls, like leaf and branch, diffuse the light while thin arms, raised to either side of the door frame, become limbs of bark not flesh. Drawing myself back further into darkness, I fix my eyes on the place where this shadow stands and waits.

One, two, the great hall clock ticks on through the silence, unaware that anything magical or macabre has intruded upon its busy order. A rustle of cloth, a sigh, and the shadow turns away, dropping one branch and then another before moving away. I move into the light, toward the thin slice of sunshine, the boundary between my quiet place and the lofted hall. Was she real or illusion: Ent, Elf, sorceress,

 18   A PLACE AMONG THE THISTLES

or girl? Reality tells me that nothing magical ever comes to Strathmore House while my imagination conjures more magical beings, each one wilder then the last. As curiosity gains a stronger hold, I slide from under the table, and walk toward the door.

The movement comes before its sound, much like clouds pushed by a fast-moving wind which has yet to shake the roof tiles. She is there before me in one darting motion, her red curls framing a heart shaped face alight with iridescent gray-blue eyes. I recoil at the quickness of the motion, at being spotted, at being found to hide like a child when I'm meant to be a man.

"I heard you move," the girl whispers in an *I caught you* voice. Though I am taller, she is older than me by maybe two years if not more. None of this registers as I take a step back.

"Where did you come from?" I watch her watch me, her eyes alight with a curious almost soulful stare.

"I came to find you." She turns toward the windows, her accented words ringing in the room. I look past her, past her golden red hair and white sundress toward the drive where a Mercedes stands half hidden by the yew hedge. Alma, the housekeeper, stands with a woman in a pale-yellow travel coat and a third figure, a man I recognize as my long absent father. The momentary shock makes me dizzy. The room spins imperceptibly. I blink, forcing reality into its place. But the loneliness will not give way, and try as I might I cannot accustom myself to this new and sudden vision because *nothing* has ever induced my father to come home to Strathmore House.

"You should go...go and say hello," the girl murmurs, disturbing my thoughts before leaving the way she came. I watch for her reappearance behind the panes of old window glass, her hair a golden torch in the bright sunlight. "I found him," I hear her call from the front step as the man I recognized as my father looks toward her.

"Gidra, you should have waited!" he reprimands, but Gidra seems not to hear him. Instead she turns toward the orchard and walks away.

I follow Gidra through the house, past the western windows, through the library, my feet skidding over the stone floors while I mark her path, finding her again and again in each consecutive window. Only when I reach the southern library casement do I find her again through French doors that lead to the veranda overlooking the koi pond.

She is there like spun gold and spring petals, leaning over the pond, her hair falling around her face. She watches the fish move toward her, splashing and rolling at the water's edge. Her high sweet giggle chimes through the shimmer of refracted light to where I stand. Her gaze rises to meet mine, searching me out in the shadowy depths of the library casement.

Frozen, I could stand here for the rest of my life, transfixed as I am by this girl beside the pond. Her beauty is on fire in the spring sunshine, her luminous figure framed by lilies, green leafed trees and the happy frolic of orange and yellow fish. Yet, my hand moves without me, my mind operating on its own as I feel myself pass through the open door to the veranda, only half aware that some part of me has decided to join her.

"What do they want?" Gidra laughs. In the water the fish begin to boil, mouths open, pushing, begging, and gulping for her attention.

"Food," I say, my voice so low it is a stranger to me. I walk to her holding the jar of pellets I keep by the door, surprised to find my feet on the worn stone steps that lead down to the southern garden. Gidra's laughter rises when a fish splashes her, sending droplets of water to cling to her cheek and hair.

I lift the jar out toward her, free of its tin lid. Gidra reaches in with both her hands, grabbing fistfuls of food. She throws the food into the air, high above the pond where I see the pellets aloft for an instant against the blue sky only to rain down like hail over the water's surface. The fish dive in every direction, their large whiskered mouths straining to catch every falling piece. Gidra laughs again; the music of her laugh is as alive to me as are the fish writhing in the water. But I can no longer see the fish. Strathmore House, the gardens, the entire world, disappear when I hear Gidra laugh. Again, I am aware of the gold light which follows her, perhaps the result of sunlight on beauty. Or perhaps *it* is something more.

22   A PLACE AMONG THE THISTLES

GIDRA

I am so glad to be free of the car, so glad to leave Mama and J.S. behind, that I exit the Benz, and walk straight toward the house. It is a daunting old place, gothic with its pointed arches and heavy Blue Ridge granite. The original plantation house was burned down in the Civil War, yet this new version of Strathmore House looks more suited for the drizzling rain of the English countryside than for the sun bright south.

I think I like Virginia. It's beautiful. Not since leaving Europe have I seen so many thousands of acres of unspoiled green beauty. It reminds me of Austria, only warmer.

I'm nearly to the house when I see movement through the windows. Two dark skinned women disappear into shadow leaving the front hall empty on my approach. No one comes to welcome us. I study the heavy wooden doors with their weather-beaten exterior, sun bleached to a dull unwelcoming gray. This deterioration renders them as colorless as the cool stone they are set in. The left handle looks more worn with use then the right and grasping the hot metal I open the door, which swings lightly on its well-oiled hinges.

A musty, unwholesome air envelopes me. I lean into the cool darkness of the room, the hot sun casting my shadow in strange lines across the stone floor. The scented breath of this old house stinks of the past, of too many closed windows and tucked away memories. It is the scent of a tomb rarely visited, its few inhabitants forgotten by history, by their family, and by time. This house is England all over again. The odor of moist stone and rooms filled with moldering antiques repels me, but the moment I turn to go a noise catches my ear. It sounds very much like the shuffle of an old dog or something else worth investigating. I'm over the threshold in a movement, coming face to face with a boy who is so like Albert that I can't disguise my shock.

"I heard you move." My words sound childish and absurd, spoken only to excuse my sudden intrusion. His eyes are that same dark brown chocolate I loved so much in childhood; warmly lit and beautifully edged with heavy dark lashes that frame their distinctive almond shape. Looking away I cast my gaze through the old warped glass to the place where Mama and J.S. unload the car with another woman who has appeared to help them.

"Where did you come from?" the boy who must be Parker asks. The figure before me becomes obscured by a fine mist of tears because his voice is equally rich and familiar.

"I came to find you." I look again on this boy who is the man I loved, only so young, so delicately formed and sweet, that he is at the same time unrecognizable. *I came here to find you*, I repeat to myself, acknowledging the longing in every syllable. Yet even while I stand studying his face, his high cheekbones and strong nose, the likeness dwindles, and Parker is again the son J.S. has plagued me with–the private school boy who needs breaking in before the world has a chance to ruin him with its manifold proprieties.

"You should go…" I say, warning him away, "…go…go and say hello." I walk out onto the gravel drive and call, "I found him." J.S. scolds me but I don't wait to hear why. In this perfect sunshine, I am free of Parker and my memories,

 24   A PLACE AMONG THE THISTLES

free of the odor of the house and of Mama and J.S. I follow my feet around the house to a beautiful fish pond. But no sooner do I reach the water than I feel Parker again, his eyes warming that cool empty place in my chest. I lift my eyes to where he stands watching me from a window. He is drawn to me like a flower that turns its face to the sun. One look gives him all the encouragement he needs to join me. We stand watching the play of light on these wonderful fish, their freedom and joy in the moment matching my own. A free, easy, uncalculated laugh escapes me.

"What do they want?" I ask, smiling up at him.

Parker mumbles something which sounds like *food*, and presents me with a jar. Grasping two handfuls I loft them high over the pond. Looking up again I find Parker's eyes have never left me. For one moment more I see my Albert smiling, his face soft with peace instead of lined with illness and worry. I've stared too long. I'm being rude but to look away now would be to lose this moment, the last moment in which I think I will ever see Albert happy. For propriety's sake alone, I drag my eyes from his face, smiling again on the fish. For some incomprehensible reason my heart warms with hope. Maybe this is my second chance to live and love as I wasn't allowed to before. When I look again at Parker, I feel the warmth of our connection intensify, its bright heat lighting my soul and the small space between us.

No matter what Mama says, I will not play the courtesan with Parker. He is not an easy mark to be targeted, lured, and exploited. I will be myself with this boy. I will ruin him for the world if only to keep him for myself. With a sudden rush of covetous need I know that I want him, no matter the consequence.